Dana Pierson Book #2

"Jones makes the most of her setting, Tuscan wine country, in her captivating sequel to 2015's *Lost and Found in Prague* . . . keeps readers guessing as to what lies behind the violence. Armchair travelers will be rewarded."—*BookLife*

". . . there are enough characters and relationships and crossed wires to keep the story humming along nicely, and the Italian setting is marvelous. . . a satisfying batch of both comeuppances and happy results by the end . . ."— Barbara Lloyd McMichael, *The Bookmonger*

LOST AND FOUND IN PRAGUE

Dana Pierson Book #1

"Many layered, intelligent and atmospheric, with an unusual cast of characters, this is addictive stuff from Kelly Jones."—Elizabeth Cooke, author of *Rutherford Park*

"*Lost and Found in Prague* captures the reader with a complex plot and engaging characters as it explores the interrelationships of good and evil, of faith and doubt."—Donna Fletcher Crow, author of *The Monastery Murders*

continued . . .

EVEL KNIEVEL JUMPS THE SNAKE RIVER CANYON AND OTHER STORIES CLOSE TO HOME

"... Jones tells an endearing story ... a fast and pleasantly bumpy ride through the lives of idiosyncratic characters trying to find their way across one kind of chasm or another,"—Bill Wolfe, *Read Her Like an Open Book*

THE WOMAN WHO HEARD COLOR

"You will not be able to put down this extraordinary story of condemned art, unshakable family loyalty, and secret passion in a time gone mad."—Stephanie Cowell, author of *Claude & Camille*

THE LOST MADONNA

"Jones' vivid descriptions of Florence, and the involving story, will captivate art and fiction lovers."—*Booklist*

THE SEVENTH UNICORN

"... absorbing, thoroughly satisfying debut."—*Publishers Weekly*

"Along with her fine writing, Jones delivers a nice feel for place, while taking the reader on a bit of a tour, from Paris to Lyon ..."—Dana Dugan, *Idaho Mountain Express*

ANGEL BOY

Kelly Jones

Ninth Avenue
PRESS

Ninth Avenue Press

Angel Boy
Copyright © Kelly Jones 2021
All rights reserved, Ninth Avenue Press, 2021
No part of this book may be used or reproduced, except for brief quotes in articles and for review, without written permission. For more information, contact kelly@kellyjonesbooks.com

ISBN   978-0-9914468-4-1
e-ISBN   978-0-9914468-5-8
Cover Design by Brian Florence, Steamroller Studios
Author Photo by Jim Jones

Acknowledgments

I will begin where I usually end up—with gratitude for my husband, Jim, who has seen me through seven books with multiple readings and many words of encouragement. The final frustrating edits were done during our time in isolation due to the Pandemic, and we seemed to have made it through. Thank you, Jim.

The women in my writing group critiqued Angel Boy chapter by chapter at our coffee-shop meetings, then moved to Zoom during 2020. I am so thankful for each of you, Erin Anchustegui, Glida Bothwell, Judy Frederick, and Laura Kelly Robb.

Additional early readers include my sister-in-law, Renie Hays; a high school classmate, Anne Holladay Egbert; and my sister, Mrezzie Putnam. Your support and suggestions are so greatly appreciated.

The setting is Boston because the real story that moved me to write this fictitious one happened there. I intended to visit Boston, but the trip and everything else in 2020 got canceled. So, I had to rely on those who know Boston well to help me out. The Fabulous Fulhams of Boston have assisted me by reading drafts, answering my questions, and sharing knowledge of their city. Tom, Christina, Nicholas and Rosemary, please know I am grateful for your suggestions. If I asked the wrong questions or misinterpreted your answers, the errors are all mine.

I would also like to thank the real State Fire Marshal of Massachusetts. I never met Peter Ostroskey in person, but he graciously answered questions by email. Again, if I got the questions wrong, misread his replies, or used my fiction writer's license too liberally, I take full responsibility for all inaccuracies.

Though parts of the story are true and made international headlines, this is a work of fiction, and the people, the churches, Mia's school, the events, and the plot are purely fiction.

*A*ngels hover, wings dipped in gold, halos strung with stars. Altars blaze with candlelight. Saints in alabaster robes stand overhead, watching, unmoving. Doing nothing.

"Take my hand . . . come with me."

A spark fights to ignite, the devil fanning the flame, nurturing wicked cravings that might have been doused, had anyone noticed, had anyone cared. It flickers and rises, glowing, the scent of sulfur assaulting the sacred air, spreading, reaching out, enfolding the innocent.

"Come, my love . . . I have something special for you."

Fonts of water, blessed sacramental offerings do not extinguish flames, nor sate the acrid heat of desire.

"No one need know our secret . . ."

Evil burns within one's soul, spirits tormented by unpardoned sins. Hell. Damnation.

"Don't be afraid . . . I will take care of you."

Night to day. Light, then dark. Cold, then comfort offered, soft and warm. Time passing, yet going nowhere. Someone waits.

"Be still, lovely boy . . . be still, my son."

Flames expanding, swirling, dancing, scorching, spreading, devouring. Crimson, gold, orange, and blue. A voice rises up. "Do you hear us now?"

Burn, fire, burn.

CHAPTER ONE

Dana Pierson stood, waiting, scanning knots of incoming travelers at Logan International, searching for Mia. The flight from Rome, according to the digital display board, had landed on schedule, and Mia should have passed through customs by now. Dana, concerned that her young guest from Italy might arrive with no one to greet her, had allowed herself plenty of time to drive from her Boston apartment to the airport. So, here she stood, waiting, a bundle of nerves tightening in her stomach. Arriving passengers continued to flow, moving quickly, voices echoing through the expanse of the terminal. Dana shifted her weight and adjusted the strap of the handbag slung over her shoulder.

She and Mia had kept in touch since they met four years ago, sending emails and even old-fashioned letters and notes tucked into birthday and Christmas cards. Dana was fond of Mia, yet their person-to-person time had been limited. Even when Dana visited Rome over a year ago to attend Giovanni and Gia's wedding, she'd had little time to spend alone with the girl.

Now, she would be taking a seventeen-year-old into her home for the school year, and she knew little to nothing about teenagers. She had teenage nephews and a pre-teen niece, but this was different. Logistically, at least, Dana felt prepared—new bedding on the foldout sofa, guest bathroom stocked with fluffy, recently purchased towels, fridge and freezer filled with foods she thought a teenage girl might enjoy. She'd done the prep work, and yet, the nerves . . .

She glanced at her watch, and when she looked up, she saw not Mia but someone else, someone she easily recognized, though she had not seen him in almost eight years. Heat shot up through her chest, warming her cheeks as she took a deep breath.

He was checking his cellphone, and then he gazed over, making eye contact, shaking his head in disbelief. He walked toward her, a perplexed look on his face.

"Dana Pierson," he said in greeting.

She felt as if she'd been socked in the chest. His voice alone could do that to her. She was already attempting to push away the clawing of self-inflicted doubt, the inner voice questioning, can I really do it? And now this. Him. Drew.

"Andrew Monaghan," she said.

"Dana Pierson," he said her name again. It was something between them. This calling each other by their full names. It had started as a joke but had become something different, verging on defiant.

She had refused to take his last name. No, refused wasn't the correct word. There was nothing malicious or disrespectful in her decision. She'd established a career. She had a byline. She didn't want to change her name.

He extended his hand. She felt her spine stiffen. Their final parting had nothing to do with names. She had pushed him away. Yet, they would always be connected by the loss they had shared, one they eventually were unable to share.

"It's been a while. You look good, Dana," he said, releasing her hand. "I like the blonde." She'd been brunette when they met, brunette through the extent of their marriage. And now, the blonde was mostly a way of masking the hints of gray.

"You, too, Drew." His dark hair was touched with silver, and fine lines fanned out from the corners of his eyes. Maturity played well on Drew. "Meeting someone?" she asked, then glanced down at the wheeled travel bag and realized he was returning from a trip.

4

"Just spent the week in Paris," he replied. "And you?"

"Picking up a guest." She was about to explain about Mia when a woman appeared and slipped her arm through Drew's. Had this woman been standing there all along? No, of course not. Dana would have noticed. Had she stopped off at the restroom while Drew forged ahead to find a ride into town?

"This is Amy Beck," Drew introduced the woman as she held her hand out to Dana. "Amy, Dana Pierson."

Dana waited for more as she took the woman's hand. A description, an addendum, a qualifier? *This is Amy, my girlfriend,* perhaps? *My new wife. My lover. My business associate. My junior partner.*

But, this was all he offered, and the woman's expression, both guarded and curious, told Dana that Amy knew who *she* was. Several years younger than Dana, though probably not at her best, Amy appeared slightly disheveled, weary from a long flight. She had a travel bag too, and it was obvious to Dana, as Amy and Drew exchanged a quick glance, that no further explanation was necessary—they'd just shared a week in the most romantic city in the world. But why was Drew here in Boston? He'd left Boston years ago.

They stood awkwardly, saying nothing, Amy's arm laced through Drew's. She had a round, pleasant face, an ample, curvy figure.

He asked, "You're meeting someone?" Arriving passengers maneuvered around them, voices mingling, the sounds of footsteps and rolling bags bumping along the floor.

"A friend from Italy," she replied. Drew's cellphone rang. He reached into his pocket, nodded toward Dana.

"Well, nice to meet you," Amy said, clutching her bag as Drew motioned toward the terminal exit, speaking rapidly into his phone.

Drew shot Dana a nod and wave. "Enjoy your guest," he called out, phone still to his ear. "Good to see you."

Dana stood, stunned for a moment, and then turned her gaze toward another incoming crowd as the roll and click of Drew and Amy's bags, their steps, faded behind her.

Then, there she was. Mia coming toward her. She wore skinny

jeans, cuffed in the latest style, short leather boots with heels that added a couple of inches to her five-foot-two. She was tiny, darling. Her long shiny hair, sleek and dark as raven feathers, fell over one shoulder. Mia adjusted her carry-on. She grinned, moving quickly, wheeling behind her a large bag, almost as big as Mia herself.

"Mia," Dana exclaimed, taking the girl into an awkward embrace, encumbered by her bags. "Welcome to Boston."

"I'm so happy to be here," Mia said. "Long flight." She sighed with exhaustion as Dana took over maneuvering the larger bag. The two chatted as they left the terminal and headed out toward Dana's car. Dana inquired about Mia's father, Leo, her grandmother, Estella, her great-uncle Zio Giovanni and Gia, and Fabrizio, a young man employed at the family vineyard for the past several years.

As they pulled out of the terminal parking, the image of Drew flicked through Dana's mind, even as she attempted to push it aside.

She glanced over at Mia, who offered a smile, equally tentative and thrilled—a smile that seemed to announce, *I'm ready for this, are you?*

CHAPTER TWO

Mia stared into the darkness, fully awake. Earlier, after arriving in Boston, she'd felt so tired, but now, she found it impossible to sleep. The bed was reasonably comfortable, though Dana had said she would get her a real bed if it didn't work out. She'd explained that Mia's bedroom was formerly Dana's office, and the bed, not really a bed, but a foldout sofa used for her infrequent guests. Dana had moved her desk, a bookcase, and most of the file cabinets out of the room and set up a small desk for Mia to use.

Mia shifted from back to side, adjusting herself, aware it wasn't the foldout bed that was making it difficult to sleep. It was the conversation they'd had over dinner. Yet, it wasn't what Mia had said, but what she hadn't said that was causing this restlessness.

Dana's mom had invited them for Sunday dinner, and Dana told Mia they were all looking forward to meeting her, especially her nephews and nieces, Kiki, Olivia, Quinn, and Zac, who was the same age as Mia.

After a while, she sat up and reached for her cellphone on the file cabinet Dana had left in the room to serve as a nightstand. During dinner, to be polite, Mia had left the phone here. Then, exhausted after her long day of travel, getting settled in, Dana going over their schedule for the next couple of days, she'd fallen into bed as soon as she stepped back into her room, hadn't even bothered to check for messages or texts. Now, wide-eyed and fully awake, she clicked on her phone and noticed a message. It was from Zac, and he'd sent it about three hours ago.

She opened it with a tingle of guilt. *You here?* She should have told Dana that she and Zac had already met. Not really *met*, but they had connected online. She was curious after Dana mentioned him in her emails.

So, she'd found him on a couple of her favorite social media sites. He was about as cute as a guy could get. Dark hair slicked back like some guy out of the fifties. In some of his pictures, he wore a baseball cap. Forward or backward, depending on his mood, he'd explained to her in one of his early messages. His eyes were dark, and his smile, a little bit naughty, turned up ever so slightly in the corners in a sly way. Showing beautiful sexy teeth. Could teeth be sexy? And a single dimple on the left cheek. She'd shown some of his pictures to her girlfriends in Italy, and they were all eager to hear if he was as gorgeous in person.

After she'd initially checked him out digitally, she sent him a message and introduced herself. He messaged back, told her his aunt had mentioned her. He said he liked her profile picture.

This had started a friendship of sorts. Maybe she should have mentioned it to Dana, but it wasn't like they were doing anything wrong. She and Zac hadn't exchanged anything improper, no sexy pictures or inappropriate words. He said her English was really good. How did she know all the latest American slang? He asked how she learned to speak English so well, which made her laugh because he'd never heard her speak, and she sent a smiley face emoji and said she watched a lot of American TV shows. That was partially true. That's how she updated her vocabulary to talk the way people in America actually talked. But she'd also been studying English in school since she was five.

He said he admired her, that American kids could barely speak English. He said he was taking French for his language credits. He'd already taken two semesters, and about all he could say was *parlez-vous francais?*" He asked if she spoke French, and when she replied,

"Oui," he said maybe she could help him out. She liked that idea. She could already imagine study sessions with Zac, though they would be going to different schools.

She stared at her phone now, thinking it was too late to reply. But maybe he'd still be up. It was Friday night. He might be out with his friends.

On a private message, she answered, "Settled in. Your Aunt Dana served cheeseburgers for dinner. Is that all American kids eat? Will I have to eat cheeseburgers every night for the next year?"

He messaged right back. "Pizza, tacos, maybe some Chinese. Or Sushi. You like Sushi?"

"Hate it."

"What are you doing tomorrow?"

"Dana's got a tour set up for me. The Freedom Trail?"

"If you're into history, it could be fun. Follow a red line on the sidewalk and learn some history."

"I've already been studying the history of Boston. I'm going to be here for the school year, so I want to know more about my new city." As she hit *send*, she wondered if this sounded too nerdy.

"Good place to start then. When will I get to meet you?"

"Sunday at your grandmother's."

"Great eats at Gma's!"

"Looking forward to it."

"Really?" Smiley face.

"Really."

"You'll get to meet little bro Quinn, my sister Olivia, and the fabulous Miss Kiki."

"Fun!" She hoped that didn't come across as sarcastic but then realized it might be better if Zac did think she was being flippant. Truthfully, she thought dinner with Dana's family would be fun. She didn't have any brothers or sisters, and Zac had filled her in on his through earlier messages. Quinn, he'd told her, was shy but a good kid, and Olivia—he hoped Olivia would behave herself! She tended to be a little pouty. Kiki, he said, was both adorable and spoiled. "Do you know what that means?" he'd asked Mia.

She replied that she was an only child and had been accused by some of always getting her way. "Is that what spoiled means?"

"So, you are a brat?" Zac had asked.

"You'll have to find out yourself," she'd replied. "Oh, and I'm also adorable."

"Yes, I can see that," Zac came back.

Mia *was* looking forward to meeting Zac's family, even his grandmother, but she didn't want him to think she was totally uncool. In Italy, she lived with her father, her grandmother, and until last year, Zio Giovanni. He'd been living in Rome when he was a priest but had retired to the family estate in Montalcino, then split his time between the family home and Rome when Gia Veronesi had reentered his life. That was quite the family scandal but a delightful addition to Mia's usually boring life.

Thinking of her family, Mia felt the tiniest bit homesick. She'd just arrived, and she hadn't anticipated that she'd miss her family on the very first night. But, she did.

It was a dream Dana hadn't had in years, not with the vividness she was experiencing now. Drew was young, his hair dark, without grey. He stood beside Dana, hand on her shoulder. She could feel his touch, but oddly she could also see him because she floated above the scene, an observer, not a participant. Yet, the younger Dana sat in a chair, the old rocking chair she'd inherited from her grandmother many years ago. She'd given it away to a cousin. Dana couldn't bear to sit and rock, arms empty. But in the dream, she was holding an infant. Joel looked up at her, eyes wide. He reached for his mother just as the phone rang.

She didn't want to lose this moment, but the familiar, oddly melodic, yet irritating sound of her cellphone was forcing her to release the dream. If she could stay a moment longer, it would silence itself. *Damn phone.*

Through squinty eyes, she focused on her nightstand, phone plugged in, charging, still ringing. As she reached for it, a brief flash of panic shot through her. *Mom?* But as her eyes adjusted, she could see from the contact name that it was Kip.

"Kip, what's up?" she asked groggily.

"You awake?" he asked. It came out *you wake?*

Dana and Kip Connor had worked as part of a team of investigative journalists off and on for over half of Dana's career, and recently, the two had collaborated on several articles. Sometimes when they were working on a story, Kip would call at an odd hour, particularly if he had some leads, something that couldn't wait until the following day. They were currently considering a project on fraud and abuse in eldercare. Surely this would not warrant a late-night call.

"Well, I am now." Rubbing her temple, pushing her fingers through her hair, Dana thought of another reason Kip might call at this odd hour, had on occasion called. "What's up? It's one-forty-seven," she added, taking in the bright red digital numbers on the clock perched on her nightstand. "In the morning."

"There's been another fire," he said. His words slurred—it sounded like he said *a mother fire*—confirming Dana's second notion as to why Kip was calling. It was Friday night, and he'd been drinking.

She was tempted to ask if it was a *mother fucking fire,* but instead, she said, "Another fire?"

"The freakin' frames are shooting out of—goddamn it. Did you hear that?"

Dana heard something in the background, a muffled conversation.

"I's just on my way home," he said, "and we saw these flames shootin' up in the air, so I ask the driver to drive by real slow, and now we're stopped, and we're watchin'."

"We?" Dana asked. "You and . . ?"

"Uber driver. Didn't you hear me?" He spoke with a broken rhythm. She could sense his effort in putting his thoughts and words together, which was difficult considering his obvious excitement mixed with alcohol. "I said there's 'nother fire. Oh, shit!"

A siren wailed in the background. Faint at first, then louder and louder, getting closer.

"*Another* fire? Where are you, Kip?"

"I'm gettin' out," he said, and then, voice fading as if he wasn't even speaking to her, "Wait here."

Dana was about to say *I'm here* when she heard another garbled voice in the background. "Where are you, Kip?" Dana asked again.

"At church." He laughed. "I told you. St. Barbara's," he added, though he hadn't, and then again, he was talking to someone else, but his words were faint and unclear as if he were holding the phone a foot away from his mouth. "Looks like all hell's breakin' loose." She could hear him again, and then he laughed, though it wasn't a *ha, ha, isn't that funny* laugh, but a deep-throated peel of gleeful delight. "The fires of hell. Dante's Inferno." His voice was rising.

"St. Barbara's? Didn't the archdiocese finally sell St. Barbara's?"

"Sure did," Kip replied quickly.

St. Barbara's had been in the news recently, finally sold after a twelve-year vigil by the parishioners, determined to keep the church. Dana had no idea how many fires were reported in Boston each year, but she'd guessed there were hundreds, maybe thousands, most of them not even making the news unless there was substantial damage or loss of life. This one, because of the recent headlines, would likely make the news.

"You said *another* fire?" Dana heard something loud that she couldn't identify over the phone. A burst, a blast, a detonation.

Kip said, "Goddamn, one of the windows just exploded." Dana imagined firefighters breaking windows. Or beautiful stained glass, bursting into a million pieces from the force and power of the flames, the heat. Beautiful colors, exploding like fireworks in the dark, then fading and falling to the earth.

"Couple firetrucks here," Kip said. "WBZ van just pulled up. I'll call you back." Then he was gone.

Dana replaced her phone on the nightstand and lay, wide awake now. She rose and went to the window. In the distance, a plume of smoke rose into the night sky, to the east, the direction of St.

Barbara's. She opened the window and took a whiff, but she could not smell the fire. Not yet.

St. Barbara's? Though the building had just been sold, it hadn't been used as a Catholic Church for over a dozen years. When the archdiocese barred the doors and slapped a FOR SALE sign on the building, the congregation had rebelled, set up a vigil, and appealed to the Vatican Court to reinstate the official parish of St. Barbara's. To no avail.

As Dana stared out into the night, she recalled a friend's wedding at St. Barbara's and pictured the lovely marble altar, the colorful stained glass. From her window, she saw only billows of smoke.

She returned to her bed but couldn't sleep, her mind abuzz. Kip had said there was another fire? What was he talking about? Then she remembered there had been a fire at St. Aloysius about a month ago. She and Kip had never seriously discussed it, other than a fleeting mention of the small fire that had quickly been extinguished with minor damage. It occurred in mid-July, the middle of summer. It hadn't warranted great concern. That church, too, had been closed down for at least ten years, though Dana believed it was still owned by the archdiocese. As far as she knew, it hadn't been sold. In a rundown neighborhood, it wasn't the greatest location for a commercial enterprise. She'd heard it had been used by the homeless to keep out of the weather, and the fire was attributed to someone *camping* inside. The fire had done little damage, other than charring a couple of old wooden pews. Barely a news bleep, though Dana remembered now a quick, fleeting thought she'd had even back then—had it been cold enough in mid-July to require a fire for warmth?

She must have dozed off. When she awoke and checked the time, it was 3:54. She snuggled back in bed and lay watching the red numbers on her digital clock flip over. 3:57 . . . 4:11 . . . 4:24 . . . 4:30. Then the phone rang again.

"Looks like it's under control, but substantial damage," Kip said. "Not much left but a stone shell of a building."

"Was anyone hurt?"

"Not that I'm aware. It's the middle of the night, so probably not." His speech was much clearer and quicker than during their earlier call. He still sounded excited, though relatively sober, as if during the almost three hours since his last call, the heat and excitement of the fire had drawn the alcohol out of him. Like a simmering stew.

"The other fire you were talking about," Dana said. "St. Aloysius? That church has been closed down, too."

"Bingo," Kip replied. "St. Al's. But, here's an interesting little tidbit. I overheard one of the firefighters say this was the third church fire this summer."

"Seriously?" she asked. "Catholic Church?"

"Not sure, and the firefighters aren't exactly accessible now, but I'm gonna stick around, see what I can find out."

"The fire at St. Al's was started by some vagrants," she said. "Any chance of that at St. Barbara's?"

"Don't know," he replied quickly.

"Take a good look around," she said. "If *someone* started the fire, they could be watching right now. Is there a crowd of onlookers?"

"Hell, yes," Kip answered.

"Why don't you scan the crowd with your phone."

"Good idea." She thought he might hang up, take some pictures, but he kept talking. "Big crowd. Looks like mostly neighbors." She heard more voices in the background, but she couldn't make out the words. "Why don't you hop in your little car and come over," Kip suggested.

Dana swallowed, rubbed her eyes, swung her legs over the side of her bed. She stood, stepped to her dresser, grabbed her jeans from the lower drawer, started to slip them on, cellphone pressed between her shoulder and ear. *On my way*, she was about to say when she realized her situation, her life had changed completely in the past twelve hours.

Surely Mia didn't require a babysitter, but it would be a terrible, thoughtless gesture for Dana to leave her alone on her first night.

"Damn. I can't," she told Kip.

"Why not? Got someone there with you?" he added with a chuckle. As if she had some sleepover-romance thing going, Dana thought. Over the years, Kip had attempted to set Dana up with his friends, but it never worked out. Kip, also single, wasn't great with relationships either, and it was almost a joke between them. They were a good team, professionally speaking. They both agreed they would be an awful couple, something that likely contributed to their continuing success. They were colleagues and friends.

"Mia arrived this afternoon," Dana said.

"Oh, that's right," he said thoughtfully. "Well, I'll be in touch, then." Dana could hear the disappointment in his voice. "I'll let you know if there's anything to . . ." His voice was fading. "Gotta go," he said urgently.

"Call me," Dana replied.

"Will do."

CHAPTER THREE

She was up now, unable to sleep as she envisioned Kip throwing questions at every first responder emerging from the scene, firefighters with serious, weary, defeated expressions and soot-covered faces, bodies reeking of smoke. Kip, quizzing those in the crowd of spectators and curiosity seekers.

She grabbed her robe from the closet, pulled it on as she slid into her slippers, and headed to the kitchen to make a pot of coffee.

She was tempted. She could leave a note. Maybe Mia would sleep 'til noon. Didn't teens do that anyway? Pammie said they'd stay up all night and sleep all day if you let them. But what kind of jerk would she be if she left Mia alone when she'd just arrived. Even if her guest were a full-fledged adult, it would be inconsiderate to up and leave. Kip could handle it, and he'd let her know if he discovered anything important.

She sat, sipping coffee, staring out the window, waiting for the darkness to lift, waiting for the sunrise, which this time of year she could enjoy from her kitchen window. She went back to her bedroom, got her laptop, set it up on the breakfast bar, and signed on to Google.

She typed in *St. Barbara's. Boston*. A slew of articles appeared. She clicked on the first.

St. Barbara's was just one of many Catholic churches closed in the archdiocese over the past fifteen years. A total of sixty-five churches had been closed. Forty-five had been sold, St. Barbara's one of the most recent. The asking price had been 3 million. It had gone for just under 2.5 million. Purchased by another denomination, it would now serve as a Coptic Orthodox Church.

It was no secret that the archdiocese had been in serious financial trouble for at least the past fifteen years. Many churches were closed, and the archdiocese claimed these closures were due to the shifting population of parishioners. The number of young men entering the seminaries was falling, and the average age of those currently in service was nearing sixty. There weren't enough priests to serve so many parishes. Some of the smaller parishes with diminishing attendance had been consolidated with others. Buildings in failing parishes were put on the market to support parishes that would continue to serve the remaining parishioners. Church officials had emphasized these points, but everyone knew the archdiocese had incurred enormous debt and, adding to this unfortunate financial situation, donations were substantially dwindling.

Dana clicked on another article. It told about the vigil that had gone on for over a dozen years, the appeal to the Vatican to spare St. Barbara's. Now, recently sold. And, now, according to Kip, gone up in flames. It didn't appear the new owner had moved in yet.

She did a separate search, typing in *St. Aloysius,* and found the brief article reporting the fire in July, over a month ago. Few details in the short piece, less than a dozen lines in the Metro section. Then she found an older article. The building had been closed, but held by the church, perhaps waiting for the real estate market to surge again.

Dana checked online sources to see if there was any mention of the fire at St. Barbara's that morning. The print paper for Saturday—today was Saturday, she realized—went to press too late for any mention of the fire. She found a *breaking news* story on the *Globe* online site—just posted—though there wasn't much there. A fire had broken out in an empty church, called in at 12:14 A.M. The story was still being updated. A photo was included, but the image was too dark and murky to see any detail.

She found an online news story live from a local TV station. The bright shiny face of one of the local reporters, a woman who barely looked old enough to be out of high school, reported live from the scene.

"We're unable to talk to any of the firefighters, but it appears the fire is under control." Dana didn't recognize the reporter, but she knew the type. Young and ambitious, they came and went so quickly it was difficult to keep track. Someone perfectly willing to set out in the middle of the night to cover a fire, an incident that might barely be mentioned in the print news the following day.

Dana could see the smoldering edifice in the background, smoke but no flames.

"Our team is live on the scene," the young reporter reported. "We'll update as details become available."

She scanned the background, looking for Kip, but didn't see him. She wondered if the *Globe* reporter, likely a rookie on the night shift, was aware Kip was there. The crowd gathered at the scene appeared to be neighbors, awakened in the night by squealing sirens, the smell of smoke. Some wore robes and jackets over their nightclothes. A few were fully dressed.

The sun was lighting the sky outside Dana's apartment. She got up to pour more coffee, then sat at her laptop, rubbing her head.

"I'm afraid I'm having some trouble." Dana turned to see Mia. "My body doesn't know what time it is." She wore a terry robe, pulled over what looked like an oversized T-shirt, belted around her tiny waist, thin legs bare, flip flops on her feet.

"It might take a while to adjust." Dana glanced down at her laptop again and hit X. She rose and pulled a cup out of the cupboard. "Coffee?"

"Yes, please." Mia sat down at the breakfast bar as Dana poured her coffee, got some milk out of the fridge.

"You hungry?"

"Just coffee for now." Mia added a generous amount of milk and stirred.

ANGEL BOY

Dana thought of the wonderful European breakfasts she'd been served in Italy when she visited the Antonellis. Homemade breads and pastries, fresh fruit, cheese and salami. She'd bought bacon and eggs but didn't know if Mia would want an American or European breakfast. She had cheese and bread too. Dana usually just grabbed a banana or orange on her way out. She had some boxed cereal, but nothing very exciting, no bright colors or rainbow marshmallows. And even her meager selection consisted of half-full boxes that were probably stale. She hadn't purchased any new cereal since she didn't know if Mia would eat it. Maybe she should take her shopping.

"You working?" Mia glanced at the laptop. She took a sip of coffee, the dark liquid turned a pale, milky brown.

"Just doing a little research," Dana replied. She attempted to clear her head, push all thoughts of fire and hell and damnation out of her mind, even as she glanced at her phone.

Over a breakfast of toast and fruit, they talked about plans for the day, then Dana scanned the morning digital papers while Mia checked her phone for messages. Dana found nothing more than what she'd already read.

"I've got time to shower before we take off?" Mia asked.

"Plenty of time."

About ten minutes after Mia left the kitchen, Dana's phone rang.

"No one is allowed inside. What's left of the inside. The fire appears to be out."

"Were you able to speak with any of the firefighters?"

"Briefly," Kip replied. "The other fire was in June at St. Lawrence's."

"All three Catholic churches," she considered.

"I Googled to see if I could find something on that fire, but nothing, and I was unable to get anything more from the firefighter who mentioned St. Lawrence's. They're keeping a good eye on things here at St. Barbara's, even though the fire appears to be contained. I chatted up some of the neighbors."

"Learn anything?"

19

"Nope. No one knew anything. The fire was going pretty good before anyone came out to gawk. Most of the surrounding buildings are residential," Kip said, "No one I talked to had any knowledge of how it might have started, though they had plenty to say about the building itself. It's common knowledge that the church has been vacant for years. One of the neighbors said it had been sold, but then another contradicted and said the Church still owned it. Naturally, there was the Church-hater who said it was a good thing it was destroyed, all that fornication and child abuse going on inside."

Dana had heard such comments many times, particularly as the details of their long-ago investigation came out.

"We'll have to get our hands on the fire incident report," Kip said.

"Did you see a reporter from the *Globe*?" Dana told him there was a brief online article, but Kip said he didn't see anyone.

"Maybe leave this to the reporter officially sent out," Dana said, "or if it turns out to be arson, a crime reporter."

This didn't seem to dampen Kip's enthusiasm. "I'll set up an interview with someone from the fire department."

"You think there's something here worth exploring?"

"I'm just thinking, that's all."

"Well, then, I'll talk to you later," Dana said. "I'm taking Mia out this morning. Showing her some of the historical sites in Boston."

"Have fun," he said. "We can talk later."

Mia returned to the kitchen as Dana clicked off her call. Mia refilled her coffee. One of Dana's recent purchases, a fluffy, mint green towel, was wrapped around her damp head. "I could hang out at the apartment today if you have work to do." She tilted her head, and the towel started to unravel. She yanked it off, settled it on her shoulders as she tossed her head, then fluffed her hair with her fingers. "You know you can leave me alone. You don't have to entertain me. Or babysit. I'm seventeen."

"Let's plan on having fun today," Dana told her. "I'm not currently working on anything urgent. When you start school full days on Thursday, I can go back to work, too. Today I'll introduce you to Boston."

Dana went back to her room to shower and change. Half an hour later, they were off for their introductory tour of the city. They headed downtown, followed the Freedom Trail, Mia interested, as Dana had hoped, in knowing more about the history of Boston. At noon, they stopped for lunch at a place near Faneuil Hall.

Over lunch, they talked about making a weekend trip to New York City. Dana told Mia they could take the train and be there in about three hours.

"How about next weekend?" Dana asked.

"Yes, that would be great."

Dana told her about some of the things they could do in New York—Central Park, The Met, boat out on the harbor to see the Statue of Liberty. They could leave Friday evening, then come home late Sunday.

After lunch, they went down to the harbor, walked around, popped into a couple of shops, then took a short cruise, Dana pointing out landmarks, giving Mia a feel for the layout of the city.

Back home, Mia said she wanted to go over her class schedule and check out the textbooks she'd had delivered to Dana's address. After she went to her room, Dana pulled out her cellphone and called Kip.

"I talked to the reporter sent out by the *Globe*," he said. "She didn't know I was there. And I sure as hell didn't know who she was. New, I think, working with one of those summer interns who took the photos. A couple of kids. I asked her to send me any pictures they got, but not much there."

"Did she ask why you were interested?"

"I told her I just happened to be driving by," he answered quickly, and then, as if brushing the young reporter aside, "I called St. Lawrence's, hoping to talk to the pastor, Father Michael, learn something about that fire."

"St. Lawrence's, still a functioning parish?" Dana knew the other two churches, St. Al's and St. Barbara's, were no longer being used.

21

"Must be. I got a prerecorded message with times of daily and Sunday Masses."

"Well, I guess that tells you when and where you might find the priest," she offered. "Tomorrow's Sunday. Father Michael will be saying Mass."

"Good thought," Kip answered. "Maybe that's why I thought of it myself. Want to go with me, so I'll know when to sit, stand, kneel, and pray? It's been a while."

"It'll come back," Dana said.

"Like riding a bike," Kip replied with a light laugh.

"I'm taking Mia to St. John's." She'd asked Mia if she'd like to attend Mass at her home parish. Dana didn't tell her she rarely went herself.

"Well, then, I'll just catch up with you later."

After they spoke, Dana went online to see if she could find any mention of a fire at St. Lawrence's in June. Just as Kip told her, nothing reported anywhere.

There were some files in the file cabinet in Mia's room that she wanted to grab, some personal notes, as well as copies of news articles. The articles she was most interested in now were those that had come *after* the big story. The stories that told of the closing of so many parishes, putting many of the properties on the market for some quick cash.

Yet, it all went back to the first stories. Back over a decade and a half ago. Her big break in journalism. Kip's, too. Events that still reverberated through the Archdiocese of Boston, touching those involved, emotionally, financially, and to the very core of their faith.

As a team, she, Kip, and three fellow reporters—all moved on to different jobs now—had uncovered a scandal that had rocked the Catholic Church, first in America, then reverberating around the world.

Their series of articles had started, as stories usually do, with one. A Catholic priest had been accused of molesting a child, then another, and more, some as young as five. He would target children particularly vulnerable, often the families of single mothers.

Mothers who would welcome the influence of a man of God, flattered and grateful for the attention they lavished on a boy in need of a father figure. He'd take them out for ice cream, visit the family at home, often say evening prayers with the children, tucking them into bed.

Dana remembered interviewing victims, concerned about victimizing a victim all over again. Now, thinking, even of the aftermath—selling church-owned properties to help pay the legal costs, the financial payments to the abused—was dredging up so many awful memories. Yet, memories of their discovery, bringing it all to light. Out in the open. Because these horrific deeds had been known, buried deep by those who felt they held forgiveness in their own tainted hands.

Those accused or suspected had been shipped from one parish to another, often with the sincere belief—or so said the higher-ups—that the sins had been confessed, the priests had received counseling, they were no longer a threat. Such stories had come up before. Payoffs had been made. News articles had been written. Then largely forgotten. Their team wasn't the first.

But their story had used a different angle, something more to the story, an even deeper level, adding to the horror. Their story was one of a coverup. The hiding of facts. If these reports had been made public earlier by Church authorities, thousands of children could have been protected.

Dana was pregnant with Joel at the time they started their investigation. She had given birth just months before the first story appeared. For the next year, she had spent every moment doing research, at times taking Joel with her, baby strapped to her back, or rocking him in the portable car seat that fit neatly into a stroller that she would wheel into the building, the office, the church. When he started to sit up on his own, eventually crawl, she hired a nanny. Should she have quit her job? If she had only known, if she had chosen differently, put her entire being into mothering rather than into uncovering every evil detail of this story. But how was she to know?

In the end, their stories had resulted in charges against five priests, though Dana knew there were more.

Father Joseph Jennings, the priest who had been at the center of their series of articles, the benchmark of all evil, so to speak, had been killed in prison. He'd been placed in a cell with a violent criminal. Had the authorities done this on purpose? A child molester, particularly one who falsely held himself up to the world as a man of God, was not safe in prison unless in solitary confinement. Dana had felt not an ounce of sadness when the old priest died. Had she herself been sucked into this evil? This thought had sat heavily upon her for many years.

There had been accusations in the parish of St. Aloysius, though the priest accused was never prosecuted. He died in the midst of their investigation. Father Jennings, the priest killed in prison, had once been assigned to St. Barbara's.

Dana checked on Mia to see if she was ready for dinner and found her curled up on her bed, asleep, cellphone clutched in her hand as if it were a puppy or teddy bear, a source of comfort. Dana wondered if she'd been calling or texting family or friends back home, or posting on social media, sharing secrets. She looked so young, so innocent, and Dana wondered again if she could really do this. There was so much involved in having a child, even a half-grown child, a teen, in her home.

CHAPTER FOUR

Sunday morning, they took an Uber to St. John's for Mass. Dana described this as her childhood parish before her mom and dad moved to Sherborn, but Mia noticed Dana didn't talk with any of the other parishioners. She seemed distracted during an admittedly boring sermon and didn't go up for communion with Mia.

On the ride home, Dana asked what she thought of the church, and Mia replied that it wasn't as old or large as the churches in Italy, but she liked the intimacy of it. Dana suggested they change into jeans for the family dinner at her mom's. She said it was always casual.

Mia and Dana were the first to arrive, and Mia suspected that Dana had planned this so she could meet her mom before the rest of the family showed up.

To Mia, Ann Pierson looked like a movie star from her grandmother's era. She wore red lipstick, eyeshadow, and mascara. Mia had seen a picture of Dana's parents in the hallway of the apartment, and Dana explained it was taken before they married, that Ann Pierson had worked as a secretary for the Boston Red Sox when she was young, that Dana's dad had been a professional baseball player. After they married, Ann stayed home to raise her children.

Even in the old black and white picture, Ann appeared very blonde, and the floral print dress she wore showed off her feminine figure and shapely legs.

Mia thought of how people often said she looked like her mom, but she saw little resemblance between Dana and her mother. She wondered if Dana, who towered over her mom, took after her dad. Yet, Dana had just enough of her mother's genes to be pretty while not as beautiful as the young Ann Pierson in the photo. The older woman, still blonde and perfectly coiffed, obviously dyed her hair. Dana wore hers casually, a more modern style, streaked with honey-colored highlights. She used little if any makeup, maybe a touch of mascara.

"Oh, Mia, so pleased to meet you." Dana's mom gave Mia a warm hug, then stood back to study her. "You are just as Dana described you. You are darling," she exclaimed with such enthusiasm Mia thought she might give her another hug.

"Thank you for inviting me for dinner," Mia said as Ann motioned them from the front foyer into the kitchen where the smells of roast meat and freshly baked rolls that had greeted them as they arrived intensified and wafted in the air.

"I'm a little behind," Ann said, swinging an arm across the kitchen table where she'd set out stacks of dinner plates, silverware, and napkins.

"We'll set the table," Dana said, grabbing half a dozen plates. Mia picked up the remaining plates as Dana motioned toward the formal dining room, which they'd passed on their way to the kitchen.

Dana set out plates. As Mia returned to the kitchen for the silverware and napkins, she heard the front door open, several people talking, a man, a child, another man. Dana's voice mingled with those newly arrived.

Dana walked back into the kitchen, a little girl holding her hand. Her curls were golden, her eyes wide and blue. Mia thought she looked like a doll. Two men followed, just steps behind.

"I'm Kiki. I two," the girl explained, holding up two fingers. "I be three November twenty-seven. You come to my birthday party?"

Mia had not been around many small children, but she didn't think most kids Kiki's age were this verbal. Kiki, Dana had explained on the drive, had been conceived through a surrogate. Dana's brother Ben and his husband Sam had both donated to the possibility of parenthood—Dana actually used those words, staring straight ahead as she drove. Mia thought Dana was too embarrassed to use the words *sperm donor*, but when she added, "They've decided not to find out who the biological father is," Mia realized that Dana had just shared something likely known only to family members. Kiki was too young to understand any of this, but Mia wondered if someday she might want to know. Wouldn't she want to know exactly where she came from?

"Mia, this is my brother, Ben," Dana introduced the tallest man. "And his husband, Sam."

"Pleased to meet you," Mia said, extending a hand to each, eyes flickering from one to the other, studying the two men.

Additional family members had arrived and were migrating to the kitchen.

"And this is Jeff, his wife Pammie," Dana introduced them. "Quinn, Olivia." She glanced toward the end of the procession, as did Mia. "No Zac?" Dana asked.

Mia felt a flush of disappointment, and then Pammie said, "He's coming. He's got a new car, well not new-new, but new to him. The old clunker gave out, and with all the stuff he's got going, he needs his own transportation." Pammie had short-cropped black hair and wore wide-rimmed plastic glasses. She was even taller than Dana. "Welcome," she told Mia with a warm embrace.

Family members chatted back and forth, the women scurrying between kitchen and dining room. Ann lifted the roast out of the oven.

A deep voice came from the dining room. "I'm here! We can eat!"

Mia and Zac's eyes met as he sauntered into the kitchen, removing his cap, giving his grandmother a hug, tossing a grin over her shoulder, landing right on Mia, who felt her heart skip a beat.

He was even better looking in person.

"You must be Mia," he said in a voice both casual and confident. She wondered if she should offer her hand but decided that was too much of a wannabe adult thing to do, so she just shot him a little wave. Though they hadn't really agreed, she knew instinctively that they would not reveal they had been talking through social media. They had never specifically said it was a secret, but they both knew, and Zac seemed to understand she hadn't told his Aunt Dana.

"Zac is a senior this year," Jeff told Mia, placing an arm around his son's shoulder.

Zac offered Mia another smile, and she noticed the dimple in his left cheek.

"He's on the football team," Quinn, his thirteen-year-old brother, informed Mia, and she smiled and nodded as if she had no idea, though Zac had already sent her his schedule, hoping she might come to a game. Quinn and Zac both had dark hair, like their mother, but Olivia, who just listened, eyeing Mia suspiciously, was a combination of her mom and dad with brownish hair. Like her mother, Olivia wore glasses. Mia didn't quite know what to say to this sullen eleven-year-old girl, so she just offered a smile, and Olivia returned a shy, guarded grin with a mouth full of braces.

"Everything's ready," Ann said.

Within minutes, they were seated around the table, Mia between Dana and Pammie, across the table from Zac, who glanced up at her quickly just as the others bowed their heads in prayer.

Dinner was filled with more chatter, a little bickering between Quinn and Olivia, who both wanted the end piece of the roast.

"There's plenty for everyone," their father admonished.

"So, Zac, when's your first game?" Ben asked.

"Friday night."

"How's the team?"

"We lost some of our star seniors, and we're having a tough time with the new quarterback. But we'll do okay."

"I don't suppose you watch much football in Italy?" Jeff said to Mia, thoughtfully including her in the conversation.

28

"Soccer is football in Italy, so, no, not much American football," Mia replied. She'd never watched an American football game.

"Are you going to the game Friday?" he asked, glancing from Mia to Dana.

"You're invited," Zac said.

"I'd like to, but we're going to New York this weekend," Mia said. She had little interest in American football, but she would like to watch Zac play.

"Dana, why don't you come to the game," Pammie said. "You could catch an early train into New York Saturday morning and be there by ten. If you leave Friday after school, you'll get there too late to do much, and that extra night in New York, well, you can't get a room for much under three hundred."

"That's a possibility," Dana said, exchanging a look with Mia. "It'd mean getting up really early."

"I can always sleep on the train."

"We'd love to have you come to the game," Pammie said. "Give it some thought."

"We will," Dana replied.

Ben offered to carve more roast as Zac and Quinn refilled their plates.

As they were finishing up the meal, Jeff leaned toward Dana and said, "I heard something the other day. You know there is an opening on the Supreme Judicial Court." His voice was low, like this was just for Dana. Pammie was engaged in a separate conversation with Ann, something about the bulbs she was planting in her garden.

Then Ann asked Quinn and Olivia if they'd help serve the pie.

"I help," Kiki shouted.

"I'll take orders," Ben said as both he and Sam popped up to help Kiki out of her highchair. "Who wants ice cream?" Sam lifted the little girl, and they started toward the kitchen.

"May I help?" Mia asked.

"You're our guest today." Ben laughed. "After today, you'll have to fend for yourself."

29

"Yes, ice cream, please," Mia said.

"I heard that, too," Dana said, turning to Jeff, "I heard about the opening on the court. You interested?"

"No, no, not at all," Jeff said. Dana had told Mia her older brother was an attorney. He had an informative, official-sounding voice, as if he were accustomed to delivering news in a matter-of-fact, non-emotional, nonjudgmental way.

"We're hearing the governor is considering Drew," Jeff continued.

Dana's back straightened, and she blinked. After several moments, she said, "I saw him. I saw him at the airport." She swallowed. "When I went to get Mia." She glanced at Mia just as Pammie attempted to draw Mia into another conversation about St. Gertrude's, how a good friend had graduated from St. Gert's.

Attempting to be polite but more interested in what Dana and Jeff were talking about, Mia smiled and nodded at Pammie. Mia had seen no one at the airport with Dana when she'd come to pick her up.

"St. Gertrude's has a great reputation," Pammie said. "Always looks good on a resume."

"Yes, my father was pleased with what we learned about the school."

Jeff said to Dana, "Just thought I should share this information with you."

Quinn and Olivia were delivering dessert, passing plates around the table.

"Thank you, Quinn," Dana said, smiling at the boy, then turning back to Jeff. "And thank you. I appreciate it. I'm not sure how I would feel having him back in Boston." Mia heard something in Dana's voice and knew there had to be a history. Judging from Dana's reaction, a romantic history. A thought flickered through Mia's head. *I wonder if Dana goes out on dates. I wonder if I want to go out with a boy, will Dana have to approve?* She glanced across the table at Zac, who was now devouring a piece of pie. He glanced up, raised his fork, and shot her a smile.

After plates were cleared, Mia offered to help fill the dishwasher, and Dana's mother reluctantly agreed.

"I guess you are officially part of the family now," Ann said. Zac offered to help, and his grandmother gave him a smile that moved on to Mia.

The younger children had gone upstairs to play Monopoly, Uncles Ben and Sam supervising.

Mia said, as soon as they were alone in the kitchen, "Thanks for not telling your Aunt Dana that we've been talking." Her eyes widened. She felt herself blush. "You didn't say anything? Did you?"

"No problem." Zac smiled. The dimple in his left cheek deepened. He handed Mia a plate, and she rinsed it off and stacked it in the dishwasher.

Voice low, Mia said, "I didn't say anything. And if you didn't either, maybe if we did now, Dana would think something—"

"Unsavory," Zac said, "she might think something unsavory was going on?"

"I'm not sure what that word means." But she did. Unsavory meant distasteful, or disagreeable, morally offensive, in the worst-case scenario.

"I agree," Zac said, not bothering to define his choice of words, perhaps aware that Mia did understand. "No need to confess anything if Aunt Dana believes we are just now getting acquainted."

"Oh, so nice." Zac's grandma had come into the kitchen and approached the two teens, placing her hand on Zac's shoulder. "So nice to see you two young people getting acquainted." *There,* Mia thought—*Grandma confirms that we are just now getting acquainted.* No one knew.

Zac turned, wiping his hands on his jeans. Ann removed her apron as Zac sliced himself another piece of pie, devouring it in a couple of bites, not bothering to put it on a plate. Italian boys, American boys, not much different, Mia observed.

Now Kiki had joined them in the kitchen, wrapping her arms around her grandmother's leg.

31

"Quinn say I too little to play," she whined.

Her grandmother lifted her and planted a kiss on her forehead.

"Well, let's go see if we can find you something else to do," Ann said. "I've got crayons and paper in the desk. We can draw a picture."

"But, not Quinn," Kiki said as the two left the kitchen.

Mia glanced at Zac, remembering he'd said Kiki was both spoiled and adorable. He motioned to Mia and they returned to the dining room, where Dana sat still chatting with her oldest brother and his wife. The others were coming down the stairs.

"Who won?" Zac asked.

"I had the most money," Quinn bragged.

"But we didn't finish," Olivia whined, attempting to jab him in the ribs. Quinn snickered and deflected her attack in a quick move.

"We'll play again when we have more time," Uncle Sam said. "You should have at least a couple of hours to play a proper game of Monopoly."

As the troops were gathering to leave, Quinn told Mia they were happy she was in America and that Aunt Dana would take good care of her. Olivia said, "Welcome to America. I hope you enjoy living here." She smiled, tight-lipped this time, without showing her braces.

Zac asked Mia if she'd like to take a look at his new car.

"There's a party tomorrow night," he said as they walked out to the back driveway. "An end-of-summer get-together. Do you want to come?"

"I don't know. I should check with Dana."

"I told her about it, and she said you could go if you wanted to. She gave it some serious thought before she said okay, so I'm not sure she's all in on the idea. I guess she's your Mommy for the year." Suddenly the cockiness that seemed to be part of Zac's personality was draining away. Mia sensed he'd said something he wanted to take back. Did Zac know that Mia did not have a mother? That her mother had died when Mia was eleven?

"She said I could go?" Mia asked.

"She asked if parents would be there, if I could guarantee there would be no drinking or drugs."

"What did you tell her?"

"I said most likely parents, but I didn't know for sure. I told her we would be good."

Mia laughed, more of a snort laugh. "So, she said I could go?"

"She said she would trust that we would both use good judgment. That I was to keep an eye on you." He smiled his dimpled smile. "Do you drink?"

"I grew up on a winery in Italy."

"That's a yes?"

"Everybody drinks wine in Italy, but I can't stand the taste of beer, and I don't do drugs. Is that a problem?"

"Well, then I don't think Aunt Dana has anything to worry about. Wine isn't the beverage of choice at our parties, and I never drink and drive. I'll pick you up about seven."

CHAPTER FIVE

On Monday, Dana drove Mia to her new students' orientation at St. Gertrude's. There would be an introduction program, then lunch with staff. Classes would start Wednesday with a half-day, then full-time Thursday.

"Please call when you go to lunch," Dana said.

"I could come back home on the bus," Mia said. "I've got the schedule and pass in my bag, the app on my phone."

Since her private school did not provide transportation, Mia would take the T, a short distance on the subway, and then a couple of buses to St. Gertrude's. Dana thought it was too complicated to let Mia undertake this on her own without a trial run.

"I'll be back to pick you up, at least on your first day," Dana told her, and Mia just nodded okay.

Dana wondered if Mia was nervous as they maneuvered through thick, halting, morning traffic, and she tried to engage her in light conversation, pointing out landmarks, talking about the weather, Mia's upcoming classes.

During lulls in the conversation, Dana's thoughts turned to Zac's invitation. She was aware that Mia might want a social life. She was going to an all-girls school, and Dana had found some comfort in that, though she remembered the girls from St. Gertrude's were always the most *boy crazy*, a term her mother liked to use. And here was Zac, cute as can be.

Then her thoughts switched on to another track—her conversation with Kip when he called Sunday evening after they returned from dinner at her mom's.

"Father Michael didn't say Mass at St. Lawrence's this morning," he'd told her. "But I've set up an appointment to speak with him tomorrow. You able to go?"

"What time?" Dana had asked. "Did you mention why we wanted to talk to him?"

"Told him we were doing a series on fire dangers in old buildings. He said he'd be in his office until noon. He usually arrives about eight."

"How about ten? Mia's got her orientation from nine until early afternoon."

"Perfect," said Kip. "See you at St. Lawrence's."

A story about the St. Barbara's fire had appeared in the Sunday morning Metro section with a couple of photos and brief quotes from neighbors, telling how they had heard the siren and smelled the smoke. A fire department spokesman said the cause had yet to be determined. Nothing about any connection to other fires. Nothing about St. Al's or St. Lawrence's. Neither Dana nor Kip had any part in writing the story.

Dana pulled up in front of St. Gertrude's in the drop-off area. Mia opened her door, glanced over at Dana, who offered her a smile. "Have fun," she said, then watched Mia walk up toward the school with enough confidence to almost put Dana's mind at ease. Mia glanced back, giving Dana a little wave, conveying a message somewhere between, *please leave*, and *I'm just fine*.

Father Michael was one of the oldest-looking priests Dana had ever seen. His hair was white and thinning, and little tufts of hair protruded from his nostrils as well as his ears. He wore a pair of glasses with visibly lined bifocal lenses.

He met them at the reception desk in a building attached to the church, then invited Kip and Dana into his office, and they followed as the tap, tap, tap of the stooped man's cane led them

35

down the ancient hall, over wooden floorboards, scratched and faded. He motioned for them to sit. Books and papers, old manila folders, were stacked around the room. A hoarder, Dana instantly thought. If an arsonist wanted to burn the place down, this is where he should have started. Plenty of kindling and fuel.

"You are here to talk about the fire?" the priest asked, "this past summer?" His glasses slipped down, resting on his large bulbous nose.

"If you'd share with us what you discovered," Kip said, "how you discovered the fire."

"Not much of a fire," the priest said, "In the chapel. Some boys playing with matches."

"The chapel?" Kip asked. "Not the church?"

"Yes, the chapel. We don't use the chapel anymore. Too dangerous. Used only for storage now."

This piqued Dana's interest. *Too dangerous?* she thought but asked, "The boys started the fire?"

"Well, yes, yes, I'm sure they did. Of course they did. Caught them red-handed."

"What alerted you to check the chapel?" Dana asked.

"They were attempting to put it out," Father Michael said, then circled back to Dana's question. "I smelled it. That's why I went down."

"What made you think the boys had started the fire?" Kip asked. "If they were attempting to put it out?"

The old man rubbed his head, removed his glasses, and ran his thumb over the lenses, attempting to remove a smudge. "Well, there *was* a fire." He spoke defensively as if they thought he was making the whole thing up.

Dana wondered why they would be messing around in the chapel, used only for storage, according to Father Michael.

"Why is the chapel too dangerous to use?" she asked.

"Of course, they started it," Father Michael said indignantly. "Trying to blame a ghost," he said with a laugh that turned into a cough. He pulled a tissue from his pocket and wiped his mouth.

Dana and Kip exchanged a quick glance.

Father Michael placed the tissue back in his pocket, folded his arms defensively over his wide chest, and rested his arms atop his protruding belly.

"They blamed someone else?" Dana asked. "What exactly did they say?"

"You know boys!" He looked directly at Kip, dismissing Dana as if she knew nothing about boys. As if all boys would blame someone else.

After several moments, sensing this was as much as Father Michael would reveal, Kip asked if they could take a look inside the chapel.

The priest rose slowly and explained they would have to enter the chapel from outside, that the staircase leading down from the interior of the church hadn't been used in years. It was a safety issue, he told them, and the church would be liable if anyone got hurt.

Was this the danger? Dana wondered. Merely a question of safe access?

They walked slowly down the hall, exited the building, and then, with great effort on Father Michael's part, they circled around to the left side of the church and entered an unlocked door—a fact Dana tucked away in her mind—and down a narrow, dimly lit staircase that led to a small chapel. A hint of mildew and maybe a touch of leftover incense lingered in the air.

Father Michael showed them where he found the boys, directly in front of the altar, where, he explained, they had started the fire.

"Is the outdoor entry the only one used now?" Dana asked.

The priest didn't answer, maybe didn't even hear her. "The school uses it for storing supplies," he finally said.

Dana wasn't aware that the school was still open. So many had been closed. Kip was already exploring as Dana stood, scoping out the interior of the chapel. The altar had been draped, as well as several small statues. Not the large, bigger-than-life versions normally found in the sanctuary of the main church, but smaller icons. Dana remembered years ago, during Lent, the statues were draped with purple fabric, the color of sacrifice and penance leading up to the Easter holidays, the Resurrection. These were covered in what appeared to be old white bedsheets, the kind that kids used to make into Halloween costumes. Cut some eye holes, and voila, you have a ghost. *Ghosts?* Dana considered.

Kip opened a door to the left of the altar and pointed out a stairwell leading to the interior of the church.

"No, no, you must not enter," Father said. "The wooden steps are falling apart. Much too dangerous. One might be injured."

Dana saw another door leading to an area that she guessed was partially beneath the stairwell. She opened it and flicked on the light. Both Father Michael and Kip were right behind her. She and Kip had to duck their heads to enter the space. Without asking, Dana opened a cupboard. Stacks of paper, both white and colored, hymnals, and daily missals were stacked on the shelves. In another section, garments hung on wire hangars along a wooden bar. Black cassocks, white surplices. Altar boys. She could smell something distinct, again a combination of mildew and incense. And something else. A singed, burnt smell. She touched one of the garments, even as Father quickly shut the closet door. But not before Dana saw a distinct brown marking on the hem of a once-pure-white altar boy's surplice.

"You should speak with one of the firemen," Father Michael told them, "They can verify that the fire was completely out when they got here."

"A fireman spoke to the boys?" Kip asked, tossing a look toward Dana.

"Oh, no, no," Father Michael said, "I had sent them home, the boys, to their parents by then."

"How long did they stay?" Dana asked. "The firemen?"

"Oh, not long at all. Everything was under control." He squinted, studying the two reporters, then said, "Everything under control. Check with the Fire Marshal."

"Boston Fire Marshal?"

"State Fire Marshal," he said.

"State Fire Marshal?" she asked, wondering if Father Michael was confused. She found this strange, and she also wondered why a report had not been filed if someone from the fire department had come out. Even if the fire had been extinguished by the time they arrived, wouldn't there be an official, publicly accessible record?

"Thank you, Father Michael," Kip said as they walked back up the stairs that led outside. He and Dana headed to their cars as Father Michael returned to his office.

"No record of this fire?" Dana asked.

"Not that I could find," Kip replied. "Sometimes those take a while, I imagine."

"State Fire Marshal?"

"That doesn't make much sense."

"Ghosts?" Dana said after a while. "Father said the boys saw ghosts?"

"Well, I saw them, too, didn't you?" Kip asked, shooting Dana a grin.

"Looked like ghosts to me," she agreed with a laugh and then asked, "Did you notice a smell?"

"The whole place reeked of mold, musty old smells," Kip said.

"When I opened the storage closet, I got a whiff of something. A smoky scent. Something scorched."

"I didn't smell it. The fire was like two months ago."

"It smelled like scorched cloth," she said. "Ever burn something with an iron?"

"I'm a wash and wear fellow all the way myself."

"The altar boys' surplices."

"You think someone attempted to burn them? Then returned them to the closet?" Kip asked.

"I don't know," Dana replied. "But there was a discolored area on the bottom of one of them."

"Discolored?"

"Singed, maybe," Dana said.

"As in a fire."

"Rescued perhaps," Dana said slowly. If the boys had attempted to burn the cassocks and surplices—if it truly was the boys who started the fire—someone had returned them to the storage closet.

"Father said nothing about those."

"No, he didn't," Dana said.

When Dana picked Mia up after the orientation at St. Gertrude's, she asked, "How was it? Did you meet anyone?"

"A couple of girls," Mia replied.

"A couple?"

"One a transfer from public school."

Dana remembered back in her day the public-school transfers were often the troublemakers. Kids whose parents were trying the "religious" school as a last resort.

"Oh," Dana said, glancing at Mia, brow raised, hoping for more information. "The other girl is new to the area? Where is she from?"

"Somewhere out west. Oregon?" Mia pronounced it clearly with three syllables.

Dana waited for more, then finally said, "That's good, I mean that you are making friends. Was the orientation helpful?"

"Mostly what I already knew," Mia replied vaguely. "Information emailed before. The tour of the building was helpful. Really, I'll do fine," she said, clearly trying to put Dana's mind at ease. "Everyone was helpful. I like the principal, Sister Mary Ellen."

A nun for principal, though hardly the type who showed up in full habit in Broadway plays and cartoons. A modern woman who wore a business suit and ran the school as though she were CEO of a major corporation, which was probably a good thing as so many of the schools had shut down. The girls from St. Gertrude's were known for their academic achievements, as well as involvement in social causes and projects to help the community.

Back at her apartment, Dana suggested Mia try on the school uniforms she'd ordered and had sent to Dana's address—they'd been allowed to wear whatever they wished to orientation. They were both relieved that they fit, especially Dana, who wasn't one to do alterations and didn't even own a sewing machine, though she knew her mother would help if need be.

"Should I fix dinner?" Dana asked. "Will they have dinner at the party Zac's invited you to?"

"I don't know," Mia replied with a lift of her shoulders. "Zac is picking me up at 7:00."

To make sure she didn't go hungry, Dana tossed some spaghetti in a pot of boiling water, heated a jar of pre-made sauce, and threw a salad together. She took a small loaf of French bread out of the freezer and thawed and warmed it in the microwave. She wondered what Mia thought of her "authentic" Italian dinner, but the girl ate little and spoke even less. Dana sensed she was thinking about the party, maybe concerned about meeting Zac's friends, perhaps more concerned than she had been about starting a new school.

CHAPTER SIX

"Mia, this is Hick, this is Tanner, Rachel, and Elli," Zac introduced his friends.

Again, Mia wasn't sure how to greet them, so she just offered a wave.

Elli said, "You're going to St. Gertrude's? My cousin Kaylee Westover is a sophomore there. You're a senior?"

"Yes," Mia said, though technically this wasn't correct since the schools in Italy did not recognize the four-year system of U.S. high schools, and her acceptance at University was based not on graduation but on final exams she'd take back home. "My first year, so I don't know anyone yet."

"Can I get you a soda?" Hick offered.

On the drive over, Zac had explained that the party was at Hick's, that his parents would be there, but the kids were upstairs in what Zac called their family room, which was complete with TV, video games, a pool table, and a bar that didn't appear to offer anything but water and soda, for which Mia was grateful. She didn't want to have to decide what she would do if she were offered a beer. She didn't want Zac to think she wasn't any fun.

"Just a water, please," Mia said. Her stomach felt tight and twisted as if the spaghetti Dana had served for dinner was tying itself in knots inside her.

"Water's good," Zac echoed. He took Mia's hand and led her

over to the bar where snacks—chips, dips, veggies, cheese and crackers, had been set out. Probably by Hick's mom as they were in matching bright blue bowls, with napkins with football motifs fanned out beside them.

"See, nothing for Aunt Dana to worry about," Zac said, glancing around, taking a swig of water. He waved to a couple of boys, big guys standing outside on a deck that looked out onto the street. Mia noticed they were both smoking cigarettes. If that was as bad as it got, she wouldn't have to worry.

"She let you come tonight," Zac said.

Mia glanced back toward the balcony and said, standing on her tiptoes as if she could see down to the street, "Maybe she followed me."

They both laughed as a couple of guys came up to them. One of them gave Zac a punch to the shoulder. "You ready for that big game Friday night?"

"Friday under the lights," Zac replied with a grin.

"More likely under the microscope," the biggest said. "Ol' Coach Pickson is going to be watching to see who he's gonna throw off the team."

"Not me," Zac said, holding up his water bottle. "I'm in training, keeping healthy." He picked a carrot off the veggie tray, pointed it at the big guy, and then took a crunchy bite.

"Whatever," the biggest fellow said in a mocking tone. He pulled a vape pen out of his pocket and headed out to the balcony. His friend raised his shoulders as if to say, *isn't he hopeless*, and followed.

"So, seriously, how's it going?" Zac said to Mia after the two had left. He picked up a chip, dipped it, then stuffed it whole into his mouth and chewed. "With Aunt Dana?"

"Fine. So far just fine."

Zac laughed. "You know she's going to keep an eye on your every move."

"Isn't that what parents," Mia said, then corrected herself, "or sponsors, or guardians, or whatever she is, are supposed to do?"

"Yep."

Zac asked if her dad was strict, and Mia told him a little about her life back home. "My father trusts me. So, I hope Dana will too."

"Your dad's been doing this for seventeen years. Dana doesn't have much experience, especially with a teenager. Aunt Dana does not have a single clue," he said, emphasizing each word.

"I don't plan on giving her any trouble," Mia said sincerely.

"You are a sweet girl," Zac said, and Mia thought that was a compliment, but she wasn't sure. He touched her cheek, and for a moment she wondered if he might kiss her. "If you don't plan on giving Aunt Dana any trouble, then neither will I." He withdrew his hand and said, "You play pool?" He glanced over at the pool table.

"Not really," she said as Zac took her hand and led her over to the table. He pulled a dollar bill out of his pocket and placed it on the table.

"Ah, a challenge," one of the boys said, chalking his cue stick, pointing it in Zac's direction.

A woman came into the room, carrying a tray. Hick's mom, Mia guessed. She stopped to say hi to Zac, and he introduced Mia, explained that she was here for the year, staying with his aunt, going to St. Gertrude's.

"That's a good school," Hick's mom said with approval. "So glad you could come this evening," she added graciously, then went on to fill the bowls of chips and crackers, which were almost empty, and to freshen up the veggies, which had hardly been touched. She checked the minifridge, Mia guessed to make sure there was nothing there but water and soda. She moved around the room casually, stopping to talk to several of the kids before leaving.

Zac was on to a game of pool. Mia stood watching, feeling out of place. A tall girl approached and introduced herself as Mimi. She had to be at least 6 feet tall. Soon, two more girls joined them, both almost as tall as Mimi.

"Well, here's the team," Mimi said, and Mia guessed by the size and confidence of the trio that they were a winning team. She glanced around the room, deciding that Zac was part of the popular crowd. She thought she might like hanging out with these kids. But she wasn't sure. None of them would be going to her school. So maybe it didn't matter.

Dana and Kip sat at the dining room table. She'd made coffee, sliced a couple of pieces from the pie she'd brought home from her mom's.

Initially, they'd set up this get-together to go over notes for the eldercare story they were working on and review their interview schedules. Dana had arranged to talk with several elderly Boston residents who'd received home health care from a company whose services they thought might be fraudulent. Kip was looking at nursing homes where patients had died due to neglect, according to some family members.

But as soon as Kip sat down, Dana knew they were about to veer off course as he lifted his battered briefcase onto the table and pulled out copies of the blurry photos taken by the *Globe* photographer at St. Barbara's the night of the fire. Dana flipped through them. There were several of a crane reaching into the dark sky, a few of firefighters, unidentifiable, indistinguishable in their protective gear.

"You still have those files?" Kip asked, "on the churches that have been closed down or sold over the past ten years?"

"I thought you came over to go over our eldercare project," she said, and then, "You didn't get any shots yourself?"

"Nope." He defended himself by telling her that his phone battery had been running low, and he didn't want to be without power since his Uber driver had deserted him. He didn't mention Dana's inability to pick him up, and she did not mention his diminished mental capacity and judgment. After all, he'd merely come across the scene. It wasn't like he'd been drinking on the job.

"Something's going on," Kip said. "Someone purposely started those fires. And we might just have possession of one of the greatest archives ever on Catholic Churches in the Archdiocese of Boston."

Dana could see Kip wasn't about to let this go, and after their meeting with Father Michael, she was curious, too.

She stood, went into her bedroom, got a key from her nightstand, went to her office—Mia's room now—unlocked the file cabinet, pulled out a stack of files, then returned and placed the pile on the table before Kip. He stared at them for a moment, then shot Dana a conspiratorial smile before opening the top file folder.

The folder contained a printout of a spreadsheet of churches that had been closed or sold, transactions obviously timed and related to the financial difficulties the Church had suffered as a result of the lawsuits. Dana had updated the information sporadically over the past ten years. She wasn't sure if it was current or not, as they hadn't added anything in the past couple of years. Both St. Aloysius and St. Barbara's were on the list, but not St. Lawrence's.

"What are we looking for?" Dana asked.

"Not sure," Kip replied. "I've got an interview set up for Wednesday with Ryan Kelly, the Fire Marshal."

"Oh?" she said, wondering why he hadn't mentioned this earlier. "I've got some interviews scheduled." She gestured toward the eldercare notes.

"I can go on my own," Kip said. "Report back to you if I discover anything that might help us."

"What time is the interview?"

"One. Wednesday afternoon."

"My appointments are in the morning," Dana said slowly as she thought this through. "Mia's got a half-day on Wednesday." Mia had a key to the apartment, she reasoned, and could let herself in. "Yes, I'll go."

"Great, then." Kip took a drink of coffee, the last bite of his pie. "Did you make this?" he asked skeptically. Kip had a sweet tooth. Until the past couple of years, the guy could put it away without showing, but now he was starting to develop a mid-age paunch.

"My mom did," Dana said. "Leftovers from Sunday's dinner."

"Oh, yes," Kip said. "How did that go? Family dinner with Mia?"

"She's a nice girl. She fits in well with the family." Then Dana thought of what her brother had told her at dinner, something she was able to shove from her thoughts, or at least into a corner of her mind because she was overwhelmed with other things—Mia, Kip's insistence on looking into these fires. "My brother Jeff said Drew is considering a position here in Boston."

"Oh?" Kip looked up from the file. "How does that make you feel?" He sounded like a shrink, encouraging his patient to share her feelings. "Having him back in town?"

"Not sure he is coming back. Just considering. There was a woman with him—"

"With Drew?" He glanced up again, brow wrinkled in confusion. "I thought you said it was your brother who told you. You talked to Drew?"

"I saw him."

"He stopped by? With a woman?" he asked incredulously.

"No, no, I ran into him at the airport when I went to pick Mia up on Friday." Dana wasn't sure how she would feel if Drew came back to Boston. Most likely, she wouldn't even see him. They had nothing to connect them to one another anymore.

"With a woman?" Kip asked again.

"They were returning from a week in Paris."

"A serious relationship? You don't spend a week in Paris unless it's serious. Or great sex."

Dana could feel her brows lift as she shot him a look. "Are we really going to talk about my ex's sex life?"

"Inappropriate?" Kip asked with a chuckle.

"One might consider that inappropriate," Dana replied, shaking her head. She'd had the same exact thought—Drew and Amy were having great sex. Or they were in love. Maybe both.

The bedroom was not the problem between Dana and Drew, at least during the early years of their marriage. But, after they lost Joel, the first time he'd taken her into his arms, run his hand down her body, caressed her breasts, a prelude to lovemaking, she wanted to scream. She felt as if he were telling her that life must go on.

47

"So where is she now?" Kip asked, glancing up.

"The woman?" Dana asked, confused.

"Mia." Kip looked around as if the girl would pop into the room, as if just realizing she wasn't there.

"My nephew Zac took her to a party. An end-of-summer, beginning-of-school party."

"A *party*?" He pronounced the word *party* with a flair that made it sound dangerous. *Drinking, drugs, and debauchery*, he might as well have said. He raised a dubious brow as if to say, *you sure this is okay?* Dana hadn't known Kip in high school—he'd grown up someplace out West—but she imagined he'd been a partier during the day and had a pretty good idea what went on at high school parties. Dana had been a bit of a nerd herself, which put her at a disadvantage in this particular situation.

"She's a good girl," she said. "Zac's a good kid."

"I'm sure they are," Kip said, then paused as if to consider a smart-ass remark.

"By the way," Dana said, "thanks again for helping set up the desk for her room."

"So, it's working out? Mia's room, the desk?" Then without waiting for an answer, he stood. "How about another piece of pie?" He grabbed his empty plate.

She smiled. "Yes, please go ahead. I'm good. I'll let mom know how much you enjoyed the pie."

Kip made his way to the kitchen, came back with another slice of pie, sat down, took a large bite. "So, what's the connection," he asked, picking up a file. "St. Al's . . . St. Barbara's . . . St. Lawrence's?"

A cute, tiny blonde wearing expensive-looking embroidered jeans came up to Mia and said, "You dating Zac?" Mia couldn't tell if she approved or not. She had a sour look about her. Mia wondered if she did too—have a sour look—and this girl was just reflecting Mia's own demeanor. Mia turned her eyes from the girl to Zac, who had all but deserted her. He just kept winning, sliding those colorful pool balls into the pockets, smiling over at her now and then as if she was enjoying watching him.

"Oh, no," she told the tiny blonde—a girl even shorter than Mia herself. "I'm staying with his aunt for the year. He invited me to come along."

"His aunt?" she asked. "The one that writes those horrible articles for that horrible newspaper? No one reads that anymore."

Mia wondered how she knew they were horrible articles if no one read them. "She writes for *The Boston Globe*. She's an award-winning journalist."

Before the girl had time for a comeback, another girl had joined them. She was chubby and curvy and wore extra tight jeans and a tank top with a denim jacket decorated with buttons and patches. "Meagan is going to hypnotize Becket," the girl said in a low voice. "She says she can get rid of his nerves. His low self-esteem." She glanced at Mia. "Do you believe in hypnosis? Meagan says we can win the game if Becket believes we can."

"Meagan, that witch," the tiny blonde said.

Mia didn't know if she believed in hypnosis or not, but it sounded interesting. She glanced over at the far side of the room, where a kid with reddish hair and broad shoulders sat on a chair. He wore an athletic jersey with *Barron* in bold caps printed on the back. Mia didn't know if it was the name of a professional athlete or the boy's name. Opposite him, a thin girl with dark hair, ends tipped with blue, sat. A crowd was gathering around the two.

The girl in the denim jacket motioned Mia to join her. She glanced at Zac, so involved in his game, he didn't notice when she walked over to where the boy and girl sat facing one another. The girl with the blue-tipped hair had a gold nose ring. Her makeup was severe with black cat-eye liner. She looked directly at the boy, who seemed to be in a trance. Mia thought the girl would be spouting some gibberish, but she spoke in a low voice, words kind and soothing. She told the boy, "You are fearless, Becket, you are the best quarterback in the conference. You are strong. You are smart. You are a leader. You believe in your team. You are a winner."

49

"Winner, winner, winner," one of the boys in the group shouted, and the girl with Mia shot him a look that said *shut up*, which he did.

The girl, the hypnotist, the witch, as the tiny blonde called her, did not seem fazed by the activity around her. She leaned in, still looking directly at Becket. Her eyes did not waver and neither did his. It was as if they were alone in the room, not surrounded by curious, maybe even doubtful, observers. She said something so softly that Mia could not hear. After several moments, she sat erect, back straight, but she did not lose eye contact. "Now, close your eyes, Becket," she said softly. "When I snap my fingers, you will come back. You will not recall my exact words. But this power of self-confidence will stay with you. Do you understand?"

His eyes closed, his posture drooped. "Yes," he said.

The girl leaned in, touched his hand, then released it and snapped her fingers.

Becket sat motionless, but his eyes popped open. His posture straightened, and he blinked, then glanced around.

Again the girl touched him, made eye contact and whispered something. Becket nodded.

Mia didn't know what to think. She didn't know if the two were putting on a show or if Becket had really been hypnotized. The girl sat very still for several moments, then got up, spoke to no one, and left the room.

Mia turned to see Zac standing beside her.

"What just happened?" Zac asked.

"I'm not sure," Mia said.

"We'd better get going. I told Aunt Dana I'd have you home by eleven."

Mia pulled her cellphone out of her pocket and glanced at the time. She was shocked it was already half past ten.

On the way home, he asked if she'd had a good time, and she said it was interesting.

"Interesting? Not like parties in Italy?"

"Not exactly. Was that girl really hypnotizing Becket? Is she one of your classmates?"

"So, that's what was going on."

"That's what they said."

"The girl's not in any of my classes. She's the artsy type. Don't know her," he answered curtly. "Not in my group of friends. Becket has been having issues. Not feeling confident about his abilities."

"Don't we all?" Mia said. "Have issues."

"She's a little unusual. Weird. I was surprised to see her at the party."

"You don't even know her?" There was something in Mia's voice, almost an accusation. She could hear the tone herself. "Yet, you are calling her weird? Because of the way she looks? Or—?"

"Or what? You think I'm being . . . what?" Zac said before Mia could finish her thought. "I wasn't implying anything. Though she is weird. But, you're right, I don't know her. She doesn't hang out with the people in our group."

"But, someone invited her?"

"I guess."

"She was invited to hypnotize him? To make him feel more confident, so you'd win your game. Isn't that excessive for a high school sport?"

Zac laughed. "You don't understand how important this is."

"Oh, really?" she said sarcastically and glanced over at Zac, who didn't seem to react. He was right; she didn't understand.

"Aunt Dana will be pleased that I'm bringing you home on time, completely sober."

Now, it was Mia who didn't respond. Was Zac implying that he was the one determining her behavior, her choices? They drove on in silence.

"Something I wanted to ask you," Mia finally said.

"Yes."

"Does your Aunt Dana have a boyfriend? Does she ever date?"

"She used to now and then, but no, not lately. I don't think. At least nothing serious. She never brings anyone to any family gatherings."

"Your dad was talking about someone. I could see her reaction.

Something about this man being considered for a position, coming back to Boston. I think he called him Drew."

Zac's eyes narrowed. He slowed for a stoplight. "Her ex," he said after a long moment.

"Boyfriend?"

"Husband," Zac replied. "I don't remember him much." They pulled back into traffic. "He's a lawyer. They broke up when I was little."

"Oh," Mia said, and then she hesitated, questioning if she should ask, but she wanted to know. "They had a child? They lost him?" Dana had spoken to Mia about her son just once, when they were in Italy. She hadn't explained what happened to him. She'd called him Joel. "His name was Joel?"

Zac twisted his lower lip with his fingers. Mia could see the subject made him uncomfortable. He gazed ahead, didn't look at her, didn't even acknowledge her question.

"That was a long time ago," he finally said. There was a quiver in Zac's voice, and Mia knew if she was to learn more about what had happened to Dana's son, the information would not be coming from Zac.

CHAPTER SEVEN

Dana's phone rang just as she replaced the folders in the cabinet in Mia's room. She rushed back to grab her phone off the table where Kip sat, finishing his third piece of pie.

"Hi," she said.

"It's Zac."

She could see that from the digital name on her screen. "Everything okay?"

"Of course," he answered. "Just wanted to let you know that we're back. Right on time. I told Mia I'd walk her up, come say hi, but she said she was fine."

"Thanks, Zac. Did you have fun?"

"It was interesting," he said in a way that Dana understood was probably about as much as either one of them would share with her.

"Kids are back," Dana told Kip.

"Guess I'll head out then," Kip said, standing, shaking one leg, then the other, stiff from sitting so long. His pants had bunched up on his leg, and he reached down to straighten them. He took his plate back to the kitchen, then returned and slipped on his jacket. "See you Wednesday, then, interview with Fire Marshal Ryan Kelly."

"I'll let you know if it doesn't work out."

"What do you mean? We're on. Aren't we?"

But, before she could answer, the key clicked in the lock, and Mia walked in. Dana introduced her to Kip, told Mia he was a reporter for the *Globe*, that they'd been working together for years, and Mia said, "Very pleased to meet you," and then to Dana, "See you in the morning." Her tone suggested things hadn't gone so well. Maybe she was just tired. Kip raised a brow, and Dana could see he was getting the same feeling.

"Wednesday, then," he said as he left.

The following morning, Mia and Dana started out early, walking several blocks to the T for a practice run. Dana offered a detailed commentary and history of the Massachusetts Bay Transportation Authority, the public transportation system in Boston, explaining the various color codes for each of the four main lines, telling Mia how the Boston subway was the first in the United States.

"The first tunnels were opened in 1897, and they're still in use under Boston Common," Dana said, and then she laughed. "I guess that's not very old by Italian standards." Mia just smiled.

They transferred to the first bus, then the second, and then walked from the bus stop to Mia's school. Dana suggested they practice getting back home too. After hopping on one bus, then another, they arrived back at the subway. Mia told Dana she was sure they didn't need to practice the entire route back home. Reluctantly, Dana agreed, and they headed downtown to her office.

Dana explained to Mia that the *Globe* had recently moved to their downtown space, that Dana herself was just settling in. She introduced Mia to several other reporters, a few people who were milling about. "Support staff," Dana told her. Dana's editor, Macauley Macey, was out for the day.

They stopped for a quick lunch and headed to the Museum of Fine Arts. While browsing, they talked about their upcoming weekend trip to New York, where they would visit the Metropolitan Museum of Art. They'd decided to go to Zac's game, then take the early Saturday train.

Mia felt a longing for home as she studied the paintings in the

Italian Renaissance Gallery. They lingered over Botticelli's Virgin and Child with St. John the Baptist, which both Dana and Mia agreed was the most beautiful painting in the museum. The images of the mother and child made Mia wonder how this affected Dana. She was a mother without a child. Mia herself was a child without a mother. The sweetness of the picture, the interaction between the two was so very tender. St. John lurked in the background. Mia thought of the question she'd asked Zac about Dana's child and how he had reacted. He didn't want to talk about it. She glanced at Dana, aware that she had spoken to Mia only once about her son.

They took the T back home, Dana quiet as if she were all chatted out after their busy day. Mia's thoughts turned to Zac, how their date—no, it wasn't really a date—hadn't ended particularly well, and how he hadn't even called or texted all day. Well, she guessed she could have contacted him herself. It wasn't like they were living in the twentieth century when a guy had to make the first move. But, maybe in person, she and Zac just didn't get along that well. He'd pretty much dumped her to play pool, left her alone at the party. Then, on the way home, he'd said something about how pleased Dana would be that *he* was bringing *her* home completely sober. Maybe none of this mattered anyway. They wouldn't be going to the same school and, even if she had to see him on an occasional Sunday for dinner at his grandma's, they could at least tolerate each other for a couple of hours. Mia could even go upstairs and play Monopoly with the little kids and the uncles.

Wednesday morning, Dana told Mia she could walk her down to the T if she'd like.

"I'm not in kindergarten," Mia replied with a playful lilt in her voice, and, thankfully, Dana responded agreeably with a laugh. "I'll see you this afternoon, then."

She navigated the subway, then the bus with only a few nervous flutters. Once she was on the second bus, she relaxed and studied the people around her. A plump woman with curly black hair clutched an enormous briefcase protectively in her lap. A man, backpack at his feet, held a cellphone, fingers tapping rapidly. An Asian woman sat with a child who kept glancing at Mia. She smiled and so did he, shyly cuddling closer to his mother. The bus stopped several times. Passengers got off, and new passengers got on. Mia checked the app on her phone. She was almost there.

At the next stop, a girl about Mia's age, wearing a long, tan raincoat that made her look like a spy, hopped on the bus, barely making it on before the door swished shut. She glanced around, not finding a place, then stood, grabbing a bar. She looked familiar, but Mia wasn't sure why. Then she realized it was the girl from the party, the girl that one of the other girls had called a witch, the girl Zac implied didn't fit in. The hypnotist. She was devoid of the catlike makeup, and the ring through her nose was missing. But the dark hair was still tipped with blue. What had they called her? Meagan?

Meagan shot Mia a narrow-eyed look. Did she recognize Mia from the party, too? What would she be doing on the bus this morning? Mia guessed they were some distance from where they had gone to the party, which she'd assumed was near Zac's public school.

When the bus stopped where Mia had practiced getting off with Dana the previous day, Meagan adjusted her backpack and headed to the exit. Mia was just a few steps behind her. She didn't want Meagan to think she was following her, but they were going in the same direction. Mia slowed her pace, but then abruptly, Meagan turned. "Are you following me?" she said roughly.

"Of course not," Mia replied. "Just because we are going in the same direction does not mean I am following you. I got on the bus before you did."

Meagan's eyes narrowed. "You were watching me."

"Well, no," Mia said defensively.

"You were at Hick's house on Monday."

"As were you," Mia replied.

"As were you," Meagan mocked. She studied Mia and then said, "Where are you from?"

"What do you mean? Which planet? I guess I could ask you the same thing." She remembered Zac calling Meagan weird, though she certainly didn't look as weird today as she had at the party.

"Your accent," Meagan said. "I don't think you're from around these here parts." Her voice was twangy and taunting as if making fun of the way Mia spoke.

"Italy," Mia said. She didn't think her accent was that noticeable. In fact, people usually told her she had little, if any, accent. Her English teacher back home said her English was very good. Nearly perfect. When she told her teacher she was going to Boston, she said there was a distinct Boston accent. Well, maybe Mia had not mastered that, but she hadn't noticed that Dana and her family spoke any different than other Americans she'd met.

"Italy. That's cool," Meagan finally said, and Mia detected a shift in her voice. She remembered how softly, how reassuringly she'd spoken to Becket.

They were nearing St. Gertrude's now, passing the small parking lot filled with a variety of cars. Some sporty, some shiny new, some that looked like castoffs from someone's grandmother. That's what Mia drove at home. Admittedly it was a Mercedes, though very old. A car her grandmother had given up driving years ago, that had been gathering cobwebs in the garage. Mia wondered about the girls who drove these cars, if they would be as different and varied as their transportation. Even as these imaginings flitted through her mind, Mia was aware that Meagan was walking beside her. As they approached the sidewalk leading to the main entrance, Mia stopped and took in a deep breath. Meagan stopped, too, and then she motioned for Mia to walk with her.

"How did you know I'm going to St. Gertrude's?" Mia asked.

"Duh," Meagan said, "the uniform."

Mia felt herself blush with embarrassment. She was wearing her officially approved blue and green plaid skirt, white blouse, and a cardigan sweater since the morning air was slightly brisk. Meagan wore a raincoat that Mia thought was too heavy for the current temperature and would be sweltering by afternoon.

the slightest smile, a smile much friendlier than Mia would have
imagined the girl capable of.

CHAPTER EIGHT

Dana pulled up to a green-shuttered house in the Hyde Park neighborhood, delighted to find an open parking spot so close. She walked up to the front door and knocked. It was her second interview that morning. During the first, she'd talked with a woman who'd recently lost her mother, a client of the home health therapy company that Dana was homing in on for their prospective piece. The daughter was, Dana realized, still in a state of shock and had provided little if any helpful information. Dana suggested they get together later, and the woman had agreed.

Within seconds, the door opened and Laura McClennan introduced herself. Dana guessed Laura to be in her early to mid-sixties, though the stressed look on her face possibly added years. Dana knew her elderly mother, Mary Cassidy, was in her late-eighties.

"She's totally homebound," Laura said. "It's difficult for me to take her out anymore." She smiled sadly and led Dana through the dining room and then a narrow hall to a bedroom.

A woman sat hunched in a wheelchair, facing the window. The blinds had been raised, and sunshine fell into the room across the floral print bedcover. Laura turned her mother toward Dana.

"Mom, this is the woman I told you about. She wants to talk to you about the therapy you received through Home Therapy Care."

Mary studied Dana for several moments as if attempting to place her. The woman's face was thin and lined. She wore lipstick, blush, and her brows were filled in with brow pencil to form perfect arches. Her housecoat matched the colors of her bedcover as if the woman was part of the furnishings. She adjusted the housecoat to cover her thin legs, encased in support stockings with open toes. Her toenails were painted pale pink, and Dana could see the woman still had some pride in her appearance. She guessed the daughter had helped with the pedicure. A fleeting and unexpected thought . . . *who will paint my toenails when I am old?*

"You are the woman who lost her child," the woman said in a raspy voice.

Dana felt as if she had been socked in the chest. A lump rose up into her throat.

"Mom," Laura said, placing a gentle hand on the woman's shoulder, then lowering herself to the edge of the bed, "Mrs. Pierson is from the newspaper." Dana had never been a *Mrs.* Pierson, but she didn't correct Laura, who motioned for her to sit on the damask chair next to the bed. "She's here to talk about the home care you received after your fall."

"Yes, I know who she is. She writes those stories in the newspaper."

Was Dana just imagining what the old woman had said? *The woman who lost her child.* She took in a deep breath and began her interview, though it seemed her words, as well as Mary's responses, were coming from a deep dark hole, fighting for oxygen as they rose into the room.

The woman spoke slowly and carefully, talking about this therapist, this doctor, that hospital. A litany, not of neglect or abuse, but of those who had cared for her. Dana attempted to lead the flow of conversation, questioning, then listening, trying to keep Mary from veering off from one unrelated topic to another. After about twenty minutes, Dana's head spinning, she thanked the two women and stood to leave.

Then, abruptly, Mary said, "You should not have put that priest in prison with a murderer." Dana, stunned once more, said nothing as the old woman reached out and took her hand. Mary's hand felt cold, though her grip was surprisingly firm.

Saying no more, Mary released her hand, and Dana left the room, breathing heavily now, as Laura accompanied her to the front door. Dana's heart throbbed in her ears, pushing into her brain, ready to burst out of her skull. She managed to reach her car, jab her key into the ignition, and dart out onto the street. She was shaking so badly she could barely hold on to the steering wheel. She pulled over, stopped and parked. For several minutes she did nothing but sit, head lowered against the steering wheel, trying to free her mind, even as Mary's words played through her head. *The woman who lost her child.*

Lost.

Dana had lost her child.

Mary did not say, *someone came and took your child,* or *your son was kidnapped,* or *your precious boy was abducted.* Dana was the woman who lost her child. *She* had *lost* her child.

You should not have put that priest in prison with a murderer. Dana had not. The priest had done that to himself.

Attempting to clear her mind, to push Mary's disturbing words aside, or shove them into the tightly held place within herself where she stored her pain, Dana took in a deep breath, then another. She considered Kip, his interview with the Fire Marshal. She'd told him she'd call if she couldn't make it. She glanced at her phone, muted during the interview, and saw there was a voice message from her editor Mac, Macauley Macey. She listened. He'd like to talk with her. He knew she had taken some time off, but how about Thursday morning at 10:00? If that didn't work, let him know. Dana wondered if he wanted to go over this latest project, get a clearer idea of where they were going.

Then she checked the time, realizing it would be impossible to arrive by 1:00 for the interview with the Fire Marshal. It was a good fifty-minute drive to his office in Stow, and she had no desire to make the trip. Right now, she wanted nothing more than to roll into a tight little ball. She'd been here before. So many times. And yet, she had continued. She had gone on.

When Dana finally arrived for the interview with the State Fire Marshal, Ryan Kelly, he and Kip were engaged in a lively conversation about baseball—something Dana probably knew more about than either of them. Even after her dad had played for the Sox and gone on to a second career in sports journalism, a love for the game was their special bond. Dana had played in high school. She was a pitcher and had a pretty good arm.

Kip sat across the desk from Kelly. A third chair sat empty. She apologized as she sat, blaming her tardiness on traffic, which was partially true. The Fire Marshal didn't seem to be offended, though Kip sent her a semi-annoyed glance.

"Mr. Connor here," Kelly said, waving an arm toward Kip, "is interested in knowing more about some recent fires. There's not much I can tell you at this point, other than they are currently under investigation."

His eyes, which were exceedingly blue, narrowed slightly, and he looked directly at Dana as he spoke. His gaze shifted when Kip asked, "Is there any connection between the fire at St. Barbara's on Saturday morning and St. Aloysius last month?" Kip was letting Dana know he hadn't started asking the pertinent questions until she arrived. He knew she'd show up. She always did, though it wasn't her style to be late.

"Both still under investigation," Kelly said vaguely. Dana noticed a sprinkle of freckles across his nose and forehead. His complexion was fair, his hair a faded coppery color, the natural progression of a redhead. Oddly, she imagined him as a child with bright red hair, and guessed he'd had to slather on the sunscreen in the summer, which some boys might see as a wimpy thing to do. Yet, there was nothing wimpy about Kelly. He leaned back, folding his arms across his chest. An indication of defensiveness? Or strength and authority? She was having trouble reading his body language. He leaned forward, resting his arms on the desk.

"What about St. Lawrence's?" she asked.

His eyes narrowed again for a moment and then he replied, "How did you know about St. Lawrence's?"

"We're unable to find anything," Kip said cautiously, "any report on that fire." Dana caught on that Kip wasn't answering the question and, even though he maintained his composure, she could tell Kelly was aware of that too. His cheeks had colored in an almost imperceptible way.

"An official report might not be available just yet," Kelly said.

Not a priority, Dana considered. But would it become one?

"We understand that a couple of boys were caught in the chapel," Kip said, "playing with matches. The chapel is no longer being used by the church? Did anyone talk to the boys?"

Dana wanted to tell Kip to slow down. He was throwing out too many questions at once.

Kelly replied, "The priest said they put the fire out easily, and there was no damage to the chapel." Dana and Kip waited for more, but the Fire Marshal added nothing.

"Is it odd to have so many fires in Catholic churches in such a short period of time?" Dana asked. "Three total in the last couple of months?"

"Do you know how many fires are reported each year in Boston? In Suffolk County?" Kelly asked without a moment's hesitation. His voice was calm as still water. But certainly not as transparent. And there was that definite hint of blush in his cheeks.

Both Dana and Kip shook their heads. She had no idea how many fires were reported in the city each year, and certainly not the county. Normally she would have done more legwork. One thing she knew from a quick online search—Ryan Kelly had only been on the job for a few months, he'd risen through the ranks, and he'd started out as a firefighter. She didn't know how old he was, but she guessed about her age—late forties, early fifties.

But, she'd gathered no stats on fires in Boston, and Kip wasn't the most likely to do this, generally relying on Dana. She should have known better than to come in so ill-informed. She felt a trickle of irritation with Kip.

Kelly Jones

"Seven to eight thousand," Kelly said, after allowing a substantial lull in the conversation for them to come up with an answer. "So three fires in three churches . . ." His shoulders rose. Broad shoulders, Dana noted. She knew as a firefighter he'd be required to stay in top-notch physical shape, and he still looked like a guy who frequented the gym, though his position now was one of supervision, overseeing reports, investigations, and education within the state-wide department.

Dana asked, "How many of these eight thousand fires are arson?"

"Suspected arson or proven arson?"

Dana shrugged now, glanced again at Kip.

"One hundred. Sometimes a few more," Kelly said. "A small percentage turn out to be human-caused. Intentionally," he clarified. "Many are caused by accident or human negligence, but those fires are not considered arson."

Dana reflected on how many unfortunate events resulted from human neglect or carelessness. Very few acts of God, a strange phrase that she never liked. "But, these three fires?" she asked.

"We are investigating St. Barbara's as an arson. And now, possibly St. Aloysius. Originally, that was attributed to vagrants in the empty church. An accident, not intentionally set. Grab a blanket and those pews make a decent bed. A little hard, but better than being out in the weather, sleeping on the damp ground, getting kicked out of the parks." He smiled as if he approved of allowing the church to be used as a homeless hotel.

"So, there is some concern?" Kip asked.

He paused for another moment. "I understand that you,"—his eyes met Dana's again, then slid to Kip's—"I am aware that you have done substantial investigating that relates to the Catholic Church and clergy in the Archdiocese of Boston . . . if you come across anything that might be helpful, please let us know."

Kip shot Dana a quick smile as if to say, *see, I told you something is going on here.* Even the Fire Marshal believes these three fires are related.

64

"If there is reason to believe there will be more fires," Ryan Kelly said, "we're certainly open to . . ." He seemed to be searching for more words. "If you see any similarities, anything that ties these fires to a common source." He sat quietly for a moment, letting both Dana and Kip consider what he had just shared. Dana knew he was talking about similarities that had nothing to do with fire forensics. Their seasoned investigators would handle that aspect of the investigations.

Ryan Kelly stood and motioned toward the door. "Please, if you discover anything, I'd like to know before it goes to press. Anything that might be helpful to our investigators."

Dana knew it was Kip who had contacted the Fire Marshal. Kelly had not reached out to them. But, why would he? Yet, he had, for some reason, agreed to meet with them.

She and Kip walked out together. As they approached his car, which he'd parked much closer to the building than Dana, she asked, "You didn't mention our visit to Father Michael at St. Lawrence's?"

"I didn't see that it was necessary. Not at this point."

"And neither did he?"

"Nope." Kip pulled out his keys, clicked and unlocked his car. "I'm going in to talk to Mac tomorrow morning."

"To tell him what we're up to?"

"*We?* So, you're in?" He threw her a grin, and she raised her shoulders dubiously, though she knew Kip could tell she was definitely in. "By the way," he said, "I wasn't the one who called the meeting with Mac. He called me."

"Oh . . ." Dana considered this. "I had a message from Mac, too. He asked me to come in at 10:00."

"I'm going in at 10:30."

Dana wondered why Mac had scheduled two separate meetings. Had that rookie reporter told him they were snooping around, requesting photos? If this were the case, Mac would call them in together. As Kip climbed into his car, he glanced up with a troubled expression, and she knew he was thinking the same thing.

CHAPTER NINE

Dinner that evening was canned chili and grilled cheese sandwiches. Dana told Mia it was a *fallish* meal that she had loved as a child, though her mom's chili was always homemade.

"I know that soup in Italy," Dana said with a light laugh that carried a hint of apology, "is just a starter."

"This is great," Mia said. She could see Dana wasn't much of a cook, and she did miss the fantastic dinners she had each evening in Italy. The family employed a cook, so it wasn't like Mia or her grandmother were slaving over the stove. Even Mia's mother had done little cooking. When she was alive, her mother had worked as diligently as her father—in the vineyards, the wine cellars, meeting with prospective buyers. Mia wondered if they would go to Dana's mother's again for Sunday dinner. She wondered if she would see Zac again. She thought about the girl—Meagan—whom she'd met on the bus. Why had she transferred to St. Gertrude's?

"How were your classes?" Dana asked, bringing Mia back to their conversation and the realization that these one-on-one, two-people-only dinners might become a strain. At home, with her dad, grandmother, Zio Giovanni, and often visiting guests, Mia could drift off into her own thoughts without anyone noticing.

"I'm not sure yet," Mia answered, "after just a half-day."

"Did you meet anyone new, other than the girls you met at orientation?"

"A girl on the bus."

"Oh, that will be nice to have someone to ride with," Dana said. "Someone to talk to on the way to school."

Mia didn't want to tell her the girl was at Zac's party, that Zac had called her weird, and that she wasn't very nice to Mia on the bus. "She wasn't on the bus this afternoon, so she must have had a ride."

"Maybe I could pick you up after school, then you wouldn't have to ride alone."

"No, I'm fine, really." Mia wondered if Dana would quiz her each day. Mia always had a lot of freedom at home. After her mom died, half the time her dad didn't even seem aware she was there. "How was your day?" Mia asked. She didn't want to talk about her school anymore or the weird girl on the bus. Mia was beginning to realize that Dana had a way of making the conversation about anyone but herself. Mia wondered if this was a trick she'd learned as a reporter.

"My day?" Dana said as if this would require considerable thought, as if no one had asked her the question before. "I did some interviews, talked to several older people. We're trying to uncover possible fraud or abuse in the various care services for the elderly." Dana grimaced, then laughed. "This must sound terribly depressing and maybe boring."

Mia laughed too. It did sound boring.

"You have homework?" Dana asked.

"A little," Mia said.

Dana rose, took her bowl and plate to the sink and rinsed them off. "I'll load the dishwasher so you can get to your schoolwork."

"Thank you," Mia said, bringing her dishes to the sink. She didn't really have homework. They'd only had half a day of school, and she'd already started the "suggested" reading.

Back in her room, she got out her iPad and sent a message to her dad to let him know how the day had gone, then a couple of messages to girlfriends back home. She couldn't call or facetime because it was the middle of the night in Italy. She'd already told her friends about the party, about how she didn't think she and Zac were going to be friends after all, then about the girl who was at the party, how she'd hypnotized Becket. She told them now how she'd run into the same girl on the bus, that maybe she was weird like Zac had said.

She read the first chapter of her American History book, then got ready for bed. Reaching for the lamp on top of the file cabinet that served as her nightstand, she noticed the bottom drawer had slid out a tad, so she bent down to shove it back in since she didn't want to trip over it in the morning. Then she noticed a small key still stuck in the lock. Had Dana retrieved some files and maybe forgot to relock the drawer? Mia wondered why she had a lock on a cabinet in her house. Did she think Mia would be snooping around? Or was she afraid someone might break in, searching for something?

The thought intrigued her. She knew Dana often wrote about controversial subjects, that she was an investigative journalist, though this deal with the old folks' care didn't sound like it was something that would lure robbers or prowlers to break into the apartment to retrieve valuable or incriminating evidence.

Mia reached down and slid the drawer back in. The top drawer, too, wasn't fully closed. Mia noticed the cabinet was slightly out of balance, and it looked like it needed to be locked to keep the drawers closed tightly. Or maybe there was some really important stuff in here, and that's why it was locked. Knowing she should just leave it alone, Mia pulled the upper drawer out to see what was inside. The drawer was only about halfway full, a dozen or more hanging folders on a metal rack. She could see some handwritten labels, some dates. They all seemed to be older files, dating back to the early 2000s. The year Mia was born. With her fingers, not wanting to lift a file out—that would be flagrant snooping—she separated one of the middle manila folders, labeled THE COVERUP, 2001. Opening it just enough to scan the article on top, she tilted her head to get the perfect angle to read. She read quickly, getting the general drift of the piece. It was about something that had happened in the Archdiocese of Boston years ago. Priests had been molesting children. The archbishop, as well as several higher-ups in the Church, had been covering up this abuse. Mia had heard about such scandals though they didn't talk about it at home in Italy, as if it was an American thing.

She closed the drawer and considered relocking the cabinet, but she decided it best to leave it as she had found it.

Then, knowing she had already invaded, perhaps broken a trust, but still curious, she carefully pulled the lower drawer open. Her heart stopped for a moment. The entire drawer was a series of files, stuffed tightly. But even from a quick, guilty glance, she could see that each one, especially the one in the very back labeled "JOSEPH LEON MONAGHAN-PIERSON, birth certificate," held information about Dana's son. And she realized that the unanswered questions she had about Joel might be contained in these very files.

CHAPTER TEN

"I'm going to need some help," Dana told her sister-in-law Pammie over the phone. "She seems reluctant to talk to me. When she got home from the party with Zac, she didn't seem inclined to share anything about it."

"Welcome to the world of teen parenting," Pammie said with a laugh.

"But, you've had years of practice, years to prep for this."

"Just do what you're doing. Try to spend time with her. Family dinners."

"Ha, ha," Dana said dryly. "It's just the two of us in attendance at these family dinners. No diversions or deflections. No one else to join in the conversation."

"Well, true, but do what you're doing. Ask about her day. Her classes. What she's up to with her friends."

"I tried that," Dana said, thinking, *gosh I hope she's making some friends.* She'd mentioned meeting a few girls, but it was too early to tell if they would become friends. This must be so difficult starting a new school, especially so far from home.

"Sometimes they'll open up," Pammie said, "share something. I can guarantee if you don't show an interest, if you don't ask, they will tell you absolutely nothing."

"Did Zac say anything about the party?"

"Not much. He said Hick's parents were there. Don't worry

about Zac. He's into sports. He's a decent student. He's a good kid. I trust him." Pammie laughed again. "Most of the time. You and Mia planning on going to the game Friday night?"

"We are. We've decided to get up early Saturday and take the 5:00 A.M. train to New York. Is that crazy? We'll have to get up at three or earlier."

"Ouch," Pammie said, and Dana remembered it was her sister-in-law's suggestion they save a night's hotel cost and go in the morning. "Have her sleep in her clothes. Or better yet, have her go in her jammies and sleep on the train."

"You're not helping me much here, Pammie," Dana said with a laugh.

"We're going for pizza after the game. If it's not too late for you, we'd love to have you join us."

"I'll ask Mia if she'd like to go for pizza."

"Zac won't be there. Let her know that. Jeff, Quinn, Olivia, and I usually grab something after the game. You and Mia should eat something before, at least a snack, because it's late when the game's over. Hope we have reason to celebrate."

"Me too. We'll just meet you at the school, and I'll let you know about pizza."

"Sounds good." Pammie paused for a moment as if she had something more to add. "Hey," she finally said, "Jeff says Drew's in town, looking at a position here."

"Yes, I know."

"You okay with that?"

"Boston's a big town, big enough for the two of us. Doubt we'll even run into each other," Dana said, realizing they already had. "Did Jeff mention he'd spent the week with a woman in Paris?"

"He did," Pammie said. "You think this might be serious?"

"A fellow takes a girl to Paris?" Dana answered.

"It's been how many years since your divorce," Pammie said, and she might as well have said, *It's time to move on.*

After they hung up, Dana lay in bed. It had been five days since she'd seen Drew at the airport. Five days? Had Mia really been here for five days now? Should Dana be counting the number of days Mia had been with her, or should Dana be counting down the days until she was alone again? She didn't like that thought at all. She remembered how happy her mom had been when Dana told her Mia was coming to live with her for the school year. "It'll be good for you," she'd said. "You spend too much time alone."

Mia glanced at the handwritten labels on the numerous files. Most of them were dated, and some had topics. The last one, the one farthest back in the cabinet drawer, was labeled JOSEPH LEON PIERSON-MONAGHAN birth certificate.

Carefully, Mia lifted the file out and opened it. The date on the birth certificate was March 27, the year after Mia was born. He weighed 8 pounds and 6 ounces and was 22 inches long. Mia herself was six and a half pounds and only 20 inches long. She thought about Zac, how tall he was, and she guessed that Joel would be too. A tiny footprint, a small ink of a step, was imprinted at the bottom of the certificate. Then Mia noticed, in the deep fold of the file folder, a lock of hair. Pale in color. She ran her fingers over the softness and felt a tear slip from her eye. She was shaking now. She had crossed a line. She had invaded the most intimate memories. She closed the folder and slipped it back into the cabinet.

She should stop herself. She knew this, but something inside her urged her to go on.

She lifted a file toward the front of the cabinet that was labeled merely with a date. It contained an article. It was dated nine years ago. A body had been found. Deteriorated to the point that it could not be identified. In a wooded area, found by a hiker.

Forensic tests were conducted. It was not Joel.

Several folders behind this one contained similar findings. Possibilities. False clues. No trace of a boy who, if he had survived, would be sixteen years old now.

Mia flipped to the back of the cabinet, the file in front of the one containing Joel's birth certificate. She imagined other files in Dana's bedroom. Or photo books. Pictures of a newborn baby. A toddler.

A preschooler. Pictures of first steps, first birthday cake, first vacation. Mementos. Perhaps drawings, scribbled in crayon. Those that Mia was now looking at were not the files of intimacy and memories. These were the files of a mother looking for her lost son. Every clue. Every possibility. Every failure.

Mia lifted the file dated Easter 2004. Joel would have been barely three.

There were several clippings, some with photographs. One Mia recognized as Dana's mother's house, Zac's grandmother's house. This is where Joel had disappeared. Yet, something looked different, as if the outside of the house had changed. It was a shot of the back of the house. Maybe some trees or bushes had grown up and covered part of the house? There was a photo of a three-year-old boy. Blond with large innocent eyes. He looked a bit like his mother, around the mouth. A little like Kiki. Mia realized there were no photographs of Joel in Dana's home. No, she didn't know if that was true. Mia had not been in Dana's bedroom. Maybe there were photos of Joel in Dana's room.

In one of the articles, Mia found a picture of the lost boy's parents who were identified as Dana Pierson, a writer for *The Boston Globe*, and Andrew Monaghan, an attorney with the prosecutor's office. Mia wouldn't have recognized Dana. Her hair appeared to be dark and straight and she wore glasses, though her eyes were closed in pain beneath the lenses. Joel's dad had a different name than Dana. Mia might have thought that they had never married if Zac hadn't told her that Drew—the man Dana's brother had mentioned at dinner—was Dana's ex-husband. Mia studied the photo for several moments, then continued scanning the news story.

According to the article, the family had been visiting Dana's mother for Easter. Joel and his older cousin, whose name was not revealed, were sharing a bedroom. The cousin told the police that someone had come and taken Joel in the night.

Another article, written several days later, stated that the boy had at first told the police someone had come in the night, but the following day he was unable to remember being at his grandmother's house. Mia felt her heart throb, and she held her hand to her chest. She was having a hard time breathing. She closed the file. Put it back in the cabinet. She locked the drawer but did not remove the key. She had no right to pry.

She lay on her bed on top of the covers, still holding her heart, which beat so violently she could feel the thump, a deep, painful throbbing within her chest. Then it seemed she could feel and hear the blood rushing through her veins.

She was crying now. She knew why Zac did not want to talk about his lost cousin. Zac had been there in the same room, perhaps in the same bed with Joel, who, after 13 years, was still missing.

CHAPTER ELEVEN

Mia wouldn't have recognized Meagan as she hurried toward the bus, barely getting on before it pulled out from the bus stop, if it hadn't been for the trench coat that flapped against her legs. She grabbed a seat across from Mia, unaware they were so close until she looked up.

"Hi," Meagan said.

"Hi," Mia returned, then, "I like your hair." It was no longer dark with blue tips, but blonde. So blonde it could have been described as white.

"Just trying to comply," Meagan said with a smile. Not a snarky smile, but one that seemed to say, *you want in on the joke?* "Since I missed orientation and apparently did not read the school manual, I was unaware that *unnatural* hair colors are *verboten.*" She used the German word that made it sound like she was talking about Nazis.

When Mia read the school manual, she had assumed the reference to *unnatural* color meant no green, blue, or pink hair allowed, but the rule said nothing about prohibiting the use of hair colors or tints. As long as they were *natural.*

Meagan fluffed her shoulder-length hair. "What do you think? Do you think this is a natural color?"

Mia thought for a moment. "My grandmother's hair is that color. And perfectly natural."

Meagan laughed and then so did Mia.

The bus jerked to a halt and more people got on, a woman grasping a bulky green burlap shopping bag, a child propped on her hip, a dad and three kids searching for seats. Meagan smiled at the mom and motioned to the bench, then moved across the aisle to sit next to Mia. The mother nodded a thank-you.

After the bus started back up, Meagan turned to Mia and said, "Sorry I was such a bitch yesterday."

Mia felt her brows rise in surprise.

"You do know what a *bitch* is?" Meagan asked.

"A female dog," Mia replied, then laughed. "Yes, I do know what it means when you call someone a bitch. I honed my English on American movies and cable TV shows, so I know."

"Yeah, well, sorry." Meagan laughed too. "Your English is very good. You've barely any accent at all, and I'm sorry for what I said yesterday."

"It's okay," Mia said. "I figured you were stressed over going to a new school."

"You're new here too," Meagan said. "Stressing much?" She didn't wait for an answer. "How you like it so far? St. Gert's?"

"We've only had half a day, so I will reserve judgment."

"Academically, it's a good school," Meagan said. "My father is pleased with that aspect of St. Gertrude's. And he's all into a Catholic education. All that social service and those required do-gooder projects."

"Mine, too," Mia said, and even as the words came out, she wondered what Meagan's mother thought about St. Gertrude's.

"Come on in," Macauley Macey told Dana as she stepped inside his office, maneuvering around boxes that, even after three months in the new building, were stacked about the room. She took a seat. She'd arrived early for her 10:00 appointment, curious why her editor had asked her to come in, why he'd invited Kip separately for a 10:30 meeting.

Mac was Dana's senior by several years. He'd been their editor for just three, and though neither Kip nor Dana flaunted it, all three knew one thing—she and Kip had a Pulitzer. Mac did not. Yet, there had always been respect going both ways. Mac had an innate ability to tell if a story was worth chasing and when to move from research to words. She and Kip had plenty of freedom and leeway to pursue their own projects. Mac seldom pushed them and infrequently probed during the initial stages of an investigation. Research might take a month or two, depending on the complexity of a story, and those going deeper had been known to take a year or more, often pulling in reporters from other sections of the newsroom if a story became time-sensitive.

"I have some concerns," Mac said as Dana sat across from him at his cluttered desk.

"Concerns?" she asked. "About?" She didn't think this was a great way to start a conversation. *Concerns?* She could see Mac was nervous, eyes flickering, meeting hers briefly, picking up an oversized paperclip, tapping it absently three times on the desk.

"I'm going to ask Kip to take some time." He glanced at Dana, eyes still unsteady.

She'd come in thinking this might be about their unofficial interest in the fires, but she knew now it was something else. "What's going on, Mac?"

"I've had a couple of complaints."

"From whom?"

"A couple of women on staff." He met Dana's eyes. "Inappropriate remarks."

"Oh," was all Dana could come up with. A thousand thoughts were whirling through her head. She thought back to some of the jokes she and Kip had shared over the years, realizing the definition of inappropriate was rapidly shifting, wondering if she should have been more aware of this. *Inappropriate remarks?*

"No formal complaints to HR," Mac said, "but I'm concerned. You know, with the sensitivity in the workplace now."

"You're not firing him. Are you?"

"Not yet." Mac scratched his bald head, then tugged at his collar as if it was too tight. "You've worked with Kip for a long time."

77

"Yes," Dana replied cautiously.

"No problems with . . . inappropriate conversations?"

Kip was her friend.

Before she could put the words together, Mac said, "I know Kip's a drinker."

"Never on the job," Dana replied. This came out without thought because it was true. Dana had never seen him drinking while working. There was the night of the fire, but he was there merely by chance, and this conversation had nothing to do with fires.

"There have been some late-night calls," Mac said slowly as if he wished Dana to add something here. When she didn't, he said, "I believe that Kip might have some problems to address."

"You're speaking with him this morning?"

"I wanted to talk to you first, find out if there is anything I should know."

Dana shook her head. Why was she feeling a wash of guilt come over her? He'd never been inappropriate with her, and yet . . . past conversations were playing through her head. An off-color story, a comment thick with sexual innuendo.

"I'd like to pull Brenda Falk in on the eldercare story," Mac said. "Maybe you could go over what you've got, get her started."

"Sure," Dana said, attempting to control her voice. She'd worked with Brenda on stories when they'd called in the entire team, but never one-on-one. Right now, she was concerned with what Mac just told her, not a prospective story.

On her way out of Mac's office—the entire meeting took just 10 minutes—Dana was relieved she didn't run into Kip, who had his appointment at 10:30. She could hardly look him in the eye, knowing what she knew. Brenda wasn't at her desk, and Dana made no effort to find her before leaving the building.

She pulled into the drive-thru at Starbucks and got a coffee, black, then drove around drinking and thinking about Kip, wondering what he would do next. Would he protest? Offer a defense? She waited long enough that she figured he'd have left

Mac's office, and then she called. When Kip didn't answer, she left a voice message. "Call me."

Lunch break followed Mia's Art History class, and she, Meagan, and the girl from Oregon, Marley, who were also in the class, headed to the cafeteria together. Like Meagan, Marley was blonde, though hers looked natural, unlike Meagan's bleached version, which had evidently passed inspection that morning.

Conversation came easily, especially after the two American girls learned Mia had grown up on a winery in Italy. Marley said her parents had invested in a small vineyard when they lived in Oregon. Kind of a hobby, though they made a nice profit when they sold their share and moved East. Meagan said she'd never been out of the country but would love to travel. They were all interested in art. They all liked the Art History teacher.

They talked about their old schools. Marley had gone to a charter school in Oregon, but they had moved to Boston for her dad's work. He worked in some kind of IT. Marley was definitely the chatty one of the trio, which Mia didn't mind. She liked her.

"I went to public school," Meagan said. "Just didn't work out. What was school like in Italy?" she turned to Mia, obviously wanting to shift the conversation.

"I lived out in the country and went to school in the small village nearby."

"That's so romantic," Marley sighed. "A vineyard in Tuscany." She sounded so enthusiastic that Mia thought she might stand up and shout to the entire cafeteria. "Mia, Meagan, Marley. We're *Three Ms,*" Marley pointed out. "Like the three musketeers!"

Mia knew the three musketeers were named Athos, Porthos, and Aramis. She'd read the original for a French-language class, though a lot of it she didn't understand. Her French wasn't as good as her English. She didn't think Marley really thought the three musketeers were all *M* names, so she didn't say anything, she just smiled and nodded.

Three new girls. Three transfer students. Mia felt like she'd found her tribe. A trio of *Ms.*

The bell rang to signal the next period would begin in five minutes.

"See you tomorrow, then," Mia said, knowing that neither Meagan nor Marley was in any of her afternoon classes.

"I'll be on the bus," Meagan said to Mia, who shot her a puzzled look as they went up to dump their lunch trays.

"I thought you have a ride home after school."

"That was yesterday." She rolled her eyes. "My dad wanted to get the lowdown. Fresh from the classroom to his ears. Catch me right away before I retracted into my shell."

Mia detected a mildly angry tone in Meagan's voice. She'd mentioned her dad a couple of times, but not her mom. Her dad was the one who wanted her to go to St. Gertrude's, the one who picked her up from school.

What about her mom? Mia wondered.

CHAPTER TWELVE

Dana called Kip several times, but still no answer, so she left another message asking him to call back. She kept her eldercare interview appointments and then the interview Kip had scheduled, hoping that Mac had changed his mind, that she'd run into Kip. But, she didn't. He was heavy on her mind as she did *his* interview with the family of an elderly man who had died in a nursing home. She saw no evidence of neglect that would have caused his death, though the family complained of diapers that were changed too infrequently, medications that were not always given precisely on schedule, meals that arrived late.

After leaving her final interview, she called Brenda, got no answer, but left a message asking her to call. Then, about to give Kip another try, Dana's phone vibrated. She didn't recognize the number but answered, sensing it might be a good idea.

"This is Ryan Kelly. I've been trying to get in touch with your colleague, Kip Connor, but he's not returning my calls. Can you meet me over at St. Aloysius?"

"What time?" she asked, remembering she'd given Kelly her card as they left his office. She was both curious and puzzled by the Fire Marshal's request. Why would he invite a reporter to meet at the site of one of the church fires unless there was a story he wanted to get out to the public?

"I'm headed over there now."

"Might take me thirty, thirty-five minutes. Will that work?"

"See you when you get there."

Half an hour later, after another futile attempt to contact Kip, Dana arrived at St. Aloysius. She saw no sign of Kelly, no sign of anyone. She caught a motion in her peripheral vision and turned to see a man riffling through a dumpster in front of a building that looked like it had been gutted and was being renovated. It would be nice to see the neighborhood come back to life, to see the building, the church, put to use. She thought of St. Barbara's in a completely different part of town. The intention of the buyer, the Greek Orthodox Church, had been to use it as a house of worship.

She started up the wide stretch of concrete stairs. Her gait felt awkward, the steps probably too narrow by today's standards, and oddly a little tricky to maneuver without taking two at a time. She soon stood before the entrance, an imposing trio of beautiful, carved wooden doors. A sign on the middle door advised that the building was closed, that all intruders would be prosecuted to the full extent of the law. There were no real estate signs on the building, though a lockbox was latched to the door. Dana thought of the homeless who had been nesting inside the church when the fire occurred. She glanced back toward the dumpster, but the man sorting through the trash had disappeared.

"Ms. Pierson," a voice called out.

Ryan Kelly stood at the base of the stairs. He took off his sunglasses for a moment as if she might not recognize him, then quickly slipped them back on. Sensitive eyes, Dana thought. Redheads have very sensitive eyes. He started up toward her, and she started down as if they had agreed to meet halfway. Even ascending, he was moving much swifter than she. He was obviously in good physical shape.

"The Realtor representing the diocese," he said, "was supposed to be here at . . ." He slid the sleeve of his jacket up and glanced at his wrist. He wore one of those substantial watches that does everything but make your morning coffee. "I think she's a no-show," Kelly said. "What about your partner, Kip?"

"Doesn't look like he'll make it either. I'll let him know what we . . . what was it you were hoping to discover?" Dana asked.

When he motioned for her to follow and started back down the steps, but didn't bother to answer her question, Dana said, "The fire's been attributed to a vagrant sleeping in the church that night?" She glanced around as they reached the bottom of the stairs, wondering how they got in—the homeless. The front door was locked.

"There's a broken window around the corner. Easy to get inside," he said as if he'd grabbed the question right out of her head. He gestured toward a sidewalk that ran along the side of the church. "I took a look around while I was waiting for you," he explained, leading her around the building. There was no fire damage to the exterior of the structure Dana observed as they walked. "The answer to your question—do you think it was a homeless person who accidently started the fire? I have some reservations."

"It was deliberate? Not an accident?"

His phone rang.

"Ryan Kelly," he answered as they continued to walk. He nodded, listening. "Yes, I understand. I've got something else going later this afternoon. I'll get back to you to arrange another time." He slid the phone into his pocket. "The Realtor representing the archdiocese can't make the appointment, but I don't believe we need her." He pointed toward a broken window—no sharp, shattered glass visible, but a missing pane, a section within a wooden frame. The opening wasn't big enough for a body to slither through.

"Breaking and entering?" Dana asked, aware Kelly intended to go inside. A quick memory flashed through her mind—her own unauthorized exploration of a church in Prague.

"Can't break something that's already broken," Kelly said with a grin, reaching inside. With ease, he pried the lock open and lifted the window. He motioned for her to go first. She hesitated, considering the legality as well as the logistics of his invitation. She was in reasonably good shape and wearing slacks—she seldom

83

wore a skirt—but the window was just high enough from the ground she knew she'd need some help. He laced his hands, making a lift for her foot, which required Dana to brace herself with one hand on his shoulder, and then, as she attempted to balance on the window ledge, to reach for his other shoulder. "Thank you," she said awkwardly. Yet, something told her he was a man who could be trusted, and this made her comfortable and uncomfortable at the same time. She twisted and reached for the window frame, lifted one leg over, then another, and dropped into the interior of the church. Within seconds he too was inside, standing beside her in what appeared to be the sacristy. She glanced around in the dim light and saw no trappings of the former occupants, nothing but empty shelves, walls with random nails and shadows outlining where pictures or certificates might have hung. Strips of once-elegant flocked wallpaper peeled from the walls. She detected no scent of fire, just the musty smell of desertion. Dana opened a cupboard, and Kelly examined the interior of the closet, finding nothing inside either.

"The diocese still has insurance on the building?" she asked.

"Yes."

"How about St. Barbara's? It was recently sold. Who carries the insurance?"

"New owner. We've ruled out insurance fraud if that's what you're asking."

"Just throwing out some thoughts," Dana said.

As they entered a small room off the sacristy, she attempted to flip the switch, but the electricity was off. Daylight coming through the small window a foot over Dana's head provided enough light that she could see it was a tiny, narrow bathroom with a toilet and sink. It reeked of urine with an unconvincing overlay of pine-scented disinfectant. A circle of stubborn rust circled the interior of the lidless toilet bowl. No sign of needles or syringes.

Kelly stepped back through the sacristy and out toward the main altar. Dana followed.

The church was still beautiful, even in its unattended state. The altar rose up toward a domed ceiling painted to look like heaven with fluffy clouds, winged bodyless angels, the Virgin and Child. Dana had never been inside this church. It nearly took her breath away. The vastness. The beauty. The emptiness. All which seemed to physically reach inside her. An unexpected sadness came over her.

Kelly ran a finger over the marble altar. A layer of dust rose and danced, spreading into the air. Outlined by a beam of light coming through the lovely stained glass, it looked like colored specks of light.

"It's a shame," he said as he approached the front pew, and Dana wasn't sure if he meant that the church was empty or that there had recently been a fire. He'd hooked his sunglasses on the pocket of his jacket. He squinted, then glanced at Dana. Very blue eyes.

The front bench was charred, but it appeared this was the only significant damage. Then she noticed the floor, too, was burned, a circular pattern in front of the altar, reaching out past the communion rail to the wooden pews. Marble, she observed, hard, cold stone would not burn.

"This is where the fire started?" she asked.

He was walking away from the altar, surveying the rest of the church. Dana, too, cast her eyes about, attempting to find something, anything, out of place.

Just as she was about to turn back, she spotted something in the last pew. She approached. It was a stack of blankets. Second-hand blankets, but clean and neatly folded. There was a note on top. She stooped to read the note, aware she shouldn't pick it up. A whiff of clean, fresh detergent rose to her nostrils. Blankets recently laundered.

You are welcome to use, the note read, *but do not take from the church. Leave for others.*

She sensed Ryan Kelly, who'd been surveying the opposite side of the church just seconds ago, standing beside her. He'd moved quickly and quietly. He picked up the scrap of paper and scanned

85

the message, then replaced it. "Someone is encouraging those without shelter to come inside." His brow furrowed in thought, then a quick, fleeting nod of approval, a smile. For a moment, she thought he might quote scripture. *Shelter the homeless.*

"Do you think they are coming in through the window?" Dana asked. "I know some of the homeless are elderly, some with physical limitations. That window was a bit tricky." *Not sure I could have made it without your help*, she thought. "There's a lockbox on the front door."

"There's also a side door." He motioned. "Locked."

"You tried it?"

Kelly nodded. "Someone is laundering these blankets. I'm guessing someone is coming in and unlocking the building at night. Relocking it in the morning when everyone leaves."

"Cleaning up, too," Dana added. She'd seen deserted buildings before, used by the homeless, by drug addicts, but there was no trace of drug paraphernalia, cigarette butts, cans, or bottles scattered about.

He motioned her back toward the altar, then into the sacristy and, without further words, again he constructed a lift, lacing his hands, and helped her out the window. He followed shortly, closing the window behind them. They circled back toward the front of the building.

Dana could see the side door Kelly was talking about. He tried it again, but it was definitely locked. "I'd like to walk," he said. "You have time?"

"Sure." Dana had already determined that Kelly was a man who used his words carefully. Dana herself had a tendency to ask too many questions, to overload, though she'd learned over the years to tamp it down, especially when she felt she would gain more by going with the flow, so to speak. At the moment, she felt like her insides were about to implode, and she wasn't even sure why.

They walked in silence. She wondered what Kelly was looking for as he turned down an alley, then on to an adjacent street, passing by a second-hand store next to a boarded-up building.

"The fire was in July," she said after a while. "I wonder how many people would have been in the church since it was probably still warm outside."

"There was the threat of a thunderstorm that night."

"So, they were seeking shelter from the storm, not the cold?"

"Yes, I believe so."

They passed a liquor store where an older man stood outside smoking a cigarette and then into an area with some run-down apartment buildings.

"What are you looking for?" she asked.

"A better question," he replied, "might be *who*."

"And why have you asked me along?"

"I'm not sure," he said.

"Aren't fire investigations generally handled through the local fire departments?" she asked.

"Generally."

"Is there a reason the Fire Marshal has been called in?" She wasn't sure why she referred to the Fire Marshal as if Kelly himself wasn't the Fire Marshal.

"That's pretty much the Fire Marshal's call."

"And that would be you?" she asked, throwing him an inquisitive smile, which he returned with a nod. Both were aware he wasn't giving her much. *Why had he invited her along?*

He motioned down another alley, lined with large green dumpsters, reeking of refuse. Dana spotted a man going through a dumpster. It wasn't the man she'd seen earlier. They were now several blocks from the church. But she sensed, as Ryan Kelly approached him, that this was exactly what—or who—he was looking for. The possibility that he might encounter someone who'd spent the night in the church or knew someone who had.

"How's it going?" Kelly said in a friendly voice.

"I'm eating out of a dumpster," the man replied. "How do you think it's going?" He jumped down, landing roughly on the pavement. Kelly helped him up. He was much younger than Dana would have imagined. So many of the homeless on the streets were older. White-whiskered and toothless. This young man barely looked out of his teens, though he did have a front tooth missing. "I ain't doing nothing wrong," the man said. "You a cop?"

Kelly wasn't wearing anything that resembled a uniform, but even Dana thought he could pass for a plainclothes detective. Just something about him. Something authoritative and confident. He wore tan slacks, an open-collared, plain white shirt, no tie, a sports jacket.

"No," Kelly replied. "Not a cop." He removed his sunglasses to make eye contact with the man.

"Then whata ya want? I ain't breaking no laws."

"I can see that," Kelly said. "I'm with the Department of Public Safety and Security."

"Well, then maybe you could get some ladders or lifts or something," the man said, "so it'd be easier to climb up into these dumpsters, so it'd be safer to get my dinner." He laughed at his cleverness.

Kelly smiled and said, "I'm with the Department of Fire Services. Just wondering if you heard anything about what happened at the church?" He waved back toward the direction of St. Aloysius.

"Somebody started that fire," the man said.

Kelly nodded, encouraging him to go on.

"I wasn't there that night, but I heard about it. Some guy was sleeping on one of them benches, and he hears somebody, and he wakes up, and the next thing he knows, the place is on fire. So he takes his ol' blanket, and he starts smacking them flames, but he can't get it out, and it starts to spread and then another fellow sleeping in the church helps him get it out, and then one of the guys with a cellphone makes a call and the fire department shows up."

"The fire was out when the fire department arrived?"

"That's what I heard. But then I read in the paper that the fire was started by some homeless people living in the church, and that just isn't true. But, what the hell, I mean what the hey . . ." He glanced over at Dana as if he was trying not to swear.

Yah, what the hell, she thought. Why believe a homeless person?

"Who told you it wasn't started by a homeless person?" Kelly asked. "You remember his name?"

"Oh, gosh," the man said, rubbing his stubbly chin. "I think it was this fellow called Pinkie that told me, but he wasn't the one in the church, he just heard about it, not sure who it was."

"Do you know where I can find Pinkie?"

"He used to hang out at the park." The man motioned in the opposite direction of the church. "But, I ain't seen him in weeks. I think he's moved on."

Kelly reached into the inside pocket of his jacket and pulled out a card, then another, not a paper business card like the first, but something that looked to Dana like a plastic credit card. "Call me if you see him. I'd like to talk to him. Or anyone else who might know about the fire."

"Hey, thanks." The man slid the plastic card in his pocket, then studied the paper card. He grinned. "So, you're the marshal." He made a gun out of his fingers and pantomimed like he was shooting into the air. "So, you're the marshal?" he said again as if Kelly was a law enforcement officer right out of the Old West.

"Let me know if you learn anything." Kelly nodded a thank-you to the man, then motioned to Dana, and they walked on in the direction of the park.

"What did you give him?" she asked.

"My card."

"But, something else. A plastic card."

"Oh," he said with hesitation. "A card to get a sandwich."

"Like a McDonald's gift card?"

He shook his head. "Sub sandwich, much healthier."

"You carry sub gift cards around in your pocket?"

"Yep," he said.

They'd arrived at the park, little more than a square of faded grass, a few wooden benches, half a dozen trees. Kelly approached a man sitting on a bench, asked him about the fire at St. Al's, if he knew a man named Pinkie, but he just shook his head. Then Dana noticed another man lying on a bench on the other side of the park, partially hidden behind a tree. She motioned, and she and Kelly walked over.

The man's face was obscured, a folded newspaper shielding him from the sun, looking like a hobo in an old cartoon. Dana noted it was a two-day-old paper, not a *Globe*, but a *USA Today*.

Kelly gave the man's foot a yank. The man, startled, jumped, and the newspaper fell to the ground.

"Whata you want?" the man said brashly.

"Just wondering if you know about the fire over at the church."

"St. Al's?" The man scratched his head, smoothed his matted hair. He had several day's growth on his face.

"Yes, did you hear anything? Talk to anyone who was there that night?"

"You a cop?"

Kelly handed him his card. The man stared at it suspiciously, apparently trying to decide if he wasn't a cop if it would be okay to talk to him.

"Tripper was there."

"Tripper? Do you know where we can find him?"

"No, I do not," the man said formally. "But, I can tell you what he saw."

"What did he see?" Kelly waited. The man scratched his head, but he didn't say anything, apparently hoping for a reward. Kelly dug around in his pocket, maybe searching for another sub card, which he evidently didn't find. He withdrew a five-dollar bill and handed it to the man.

"He said he saw an angel." The man grinned as if he'd just pulled one over on the Fire Marshal.

"What did the angel look like?" Kelly asked matter-of-factly.

"Long flowing gown. Long flowing hair."

"Wings or halo?"

The man scratched his head again. Flecks of dandruff rested on his thin shoulders. "You know, I just don't recall if he mentioned that or not." Dana got the impression he was waiting for another

90

bill to *recall*, but maybe he was just making up a story.

"Here's my card," Kelly said, handing him a business card. "If you hear from Tripper, or hear where he's taken off to, or recall anything else, let me know."

"That I will," the man said. He reached down, picked up his newspaper, tucked it under his arm, and strutted toward the opposite side of the park.

Kelly and Dana started back to the church.

"An angel?" Dana asked skeptically. She remembered what Father Michael had told them when she and Kip went to the chapel. The boys claimed to have seen a ghost. She weighed whether she should tell Kelly. She wanted to talk to Kip before she revealed what they'd learned at St. Lawrence's. *Ghosts? Angels?*

"I've heard stranger," Kelly said, and Dana wondered if Kelly too had heard about the ghosts. She had the impression that, after the St. Lawrence's fire, there hadn't been a proper investigation, but she didn't know. No official report had been issued. Not yet. But, Ryan Kelly might have also visited Father Michael. The priest had mentioned the Fire Marshal, though she and Kip thought he was just confused. She glanced over at Kelly, and he shot her a guarded smile.

They passed an apartment building. A woman was lifting a toddler out of a stroller. Baby hitched on her hip, she bumped the empty stroller up the steps and went inside.

"Thanks for your time," Kelly said.

"No problem," she said. "I'm still not sure why I'm here."

"You're good company," he said after a while. "I usually don't like hanging out with reporters. Most of them talk too much. Ask too many questions."

Dana laughed awkwardly. "That's generally how we learn things, asking questions. I take it you asked me along because you think I might have something to add, that I might have information that might help you in your investigation." She knew she was baiting him a bit, throwing it out there—though there was nothing on her hook. Nothin' at all.

"Like I told your friend Kip . . ." Kelly cast about as if looking for Kip to show up. "If you'll promise not to write anything until you've run it by me first, maybe we can work together."

She wasn't sure how to reply. She had nothing but a bunch of questions.

"I know you've written extensively on the Catholic Church in the archdiocese." He motioned toward the alley that would lead them back to the church.

"More focused on the people," she said, "the clergy, not the churches themselves."

"My mother always told me it wasn't the building, but the people inside."

Oddly, Dana thought about that little finger game: *Here is the church, and here is the steeple. Open the door and see all the people . . .*

A man, wearing a stained white apron, stepped out of the backdoor of one of the buildings, heaved a can of trash into the dumpster, then reached for a cigarette wedged on his ear.

"I'd like your word that you won't publish anything without my knowledge," Kelly said as they passed the man, now lighting up the cigarette. "I think we can work together if you'll agree. We'll both get something out of this in the end."

"I probably should run this by Kip before I agree to anything." She didn't have enough for a story, wasn't getting anything from Kelly. Dana pulled her phone out of her pocket and glanced at it to see if Kip had called. He hadn't. But, Brenda had. Dana had turned her phone off during her earlier interviews, and hadn't bothered to turn it back on, hadn't even felt it vibrate.

"You know those stories you wrote years ago," Kelly said as they headed out of the alley.

She knew what he was talking about, *those stories.*

"My mother thinks some of that reporting was . . . well, it wasn't a pleasant time for a lot of the old-timers. But a story that needed to be told. A terrible thing that needed to be uncovered. What those priests did. How it was all covered up."

He gazed down at the ground then looked up at Dana. They'd

arrived back to where she'd parked near the church. "Here's where I get off," she said, clicking her car key. He opened the door for her. "Yes, the story needed to be told." She slipped into her car. "Do you believe these fires relate to—"

"You have some time?" he broke in, still holding the door. "Maybe grab a coffee? Something to eat?" He removed his sunglasses so she could see his eyes. It was something he did, she realized—make eye contact. There was a certain honesty about this gesture that she liked.

Yet, his question took her by surprise. Dana glanced at her watch. It wasn't even four yet.

"I didn't have any lunch," he said.

"Neither did I," she admitted. "But, I've got a girl at home." *Did I really say that?* Dana asked herself. How stupid did that sound? *A girl at home?*

She could see from his expression—a squinty gaze that made his eyes look almost closed, that he found her wording odd, too. "Your daughter?"

"No, no," she said with an embarrassed laugh. "I have a girl, a young woman, she's seventeen, she's staying with me this year, going to school. She's from Italy."

"An exchange student?"

"Not officially. I met Mia in Italy several years ago through her great-uncle, who is a good friend. She's been here for less than a week. I'm sure she's fine on her own, but—"

"That's good." Ryan Kelly held up a hand. "I understand. I'll be in touch. I've got some questions, some thoughts, and I believe you might be able to help me." He stopped, bit down on his lip, looked directly at her as if she knew something he did not.

"Can you share more?" she asked, trying to keep the excitement out of her voice. Why did *he* think *she* might be able to help him? And why had he spoken of *those stories*?

When he shook his head apologetically, she replied, "I'll do what I can to help." She wasn't willing to agree she'd hold a story until she got his stamp of approval, but something inside her was jumping with the possibility that there *was* a story. "I'd like to talk again."

"I'll give you a call."

Pulling out, she waved to Kelly, who smiled as he adjusted his sunglasses. Dana realized she would like to go with him, have something to eat, attempt to pull more information out of him. Her stomach was growling. Mia would be okay at home without her.

But, she was more concerned about Kip than Mia at the moment. She'd drop by his house, make sure he was okay. She wanted to know exactly what Mac had told him. She knew it wasn't good, that it hadn't been a conversation anyone would want to have with their boss. Kip was probably nursing his wounds with a bottle of scotch.

And, she wanted to share with him that she'd gone to St. Al's with Fire Marshal Ryan Kelly, that something strange was going on with these fires.

CHAPTER THIRTEEN

On the ride home on the bus, Mia got up the nerve to ask Meagan, "You said your dad wanted you to go to St. Gertrude's?" She swallowed hard. "What about your mom?"

"She's not in the picture."

"Oh," Mia said. She could tell Meagan didn't want to talk about her mom. Kind of like Zac didn't want to talk about his cousin Joel.

They bumped along in silence.

"Your dad didn't like the public school you were going to?"

Meagan gave her a look, and it seemed maybe she was going to turn into the "bitch," again. Mercurial, Mia thought. The girl was moody.

"It wasn't that he didn't like the school." Meagan stared out the window, then turned to Mia. "I've got some issues."

Mia wanted to ask, but she was sort of afraid. She liked Meagan, the *kind* Meagan, the one she'd seen at the party. She'd looked weird with her nose ring, blue-tipped hair, and cat eyes, but she'd spoken so kindly to Becket.

Meagan smiled, not a freaky smile, but an apologetic smile. "So how come your parents decided to send you to America for your senior year?"

"Mostly, my dad wanted to broaden my horizons." She laughed. "It was my idea at the beginning, but finally, he agreed. I've lived my entire life in the same place. Oh, we've done some traveling, mostly in Italy."

"I'd love to go to Italy," Meagan said dreamily. "How did you end up here in Boston?"

"Dana, the woman I'm staying with, is a friend of my great-uncle's. He's a priest. Well, he *was* a priest."

"Were he and this woman, this Dana, were they lovers?" Meagan asked with interest as if she'd be delighted with a scandalous story.

"No, no, I'm sure they are just friends. But . . ." Mia covered her mouth to suppress a giggle. She wanted to draw it out, to allow Meagan the full effect of what she was about to say. "But, he's not a priest anymore. He got married."

"Nooo!" Meagan exclaimed. "Really?"

"Really."

"That's romantic," Meagan said.

"They're really old," Mia said to add to the effect. "I mean like really old."

"How old?"

"Like almost in their eighties."

"Still romantic," Meagan said with a grin.

They stopped, and several passengers got off. Mia knew that she and Meagan would part at the next stop. She didn't know if Meagan made another connection or walked home from there.

"Okay," Meagan said. "You next. Ask another question. Any question."

Mia wanted to know about Meagan's mother. She wondered if she was dead, but instead, she asked, "Did you really hypnotize Becket at the party? Or were the two of you just putting on a show?" She still remembered how Zac had said that Meagan didn't fit in, that she wasn't part of the group.

"Becket's a nice kid, but he has no confidence. I was trying to help out."

"So, you did? You hypnotized him?"

"I just talked to him. You know, a person can't be hypnotized if he or she doesn't want to be. I wasn't doing anything to hurt him."

Mia took this as a yes. "You sounded so kind, so gentle."

"As opposed to *bitchy*."

"That's your word, not mine," Mia offered.

After a moment, Meagan said, "It doesn't work unless the person trusts you. You have to be kind to gain their trust."

"How do you even know how to do that?"

"My dad has a bunch of books. I saw one on the shelf, and I was interested. So I read it."

Mia could feel her mouth drop, her eyes widen. "That's well, that's . . ." She didn't know what to say.

"It's not as weird as it sounds," Meagan said. "My dad's a therapist. A psychiatrist. It's a recognized tool in some types of therapy."

"But, you're just a kid," Mia said. "Isn't that dangerous?"

"Could be," Meagan said, and by then they had arrived at her stop.

Dana rang Kip's doorbell, then rang again and waited. No answer. He wasn't home, or he wasn't answering. She tried knocking, then knocked again louder. Still no response. She walked around to the side of the house and stopped to peer into the garage through the dusty window. Through a haze of dirt and cobwebs, she could see his car was parked inside, which meant he was driving his truck. She could never figure out why a single guy would need two vehicles, especially in Boston, and a huge monster of a pickup truck at that. Kip wasn't even that outdoorsy. It wasn't like he took off for an adventure in the woods every weekend.

Before she got back in her car, she made another call. Surprisingly, this time he answered.

"Where the hell are you?" she asked. "I've been trying to reach you all day."

"Well, let's see," he said slowly, casually. She wondered if he was drinking. "I think I'm somewhere between Boston and Boise."

"Boise? Boise, Idaho?"

"I hear it's a great place."

"What the hell, Kip!"

"I suppose you heard I lost my job."

"I heard Mac suggested you take some time."

"I guess that's how he put it."

"Maybe you need to—"

"Need to what?" he cut in. She was about to suggest he think about his drinking. Isn't that what a good friend should do? She wasn't sure if she should mention the inappropriate remarks. He'd been making them for years, but twenty, twenty-five years ago, they didn't seem that inappropriate. Women who wanted to get ahead put up with that shit. Younger women just weren't inclined to do so.

"I quit," he said.

"You quit?"

"I did."

She didn't know how to respond. "Oh, Kip, no." She knew he wasn't in the greatest shape, financially speaking. On occasion, Dana, who'd always been frugal and had invested an inheritance from her grandparents wisely, extended him a loan. He hadn't been good at saving, bought a new car every other year, and had recently purchased that monster of a pickup truck for reasons unknown. He'd been married twice to wives who both seemed to have hired better lawyers than Kip.

"Yep, didn't appear Mac wants me around, so I quit." His words were starting to slur, and she thought he might even be crying. "I told the office girl you'd come in and clear out my desk, my personal stuff."

Office girl? Dana thought. Part of the problem right there. "I could do that, Kip."

"Yep, gave my notice. Well, no notice." He sniffed, then laughed. "Just told Mac he could stuff his fucking job."

"How did he take that?"

"Said if that's what I wanted." He sniffed again.

"You're not driving?"

"Best way to get someplace on short notice."

"Why don't you pull over. Get a place to stay. You shouldn't be driving while you're—"

"Pissed off?" he broke her off. "Yes, yes, I know."

"I could call later, when you've found a place for the night. Talk later?"

"Let's talk now," he said, followed by an exceedingly long silence. "Okay, I've pulled over."

"Boise?" she asked after a while. "Really?

"I have a sister who lives in Boise."

Kip had never talked about a sister in Boise. He'd mentioned a sister who lived in California.

"I thought your sister's in California."

"They just moved to Idaho a couple of months ago. Her husband got a job at some tech company. They like it there, and she's extended an invitation to visit. So, I've got time."

"Well, that's good, I guess."

"So, what are your plans?"

"What are *my* plans?" she repeated.

"How are you going to survive without me?" He laughed.

"I don't know, Kip," she said sympathetically.

"Well, guess you can't join me in Idaho. Unlike *moi*, who has nothing and no one depending on him."

"I went over to St. Aloysius today," she said because she didn't know what else to say, and she wanted to share the conversation she'd had with Ryan Kelly.

"So, how'd you get in?"

"Crawled through a window."

"Oh, fun."

"I didn't go alone. Ryan Kelly invited me. He says he wants our help. He wouldn't expand on it, seemed evasive, but he asked about the stories we did on abuse in the Church, giving me the impression there is a connection to the fires."

"Holy shit," Kip responded. "That's almost enough to make me want to turn around."

They made a good team, Dana thought, and then she felt like she might cry. "We talked to a couple of men who'd been sleeping in the church, though neither was there that night. I believe the church hotel has a fairly high vacancy rate in July. However, one of them said he talked to someone who'd been there, a fellow named Tripper."

"As in tripping out on drugs." Kip laughed.

"Yeah, I'm kind of thinking that."

"So, what did Tripper see?"

"Someone in a long flowing garment and long flowing hair. He said it was an angel."

Kip laughed a good, hearty laugh. "Ghosts and angels. This is getting interesting. Wish I was there to help you out. Did you tell Ryan Kelly about the ghosts at St. Lawrence's?"

"I didn't. I wanted to talk to you first."

"That's kind, very thoughtful, but you know you are on your own on this one." A pause stretched out, and Dana thought they had lost their connection. "You spoke with Tripper?" he finally asked. "In person?"

"All hearsay."

"Not a great source of reliable information any way you look at it."

"It seems Kelly wants our help." She couldn't quite let go of the *our*, the *we*. "But, he's sharing little if anything."

"Make that *your* help," Kip came back. Dana heard the blast of a horn, then Kip shouting, "Damn, fucking drivers."

"You okay?"

"Some idiot just about hit me. Sitting here on the side of the road is more dangerous than drivin'."

"You okay?" she asked again.

"Yeah, tell me more."

"More?"

"This Fire Marshal?"

"Kelly wants us—me—to keep anything we discover under wraps until we've consulted with him."

"Not exactly how we *bona fide* reporters do it," Kip came back. "Not that I could possibly be classified as a *bona fide* anymore, but do what you wanna, Dana." Kip's tone had a bit of an edge, and she could tell he was unhappy that he wasn't in on this.

"I will," she said, and then after a moment of no reply she thought he'd hung up. "You still there?"

"Not sure where, but I'm somewhere between there and here, someplace between nowhere and somewhere. Or maybe just in the middle of nowhere."

"Be careful, Kip."

"Always."

"Maybe take this time to—"

"Consider what the fuck I'm gonna do with my miserable life?"

"Yes."

He didn't respond.

"Maybe consider why Mac suggested you take some time."

Nothing from Kip. *But, wouldn't a friend offer some help?* Dana thought. *Be honest.* "I care about you, Kip," she said. "Please call and let me know how things are going. Or, at the least, reply to my texts and calls."

"Will do."

About ten minutes later, back on the road, attempting to push her worries about Kip out of her head, Dana pulled over and sent a text to Mia and said she'd pick up some Chinese food on the way home. Mia texted right back and said that would be great, she liked Chinese food. She was home and had had a GREAT day at school. She said she'd tell Dana about it at dinner.

Even though it was just a text, not her voice, Dana was pleased, so pleased she could feel her face split with a grin. Mia had voluntarily let Dana know she'd had a GREAT day and wanted to tell her about it that evening. Dana felt a trickle of something she would have to describe as satisfaction. This positive reinforcement made her feel much better about stopping off to pick up dinner rather than cook something herself. She had more to worry about than where their dinner was coming from. But, she reflected, she'd almost made it through an entire week without grabbing dinner on the way home.

CHAPTER FOURTEEN

D ana was delighted by how chatty Mia was at dinner that evening. She talked about Marley, who came from Oregon, and Meagan, the girl who had transferred from Zac's school, how they were all in the same Art History class, and they all had the same lunch period, so they could eat together.

"That's great," Dana said.

"I like the Art History teacher." Mia wound a chow mein noodle around her chopstick as if she were eating spaghetti. "Today was officially my first class, but so far, I think it's my favorite."

"Is that something you might like to pursue?" Dana asked.

"At university?"

Dana nodded. "Yes, something you might continue to study in college?"

"Possibly. My father has encouraged me to consider something in business."

"I know he'd love to keep the management of the winery in the family," Dana said.

"I'm still not that excited about the prospect of taking over the family business," Mia said. "Fabrizio is doing wonderfully."

Fabrizio was a young man whom Mia's father had taken under his wing at the vineyards and winery. When Dana visited, she'd sensed that Mia had a crush on the young man, but she seemed to be over that now. Fabrizio was several years older than Mia—

twenty-two—and Mia had told Dana that he was engaged to a girl from Siena who loved the idea of moving to the estate near Montalcino.

"I have a cousin who majored in Art History." Dana scooped up a shrimp with a chopstick.

"Father said there are limited opportunities unless one wants to teach or work in a museum. What is your cousin doing now?"

Dana swallowed the bite of shrimp, and then she paused, realizing her answer probably wouldn't be too encouraging. "She's a nun."

"Really!" Mia squealed and then laughed.

"Yes, really." Dana laughed too. "She lives in a convent in Prague. She helps take care of a small church, but mostly, she does a lot of praying."

"Prague? That's where you and Zio Giovanni met? Did you meet through your cousin?"

"Well . . . it's a long, involved story." Dana picked up a fortune cookie and handed one to Mia.

"I don't like the taste of these. They're not really cookies," Mia said, "but I like to look at the fortunes." She cracked it open, glanced at the message and read, "A person is never too old to learn." She wrinkled her nose.

"I think that was supposed to be mine," Dana said with a shake of her head.

"No, this one is yours," Mia replied, handing Dana the other fortune cookie.

Dana broke it open and gazed at Mia, raising her brows skeptically. "Romance is in your future," she read dramatically.

"That's a good one," Mia said with a grin, and Dana laughed and rolled her eyes.

"Maybe we should trade?" Dana replied. "Definitely a mix-up here."

Mia shook her head and said she doubted she'd find anyone at St. Gertrude's. "If Zio Giovanni and Gia found love so late in life, there is hope." Instantly a pained expression twisted her lips, Mia aware of what she'd just said, suggesting that Dana was old. When Dana laughed again, so did Mia.

As they cleared the table, Dana reminded Mia that they were going to Zac's game the following evening, that they were invited for pizza after, though Zac wouldn't join them.

Mia excused herself after loading the dishwasher and went to her room to do some reading. She felt both relieved and disappointed that they wouldn't see Zac after the game and wondered why Dana had made a point of telling her he wouldn't join them for pizza. Did Dana think something was going on between her nephew and Mia?

Sitting on her bed, legs tucked under her, English Lit book in her lap, her mind continued to drift as she wondered again about Dana's personal life. As Zac said, his aunt didn't date, as far as he knew. She never brought anyone to family events. There was that man who'd been at the apartment when Zac dropped her off from the party. Dana had introduced him as Kip, a co-worker. Mia wasn't the greatest judge of what made a couple romantically attracted, but it was pretty clear even from that brief introduction that there was nothing amorous going on between Kip and Dana.

Mia set her book on the bed and glanced over at the file cabinet. She had locked it again, just left the key stuck in the slot. She didn't think Dana had come in to get any additional files. Wouldn't she have taken the key out if she had?

Just as she was ready to turn off the lamp on her nightstand, Dana's phone rang. Ryan Kelly—she'd added his number to her contact list.

"What are you doing tomorrow?" he asked.

"Depends," she said. Her single word came out sounding a little flirty, like she was asking him to come up with an offer she couldn't refuse.

"How about Mass at St. Lawrence's. They have a student Mass Friday at eleven-thirty."

"What are you looking for?"

"Altar boys," he said. "When I talked to Father Michael, oddly he couldn't remember the names of the boys he found in the church after the fire. I think he's overplaying the senile old priest role."

Dana hesitated. *Altar boys?* Had Kelly seen the singed white surplices in the chapel closet? As this thought came to her, she also realized that he had just shared, very casually, as if she already knew, that he had spoken with Father Michael. Was this his way of letting her know that he was aware that she and Kip had made the same visit? Yes, that was precisely what he was telling her. They were building trust. She wouldn't have to tell Ryan Kelly they'd been to St. Lawrence's, and she knew he wouldn't ask.

"He's fairly old," she said, contributing her part to the conversation.

"That he is, but I sense there's more to the story than he shared."

"He's hiding something?"

"Possibly. Can I pick you up somewhere?" Kelly asked. "I could run by your office, say about eleven?"

She hadn't actually said she would go, and she didn't want him to come by her office, though she was going in early the following day. Kip had requested she pick up his personal things, and she'd finally talked to Brenda, and they were getting together.

"I'll meet you at the church," she told Kelly. "Mass starts at eleven-thirty?"

"Yep, see you then."

CHAPTER FIFTEEN

The downtown office still didn't feel like home to Dana. They'd moved out of the mezzanine in the old building in the Dorchester neighborhood at one point, then into the wider newsroom, but here in the heart of the city in the Financial District, she felt oddly out of place.

Kip's computer had been removed, but notes from his interviews were still in the drawer. Dana put them in her bag. She stuffed his few photos—one of him on a fishing trip to Alaska, another of him with his sister's family—a few trinkets, a pencil holder, a plastic bobblehead of a Red Sox player who wasn't even with the team anymore, into a cardboard box. Just as she was about to heft the box and carry it out to her car, Mac appeared.

"I think he'll be back," he said.

"I hope so," Dana replied. "I hope he can get things straightened out."

Mac nodded. "You can store those in my office if you'd like."

Dana wondered why, if he thought Kip was coming back, Mac didn't just leave his desk intact.

"Sure," she said. She had no room in her apartment to store anything anyway.

Mac carried Kip's box into his office, and Dana stopped to talk to Brenda. They chatted a bit about where they each felt the story might go. Brenda's blonde hair, perfectly parted down the left side, fell over her right eye in a veil as she scanned Kip's notes and interview schedule. She looked up, tucking her hair behind her ear, and Dana noticed how young and pretty she was. "Looks like these are fairly well organized. I'll take up the interview schedule right away."

"Sounds good. Thanks for stepping in." Neither of them mentioned why Kip was no longer working on the story. Dana wondered if one of the complaints had come from Brenda, though Mac had mentioned no names.

Dana stopped at her own desk, checked the messages on her old-fashioned landline. Often, she'd check it remotely from her cellphone and listen to messages. Today there was one from someone selling life insurance, another from a marketing company, and one obviously from a scammer, something about the warranty on her vehicle being expired. Her *little car* warranty had expired years ago. Just as she was about to leave, Robyn, a recently hired office clerk, came up and said, "A call for you came in this morning." She handed Dana a form used for incoming calls to the general *Globe* number.

"Thanks, Robyn."

Dana glanced at the note as Robyn headed back to her desk. It was a call from Drew. Why would he call her at work? Had he forgotten her cellphone number? She'd canceled her landline years ago. Did Drew's call have something to do with Joel? Her heart clenched at this thought. But wouldn't he have said it was urgent if this was why he'd called? Quickly, she dialed his number and got only a recorded greeting. She left a message and then reluctantly left her office, certain that Drew would have said so if it was important. Surely, if this was about Joel, he would have said, *Call immediately*.

The students had already filed into the small church of St. Lawrence's and were seated in the pews with a teacher flanking each aisle. Dana found a place near the back and slid in, kneeling for a moment before she sat.

Just as old Father Michael hobbled in with his altar servers, Ryan

Kelly appeared. He shot Dana a smile and a nod of apology, apparently for his tardiness, then joined her as the children remained standing to begin the Mass.

Dana studied the old priest as he slowly made his way up to the altar, followed by his altar servers. The tallest was thin with long blonde curls falling down her back, the other a short brunette with hair pulled back in a ponytail.

Dana leaned close and whispered to Kelly, "So much for the altar *boys*."

He nodded and shot her a guarded grin.

Several students got up to do the readings, and Dana was impressed and touched by their abilities and apparent devotion. Some looked barely old enough to be in school, let alone get up and read scripture.

As the Mass progressed, Dana could see Kelly's eyes darting along the pews, focusing on a particular row that looked like mid-grade students, maybe third- or fourth-graders. The girls were separated from the boys, and she thought that Kelly was concentrating on the boys, maybe hoping to find the kids accused of starting the fire. Dana had considered that the hooligans—she laughed at the word that popped into her head—responsible for the fire had no affiliation with the church. The chapel had not been locked. Anyone could have entered. Maybe the fire-starter kids didn't even exist. Maybe Father Michael had made them up. But, hadn't Father said he'd sent them home to their parents, which would incline her to believe he knew them. Were they sitting in the church right now? Little Catholic hooligans? She guessed that's what Kelly thought.

Some of the kids were getting restless as they filed up for communion. One boy was elbowing another. He was a scruffy-looking kid with mussed hair and patched pants that were too short. Hand-me-downs, Dana thought, from an older brother. A teacher tapped him on the shoulder and gave him a stern look, and he settled down, bowing his head innocently, pressing his hands together in front of him.

After Mass, the children started back down the aisle, front rows first, the little ones, kindergartners and first-graders. The last ones out were eighth-graders, who came in a variety of sizes and shapes. Some of the girls looked more like women than girls, much more mature than the boys. Dana certainly remembered those awkward years.

As they left the church, Dana said to Kelly, "Looks like you didn't find your altar boys."

"Not on the altar." He grinned. "I like the idea that girls can now serve. That was happening in other parishes, including the girls, when I was serving Mass here at St. Lawrence's."

"But, not here at St. Lawrence's?" Dana attempted to keep the surprise out of her voice. Kelly had just revealed something else, casually as if she should have already known. This was Ryan Kelly's parish as a child. Is this why the Fire Marshal had taken this very personal interest?

"Girls on the altar," Kelly said, "not a chance. Let's just say that Father Michael has sexist leanings."

"He was here when you served as an altar boy?"

"He's almost as old as the church itself," Kelly said with a quiet laugh as they walked down the steps. "And, yes, it's been a while since I served as an altar boy."

"He's allowing it now. Those feminists must have worn him down."

He shot her another smile; Dana thought a smile of approval. She wondered how long ago Kelly had served on the altar with Father Michael. She guessed he was about her age, late-forties. He had a youthful face, yet a few worry lines around his eyes and mouth. She could easily picture him as an altar boy and also imagine him as the kid elbowing the other boy in the communion line.

"I think I could pick the kids out of a lineup," he said with confidence. Dana was well aware he'd been studying the boys as they sat in the pews, as they went up for communion, then filed out of the church. She wondered if he could really pick those naughty boys out of a group just by observing their behavior during Mass.

"Let's head on over to the school," he said. "Kids should be going to lunch."

They signed in at the front desk and then headed to the principal's office. She wasn't in, but the office helper asked if she could take a message. Kelly handed her a card and said he would be in touch, that the Department of Fire Services with Public Safety and Security would like to arrange some educational programs at St. Lawrence's.

The girl glanced at his card and said that sounded like a good idea. She wore glasses with wide, plastic frames, her hair pulled back in a scrunchie. Dana guessed the office helper was about thirteen or fourteen, probably an eighth-grader. *Eighth-graders rule the school*, Dana thought, remembering a chant from her own grade school days.

The girl was studying the card, writing a note on a while-you-were-out pad. *That could have been me*, Dana thought. She'd worked as an aid in the office in eighth grade. At times she felt she knew more about what was going on in the school than the principal.

"You know there was a fire in the chapel in June," the girl said. "It would be a good idea for some education. Some kids don't know how dangerous fires can be." Dana could almost hear a *tch, tch, tch* in her voice.

"How'd you hear about the fire?" Kelly asked. "It happened during the summer, before school started."

"Oh, everybody knows about it. Kelvin Stewart and Mic Mahoney were bragging about it all over the place, about how they put the fire out. They're fourth-graders this year. A couple of troublemakers if you ask me."

"They were bragging that they put the fire out?" Kelly asked.

The girl laughed. "Well, probably they started it. Even though they claimed it was someone else, they were telling everyone they put it out. But you know it was the middle of the night. What would a couple of fourth-graders be doing in the chapel in the middle of the night but causing trouble?"

Middle of the night? Dana wondered. Why had she assumed it was during the day?

"Kelvin Stewart and Mic Mahoney?" Kelly asked the girl, and Dana could see he was repeating the names to verify he'd heard correctly.

"I'll give your card to Ms. Trenton," the girl said. "You're Ryan Kelly, the Fire Marshal?" She scanned the card again as she paperclipped it to the note she'd written, then she glanced toward the door. Dana and Kelly both turned.

A woman had slipped into the room. She was slender with her hair gathered loosely atop her head. She wore a long dark charcoal skirt and grey speckled cardigan sweater over a white blouse, which she'd spiffed up with a colorful scarf with bright yellow and orange geometric designs. She held a stack of papers under one arm, an insulated lunch bag looped over the other. She set the papers and bag down on the desk.

"Why, Ryan," she said, reaching out with both hands. Delicate, thin hands, affectionately grasping Kelly's much larger hands. "What brings you to St. Lawrence's?"

"He's going to give some fire safety classes at the school," the girl said, sounding very much like she was in charge, that it was all arranged.

"Oh, that's right," Ms. Trenton said with a warm smile. "You've recently been appointed State Fire Marshal." Dana guessed she was in her mid-fifties, older than she had first appeared when she walked in the door. Streaks of gray threaded through her dark hair. She was very thin in a fit rather than undernourished way and had a healthy glow about her. She smiled again and said, "Congratulations. We're always pleased to see one of our St. Lawrence's boys do well." She studied him for a moment, the way a delighted mother might appraise a favorite child, then added, "We could certainly use a little fire safety education at St. Lawrence's."

"I understand there was a fire in the chapel in June."

"No damage, as I understand." Her eyes tightened. She paused. "What's up?" She glanced at Dana as if to ask, *and who are you?*

Dana had attempted to remain invisible during the conversation with Kelly and Miss Perfect Office Helper, but she could see the principal, Ms. Trenton, wanted to know what was going on and why the newly appointed Fire Marshal had a sidekick.

"This is Dana Pierson. She's helping me with some investigations into recent fires."

"Oh," Ms. Trenton said, then turned to the girl. "Sara, why don't you take your lunch break. Thank you so much for your help, for covering during Mass."

The girl shot Kelly, then Dana, each a tight smile, before reluctantly leaving the office.

"Please," Ms. Trenton said, "please, sit down."

Kelly pulled out one of the plastic chairs in front of the desk for Dana, who sat and then lowered himself into the other. The chairs seemed exceptionally small—grade school chairs.

Ms. Trenton sat at her desk.

"What do you know about the fire?" Kelly asked, attempting to adjust his large frame in the small seat.

"Nothing, until recently. The two boys who were caught in the chapel have been talking. There was nothing in the news this summer, nothing mentioned at the meetings as we were preparing for the upcoming school year. The chapel isn't used, other than for storage. I don't believe there was any damage?"

"What are you hearing?" Kelly asked.

Why were two young boys, fourth-graders, Dana thought, which made them about 9, *doing in the chapel in the middle of the night?* She sensed it best that she let Kelly lead the interview, even though she had a list of questions popping like kernels of popcorn in her head.

"I'm hearing that Father Michael caught the boys in the chapel," Ms. Trenton explained. "Perhaps playing around with matches, maybe trying to light some candles, not intending to do any damage, I'm sure."

And what alerted Father Michael? Dana wondered. *In the middle of the night.*

"Did Father Michael say why he was there?" Kelly asked. "How he became aware of the fire?"

"I haven't spoken to Father Michael," Ms. Trenton said. "We've learned nothing. Officially that is. It's all rumor. And I've certainly got my hands full, starting a new school year. We're short a couple of teachers. I'm afraid the pay in a parochial school can't compete with what they offer in the public schools, and even those are having difficulties filling all the positions. Being a teacher these days is a true challenge." Her lips turned downward, as did her eyes. Then she glanced up at Kelly and said, "Perhaps you should speak to Father. If the boys need further discipline . . . this didn't happen during the school year. Perhaps it's the parents who should become involved."

Dana knew Kelly had already spoken with Father Michael. Maybe he was just attempting to learn if what the priest told him lined up with the rumors flying around St. Lawrence's.

"Do you have any idea why the boys were in the chapel at this odd hour?" Kelly asked.

"Yes," she said, then gazed out the window. "I can imagine." She paused, and Dana thought she might refuse to answer, though she clearly had an idea.

"Is it something you can share?" Kelly coxed in a gentle voice.

Ms. Trenton turned, looked at him, and laughed. She had a pleasant laugh, even though Dana sensed she didn't really want to share.

"You know the chapel hasn't been used in years," she said. "There's no entry from the church itself. The staircase is in shambles."

"Why hasn't it been repaired?" Kelly asked.

"We're not a wealthy parish. Many of the families are single moms barely getting by. Nearly a fourth of the students are on scholarship, though heaven knows we can't afford it. And we hesitate to ask for financial aid from the archdiocese."

"Why's that?" Kelly asked, but even Dana could tell he already knew the answer.

"Because they tend to close churches that can't pull their weight. Add a school, and well—"

"I understand," Kelly said. "So, the reason the boys were in the chapel?"

"Some kind of challenge. Like going into a haunted house at midnight."

"Haunted?"

Ms. Trenton bit her lip.

"Is it?" Kelly asked. "Haunted?"

"There are stories," Ms. Trenton said, her voice soft and low, "that there are saints and demons that visit the chapel at midnight." She rolled her eyes as if to show she believed it nonsense, though Dana thought maybe she did believe what she was saying.

Saints and demons, Dana thought. *Aren't demons just fallen angels?*

"Could you arrange for me to talk to the boys?" Kelly asked.

"I'll call their parents. If they agree, yes. If not . . ." She raised her shoulders, held her hands up, palms open in an almost protective way. *Mother Bear*, Dana thought.

"Thank you," he said as he stood. He pointed to the note and attached card that the office aid had placed on the desk. "Give me a call."

Ms. Trenton stood to walk Kelly and Dana to the door. "How's Julie?" she said amicably.

"She's doing great."

"Tell her I said hello."

"Will do," said Kelly.

Once outside, Dana was tempted to ask, *"Who's Julie?"* She'd noticed he didn't wear a wedding band but guessed firefighters, as a matter of safety, did not wear rings. Not that Ryan Kelly was rushing into burning buildings anymore, but maybe he'd become accustomed to wearing no jewelry, had never slipped his ring back on when he became an administrator. Was Julie his wife?

But instead, she said, "Saints? Demons? Angels? Is this getting a little weird?"

"Possibly," he replied. "No report of any sightings at St. Barbara's."

"No, but . . . there were a couple of TV reporters at the scene as well as a *Globe* reporter. A rookie." She could hear a tad of condescension in her voice that she didn't like. "With a photographer. Kip and I took a look at the shots and video, but it might be worth another." Dana guessed that Ryan Kelly had taken a close look at those videos, too. "We might check out the videos, see if there are any of the aforementioned creatures observing."

"Might be worth another look."

"Though I'm not sure that angels and demons can be filmed." She shot Kelly a sideways grin and was grateful when he sent one back to her. She was joking . . . and, yet.

"It isn't unheard of that a firestarter will hang around to see how it's going," Kelly said. "See if he has accomplished his goals."

"Or hers?"

"A possibility. Equal opportunity now."

Again, Dana thought, *Open the door and see all the people* . . . Then she thought of Kip. He'd been there, outside the church, watching, but he'd been half blitzed as far as she could tell. At least when he'd first pulled up to the inferno with his Uber driver. And though Dana had suggested Kip take some shots with his phone camera, he'd failed to get any video himself. She thought of ol' Tripper, the homeless man. A druggie, hallucinating? He'd seen an angel. Had the boys from St. Lawrence's seen the saints or demons? Father Michael had said the boys blamed the fire on a ghost! She knew Kelly was determined to talk to those boys, and now, thanks to Miss Office Helper, he knew who they were.

"How about lunch?" Kelly said.

Dana glanced at her watch and was about to say, *Yes, I've got time for lunch,* but instead, she asked, "Who's Julie?"

115

CHAPTER SIXTEEN

Over lunch at a Mexican place about five blocks from St. Lawrence's, Ryan Kelly told Dana about his family, a discussion prompted by her question, "Who's Julie?"

Julie was his older sister and had been classmates with Ms. Trenton, who oddly was also named Julie. Kelly came from a typical Boston Irish family. He'd grown up with an older sister, an older brother, a younger sister, a younger brother.

"You're the middle child?" Dana asked. She wondered if he suffered from middle-child syndrome, feeling at times ignored, yet at the same time growing up with a more relaxed attitude about life.

"I am. How about you?"

Dipping chips in salsa, she told him about her family.

"I was a bit of a tomboy, myself," she said, "growing up with two older brothers, who were into sports, a dad who was a professional athlete, first basemen for the Red Sox."

"That's impressive," he said, and Dana could see he was indeed impressed. "Slim Pierson? I remember him well."

Most Bostonians worshipped their Red Sox, and it appeared that Kelly was a true Bostonian. Dana had always been proud of her father. She told Kelly how her dad had gone into sports reporting after his career and had been instrumental in getting her interested in journalism, too, after she'd graduated from Boston University.

Kelly shared that he'd spent four years in the military, was a bit of a troublemaker before that, though he'd never been in any legal trouble, finished two years at a community college, then joined the local fire department, worked his way up to chief.

Though chips and salsa were delivered shortly after they arrived, the place was busy, and getting their order seemed to take forever. Dana didn't mind. She had plenty of time before Mia got home.

He asked about "her girl," and she explained how she and Mia had met through the girl's great-uncle, Father Giovanni Borelli, how Dana had visited the family vineyards and winery in Italy. Kelly seemed interested, intrigued by what he said sounded like an exciting life.

He told her he had a daughter now in college in D.C., how she divided her time between him and her mother, Ryan's ex, when she was home from college. Dana said nothing about Joel but guessed he might know. Anyone living in Boston probably knew about Joel. Though it had been 13 years since he disappeared, and if something doesn't affect you directly, you forget. Even something in the headlines for days, weeks, months . . . people forget. As a journalist, Dana knew that. People forget.

Dana realized how easily they had slipped into a personal conversation, that is until they started talking about the fires. He was the one who brought it up when he asked about Kip, and Dana said he'd moved on to something else.

"I'm curious about the boys who discovered the fire at St. Lawrence's," Kelly said. "I plan on talking to them. I know Julie Trenton will set something up. She wants to know, too."

"Is it unusual," Dana asked, "for the Fire Marshal to get involved in such a personal way?" He'd avoided the question before, but she sensed they were establishing some trust, and he might be more open now.

"We've got seventeen fire investigators associated with our office. Generally, fires are handled by the local fire departments. Our investigators get involved if it is something unusual or within certain parameters."

"Which you supervise?" He was still being vague, she noted.

He nodded. "We generally only get involved in any depth if arson is involved. Fires as crimes. Terrorists. Bombs."

She pondered this for a moment before asking, "But your present position is one of administration, supervision?"

"That's pretty much my call," he said, dipping a chip in salsa. "I'm free to involve myself in any aspect of the investigation or rely completely on our investigators. They're good, well trained, well educated." He smiled. "Our department handles firefighter education. We supervise the training of investigators. We've got a good program. Our men are all top-notch."

"Do you miss being out there? Fighting fires?"

"Sometimes." His eyes narrowed in thought. She sensed he was physical, a doer, and maybe this new job involved too much desk work. Though he'd certainly been out in the field the past few days. Climbing up stairs, slipping through broken windows. She'd always liked this part of reporting too. The leg work, the physical part of investigating. She wasn't good at sitting at a desk all day, either.

"I served as Deputy Fire Marshal for five years before being appointed State Fire Marshal," he continued, "so the transition wasn't sudden. I worked my way up."

The server delivered their main course, a more substantial meal than Dana generally ate for lunch. She'd ordered seafood enchiladas, and they came covered with sour cream cheese sauce along with a pile of beans and rice. As she surveyed her heaping plate, she thought of what Pammie said about pizza after the game and her advice that Dana and Mia get a snack before. As these thoughts sifted through her mind, Dana realized how long it had been since something as simple as eating a meal became part of a plan that included another person.

She glanced at her watch. It was already almost two-thirty, and she surely wouldn't need to eat before Zac's game. There was still leftover Chinese for Mia if she was hungry. Dana would probably get a take-out box after lunch, too, as she'd eaten enough chips and salsa to make a meal, and there was plenty heaped on her plate, even as she worked away at it.

"Your interest in these fires?" Dana asked. "Does it have anything to do with your affection for St. Lawrence's?"

"Affection?" he asked after a moment, after a large bite of his beef taco. He placed the remainder of the overstuffed shell on the plate, wiped his chin with the paper napkin. "You like the food here?" he asked as if he'd picked the place just for her. Also, avoiding her question, she noted.

She nodded with a mouth full, then swallowed. "It's good. Yes, I like it. That was your parish when you were growing up."

He pushed the rice around his plate with his fork. "Yes, I have a special connection to the place." He lifted a bite to his mouth, chewed thoughtfully, washed it down with a slow drink of water, then said, "How did you and Kip know about the fire at St. Lawrence's?"

It was a reasonable question at this point. "Kip happened by chance to be driving by the night of the fire at St. Barbara's. He stopped. He overheard one of the firefighters say something about a fire at another church several months ago."

"St. Lawrence's," Kelly said, eyes narrowed. "He specifically named St. Lawrence's?" Kelly's mind seemed to be sorting through something she sensed he wasn't going to share.

"Kip happened to overhear something, no details, but yes, St, Lawrence's." She paused, hoping Kelly would share more. "We found nothing about that fire. Nothing in the media, on the news, no report."

"The call," he said, "came in an unusual way."

"No five-alarm fire?" She smiled, but she was proceeding cautiously as it seemed he was on the verge of telling her more. When he didn't reply, she asked, "Can you share?"

"Father Michael called."

"He called *you*? The Fire Marshal? In the middle of the night?"

"He called, but not me."

"The local fire department?"

"He called my mother."

"Your mother?" she asked, surprised.

"Yes." He smiled. "Father told her he was anxious because there had been a fire in the chapel. It was out, but he couldn't sleep because he thought something might reignite. He worried that it was smoldering. He asked her to have me come over."

"So, you went? Unofficially? To check it out?"

"I did."

"How did the fireman Kip overheard know about it?"

"I called the district chief, asked if he could send one of his men over to meet me."

"You didn't want the Chief to think the Marshal was interfering on his turf?"

"I suppose that was what I was thinking."

"The fire was out when you arrived?"

He nodded.

"No official report?"

"I left that up to the Chief."

They seemed to be sharing, nicely, Dana thought, and so she asked, "You think all three fires are related?" She recalled what the man in the park said about the angel, what Julie Trenton revealed about stories of saints and demons in the chapel, how the boys said they'd seen a ghost.

"There was almost something . . ." He paused, considering. "Something ritualistic about the way the fires were set. In front of the altar in each incident. Yet, there was something distinct about each."

"Something different about each?" Dana thought he might add more, fill her in on some important details, but after a stretch of nothing, she asked, "Like they were set by different people?"

"Possibly."

"But, part of a group?"

The server approached their table to offer refills on their water, and just as he left, Kelly's phone sounded.

"Tomorrow at ten," he said, nodding. "Sure. No problem. I'll be there. Thanks, Julie." He slid the phone back in the inner pocket of his jacket.

"She's set something up with one of the kids. His mom is off on Saturday, and she's agreed to bring him over to the school. Julie said she'd meet us there at ten."

"Us?"

"I'd like you to come."

"I'm headed to New York tomorrow with—"

"Your girl?" Kelly asked with a slow grin.

"Yes, Mia and I are taking off for the weekend." Dana wondered why he assumed her trip to New York was with Mia. She could be taking off with her boyfriend for all Ryan Kelly knew.

She explained how they were going to a football game that evening, then for pizza, then up early to catch the train. She grimaced and said, "I'm not sure I'm young enough to keep up with all this activity."

"Just be grateful that you can do this. Enjoy it." He called the server for the bill, pulled out his credit card. "I miss having those opportunities to spend time with my daughter now that she's away at college."

Kelly reached for the bill when the server delivered it to the table, even as Dana realized she should have asked for a separate ticket.

Journalistic ethics, she thought. "I'll pay my share," she told him and he nodded.

As they got up to leave, Dana realized how much she wanted to go with Ryan Kelly to talk to the boy. Mostly because she was curious about what they might learn, but also because she liked spending time with him. Yet, she was looking forward to the weekend in New York with Mia, though not the very early rising the trip would require.

CHAPTER SEVENTEEN

Mia sat next to Zac's brother Quinn at the game, which was probably a good thing. Mia understood the general objective of the sport. A large field, a goal post on each side, one team attempting to prevent the other from reaching their goal. Quinn had to point out which player was Zac—he was a defensive lineman—but he was so padded up, with a helmet hiding his face, that without Quinn's help Mia might not have been able to identify him. Zac was tall, but all the players were big. Some appeared as wide as they were tall. Mia wondered which player was Becket, the boy Meagan had hypnotized. When Zac's dad said something about the quarterback doing exceptionally well, Mia remembered that Meagan had called Becket the quarterback. Maybe Meagan's attempt at building his confidence had paid off.

Mia and Dana had arrived after the game started because Dana was confused as to where to park. She'd come home later than usual, had insisted that Mia eat some of the leftover Chinese food, then suggested they change into jeans for the game. Dana also told Mia that the team colors were blue and white, so it was always good to wear your team colors. Dana didn't know the opposing team's colors, but it would be a football faux pas if they showed up in the enemy's colors.

So, they found the appropriate fans without difficulty, merely following the colors. Zac's family had saved two seats for them, and the stadium was full. Once, during the early part of the game, Mia thought that Zac looked up to where they were sitting, but with the helmet it was hard to tell. She hadn't heard from him all week. No calls. No texts. Nothing.

After the game, which Zac's team won, they all met up at the restaurant. Just as the server delivered their pizza, Pammie called Quinn and Olivia, who were off playing some video games, back to the table and Zac strolled in. Maybe *strutted,* Mia considered. A much more appropriate word to describe what she saw. *Pavoneggiarsi.* He definitely looked like a triumphant athlete.

"Well, what a nice surprise," Pammie said, throwing her son a grin. Zac shot one back to his mom before his eyes landed on Mia and his smile grew wider.

Big wooden tables with benches required some maneuvering to get everyone in and out. Quinn popped up, offering his brother a seat next to Mia as everyone told him what a great game he'd played.

Zac's hair was still damp, fresh out of the shower, maybe, but definitely not dripping with sweat. He smelled like spicy soap or cologne. He offered Mia another friendly smile as if he hadn't been avoiding her all week.

"Good game," Quinn said as he slapped his big brother on the shoulder and plopped down next to him on the outer edge of the bench.

"What did you think?" Zac asked, turning to Mia.

"It was . . ." She was going to say interesting but instantly realized that wasn't the right word, was probably a terrible word to use on just about any occasion. This was a boring, adult-like word. "Fun," she said. "Thank you for inviting me. I'm just learning the rules. You did great!" She knew he had because his mom and dad had jumped up and down, shouting, "Way to go, Zac," throughout the game.

"Thanks," Zac said. "I'm glad you came." Mia could see he was—glad that she'd come. "Next week we're out of town, but maybe the following week you and Aunt Dana could come again."

"I'd like that," she said, and just like that, it seemed they were friends again.

After finishing their pizza, the younger kids playing more games, Mia telling Zac about their plans to take the train the following morning to New York, he asked her if he could drive her home.

Mia shot a look toward Dana, sitting opposite them, next to Pammie on the other side of the table. From the concerned expression on her face, Mia thought Dana had heard the question. She'd been glancing at her wristwatch throughout dinner, and Mia guessed she was thinking about their early morning train to New York.

"I'll drive her straight home," Zac said. "We'll probably get there before you do, Aunt Dana."

"Okay," she said, surprising Mia, "but don't drive too fast just to get home first. Don't stop anywhere. You know we have to get up early."

"Yeah," Zac said. "Mia was telling me about your plans."

Mia noticed, as they headed toward Dana's, that Zac was driving extremely slow—she thought so they would have more time together, not because Dana had admonished him.

"I want to apologize," he said, "about the other night."

Mia wondered exactly what he was apologizing for. There were numerous possibilities why he might owe her an apology. Deserting her at the party to play pool. Implying on the drive home that it was his responsibility to make sure she didn't drink or do drugs. She really couldn't include the way he'd given her the silent treatment when she asked about his cousin Joel. She could understand why he might not want to talk about that.

"When you asked about Joel," Zac said, "I didn't answer because, truthfully, I don't remember."

"You don't remember your cousin?" Her voice was low, supportive without being overly sympathetic or condescending.

"It's that night I don't remember. The night he disappeared."

The first article Mia read from Dana's files said that an older cousin was sharing a room with Joel, and Mia knew that had to be Zac. He was the only older cousin. She guessed that Quinn and

Olivia weren't even around back then. And certainly not Kiki. The article also said that the boy told the police that someone came and took Joel. In a later article, it was reported that the cousin had no memory of what happened.

"But I remember my cousin," Zac added.

"How old were you when it happened?" Mia asked.

"Just four. Joel was three. But I do remember him." There was something almost defensive in his voice now, as if he had to defend the possibility that a kid could forget his cousin. "We were friends, though he was a year younger than me. Only three." Zac bit his lower lip. "Can you have memories from when you are only four years old?" He asked as if this had been challenged.

"I do."

"So do I. Just not about that night. Though sometimes . . ." His voice faded, and Mia thought maybe Zac was done talking about it.

"Sometimes what?" she coaxed gently.

"Sometimes . . . something comes back to me . . . I don't even know what it is . . . the smell of my grandmother's house . . . it triggers something."

Mia knew from the photo in one of the articles that the place where Joel had disappeared was the same house where Zac's grandmother lived now. She wondered if it was difficult for the family to still gather there. Especially Dana. Or did her mom, Ann Pierson, as well as the rest of the family, want to be there just in case Joel found his way back to where he had gone missing. *He's probably dead*, Mia thought, then instantly pushed this awful feeling from her head.

"What do you remember about Joel?" she asked.

"His hair was very pale. Yellow, I guess you'd say. And he was smart. I remember that. Maybe because the adults said so. And I remember his birthday. He always told people his birthday was March 27. I remember that. That stuck with me."

"Like Kiki," Mia said. "That was one of the first things she said when I met her."

"That's a big deal for a kid," Zac said. "Birthdays are a big deal."

They slowed and stopped as the light changed from yellow to red. She knew Zac could have shot right through if he'd just sped up a bit. She glanced back, thinking maybe Dana was behind them, but she wasn't. It seemed Zac was driving slow on purpose. When he'd driven her home from the party Monday, he was going much faster. Showing off a little, she realized now.

"Sometimes," Zac said, "I think my parents were talking about Joel, and I overheard them, and I'm not sure I really remember him. Or, maybe something my therapist said."

Mia didn't think therapists were supposed to put ideas into a kid's head. "Your therapist talked about Joel?" she asked.

"That was a long time ago," Zac said quietly. "Haven't been to the shrink in a while."

Mia wanted to ask more about the therapist. Her Dad had sent her to talk to a counselor after her mom died. "Does Dana talk about Joel?" she asked.

"Not really." He paused as if attempting to bring up the memory of when she did talk about him. "What do you remember from when you were four?" he asked, turning and glancing at Mia.

"I remember going out to the vines with my mother," she said. "She'd scoop up a handful of soil and smell it, then I remember . . . she put a small dab on her tongue." Mia laughed. "And I remember that I took a handful and put the whole thing in my mouth. My grandmother used to tell that story. She said I was only three or four."

Zac said, "If a story is repeated enough, sometimes it feels as if you were there, that you're not really recalling it from a personal memory. That's why I sometimes wonder if I remember Joel. Do you actually remember eating dirt?" He grinned.

"I'm sure I remember. It tasted awful."

"Your mother didn't really taste the soil?" Someone who'd pulled up behind them honked, and Zac started up, just now aware that the light had flicked to green.

"No. I mean yes. She did. She did taste the soil. She could tell if the soil was good from the smell, the taste. It has something to do with the makeup, the chemical balance of the soil. When growing grapes for wine, the right soil is essential. Some people can tell if it's good by smelling it. Tasting it."

"Really?"

"Yeah," Mia said. "She tasted it. But she didn't stuff in a fist full like I did."

Zac laughed. "How old were you when your mom died?"

"I was eleven."

"So, you have lots of memories? Real memories."

"I do," Mia said. "Lots of good memories."

CHAPTER EIGHTEEN

Mia slept during most of the train ride, and Dana wondered about the wisdom of starting their New York adventure at this ridiculous hour. Unable to nap herself, Dana's mind looped back to Drew's call, which she'd returned twice now, her second attempt to contact him just before they took off for Zac's game. Since Drew had not called back, it couldn't be about Joel. Could it? She left another message, telling Drew she'd be away for the weekend, but if it was urgent, please call. Then, she'd placed a call to Christopher Prinz, the detective who'd been assigned Joel's case for the past thirteen years.

"Have you spoken to Drew?" she'd asked, hearing a crack in her voice. "Have you discovered something new?"

"You know I'd call you right away if we did," he'd replied, and she knew he would.

"Thanks, Chris. It's just that Drew called, and I thought maybe—"

No, nothing new," he'd said.

Nothing new, a familiar refrain, always delivered with equal parts professionalism and kindness.

Dana pressed her head to the window, feeling the even rhythm of the train, gazing out as the sun slowly announced the day with an offering of pink and gold in the early morning sky. She glanced at Mia, who seemed to have the ability, as many young people, to sleep just about anywhere.

When they arrived at Penn Station, Dana nudged Mia and said, "We're here."

As they stepped off the train, Mia perked up considerably. After dropping their bags off at the hotel, too early to check into their room, they took an Uber to Central Park and spent the morning wandering, checking out the gardens, the fantastic view of the New York *skyscrapers*—a word Dana always liked—from the south end of the park, and then on to the Metropolitan Museum of Art which delighted Mia. After lunch at the museum cafeteria, they walked down Fifth Avenue and stopped at St. Patrick's Cathedral. Mia reverently lit a candle and said a silent prayer. Dana wondered what the girl was thinking as she bowed her head. When Dana was a child, lighting candles in church seemed like a reverse version of making a wish while blowing out birthday candles. She no longer believed in wishes, and many of her prayers had gone unanswered. Maybe there was no difference between a wish and a prayer.

They crossed the street, strolled through Rockefeller Center, the numerous flags waving in a light breeze, then checked into their hotel just off of Times Square. After a short nap, they ventured down toward Broadway and surprisingly were able to pick up a couple of tickets for *The Lion King*. They had an early dinner at an Italian restaurant—which they both enjoyed—before strolling down to the theater. Dana watched as Mia sat, literally on the edge of her seat, eyes wide, awestruck by the colorful costumes, the oddly authentic movement of the figures on stage, the rhythm, the beat of the music. This was the second time Dana had seen the performance, but she found it as captivating, if not more so, as the first. Mia talked about it all the way back to their hotel, where they fell into bed and slept soundly until morning when they awoke, made coffee in the room, and then headed back to St. Patrick's for Mass.

All through Mass, Dana thought about the churches in Boston, the fires. And she thought about Ryan Kelly. He would have met yesterday with Julie Trenton, the principal, one of the boys and his mother. Dana wondered what Ryan had learned, if anything. She wondered what he was doing this morning. What did a single guy like Ryan Kelly do on a Sunday morning? Did he still go to Mass? Did he meet friends for a Sunday brunch? Did he sleep in? If it wasn't for Mia, Dana would probably be up, having coffee, watching the Sunday morning shows.

Then, briefly, again, she thought of Drew. Her brother Jeff had told her that Drew was being considered for a position on the court, which would bring him back to Boston. Maybe this was why he had called.

After Mass, they took an Uber down to the 9/11 Memorial, both Dana and Mia pensive and quiet, then speaking of the impact this had on the entire country. Dana thought of the heroic actions of the first responders, an image of Ryan Kelly turning once more through her mind. They took a quick boat ride into the harbor so Mia could see the Statue of Liberty. Late that afternoon, they hopped on the train back to Boston. Mia slept as Dana stared out the window, thinking of candles and lights and fires and wishes, thinking about getting together with Ryan Kelly in Boston.

As they were taking a cab back to her apartment, Dana's phone bleeped with a message. Her heart did a little flip when she saw the name Ryan Kelly pop up on her screen. *Meet for coffee Monday am?*

She wondered if he had been thinking about her, too. Or was there something he wanted to share about the interview with the boy from St. Lawrence's?

Sure. When? Where? She texted back.

She could see by the DOT, DOT, DOT in a bubble that he was texting at that very moment, and something about that immediate and personal connection tightened an anxious knot in her chest. Another message popped up on the screen within seconds. *Is 8:00 too early?* She could almost hear the words in his voice.

She texted back that 8:00 was fine, and he sent the name of a coffee shop that was conveniently close to her apartment, though she'd never told him where she lived.

* * *

The following morning, Dana checked on Mia to make sure she was up in time to catch the T. Dana herself had plenty of time since her appointment—or was it a coffee date?—with Ryan Kelly was close by and not until 8:00. She made a pot of coffee and cut some fruit. They had established a morning routine. Mia ate little in the morning other than fruit and toast. She always appreciated the coffee.

"That was fun," Mia said, slowly sipping her coffee. "Thank you for taking me to New York. It's a great city." She was dressed in her uniform, ready for school, but her hair was damp from the shower, and Dana knew this morning she intended to let it air dry. Dana didn't like her going out with damp hair, but she wouldn't say anything. Her own mother would have thrown a fit if Dana had left the house with damp hair.

"We'll have to go again," Dana said, "maybe spend more time."

"Maybe take a later train," Mia replied, gazing up over her cup with a sleepy grin.

Within fifteen minutes, Mia was out the door. Dana showered and dressed, then poured another cup of coffee and sat, staring out the window, thoughts drifting to Ryan Kelly, their meeting that morning, then thinking of Kip, wondered how he was doing. She grabbed her phone and called. A voice message picked up the call, for which she was at least partially grateful, realizing if Kip had made it to Idaho, it wasn't even 6:00 A.M. yet.

This is Kip Connor, the message said, *and I'm holed up in a remote mountain cabin in Idaho. I plan on being here through the winter, so leave a message and I'll get back to you after the spring thaw.*

Dana couldn't help but smile. His voice sounded good. Sober. She wondered if he could make it through the winter isolated in a remote Idaho cabin. Maybe this was exactly where he should be right now. She hoped the place wasn't filled with bottles of alcohol.

She went into the dining room and glanced over at the files she'd put together on eldercare. She had set up another couple of interviews—before Kip had quit—and, though she wasn't particularly enthusiastic about continuing the project, she didn't intend to cancel. They were later in the afternoon and wouldn't interfere with her coffee date with Ryan Kelly.

She grabbed a sweater and took off for the coffee shop. It was close enough she could walk, and she planned on arriving before 8:00. She liked to arrive early for an interview if she was meeting someone at a neutral location. This tactic put her at an advantage, allowing her to choose the most advantageous spot to sit. She wasn't sure why these thoughts had entered her head. She wasn't interviewing Ryan Kelly. This was more of a cooperative effort. At least that was what she thought.

He was sitting when she arrived, skimming a morning paper. It appeared he was waiting for her to order. There was no coffee cup perched on the table.

"Thank you for meeting me," he said, rising, reaching for her hand as if they were here to finalize a business deal. She liked his touch, the warmth of his hand. "What can I get you?" he offered. "I'm having a breakfast sandwich. You want one?" He folded the paper neatly on the table.

"Coffee, black," she said. "Just coffee is good."

"Black coffee it is." He was already up and, with a few broad steps, he was at the counter placing his order. She sat, glanced at his paper—*Boston Globe*, well good for him!—and shortly, he brought two coffees to the table.

"Checking to make sure I haven't published my story yet?" she asked, motioning toward the newspaper. There had been a story on St. Barbara's two days after the fire, since the church had pretty much been destroyed, but it included nothing linking it to the unreported fire at St. Lawrence's, the underreported fire at St. Al's. Neither Kip nor Dana had any part in writing the story, and there was no byline.

He smiled. "I trust that you'll let me know when you publish *our* story."

Our story? She kind of liked that. "So," she asked, "How did the interview go?"

"Surprisingly well."

"You learned something helpful from the boy?"

"Those boys didn't start the fire," he said with certainty.

"Father Michael isn't telling the truth?"

"I'm not sure what he honestly believes." Ryan took a sip of coffee. "The boy told me that by the time Father Michael arrived, they were just trying to put the fire out, but the kid swears they didn't start it."

"Did they see who did? Did they claim the ghost defense?"

"Julie Trenton was right. The boys had gone to the church that night on a dare. The kids all believe the chapel is haunted."

"What about the priest? Why was he there at night?"

"I went and talked to him again, too. He said he often has trouble sleeping and goes over to the chapel at night."

"To pray?"

"I suppose."

"Do you believe him?'

Ryan Kelly raised his shoulders, and the slow, thoughtful motion seemed to imply not doubt, but a sense of *I'm not sure what to believe about Father Michael.* "I asked to take a better look around the chapel, check out the storage closet." His eyes met hers and held as if giving her time to reply, to add to this conversation.

"You saw the singed altar boys' surplices?" she contributed because she wanted him to feel he could trust her.

"I did."

"You hadn't noticed them before?"

"I hadn't looked in the closet on my first visit."

"What do you think?"

"I think it's strange that Father Michael didn't mention this. Or the boys."

The girl at the counter called out *Ryan*, and he went up and grabbed his sandwich. He sat down, took a bite. "You sure you don't want one?" He held it up as if offering her a taste of *his* sandwich, and there was something sweet and intimate in the offer. "They make great sandwiches here. From scratch, not those pull-it-out-of-a-cardboard-box breakfasts."

"Thanks, I'm fine," she said, then asked, "You come here often?"

"Once in a while."

She found that odd that he would frequent a coffee shop in this neighborhood, though she had no idea where he lived. His office was at least 40 minutes from here. She waited for him to add more, but when he didn't, she asked, "You think the priest is hiding something?"

"I haven't figured that out yet."

"Did the boy claim they saw a ghost, one of those spirits haunting the chapel?"

Ryan laughed. No doubt he'd seen the statues in the chapel covered with white sheets, too. "Let me show you something." After taking another large bite of the sandwich, which left little on his plate, he wiped his fingers with a paper napkin, then pulled his phone out of his pocket. He turned in on, tapped and swiped several times, then leaned in close, over the small table, tilting the phone so they each had a good angle to view the video he'd pulled up. "Here, is that okay? I don't want you to get a glare."

She nodded okay, their eyes meeting. He was close enough now she could almost feel his breath on her cheek, smell his aftershave and shampoo. He smelled like he'd just stepped out of the shower.

The video was one Dana had watched the morning after the fire at St. Barbara's. A production from a local TV station. They watched in silence.

"Do you want to tell me what I'm looking for?" Dana asked.

"I know you reporters are trained to observe. I want to know what you see."

He took the last bite of his sandwich, then swiped back to replay the video. On the second viewing, Dana paid closer attention to what appeared in the background rather than the reporter and church. It showed a crowd gathered. A couple of people, most likely neighbors, stood gaping at the scene, heads shaking. One man in a bathrobe pulled over what looked like pajama pants gazed at the fire, hands stuffed in his pockets. A woman, most likely his wife, wearing a sweater over a pair of sweat pants, huddled next to him. A short distance away stood a person whose face was turned away. This person, too, appeared as if suddenly awakened, had rushed out still wearing nightclothes. A formless sweatshirt had been pulled over a nightgown, perhaps hastily, a neighbor alerted in the wee hours by all the commotion in the neighborhood. There was something about the garment—flowing, that's what it was. And the hair, pale, and long, and loose. She thought of what might appear as a ghost to a child. A flowy nightgown caught in an evening breeze or in a quick movement through the chapel might pass for a ghost. Or an angel's gossamer gown.

"You played the video for the boy?" she asked. "Mic or Kelvin?" she added, remembering the two names the student clerk had mentioned.

"Mic," he said with a nod of approval as if aware she was picking up details, and she could tell he liked that about her. "I'm not sure Kelvin's parents will allow him to talk to me, but Julie Trenton is still working on that."

"I assume you think whoever started the fire was out there watching." Though Kip had failed to take a video or photos, he might be an eyewitness, at least to the crowd gathered as the firefighters were fighting to put the fire out. Kip could have seen something that might be helpful, but he was off in a remote cabin in the Idaho mountains. The *Globe* photographer on site had taken nothing but shots of the church and firefighters, a crane from the firetruck rising into the dark night.

"I did. I showed him the video. After I'd questioned him thoroughly," Ryan replied. "With his mother right next to him," he added.

"Did he see anything familiar?"

"He did."

Dana wasn't sure how Ryan was keeping the excitement out of his voice. He was as cool and smooth as a chilled summer mocha.

"He said this person,"—he started at the midpoint in the video and pointed to the person in the flowing nightgown—"He said that looked kind of like the person they had seen in the chapel."

"The woman in the nightgown?" Dana said, trying to meet Ryan's calm with her own, though her voice jumped with excitement.

"But, no sweatshirt over the nightgown in the chapel, and Mic said he thought it was a man. The boy seemed slightly apprehensive, somewhat confused. Maybe a little frightened."

"I don't know about ghosts, but angels are androgynous, I believe," Dana said, glancing up with a half-smile, which he returned. She motioned for him to go back again to the video where the person appeared in the background. The figure was slender, not particularly masculine, but with the bulky sweatshirt, it was hard to tell the true shape of the body. The face was not visible. "So, this person spotted in the crowd outside St. Barbara's was the person who started the fire in the chapel at St. Lawrence's?"

"It's possible. Or someone dressed in a similar fashion."

"Or it's possible you put this idea into Mic's head by showing him the video?"

"That's also possible," Ryan said thoughtfully. "Did your friend Kip mention anyone suspicious-looking in the crowd?"

"He didn't." She told him about Kip taking off to visit his sister, how he was staying in a cabin somewhere in Idaho. She didn't reveal why. "Did the man speak to the boys?" Was it his voice that led Mic to identify this ghost-like figure as a man?

"He turned and fled, but Mic seemed to think he saw them."

"But, they didn't chase after him?"

"They were attempting to put out the fire."

"Which they did."

Ryan nodded. "Though Mic didn't say so, the boys were frightened. They'd come to see a ghost in the chapel—"

"And they did."

Ryan raised his shoulders, gazed down at his empty cup, then Dana's. "More coffee?"

"Yes, please."

He grabbed his empty plate and napkin off the table, put the plate into the plastic bin, the napkin in the trash can, then got them each a refill, and returned to the table. He looked like a man who was used to taking care of himself, cleaning up after himself.

"I also talked to the Realtor on Saturday," he said, sitting again. "We went to St. Al's for a second look. I asked about the blankets left in the church, how the homeless were getting in and out."

"And?"

"She was sheepish at first but then admitted she was aware that someone from the parish was laundering blankets, going over late each evening, unlocking the door, then coming back in the morning, making sure everyone was out, relocking the door during the day. She said during the winter, the place often accommodated many homeless people, during the summer months, not so crowded."

"But, there *were* witnesses the night of the fire."

"She didn't know, but from our joint visit to St. Al's, talking to the man at the park, I think we know. I'm still hoping to talk to that fellow Tripper."

"Did the Realtor know who's been providing clean blankets, opening the church?"

"It's a woman named Angela Jenson. I visited with her at her home Saturday afternoon."

"Angela?" Dana said pensively. "A real-life angel."

Ryan nodded. "She said there was a group of homeless people who used to hang around the church when it was still operating as a parish, especially on Wednesdays when they offered a free lunch, and then she started to notice, even after they had closed the church, especially when it got cold, that some of them were sleeping on the ground, bundled in blankets. The way the church is built, there were places that provided some shelter, even on the exterior, where people could get out of the weather. So, she thought, why not just unlock the door at night. She gathered blankets from parishioners, opened the church at night, then came back early in the morning to make sure they were up. Most of them made their way over to the shelter for breakfast. They could spend the night there but would have to listen to Bible readings and preaching, and some of them didn't want to do that. She seemed proud that at St. Al's, no questions asked, no biblical reading required."

"She had a key to get in?" Dana asked. She knew there was a lockbox on the front door of the church, and they'd crawled in through the broken window.

"She used to work part-time in the office, and I guess no one bothered to change that lock on the side door," he replied.

"Did she know anything about the fire?"

"She doubted the fire was started by vagrants. There would be no reason to light a fire in July."

"Maybe someone was smoking. Fell asleep? Or trying to cook some supper?"

"We've found no evidence of either," Ryan replied.

Dana realized Ryan had a crew of well-trained investigators on the job. So, why did he want her help? "You said there were similarities in how the fires were set, but there were also differences. Can you tell me more about that?"

"Not yet." He took a sip of coffee. "Our investigators are still working it out. I do believe we can work together." He didn't look at her as he said this, and his smooth, steady voice conveyed no clue as to why he thought they could work together.

Did Ryan think she knew something that he didn't? She sensed that he liked her company. But, surely, this wasn't an excuse to spend time with her. Was he looking for something from her? Did she know something that Ryan thought might help him or his investigators?

They sat silently for some time, finishing their coffee.

"Did you have fun in New York with your girl?" Ryan asked.

"I did," Dana replied. "We had a great time."

Mia was disappointed when Meagan wasn't on the bus. She wanted to talk to her about Zac. She'd been thinking about the conversation she'd had with him after they had pizza Friday night. Zac said he couldn't remember what had happened the night Joel disappeared, but the article Mia found in Dana's files said the older cousin had seen someone come into the bedroom the boys shared. Could Zac's memory be recovered? She'd heard about people being hypnotized to recover memory. She wondered if Meagan could do that.

When Mia arrived at her Art History class later that morning, she was happy to see Meagan sitting in her regular spot. The classroom was set up with tables, with places for two people to sit, rather than individual desks. The tables were slanted, used for the art classes as well as Art History.

"You weren't on the bus this morning," she said as she slid into the seat next to her.

"Slept late," Meagan said with a yawn. "My dad gave me a ride. How was New York?"

Mia told her about going to the Met, seeing *The Lion King*. Meagan had seen the musical and said she thought it was great, too. Just as Mia was about to say she needed to talk to Meagan about something important, the teacher came into the room and started their class.

At lunch with Marley and Meagan, Mia decided she wanted to wait to ask about Zac. She didn't want to share this with Marley. She might think it was weird, and Mia didn't even know if it was possible to bring up a repressed memory. Maybe it would be dangerous or harmful. After all, Meagan wasn't a professional. And what good would it do, anyway, even if Zac could remember something? How could this possibly help to find Joel? He likely wasn't alive after all this time. Maybe she should just leave this alone.

But, later, on the way home on the bus, Mia decided to tell Meagan about Zac and the disappearance of his cousin Joel.

"That surprises me," Meagan said. "That he went through such a traumatic experience when he was so young. Zac always seems like he's got it together. He's one of the *popular* kids." She pronounced the word *popular* with a hint of contempt, and Mia gathered that Meagan had never seen herself as popular. That she probably looked down on those who thought they were. Mia would have to admit she was probably *popular* back home, but here, she didn't know exactly where she fit in. She liked that. Not having to hold up to any expectations.

"He's dealing with some heavy stuff," Meagan added thoughtfully.

"Do you think his repressed memory can be retrieved?"

"What do you mean?" Meagan asked.

"When you hypnotized Becket?"

"I don't know," Meagan said slowly. "There wasn't much at stake there." She laughed. "Football game?" She rolled her eyes. "But, that was merely a suggestion, building his inner confidence. I wasn't pulling up memories."

Mia wondered if Meagan had done that just to be in with the popular crowd, gone to that party to hypnotize Becket. Maybe Meagan *did* care. From the beginning, Mia didn't see Meagan as a person who'd be concerned about her social status, and maybe that was exactly what she liked about her. But maybe it wasn't even true. Maybe Meagan did want to be popular. People were really hard to understand.

"According to Zac, winning that game was pretty important," Mia said. "Everyone was sure excited about how the game went." Mia told her about going out for pizza with Zac and his family.

"So, you're dating Zac now?" Meagan said flippantly, but then she laughed.

"I think since I'm living with his aunt, we're kind of like cousins."

"Well, don't marry him, then," Meagan said. "You'd have some freakish-looking kids."

"Mentally deficient," Mia said and they both giggled.

They'd arrived at the stop where they would part ways.

Meagan stood, started down the aisle, then turned back to Mia. "See if you can come over, spend the weekend. We can look at some of my dad's professional journals and books, see what we can come up with, maybe find something to help Zac remember what happened."

"I'd like that," Mia said, though she wasn't sure that trying to get Zac to remember something so horrific was a good idea, that maybe it might even be harmful. She wondered if Dana would approve of her spending the weekend away. Maybe she'd have to meet Meagan's dad before she'd allow a sleepover. Maybe she wouldn't allow it at all. Again, Mia thought about Meagan's mother. The girls had never talked about their mothers. Had Meagan's mother died, too?

"I'll check with Dana," Mia said. "I'd like to spend the weekend if it's okay with your dad."

"I'll talk to my dad." Meagan grinned. There was something almost conspiratorial in her smile. "I won't tell him what we are up to though."

CHAPTER NINETEEN

That evening at dinner, Mia asked Dana if she could spend the weekend at a friend's.

"For a sleepover?" Dana asked, surprised by the request. She was happy that Mia was making friends, but shouldn't Dana meet the parents first? "Is this Meagan or Marley?" Mia had shared the names of two friends, and Dana felt this in itself was a good sign.

"Meagan."

"The girl who transferred from Zac's school?" Maybe Pammie would know something about Meagan's family. Dana already had a perception of Meagan as someone who transferred because she was having trouble at public school.

"Yeah, Meagan. She's a nice girl. Her dad will be there."

Dana could hear in Mia's tone that she was making a sales pitch.

"Meagan asked her mom if it's okay?"

"She's checking with her dad to see if it's okay."

This would buy Dana some time to figure this out. "We'll see what her dad says." *We'll see. We'll see.* Now, Dana realized why her mother had used that phrase so often. It wasn't a no, but it wasn't a yes. She wondered if Meagan's parents were divorced. Did she live with her dad?

"Okay," Mia said. She was smiling. Dana could see Mia was counting on her saying *yes*.

Later that evening, as Dana was getting ready for bed, her phone rang. She'd called Pammie earlier and had left a message, so maybe she was returning the call. She sprinted from the bathroom, where she'd just squeezed some toothpaste on her toothbrush, and grabbed the phone off of her nightstand. She could see it wasn't Pammie, and though he wasn't listed in her contacts, she recognized the number.

"Hello."

"Hi, Dana. It's Drew." There was a pleasant, even rhythm to his voice. She'd always liked the sound of his voice. An awkward pause expanded between them.

"I'm considering coming back to Boston," he said.

"Yes, I heard you were looking at something here with the court."

"The timing wasn't right on that," he answered vaguely. "Not yet, but . . ."

So why did you call? The *but* hung clearly at the end of his sentence. *But what?*

"There's something I want to tell you."

"Yes? What is it?"

"At first, I wasn't sure if I should share this because, well . . ."

"If you are calling," Dana said, "you must believe that you have something I should know."

"I'm getting married," he said.

She paused, attempting to conjure some verbal response of gratitude for his calling to let her know. She wasn't sure if she would do the same for him. If she was getting married.

"Well, congratulations," she said. Her voice sounded sincere, surprising Dana herself. *Well, good for you, Drew*, she thought, thinking maybe she might even be happy for him.

"She lives here in Boston," he said.

"So, you *are* moving back?"

"We're exploring the possibilities. That's why I'm looking for something here."

"Do I know her?" Dana asked. Of, course it would have to be Amy.

143

"You remember Ray Beck?"

She laughed. "You're marrying Ray?"

He laughed too, but she could tell he didn't think she was funny.

"Sure, I remember Ray. He's with Beck, Cooper, and Bailey. They specialize in copyrights and intellectual property."

"Yes, that's the firm." Drew paused and then continued, "His daughter Amy—well, you met her at the airport—she joined the firm several years ago."

Dana guessed that Ray Beck was a few years older than Drew, early to mid-fifties. His daughter couldn't be much over thirty, if that. Dana had noticed she was younger than Drew, younger than Dana.

"We got engaged this summer," Drew said.

"Well, congratulations, then," Dana said again.

"Thank you," he said, and then, the words shot out, "Amy's pregnant." He took a breath so deep she could hear an intake over the phone.

She attempted to pull up the correct words, but nothing would come. Finally, she said, "Well, congratulations, again." Her heart dropped at the realization that Drew would get another chance at parenthood. "Ray's not standing over his future son-in-law with a shotgun?" she said lightly, even as she felt her grip on the phone tighten.

"I wanted you to know, Dana," he stuttered. "I didn't want you hearing this from someone else."

"I'm happy for you," Dana said with a deep swallow.

"Thank you." His voice was the oddest mixture of sadness and elation as if such a tone could exist. Dana knew this was why he had called—not to tell her he was getting married, but that he was going to be a father. Dana felt her face grow warm, even as she declared with an even, steady, cheerful voice, "I'm happy for you, Drew. I really am." She knew, in a way only someone with whom you'd shared such a devastating loss, that this was something she needed to know before it happened. She hoped she would do the same for him, but she knew she would never have this opportunity.

After her call, Dana stood stunned, and then she stomped about the room, then dropped to her bed and grabbed the throw pillows scattered about on top and threw them individually and violently against the closed bedroom door. She stopped abruptly, realizing she was not alone in the apartment. Could Mia hear the stomping, the pillows slamming the door with such force it rattled?

Dana left the room, walked through the hall into the kitchen and pulled a bottle of wine out of the cupboard. It was a Borelli Brunello. A wine sent last Christmas by Father Giovanni Borelli from his family vineyards in Italy. Mia's family's vineyards. Dana knew the single bottle was worth well over a hundred dollars. Mia's father had once sent her a bottle of wine valued at over a thousand dollars. A wine for a special occasion. She'd shared it at her mother's seventy-fifth birthday party.

She poured a glass, sipped slowly, then went to the window and stared out into the dark emptiness of the city. She raised it in a toast. "Congratulations, Drew and Amy!"

She poured another glass and drained this one much quicker. A special bottle of wine. A bottle of wine to celebrate a special occasion. Drew, the father of her child, was having another child. She poured more wine until it reached the top and took a long, slow swallow. An expensive Borelli Brunello down the tube as she attempted to ease the sharp, painful lump which had started in her heart and then had swiftly filled her entire being.

CHAPTER TWENTY

Dana awoke abruptly to a knock on her bedroom door, mind foggy and confused.

"I'm leaving for school," Mia said.

Dana glanced at her nightstand. In the dim room she could make out the outline of the bottle of Borelli Brunello. She reached over, lifted it carefully. Empty. She glanced toward the floor, then reached down and felt around until she found the empty wine glass. She hoped it had been empty when it fell to the floor. She vaguely remembered carrying the bottle, along with her glass, into her bedroom. She barely remembered thinking *I don't want Mia to find me passed out on the kitchen floor.*

"I've got a headache," she mumbled, sitting up, running her hand through her mussed hair, over her left temple. "Sorry I wasn't up to see you off this morning."

"I made a pot of coffee."

"Thank you," Dana said. "I'll see you this afternoon."

"I hope you feel better."

"I will. I'm sure I will." But she wasn't sure at all.

She folded the covers down, lifted her legs over the side of the bed, made contact with the floor, feeling around a bit with her foot, hoping she hadn't spilled any wine. Nothing damp. Nope. She'd drunk the entire bottle. She sat until she heard the door of the apartment open and close, until she was sure that Mia had left.

She lay back in her bed, the room still dim. Her head throbbed. She had never in her life felt like this. Worst hangover ever, shooting her theory that the more expensive the wine, the less likely to get a hangover. But, she had never finished off a bottle of wine by herself. She knew she should get up, that lying here wasn't a cure.

Finally, she rose, threw on her bathrobe and slippers, and trudged out into the kitchen. The coffee pot had a two-hour timer. She guessed with a quick glance that she had at least an hour to drink the coffee. She pulled her iPad off the kitchen counter and started to read the morning papers, skimming through several articles. More of the same. Mostly political stuff that made her feel even more depressed.

Then, telling herself not to do it, she clicked on a search engine and typed in Amy Beck, attorney Boston.

The webpage for Beck, Cooper, and Bailey popped up.

In the lawyer profiles, she found Amy Beck, who looked much better and even younger than she had at the airport. Much thinner, too. Of course, because now she was pregnant. Late twenties, early thirties at the most, Dana guessed. She wasn't beautiful, but she was attractive in a put-together, efficient, business-like, lawyerly way. The photo, Amy sitting in front of a library of law books, was obviously taken by a professional portrait photographer. *Who uses law books anymore?* Dana thought. Jeff had attempted to sell his because everything was online now. Didn't have a single inquiry, he'd told Dana.

She stared at the photo of Amy, and then she imagined Amy pregnant, hiring a nanny after the baby came, continuing to work. Then Dana imagined herself pregnant. She was 49. She felt a tightness in her chest.

She picked up her cellphone.

Pammie answered on the first ring as if she'd been hovering over her phone, waiting for Dana's call. "I was just about to give you a call," Pammie said.

"Drew is getting married," Dana said.

"Oh," Pammie replied, slowly, sympathetically, and then,

"How'd you find out?"

"He called."

"You okay?"

"I drank an entire bottle of wine, all by myself. Expensive wine." Dana paused before saying, "They're pregnant." She felt something rise up from her chest, into her throat, and then she exploded in tears, so many tears she could not speak.

"Oh, Dana," Pammie said. "I'm sorry."

Dana couldn't even reply through her sobs.

"Oh, sweetie," Pammie said.

Dana cleared her throat and said, "He didn't want me to hear this from someone else. In a way, I appreciate that he called."

"Do you want to get together, talk? We could meet for lunch."

"Okay," Dana said. "I'd like that."

"So, can you come over this weekend?" Meagan asked Mia as they sat on the bus.

"Something weird is going on with Dana. I heard her stomping around the apartment last night. Then she was throwing something against her bedroom door."

"Bad timing on the invite?"

"I'm not sure. She said she had a headache this morning, but I didn't see her. She was still in bed when I left."

"My mom used to get these headaches. Sometimes she couldn't even get out of bed for days."

Mia gulped, thoughts running through her head. This was the most that Meagan had ever said about her mom. "Did your mom die?" she asked.

Meagan looked at her like she'd just asked the stupidest question in the world. "No. Why would you say that?"

"It's just that . . ." Mia's voice was cracking.

"No, she's not dead." They'd arrived at their stop. "She just doesn't live with us anymore."

They got off the bus, walked toward the school, not speaking. Mia was trying to figure out what just happened. She thought maybe

Meagan was mad at her for talking about her mom. Maybe it was better to have a dead mom, not one who didn't live with you.

"My dad says it's okay," Meagan finally said. "He said he'd talk to your mom, I mean your aunt, or your, whatever she is. He said he'd talk to Dana to let her know it's okay."

"Okay," Mia said. "That's good. That's great."

Dana went to the coffee shop where she'd met Ryan Kelly and attempted to eat an egg sandwich, alternately sipping from her coffee, taking small bites. She wasn't sure why she'd come here. Maybe to see him. He'd said he came here sometimes, and maybe he'd just show up. She wasn't even sure why she wanted to see him. She felt awful. Likely she looked awful, too. Her stomach felt sloshy and bloated. Maybe it was all the coffee she'd thrown in there. Half a pot at home, another cup here. She wasn't sure about lunch with Pammie, but she wanted to talk to her about Drew and the baby, and also about Mia's friend Meagan. Dana was about to gather up her still-half-full cup, her half-eaten sandwich, when her phone rang. It was Ryan.

"I've tracked down Tripper. He pulled a knife on one of the preachers at the shelter. He's in jail."

"Must have been a really bad sermon." She pressed her fingers against her temple. Her head throbbed.

"Must have been." He laughed. "You alright?"

"What do you mean?"

"You don't sound so good."

"I've got a hangover." Now why was she telling him that? And how could he tell from the few words she'd said over the phone that she was feeling like shit? She liked his perception. She liked *him*.

"Out late partying?" he said in a tone that told her he didn't believe this for a minute. Was it so evident she wasn't the partying type?

She didn't want to tell him she'd consumed an entire bottle of wine by herself. Expensive wine that should never, ever be drunk alone. If she'd had a cheaper bottle in the house, she'd probably feel even worse. "Do I sound awful?"

"You don't sound great. Want to talk about it?"

She didn't know what to say. She was confused. Were they developing a friendship, or something more? "Actually, I do."

"Are you at home?"

"No."

"Where are you?"

"I'm at our coffee shop," she said, feeling stupid for calling it *our* coffee shop. "I've got half a sandwich sitting here on the table. I'll save it for you."

Within seven minutes, he was there, sitting opposite her at the table.

"You live nearby?" she asked. "Or, are you stalking me?"

"Neither," he said. "I was just close by."

She didn't know if she should believe him or not. "But, you know where I live."

"Firemen know where everyone lives." He glanced at her half-eaten sandwich. "If we don't, it's easy to find out. What happened? Tell me what's going on."

And then it all spilled out. Her story. Drew's story. His upcoming marriage. A new baby. Their child. Joel.

Ryan listened, the unfinished sandwich sitting on the plate between them. "I'm sorry," he said. "I remember reading about Joel. I couldn't imagine. I couldn't imagine then, and not now, how that would feel."

She was grateful for his words. After Joel disappeared, people offered sympathy, in any and every form imaginable. *I can imagine how you feel,* they would say. But, they couldn't. She wanted to shout, *No, you can't imagine. Don't tell me you can imagine.* Even those in the grief group she'd joined for a short time. No one could imagine how she felt.

"I've never been a drinker," Dana said. "Maybe that's why I feel so rotten." She pointed at her sandwich, encouraging him to finish it for her. "There's so much stuff going on in my life right now." She went on to tell him how Kip had quit his job, how their editor had told him to take some time off, how she was working with someone else now, but it just wasn't coming together, spilling it all out on the table for him to decide how much he wanted to take in. She even told him about some of the interviews she'd done for the eldercare project, how she found it depressing, how one of the women had told her she was the woman who had lost her child.

"I'm sorry," he said. "Doesn't sound like you are enjoying your work right now. . ." His voice trailed off as if he was considering adding more, but he didn't.

"This is good," she said, not even aware of why she had said it. But, sitting here with Ryan Kelly, even though she felt like shit, chasing down a story with Ryan Kelly, even if it turned out to be something awful. "I like the chase," she said, "chasing a story, and isn't this what we are doing?"

He smiled but didn't answer.

Dana swallowed the last of her now-cold coffee, realizing that Ryan didn't have anything to drink. That he'd come in, just sat down at her table.

"Can I get you more coffee?" he asked.

"Mia made coffee this morning. She drank some, but I had most of it. Thinking maybe it would cure the hangover. I'm not much of a drinker," she said again, at the same time thinking, *methinks she doth protest too much.* "You want some coffee?" she asked. She slowly slid her plate with half a sandwich toward him. "Please, I can't eat any more."

"I'm fine," he said. "Just ate breakfast."

They sat quietly, and then he did reach over as if for the sandwich, but instead he placed his hand over hers. "You feel up for a bit more investigating?" He smiled, his expression touched with kindness. She liked this man, and as they sat, neither speaking for many moments, she sensed an unspoken understanding and connection that she had not felt in a very long time.

"That's what I do," she said, "investigate." She didn't want to leave the coffee shop just yet. She liked sitting here with him. She liked his touching her. "I need to do something. Keep my mind busy. And, someone else might start putting two and two together, or one plus one plus one, three Catholic churches, and come up with a story before we do." She was blathering, she could hear it in her voice, her tone.

"If we are going to get you a story," he said, lifting his hand from hers, pushing his chair back, "we better get moving. Go by and talk to Tripper. I also want to swing by St. Barbara's. See if we can talk to some of the neighbors. You have time?"

"Yeah," she said. "I've got plenty of time." Yet, that wasn't exactly true. She had a lunch date with Pammie, and she wanted to be home when Mia returned from school, especially since she hadn't been up to having breakfast with her that morning. And there was the eldercare story she was supposedly writing with Brenda Falk.

She'd walked to the coffee shop, but she had no idea how Ryan had arrived so quickly after they spoke on the phone. "You don't live close by, and you're not stalking me," she said as they stepped out, "so, how did you get here so quickly?"

"Like I said, I was in the neighborhood." She looked at him with enough skepticism to raise her brow an inch or two.

He glanced at his watch and picked up his pace, and so did she. "My car's just down the street."

"We're nowhere close to the jail," she said. "Isn't that where you are going . . . so why are you parked—?"

"Here?" They'd arrived at his car, which she noted was parked in a two-hour space. He opened the passenger side door. When she gave him another questioning look but didn't move, he said, "My sister and her husband own a triple-decker here in the South End. They've rented the top two units to help pay off the mortgage. When the second-floor renter passed away, they decided to keep it available for the kids and grandkids when they visit. My mom just moved in with them a few months ago on the first floor. I stopped by to have breakfast with her."

"Oh," Dana said, realizing this story was too complicated, too detailed for him to have made it up. "So, you *were* in the neighborhood?"

"Yes, I was. Conveniently." He shot her a smile and motioned for her to get in the car, which she did. He drove a Honda Accord. Nothing fancy. Several years old. Just a practical car. Like Dana.

"So," she said, "Where do you live?"

"Marlborough," he answered without hesitation, "I have a condo in Marlborough."

"Not far from your office in Stow."

"It's convenient. Close to work. Easy access to the Mass Pike."

Again, what he said made perfect sense. And she was well aware of the personal information he'd just shared, details about his family, where he lived. Yet, a vague sensation lingered, a feeling that he was holding something back.

They pulled out onto the street, and after a while, Dana asked, "You still think the person in the background on the TV video was involved in setting the fires? The person that might be mistaken for an angel, or a ghost, or—"

"Let's see what Tripper has to say."

Within half an hour, they had signed in and were sitting in what appeared to be a visitors' room with Tripper, though Dana knew it wasn't officially visiting hours. A Fire Marshal was a *marshal*, a law enforcement officer, and evidently entitled to speak with an inmate. Tripper likely had a court-appointed attorney to defend him on his assault charges. She guessed Ryan had cleared this interview through the public defender. Their inquiries had nothing to do with the assault charges. Tripper himself didn't seem to have any qualms about talking to the Fire Marshal, though he kept eyeing Dana, who Ryan introduced simply as Dana.

"Tell me what you saw the night of the fire at St. Al's," Ryan started out.

"Well," Tripper said, "I'm not sure what I saw. I was half asleep, and at first I thought it was part of a dream. But then I was smelling it, the smoke, and I knew damned well it was a fire, and this other fella and I, well I'd never seen him before, and I ain't never seen him since, but we grabbed a couple of them blankets—using them rolled up like pillows, 'cause it wasn't cold at all that night—and we was trying to smother the fire out."

"Did you see anyone else? Did you see who started the fire?"

"I did. I did." The man smiled broadly. "Though I don't expect anyone to believe me."

"Can you describe the person?"

"Well, technically . . ." The man pronounced the word using several more syllables than necessary. Tech nic call ill lily. "I can't say for sure I saw anyone start the fire."

"The fire was burning when you woke?"

"Now, come to think of it, yes, but no, somebody was screaming *FIRE FIRE*, so I'm thinking that the screaming was what woke me. But then, yes, then I could smell it, and well, feel it too. Fire is pretty damn hot, but you know that? That's your profession? Right? Putting out fires? So, you been round lots of fires. You know how hot a fire is when it gets going. How fast it can burn things. And that's another thing. There was definitely something to burn. A bunch of papers or books or maybe prayer books or something. Like a big ol' bonfire of the varieties."

Ryan nodded, and Dana couldn't help but smile, unsure if Tripper was playing with the words—Bonfire of the Vanities—or if he really thought it was Bonfire of the Varieties. Bonfire of the Vanities? Savonarola? Getting rid of the printed word, the occasion for sin? Or maybe the Tom Wolfe variety?

"Was it the fellow that helped you put it out?" Ryan asked. "Was that the fellow you heard screaming?"

"Yes, that was the fellow." Tripper scratched a scab on his cheek, then continued. "I believe so. There just weren't that many in the church that night. Still warm outside, and that's where a lot of the fellows like to sleep when it's warm. Out under the stars, you know."

"You saw who started the fire, but you didn't actually see him *start* the fire." Ryan's inflection didn't imply a question or doubt, just a restatement of what Tripper had already told them.

Tripper nodded a yes. "Yes, I saw someone running. So, I figure if the fellow was running, not helping put out that fire, well, logic tells me that this is the fellow who started the fire. Do you see what I'm saying here?"

"I do." Ryan nodded. "Did you get a close look at him? The fellow who was running away?"

"Well, you know, had he been an ordinary man. Or woman," he said slowly as if this required a great deal of thought. Again, he scratched his cheek. The scab had started to bleed. Dana pulled a tissue out of her bag and handed it to the man. He blotted the blood, then continued. "But, this person was, well, dressed a little unusual."

"How's that?" Ryan asked.

"Like this person was wearing this, well for lack of a better word, I'd say it was a nightgown."

Ryan's eyes widened and he and Dana exchanged quick glances. "A nightgown?"

"Not sure, kinda soft like, and flowy. Maybe white."

"What else do you remember?"

"And his hair, well, truthfully, I'm not sure it was a man. Maybe a woman. Longish hair." Tripper tugged at his own hair, which was fairly long, though thinning, with patches of pinkish scalp showing through. Dana could see him tighten, then loosen, his grip on the tissue. His hand was shaky, nervous.

"What color? The person's hair?"

"Well, it was dark inside the church," he replied. "No, no, the fire was lightening things up. And that's how we saw this person. Well, like an angel or something. Everything kind of flowy like." The man fluttered his fingers and then got a confused look on his face. He dabbed again at his cheek. "I don't expect anybody to believe it. Sounds kind of like some drug-induced hallucination. Doesn't it? Here we are in church and there's this angel flying about. Like a vision."

Ryan pulled his phone out of his pocket. His fingers moved quickly. He leaned into Tripper. "Do you see anything that looks familiar?"

Dana couldn't see the screen on the phone, but she could hear the audio and recognized the reporter's voice and the words from the night of the fire at St. Barbara's. The same video that Ryan had played for Mic at St. Lawrence's just two days before.

"Let me see that again," Tripper said.

Ryan played the video again.

"Can't say I'm seeing anything familiar," Tripper said, squinting. "I read about that fire at that big church. St. Barbara's, wasn't it? Two church fires lately." He grinned at his observation as if he were the first to realize this.

"What about this person?" Ryan pointed, though Dana could see a glaze of disappointment come over him. Tripper hadn't noticed the person in the white nightgown visible beneath the sweatshirt, and if he did now, even Dana would have to admit he'd been coached.

"Well, I'll be, that does look familiar. Don't think it's the same person, but well, he, or maybe she, just might be part of the same group. This person, a lot skinnier, maybe taller than the person we saw at St. Al's. What do you call a group of angels?" Tripper grinned at Ryan, then Dana, as if this was a riddle with a clever answer. "Maybe a flock?" He laughed.

"But, you don't think this is the same person?" Ryan asked.

"Can't say for sure," Tripper replied. "Some similarities for sure, but just can't say I could honestly testify in a court of law."

As they left the building, Ryan was quiet, then glanced at Dana and said, "What are we dealing with here? A flock of angels as Tripper called them?"

"Your forensic team is finding similarities, but also differences in the ways the fires were set? More than one person involved?"

"The descriptions given by witnesses are possibly of different people, but dressed the same, same long hair. Maybe a group? A flock of angels?"

"I believe a group of angels is referred to as a *host* of angels," Dana said, shooting Ryan a half-hearted smile. "And yes, it sounds like a host of angels."

He returned her smile.

"Maybe some confusion," Dana said, "as those waking to a fire might find themselves disoriented, in a chaotic, agitated state of mind. A person attempting to put out a fire might not have gotten a good look at the person fleeing the scene?"

"But all with similar physical descriptions . . . the dress, the hair. The ambiguous gender identities. Like you suggested," Ryan said, "angels are androgynous." They had arrived at his car. He clicked his key to unlock the door and opened the passenger side door for Dana. She slid in.

"A host of angels?" Ryan said as he got in the driver's side. "So what do you call a group of ghosts? Or demons?"

Dana rubbed her left temple, realizing her head still ached, though the distraction of the interview had made her not so completely consumed with her pain. Or maybe it was Ryan Kelly, the reason she was feeling better. She liked spending time with him. Though this was a weird way to spend time with anyone, especially since there was nothing official about their working together. She dug into her purse and pulled out a couple of ibuprofens. Ryan reached to the back seat, grabbed a bottle of water and handed it to her.

"Thank you," she said. She unscrewed the cap, took a good swallow and downed two pills, then pulled her phone from her bag, clicking on her search engine.

"You up for a trip over to St. Barbara's?" he asked, and she nodded a yes.

"A congress of ghosts," she said, glancing up from her phone. "A legion of demons."

CHAPTER TWENTY-ONE

The blackened stone, remnants of St. Barbara's, loomed above them. Though a yellow tape restricted access to the building, there was no one there to tell them to stay out, and Dana knew, as the State Fire Marshal, Ryan was officially authorized to enter. Likely, it was a team several rungs lower on the firefighters' ladder that had taped the perimeter. They climbed the front steps and entered through the arch where doors had once opened to greet worshippers.

Dana stood staring at the seared stone walls, the embers of the wooden pews. The place reeked of fire and soot and destruction. Ryan walked down what would have been the aisle to the main altar. The massive marble altar stood on a platform, two steps up, fenced off by the ashes of a wooden communion rail. Ryan hunched down on the stone floor and pointed to the dark, irregular circle before the altar where the fire must have started.

Ritualistic, Dana thought, a word Ryan had used.

He nodded as if he had heard her, and then he rose.

"Kip described it as *just* a shell," she said, gazing up, then around the interior of the church, which felt vast and open and vulnerable. A metal rack that had once held votive candles stood before a charred statue, the features scorched off the face.

"Anything inside that was capable of burning pretty much did," Ryan said. "A shell, that's a fairly good description."

A shell of a church, Dana considered, maybe an accurate description of the Archdiocese of Boston for the past fifteen years.

"Have you heard any more from Kip?" Ryan asked.

"Nothing more."

"You're good friends?"

"Working partners for years. I miss him."

Ryan shot her a questioning look.

"Friends. We've been good friends for years."

Ryan nodded, but asked no further questions. He started back toward the altar, gazed around, then motioned, and they walked back down the aisle and out onto the street.

It was a much nicer neighborhood than the one where St. Al's was located, a middle-class residential neighborhood with tiny well-kept patches of grass. These were the neighbors, Dana thought, who had fought so hard, who had petitioned to keep their church open. The building had been sold, was no longer the property of the Catholic Church. She thought of the video that she and Ryan had watched half a dozen times now and envisioned the neighbors out in the night, awakened by the wail of sirens, jackets and coats thrown over nightclothes, looking on with a mixture of sadness, fear, and disbelief.

They strolled down the sidewalk across from the burnt edifice and stopped about mid-way down the block in front of a house. A trio of gnomes, a fairy, a mushroom, sat huddled in the tiny flower bed amidst an array of late summer blooms. She followed Ryan up the walk and then up the steps. He rang the doorbell. An elderly man answered.

"Yes," he said, squinting.

Ryan pulled out his ID. "We're in the neighborhood, trying to determine if anyone saw anything the night of the fire at St. Barbara's."

"Fire Marshal?" he questioned, and Ryan nodded as a woman appeared behind the man.

"They're asking about the fire in the church," the man said.

"Punishment for selling the church," the woman said.

159

"Now, now, Ruthie," the man said, "you know that's not how God works."

"That's a Catholic church. Been there all my life," the woman replied, anger in her voice.

The man continued, affably, as if he hadn't heard his wife. "Quite the deal, wasn't it? Just lucky that fire didn't jump over and take out some of these houses." His eyes swept across the neighborhood.

"Did you notice anything unusual in the neighborhood? Maybe the day of the fire or after?"

"We weren't at home the night it happened," the woman said. "Visiting our daughter in upstate New York. But the neighbors said you could feel the heat all the way up the street." She waved off to her right. "And the smell—" Her nose wrinkled as if the smell still lingered.

"You should go talk to Frank or Em Carrington," the man said, eyes darting in the direction the wife had motioned. "They witnessed it all."

"I saw Em take off about an hour ago," the wife said, "probably went down to the market. But, Frank . . . he's home, never goes anywhere. Up half the night, too. Never sleeps. Check with Frank."

"If he can recall what he saw," the man added with a chuckle.

"Thank you," Ryan said, "We'll check with the neighbors."

As they started back down the steps, Dana knew they were on the right track. Best source of information was often the elderly, the ones that were home all day, bored, with little to do. If they didn't sleep at night, that was even better.

Just as the wife said, Frank was home and more than willing to talk.

He told them he was the one who called in the fire, though the flames were spreading so quickly, so powerfully, that by the time the fire engines arrived, it was too late.

"What alerted you to the fire?" Ryan asked.

"Those sirens were mighty loud."

Dana could see the man was confused. If he'd called it in, it couldn't have been the sirens that alerted him. Dana also realized that Ryan would have access to records and knew how it had been called in and the source of the call.

"Did you see anything unusual? Hear anything before the fire started?"

The man scratched his head. "No, it was late. I don't sleep so well. Maybe it was the smell. I think the smell. Maybe the flames shooting out of the windows. Did you know that glass shattering can be really loud? My wife's the one probably can answer your questions," he said, seemingly confused.

"Can I help you?" A woman pushed a small metal shopping cart along the narrow sidewalk, then up to the house.

"They're asking about the fire," Frank called down to her. The woman stood below the steps, the small patch of concrete porch too small for more than two people. Frank remained in the open doorway.

Ryan stepped down and showed the woman his ID, then lifted the two cloth shopping bags from the cart.

The woman said, "Some kind of inspector was here day after the fire."

"Part of the investigative team," Ryan said.

"You're the boss? Chief investigator?"

"State Fire Marshal," he replied.

"So sad about the fire," the woman said, folding the shopping cart. "We heard the church was sold, and we were happy it would finally be used again. It's been sitting idle for almost a dozen years. A building like that should be used. Simply a beautiful building. The stained glass alone . . ." Her voice faded with sadness. "It should never have been shut down. You think it was arson, don't you?" Dana had stepped down to allow Em to come up on the porch, Ryan pulling the cart, still holding both bags.

"We're attempting to determine what might have started the fire," Ryan said. "If someone in the neighborhood saw something, it would be helpful."

"You probably already know *what* started the fire," the woman

161

said with a sly grin. "Frankie, take the groceries in, put them on the kitchen counter." Ryan handed the old man the bags, leaned the cart up against the porch rail.

Em made a slight motion with her hand, and her husband stepped back inside. "You are attempting to find out *who* started the fire," she said.

"Did you see anything unusual in the neighborhood the day of the fire, maybe in the days before it happened?" Ryan paused for an answer, but when she didn't reply, he asked, "Anyone who didn't seem to fit in, not one of the neighbors?"

"No, can't say that I did."

"I did," Frank said, and all three turned to see he was back in the doorway.

"What did you see, Frankie?" the woman asked, shooting a doubtful glance at Ryan and then Dana as if to say, *you can't believe him.*

"Oh, darn, what were you asking?" the old man said.

"When we heard the sirens," the woman said, "we threw on our robes and slippers and went out."

"But we couldn't get anywhere near," Frank said. "They were blocking the street with the firetruck, not letting anyone close. They were using a crane to get up to the top, but didn't do much good as far as the stuff inside."

"Then the TV crew showed up," Em said. "Well, that took a while. We saw it on TV the next day."

"We were on TV." A big grin spread over Frank's face. "Our son called and said he saw us on TV."

Ryan pulled out his phone, tapped, scrolled down, and then angled the phone for both Frank and Em to view. Dana could hear the audio. She knew it was the TV video.

"Hey, there we are!" Frank exclaimed.

The couple seemed to be able to identify most everyone in the video. From the slow and silent scrolling, Dana guessed Ryan had copied various frames to get still shots of the scene.

"How about this person?" Ryan asked, pointing.

Frank squinted. "Don't recall seeing that person. Can't even see the face in that picture."

"Not a neighbor?"

"I remember," Em said slowly. "Now that I think of it, that *was* unusual."

"How's that?"

"Most of the neighbors are older folks. Been here awhile. Well, the Andersons sold their house after John died. Deb went to live with her daughter, and I thought maybe that was the new neighbor. I knew it had to be a neighbor because some random person doesn't pass by on the street coincidentally, wearing a nightie, now do they?"

"Someone you'd not seen before?" Dana asked. She'd been holding back, letting Ryan do all the questioning. He was the expert, and she was just along for the ride. But, it seemed like they were finally getting to something that might be helpful. Em appeared to be pretty sharp, aware of her surroundings.

"Kind of the hippie type," she said, "long hair. More like a woman's nightgown, or maybe what a man might wear in the olden days. Like in the Christmas Carol, you know, like Ebenezer Scrooge. Only this fellow was young, not old. Long hair. Pretty fellow, almost pretty like a girl. Long blondish hair. Maybe a gay person," she said, sounding apologetic, or maybe just trying to be politically correct.

"Did you speak to him?" Dana asked, glancing at Ryan, who nodded as if to say, *we're a team now.* He was scrolling through pictures on his phone, eyes squinting, mouth set at a serious angle.

"No, I didn't," Em answered. "He was standing off by himself, and I was talking to Betsy Carmichael." Em pointed toward another almost identical house. A solemn-looking Buddha sat on the porch. "She and Mike were out in front, and we were talking to them, and I guess the man in the white nightgown had gone back into whatever house he came from because when I turned, thinking I'd go welcome him to the neighborhood, why he'd disappeared."

"You'd never seen this person before?" Dana asked. "In the

neighborhood? Maybe at the market? Shopping somewhere close by?"

"No, never did. But being young, probably works during the day. I'd guess in some techie or creative-type job where his long hair was perfectly okay. Frank and I don't get out much." She glanced at her husband affectionately.

"Do you recognize anyone in this picture?" Ryan asked, again angling the phone. Dana, standing below the others, caught only the glare.

Em paused, considering. "Not a very good picture." She tapped Ryan's phone, and Dana could see from the movement of her fingers that she was enlarging the photo.

"Could this be the same person?" Ryan asked.

Em studied the picture. Dana stepped up, adjusted her stance, leaning in, but she could not see the photo.

Em said, "I don't know. Could be. Longish hair like that and a real pretty face. A sweet face. Almost angelic." Dana glanced at Ryan, and for a brief moment, she thought she caught a glisten in his eye. A tear? Then a quick blink. He ran his finger beneath his left eye, wiping any sign of emotion away.

Ryan thanked them, asked that they call if they remembered anything that might help with the investigation, and he and Dana walked back down the sidewalk, not speaking until they approached his car parked in front of St. Barbara's.

"I've got a meeting this afternoon," he said. "I'll drop you off. If we don't get moving, I won't make it."

"I can catch an Uber," Dana said. "I'm meeting my sister-in-law for lunch,"

"Maybe that's a good idea."

"Are you going to tell me what's going on?" Dana asked.

"I probably owe it to you," he said.

"Okay," she said as she stopped and stood waiting.

"I'll call you later," he said, "I *do* have a meeting." It was clear he was attempting to convince her he was telling the truth, not just evading her question. She sensed, ever since they'd gone to St.

Lawrence's, there was something personal in this for Ryan Kelly, and she was sure of that now. And he knew she knew.

"Em said he looked almost angelic," Dana said. Ryan glanced away, and then his gaze flickered back to meet Dana's.

"Yes, he did."

CHAPTER TWENTY-TWO

Dana met her sister-in-law at their favorite daytime restaurant, where they always ordered the soup and salad specials of the day. When Pammie asked how she'd spent her morning, Dana was vague, saying she was doing some research. She wasn't ready to share anything about the recent fires or her joint investigation with Ryan Kelly. Pammie was a bit of a gossip—and that was something she both loved and loathed about her brother's wife.

They talked about Drew and Amy and the new baby, Pammie thoughtfully listening. Dana knew she needed to push this aside for now. She had no control over any of this. She thought of the reason she'd called Pammie, why she wanted to speak to her even before Drew's announcement.

"Mia wants to spend the weekend with a friend from school," Dana told her sister-in-law.

"That's good," Pammie said. "Right? She's making friends."

"Shouldn't I meet the parents? I can't let her take off with people I don't know. Can I?"

"You're probably safe with someone from St. Gertrude's."

Dana realized that anyone with enough money to send a kid to St. Gertrude's was probably a concerned, responsible parent, but maybe that was just a reverse form of prejudice. Being rich had nothing to do with being a good parent.

"Mia said she transferred from Zac's school. I thought you

might know something about her parents."

The server delivered their lunch specials—french onion soup with chicken salad for Pammie, the tomato bisque with shrimp salad for Dana.

"The girl's name is Meagan," Dana said. "She went to Zac's school last year."

"Do you know her last name?"

"I don't," Dana said, feeling she wasn't playing this role of surrogate parent very well, realizing Mia hadn't mentioned Meagan's last name, and Dana hadn't inquired.

"I'll check with Zac," Pammie said. "Can you tell me more about Meagan? That's a fairly common name." Pammie was attempting to scoop up the Gruyere in her soup, the rubbery threads stretching like pizza cheese. She took a large bite, a piece clinging to her lips.

"She's in Mia's Art History class. Mia seems to especially like that class. She has shared that with me—her friends are into art or at least art history."

"So, the artsy, creative type, you're thinking?"

"Yes," Dana said, hesitating. "I'll ask Mia what her last name is, maybe more about her parents. Oh, something else. Mia said that Meagan was checking with her dad to see if a sleepover would work. It sounds like she lives with her dad, or maybe spends weekends with him, so I guess maybe her parents are divorced."

"That's probably half the kids from Zac's school." Pammie gathered a long, stringy slurp of cheese in her fingers. "I'll ask him this evening and get back to you."

"Thanks, Pammie. I'll see what I can find out, too, about Meagan."

Later that afternoon, Pammie called.

"Zac said her name is Meagan MacCormack. When I described her, Zac knew just who you were talking about. He said he didn't know her that well, but she was in a bunch of AP classes, and she's kind of weird. Dyed her hair blue, has a piercing through her nose. He said she was at the party last Monday night."

"Smart girl, troubled child?" Dana asked, wondering if Mia having such a friend might be something to be concerned about. "Bad influence?"

"Oh, I don't know if that's necessarily true. Lots of kids are coloring their hair. Piercing and tattooing aren't that uncommon. It doesn't necessarily mean they are bad kids."

"I don't think they let them do that at St. Gertrude's."

"If the hair's colored, they can always change it back to an acceptable color, take the rings out of the piercings."

"What about the tattoos?"

"No, I didn't say she had a tattoo. Zac didn't say she had a tattoo. I was using that as an example. Lots of kids do that sort of thing without being bad. Just a means of self-expression."

"Don't kids have to have a parent's permission at that age?"

"Oh," Pammie replied, laughing lightly, "there's always ways around that."

God, I hope Mia doesn't do something like that! Dana cringed as she imagined sending her back to her dad with a tattoo.

"Her parents are both psychiatrists," Pammie said, voice lower now. "Zac didn't tell me this, but I checked around, and here's the story . . . her mom was doing some counseling in prison, and I guess she left the dad for someone she met—"

"A prison administrator?" Dana asked.

"A prisoner. I heard she's working to get his sentence overturned. Some kind of innocence project."

"Oh, geez," Dana said, feeling a tightening in her jaw. "Why is he in prison?"

"Murder."

Dana swallowed. "Did he? I mean, murder someone?"

"Meagan's mom seems to believe not."

"Oh, poor girl," Dana said slowly. "Do you think I should tell Mia she can't spend the weekend?"

"Well, she lives with her dad and, as far as I know, he didn't murder anyone."

"Yeah, I guess I shouldn't hold this against the dad or poor

Meagan."

"Yeah," Pammie agreed. "So, you okay?"

Dana knew what Pammie was asking. "I know I have to accept this thing with Drew, Amy. The baby."

"Yeah," Pammie said. "Life isn't always the way we'd planned it would be."

That evening at dinner, Mia told Dana that Meagan had checked with her dad, and it was okay if she spent the weekend.

"Tell me more about your friend, her family."

Mia sat quietly for a moment as if gathering her words. Her serious expression told Dana that Mia knew she was concerned.

"She lives with her dad, and he's a doctor, a Ph.D. You can Google him. He's perfectly legit and reliable. He'll be there all weekend. We won't be alone. We have a project we're working on, or maybe we'll watch some movies. I promise you I won't get into any trouble. Meagan is a perfectly nice, reliable person. I like her, and I'd like to spend more time with her away from school." Mia pulled out her phone and clicked on her contact list. "This is his number. Meagan said he would call and talk to you tonight to reassure you that everything is okay." She tapped the phone. "I just sent you the number." She tapped again. "Meagan's number, too."

Dana was impressed by the case that Mia had just presented. She'd said nothing about Meagan's mother, and Dana shouldn't hold that against the girl or her father anyway. "I'll talk to Meagan's dad, and we'll go from there."

That evening she got a call from Dr. Milo MacCormack. He told Dana they'd love to have Mia spend the weekend. They planned on hanging out at home, so it would be no problem. The girls could ride the bus home on Friday, then he could bring Mia home on Sunday evening, or she could ride the bus to school Monday morning.

"I could pick her up Sunday afternoon if that's okay," Dana said, realizing that she'd just given her permission. From the address he gave her in Newton, she knew exactly where Meagan and her dad lived. It was close to Jeff and Pammie, which made sense since she'd gone to Zac's school.

"That sounds great," Milo MacCormack said. "Meagan is looking forward to having Mia spend the weekend. The girls seem to have hit it off."

Well, there, Dana said to herself after she'd hung up, *everything is going to be okay.*

She knocked on Mia's bedroom door. When she opened it with a cautious but hopeful smile, Dana said, "I talked to Meagan's dad, and you're set for the weekend. Pack a bag to take with you on Friday. I'll pick you up Sunday afternoon."

"Oh, thank you, Dana." Mia gave her a big hug, and Dana thought, *this is how it feels, coming through for your kid.*

In bed that night, she thought about what Drew had told her about his marriage, the baby. Drew could move on, but his options for moving on were much different than those available to Dana herself. She thought about how happy Mia had been simply with Dana's giving her approval to spend the night at Meagan's. How difficult it was to have a girl, a young woman, come to her without going through those years of growth and discovery. Drew would have this now. Dana would not. She wanted to put a name, a word to her feelings. It wasn't jealousy. It was so much more than that. An emotion that had no name.

She thought of her own son, *their* son. Joel would be sixteen. A teenager. She often imagined what he might look like now. Every couple of years, Christopher Prinz would send her an age-enhanced drawing of Joel, and she always wondered how true it was to how he might look as he grew. Would Drew and Amy's child look like Joel?

Struggling to sleep, her thoughts turned again to Ryan Kelly. She knew something was going on that he wasn't sharing with her. She'd found it odd that the Fire Marshal was taking a personal interest in these particular fires. Maybe that in itself wasn't odd. But shouldn't he be enlisting one of the members of his investigative team to accompany him on his interviews?

He said he'd be in touch, but he hadn't called. Dana was curious about the photo on his phone that he'd shown to Em, the one he had not shown Dana. He was sharing some aspects of the investigation, but other pieces of the puzzle—if that's what it was—he was withholding. Was he using Dana? For what purpose? She remembered something he said as they were leaving the neighborhood around St. Barbara's. When Dana mentioned that Em said the man looked almost angelic, Ryan replied, "Yes, he did." Almost as if Ryan himself had seen the man.

Over the next several days, Mia talked more about her school and her friends, particularly Meagan and Marley. She told Dana that the three of them were working on an outreach program, an art project with children at a local Head Start.

Dana realized how much she had cut herself off from her own friends, particularly the couples she and Drew had once shared. She wondered if Drew and Amy would hang out with those couples if they decided to make their home in Boston. Dana doubted any of those long-lost friends were still raising children from infants. Maybe Drew would have to make new friends. Young Amy's friends.

Dana did not hear from Ryan Kelly. She thought about calling but decided against it. He said he would contact her. Had she turned him off with her rambling, going on about her personal trauma? Yet he'd seemed so sweet, so kind, and she'd felt a connection as they sat at the coffee shop. Then, he'd taken her to talk with Tripper at the county jail, then over to St. Barbara's. Yet, he hadn't called.

She went out for several interviews with the families of elderly people who'd passed away in nursing homes. There were signs of neglect, but not abuse on a criminal level. She could find no original angle, no way to approach a story that was anything more than what had already been written. Each interview reminded her that her mother, though very healthy, was aging, and maybe she, Jeff, and Ben should talk more about this now. She also realized that when she herself grew old, there would be no one to look after her.

On Friday morning, Mia was excited about the weekend. She

eagerly placed her packed overnight bag at the front door next to her backpack for school, then quickly ate breakfast.

"What are you doing this weekend?" she asked Dana as she loaded her plate and coffee cup in the dishwasher.

"I've got a couple of stories I'm working on." Mia turned and nodded, and Dana guessed she was asking just to be polite.

She gave Dana a big hug when she left for school. "See you Sunday afternoon."

"Call me if you need anything," Dana replied.

Mia shot her a grin. "I'm sure we'll be fine. Don't worry. Have a good weekend."

Dana spent the morning at her office, working with Brenda, arranging the information they'd gathered during their eldercare interviews, combining it with what Kip had discovered. Dana sensed that if they wanted to dig deeper, there might be possible Medicare fraud, but that story had been written a thousand times. Neglect in the nursing homes? Brenda said she'd seen a lot of carelessness, attendants who were insufficiently trained. Dana pointed out how poorly they were paid.

"Maybe that's the story," Dana said, and Brenda offered her a vague nod. Could she tell that Dana's mind was a million miles away? She was thinking about Ryan, the fires. She wondered how Kip was doing. She'd called again and got the same message. He was holed up in a cabin in Idaho.

She returned home early, started a load of laundry, considered whether she should ask Mia to do her own. Yet, she wasn't throwing things on the floor or leaving damp towels in the bathroom, and she always used the hamper. Dana would rather do a full load than have Mia do a small one on her own.

She sat and reviewed articles and her own notes and lists of Catholic churches that had been closed in the archdiocese over the past 15 years. Many had changed hands. One was now a craft mall where local artists could rent spaces to sell their arts and crafts. Another had been remodeled for affordable housing. Some were still being used as houses of worship for other denominations, and others had been razed, the land used for various commercial enterprises.

She tried homing in on those that were presently vacant, either on the market or simply no longer being used. After some time, moving papers from one pile to another, she narrowed it down to 20 that fit that description, though she realized her list was probably out of date. She also attempted to determine if there were properties still owned by the Church, where parts of the buildings, like the chapel at St. Lawrence's, were no longer used for worship services. Sections of the church where there would be no parishioners gathering. This was much more difficult to determine. Almost impossible.

Just as she was getting up for a glass of water, her phone rang.

It was Ryan Kelly.

"Could we get together some time this weekend?" he asked.

She hesitated for a moment, then said, "Mia is staying with a friend, so yes, I guess that would work." She thought of their brief conversation after visiting the neighbors near St. Barbara's. She'd asked Ryan if he was going to tell her what was going on, and he'd answered that he probably owed it to her. Yet, it had been three days now.

"When did you want to get together?" she asked.

"Have you eaten dinner?"

She glanced at her watch. It was almost six. "I haven't."

"I know a great place that's close if you don't mind walking. I'll come by at seven?"

"You know where I live?" Of course he did.

"I do," he replied.

CHAPTER TWENTY-THREE

"Your dad's okay with you dyeing your hair a different color every other week?" Mia asked Meagan. Mia, wearing plastic gloves to prevent the dye from staining her hands, was sectioning and applying the hair color they had picked up at the drugstore that afternoon.

They were at Meagan's, in her private, personal bathroom attached to her bedroom in the house she shared with her dad. They lived in a house, not an apartment like Dana. It was fairly large with a kitchen and family room combination on the main floor, as well as a more formal room, an office, and a bathroom. The bedrooms were upstairs: a guest room, Meagan's bedroom, and her dad's bedroom. Meagan's room was decorated in teal and pewter, not exactly what Mia had expected. It looked like her dad had hired a professional decorator.

Meagan's house was big, but nothing like Mia's house in Italy, a villa, part of it old, some new, much of it decorated with valuable antiques. Mia's dad's office was attached to the house with a hall leading to the visitors' center for the winery. There was a chapel on the first floor. She usually didn't describe her home to people who had no chance of ever visiting. *I live in a villa in Italy* might come across as pretentious.

On the way home from school, they'd stopped at the drugstore, and Meagan had told Mia to pick out an at-home-hair-color kit with the most boring, non-descript brown so she could return to her "natural color." Mia wasn't sure if Meagan had been reprimanded at school, if she'd been told her current hair color was not acceptable, or if she'd decided this change on her own.

"I'm not sure my dad will even notice the change of hair color." Meagan laughed.

Mia had met Meagan's dad shortly after they arrived. He was tall, thin, and balding. He wore frameless glasses, and though he was pleasant enough, he was soft-spoken, and Mia was surprised. She thought a girl like Meagan would have an outspoken, with-it parent. It struck Mia that Meagan's dad might be a bit like her own father—distant at times, overly involved in his work.

"Did Sister Mary Ellen tell you to color your hair back to its natural color?" Mia asked, "Or Mrs. V?" Mrs. Valentine was the vice-principal of their school, a former nun who was now married but still dressed and acted like a nun.

"Nope, and my dad is pretty good about letting me make my own decisions." Meagan adjusted the towel she'd draped around her neck, making eye contact with Mia's reflection in the mirror. "At least in my appearance," she added as if this needed further clarification. Mia didn't think this whole St. Gertrude's thing had been Meagan's choice. "He probably thinks I'll take off like my mom if I don't get my way."

"Is that why your mom left?" Mia asked cautiously.

"What do you mean?" Meagan asked.

"Because your dad didn't let her have her way?" Mia sectioned another strand of hair and brushed on the dye, praying Meagan's hair wouldn't all fall out. She didn't think this was healthy, changing color again so soon.

Meagan said, "No, that wasn't it."

"Why did she leave?" Mia asked, the words coming slowly and carefully. The intimacy of this procedure seemed to have opened Meagan up to talking more about personal things than she had before.

"I think maybe she was bored," Meagan said, and Mia guessed

that Meagan took after her mom, not her dad. Did her dad think Meagan would go live with her mom? And then Mia wondered why she didn't live with her mom.

"My mother's brilliant," Meagan said. "She told me I could come live with her."

"Why did you stay with your dad?"

"He needs me more than my mom," Meagan said without feeling, and then after a lengthy pause, she asked, "How about your mom?" Her voice had softened.

"She died when I was eleven."

"What happened?" Meagan asked sincerely.

"Breast cancer," Mia replied, and then, "My mom was brilliant, too, as involved in the business as my dad."

"You miss her a lot?" Meagan asked.

"I do," Mia said.

"Me, too," said Meagan. They were quiet for some time, and then Meagan grabbed the dye box perched on the vanity and scanned the instructions. "We have to leave this on for half an hour. Why don't we go take a look at some of those books."

Meagan stood and stepped into the bedroom as Mia followed. They sat side by side on the bed, leafing through magazines and books that Meagan had pulled off her dad's bookshelf in his office. They included several articles on suppressed memory, one on traumatic childhood experiences, though that one looked like it was mostly about sexual abuse, which made Mia shiver. If Dana's son, Zac's cousin Joel, was still alive, Mia wondered if he'd been abused. Isn't that why people took little kids? But then, they usually killed them after that. She glanced at Meagan, whose hand and eyes were running rapidly down the page of one of the books. She kept dabbing the side of her face with the towel around her neck, though it looked like Mia had done a good job of not dying any of her skin. Her damp hair looked dark, giving Meagan a much more normal look than the bleached blonde she'd been sporting for the past week or the blue-tipped hair. Mia hoped it wouldn't take away her friend's edge.

Meagan said, "Your idea about hypnotizing the memories right out of Zac . . . don't think it's a good idea." She shook her head, then lifted a strand of hair, taking a side glance at the color with no visible reaction. "From what I've read, and I'm reading now, retrieving memories is tricky. In the hands of an amateur—the amateur being *moi*." She held a hand to her chest. "Could be dangerous." She picked up another book and handed it to Mia. "Read this."

Mia read aloud:

"Hypnosis is an altered state of consciousness. Used in memory recovery therapy, it can be a dangerous tool, as the altered state of the mind is highly susceptible to suggestion."

Mia glanced at Meagan. "That's why it worked on Becket. You know they won their first game. I was there."

"The offense is great," Meagan replied. "The defense sucks."

Meagan had told Mia she wasn't interested in her old school's activities, but she'd obviously been following the football team. Zac had texted Mia a few times since his game, but they hadn't been keeping up that much. Mia thought they were still friends, but nothing more. Maybe they *were* kind of like cousins.

Meagan handed Mia a magazine with a dog-eared page, and she scanned the first few paragraphs. *Memory is not like a video that can be replayed at will in one's mind.* She flipped to a section about repressed memory, trying to find anything on retrieving memories that didn't involve memories of abuse.

The timer on Meagan's cellphone went off. "Time to rinse," she said, standing. She gathered several large art history books from her shelf and arranged them on the desk chair she'd moved into the bathroom. She perched on the seat to elevate herself so she could lean backward over the sink while Mia rinsed the color, much of it swirling down the drain. Mia hoped they'd left it on long enough, but not too long. The odd angle made Meagan look strange, almost vulnerable. Mia could see the hairs in her nose. Her nostrils were asymmetrical, the piercing now barely visible. Meagan closed her eyes, seemingly relaxed as Mia placed her hand under Meagan's head, using a cup to pour water over her hair.

When they'd finished, Meagan reached for the towel on the rack, flipped her hair, and started drying it. After a while, she pulled a hairdryer out of the drawer. It was too noisy to continue their conversation, so Mia stood and watched. After a while, Meagan pulled a brush as big as a grizzly bear paw from the drawer and motioned for Mia to follow her back to the bedroom. As they skimmed through more books, Meagan ran the brush through her hair, hairdryer in one hand, book in front of her on the bed, held open with her knee.

"Things like tastes and smells can bring back memories." Meagan looked up from her book with interest.

Mia remembered that Zac had said the smell of his grandma's house sometimes brought back memories, but he hadn't told her what the memories were.

A knock on the door, and Meagan's dad called out, "Dinner's on."

"We'll be right there," Meagan called back. She gathered the pile of her father's books and slid them under the bed.

Ryan and Dana walked together from her apartment to a casual place that specialized in pizza and Italian food. It was a beautiful evening with just a hint of fall in the air. As soon as they opened the door, the aroma of garlic and everything Italian, including a smiling hostess, drew them in with a we're-glad-you're-here welcome.

Even though the place was only seven blocks from where she lived, Dana had never been there. Ryan suggested a couple of items from the menu, so she knew he had. She wondered if he'd come here with a date. It was that type of place, small and intimate. An odd visual of Lady and the Tramp popped into her mind, two dogs sharing spaghetti, slurping noodles until their lips met. Dana smiled at the thought, then glanced at Ryan, who smiled too. Music played in the background. *That's Amore*, Dana thought. Dean Martin. Her grandmother had listened to Dean Martin on her record player.

"There's something I want to share with you," Ryan said after she'd ordered the chicken alfredo, he the veggie lasagna. She took him for a meat and potatoes guy, and she liked the idea that she didn't know him that well, the possibility that she would have the opportunity to get to know him better.

"What is it?" she asked.

"It might have something to do with the fires."

She nodded, embarrassed by the realization that she wanted this evening to have nothing to do with the fires, that she'd wanted to believe he'd picked this romantic little place just for her, that he'd purposely leaned in across the small table as she looked at the menu because he wanted to be closer to her.

The server arrived with a pinot grigio for Dana, a Chianti for Ryan, and set them beside the large glasses of water delivered to the table shortly after they arrived. Dana stared at her glass, wondering why she'd ordered wine when she was just a few days out from her dangerously frightening overindulgence.

Ryan gazed down, fingered the base of his wine glass, then looked up at Dana without taking a drink. "When Kip called and asked for an interview," Ryan said, "I was intrigued because I knew who he was, I knew who you were, some of your work, particularly the series of articles you did on the coverup."

In Boston, it wasn't even necessary to define THE COVERUP. It had garnered international attention, started a serious inquiry, not only in Boston, but around the world, throughout the Catholic Church. Since then, it seemed new cases, in different dioceses, different areas of the country were being uncovered, spreading overseas, all these incidents of abuse finally coming to the forefront. In Ireland, England, Italy. Generally going back years, decades, and, at the least, this made Dana believe their investigations had done something to prevent the abuse and coverups from continuing.

"That's why you didn't hesitate to meet with us?"

"Initially," he replied. Ryan had slipped his sports jacket over the back of his chair. He wore a casual, navy blue short-sleeved polo shirt. His arms were covered with pale, fine hair.

"And this is why you have continued to involve me in the investigation?" she asked, sensing he was ready to reveal more.

"You asked what was different about the fires," he said.

"Yes, I'm curious."

"You know about the altar boy surplices found in the closet at St. Lawrence's."

"I do."

"It seems Father Michael did his best to clean things up before he called. There were catechism books used to get the fire going, but I believe the altar boy surplices were pulled out of the fire before Father called, maybe because—"

"They were only slightly scorched? Salvageable?"

"They appeared to be. Father Michael's eyesight . . . I question whether he even noticed."

"Catechisms and altar boy garb at St. Lawrence's? What about St. Al's?"

"Choir hymnals."

"St. Barbara's?"

"Our investigators are still going through the rubble. When the fire pretty much destroys everything inside that is flammable, much of the fire forensics are lost—"

"These are the differences you were referring to?"

"Yes, it seems, though all three fires were started directly in front of the altars, the fuel of choice—"

"Varied? Which leads you to believe they were started by different people?" *Each with a personal vendetta,* Dana wondered. Was there something significant in the individual choice of kindling and fuel?

"Yes," Ryan said, again fingering his wine glass, staring down. "I have a younger brother." The words came abruptly, out of place in the conversation but, at the same time, oddly rehearsed.

Dana nodded. "And an older brother?" And two sisters, she thought, though Julie was the only one he'd given a name. Like Julie Trenton, the principal of St. Lawrence's. She could picture them now, all the little redheaded Kellys sitting in a row at church.

180

"I do," he said. "But, it's the younger one I want to talk about."
He looked at her.

Again she nodded, sensing that listening was the best, perhaps
even expected response. She glanced at her wineglass, feeling the
need for a prop, too. She hadn't taken a drink, wasn't even sure why
she'd ordered it. She took a gulp of water as she waited for Ryan to
continue. He sat shifting nervously, saying nothing.

"What's his name?" she finally asked, knowing that giving the
younger brother a name might encourage the talk.

"Gabe," Ryan said. "Gabriel. He was, he *is* a beautiful person.
Physically, as well as . . ." He rubbed a finger under his eye, then
grasped his wineglass and took a good swallow. "I should have
known something was going on, something with one of the priests,
but Gabe didn't say anything. He's a gentle soul, a caring person."

"When he was younger?" Dana could see he needed something
from her, something to help him along. "He was abused?"

Ryan nodded. "I didn't know, not then, but it should have been
evident. I should have known something was going on." He bit his
lower lip, again lowered his eyes. His pale lashes cast a light, delicate
shadow under his eyes. A straw-wrapped Chianti bottle with
dripping wax sat in the middle of the table between them,
candlelight flickering. Ryan touched the thick, colorful wax on the
side of the bottle, then pried a small piece loose with his fingers.

"St. Lawrence's?" she asked.

Again, he nodded.

"Father Michael?"

"No, I don't think it was Father Michael."

"But, he knew?"

"They all knew. Isn't that what your research revealed? They
kept moving them around from parish to parish."

She didn't need to reply.

"Such a sweet, innocent boy." Ryan stared toward the window
with a view out to the street. The door opened, a couple stepped in.
Ryan glanced around, and Dana's eyes followed the path of his. "He
was nothing like me or my older brother." He turned his gaze back

to Dana. "Not into sports. Not causing my mom grief."

Dana wondered how Ryan had caused his mom grief—just being a typical, adventurous boy? He'd told her earlier that he was a bit of a hell-raiser, though he never got into any legal trouble.

"More interested in . . . much closer to my sisters."

"He's gay?" she asked.

"Yes, and obviously so. Very soft-spoken, very sweet. Pretty. I think you'd have to say he's pretty. It's a stereotype, I know, but if we're talking stereotypes, he fit . . . he fits," Ryan said, shifting with unease from past to present tense.

Dana thought of her own brother, as well as her brother's husband. Ben was strong, athletic, tall, what some would call masculine. While Sam would not be described as pretty, he was attractive, probably the more handsome, as well as the more sensitive of the two. "Gabe lives here in Boston?" she asked.

"I don't know. I don't know where he lives. He disappeared several years ago." Ryan took in a deep breath. "Just about broke my mother's heart."

"When was the last time you saw him?"

"About three years ago," he replied. "He was very thin."

AIDS, Dana wondered but didn't say it. She wondered if he was dead, if his family didn't even know. She thought of Joel and realized that she and Ryan shared a similar pain. A loss with an added layer of pain because neither of them knew what had happened. No closure. No certainty either way. She took an enormous swallow of wine, pushing down the lump in her throat. She reached for her water.

"Thin," Ryan repeated, "but it was more than the physical signs of ill health. There were some mental health issues going on. I suspect he was doing drugs." His voice dropped and then shifted. "But, there was always an elegance about the boy, the way he moved, the way he spoke. He'd let his hair grow. Long. Blond."

Long blond hair? Like the ghost the boys at St. Lawrence's described, the angel the witness at St. Al's had seen? The young man that Em saw in the St. Barbara's neighborhood?

182

"Beautiful, he was beautiful." Ryan smiled, and something about the soft blue of his eyes, the freckles along his forehead, a few sprinkled on his nose, made him appear young and terribly vulnerable. "We talked, for the first time, we talked about what had happened to him many years ago. I attempted to get him to go to the authorities, but he wouldn't. I suggested some counseling, but he refused."

"I'm so sorry," she said softly, instinctively reaching out, placing her hand on his arm.

"I know it was difficult for him to talk about this. Especially for a young man, a young gay man. I think he blamed himself. That it was somehow his fault."

"He was a child." She hoped that Ryan didn't think he was at fault for not reporting this. He was honoring his brother's wishes.

"He didn't want to go to the authorities," Ryan said. "For several reasons."

"Did he tell you what they were?" *Shame*, she knew this was one. *Fear* of bringing up the memories. She knew there were many reasons a boy . . . a man now, would not report the abuse.

"The money, for one thing," Ryan said. "The enormous amounts that were going to the victims, through the courts, the enormous amounts paid to the attorneys representing the victims. He thought someone should be punished, but the money, that didn't sit right with him. He didn't want to get involved in that, and he thought if he reported it, he'd be pushed in that direction. After our father died, Mother became even more devout. She was tithing, and it hurt. We didn't have much, but she felt it was her obligation, something I see now as almost a weird religious ritual. You know the parable about the widow's penny? As if the less you have and the more you give, the better your chances are to get into heaven."

"Yes," she said. "I know that story. The widow's mite."

"Gabe said it was like taking money from the poor. It was punishing the people, not the priests. Not the bishops who covered it up."

Some of them went to prison, Dana wanted to say, *some of the bishops stepped down.* The archbishop eventually resigned. *One of the priests died in prison. Murdered, in truth, by another inmate.* But, part of her wanted to agree with him. The Church, as an institution, had to be punished, and this is how it was done. Money. It always came down to money. And this was the main reason the archdiocese had had to sell so many properties, close down parishes.

"There are organizations," Dana said, "support groups that have helped many of the victims." She had worked with these organizations—no, that wasn't the correct word. She had desperately tried to remain neutral, but how could one remain neutral when the evil was so apparent? She'd met with young men active in these organizations, but even these groups had developed their own problems of integrity and righteousness. Some of these groups had been accused of corruption, inappropriate use of funds, unauthorized referrals, and payoffs to lawyers. There were lawyers involved who had made millions off of the abuse cases.

Ryan didn't reply to Dana's suggestion of support groups, so after another pause in the conversation, she asked, "Were you the only one in your family who saw him? Three years ago?"

"I told him he should see Mom, but he said he couldn't. It would hurt her too much."

But, Dana thought, *not seeing him hurts even more.*

"He knew he had problems," Ryan said, "and he didn't want her to see him like that. He was, well, he was saying some weird, disjointed stuff. About how the Church needed to be reformed, that the whole darn thing needed to be destroyed, then built up from the beginning. He said this is what Jesus did . . . destroyed the temple and rebuilt."

Dana swallowed hard. Why was Ryan telling her this? Because he feared his brother was involved in setting these fires? "Did you tell anyone?" Dana asked.

He shook his head. "He asked me not to." Ryan bit into his lower lip so hard, Dana thought it might draw blood. "I question if that was the right decision."

"You don't know where he is now?" she asked.

Ryan reached back into the inside pocket of his jacket hanging over his chair, pulled out his phone, punched in a code, then another, scrolled down, and handed it to her. "This was taken just a few months ago."

A blurry picture appeared on the screen. A young man stood in front of a church. He wore a flowing robe. His long pale hair rested on his thin, elegant shoulders. He carried a handprinted sign. Dana squinted, then expanded the shot to make out the words.

This CHURCH must be DESTROYED and built again.

She studied the background in the photo and recognized St. Patrick's, the church she and Mia had visited in New York.

"He's in New York? You saw him there?" Hadn't Ryan just said he hadn't seen him in three years? That he'd come home to Boston, and that was the last time he'd seen him? Where did this picture come from? "This is Gabe in New York? Recently?"

"A friend took this picture just a few months ago," Ryan said. "He saw this young man in front of St. Patrick's on Fifth Avenue. He took the photo because he thought it might be Gabe."

"Did he talk to him?"

"No."

"Is it? Is it Gabe?"

"I believe so. Though I'm not sure. He looks better in this photo than he did when I saw him three years ago. I went to New York after I saw this picture, went to the Cathedral. He wasn't there, but oddly, I saw two young men, and they were dressed in a similar fashion." Ryan rubbed his left temple, then his eyes, one at a time. His cheeks had reddened. The whites of his eyes were blotched with red. "I talked to one of them, and I asked him about Gabe."

"What did he tell you?"

"Some mumbly jumbly about the Church, the need for serious reform—similar to what Gabe had told me—that the Church must first be destroyed. He quoted scripture, something about the temple being destroyed."

"You think this relates to what's been happening here in Boston?"

"He said the destruction would be done with fire." Ryan stopped, looked Dana directly in the eyes before he continued. "That the fire would grow. That it would begin where it all began. That it would reach to the upper echelons of the Church. That everything must be destroyed to be rebuilt."

Dana felt her heart take an extra beat, then stop, then thump again. "Where it all began?" she asked. "Everything destroyed?"

"It was a cryptic message," he replied. "If it was a message."

"You think it's a movement?" *A host of angels. A flock of demons. A congress of ghosts.* "Destruction by fire?"

"I don't know what to think."

"The upper echelons? What do you think that means?"

"I'm not sure," Ryan said.

"It will begin where it all began?" she asked.

Ryan's shoulders rose and fell. The server delivered their meals, cautioning them that the plates were very hot as he placed a dish of fettuccini before her, a plate of lasagna before Ryan. The server offered parmesan, and each nodded as the young man grated fresh cheese until they said *okay*.

After he'd left the table, they sat quietly, staring down at their plates, the aroma drifting up, but neither taking a bite.

"When we talked to the neighbors around St. Barbara's," Dana said, "the picture you showed Em—it was Gabe?" She motioned toward Ryan's phone, which he'd placed on the table next to his water glass. The image had disappeared from the screen.

"I blanked out the sign he was carrying," Ryan said, "when I showed the picture to Em. But, yes, I believe it was Gabe."

"He was there," she whispered, "at St. Barbara's, the night of the fire."

CHAPTER TWENTY-FOUR

"Your dad's a good cook," Mia told Meagan. He'd made dinner for the three of them—meatloaf with potatoes and gravy, a salad, and chocolate cake from Trader Joe's for dessert.

"He is," Meagan said. "Dana isn't?"

"Not great." They were sitting on Meagan's bed again after having helped her dad clean up in the kitchen. He was in his home office now, doing some writing. Though Meagan said he wouldn't notice her hair color, he had. He smiled at his daughter across the table, where the two girls sat side by side, and said, "It's nice to see you looking like yourself again, Meggie. I like your hair."

Meagan had just rolled her eyes, side glanced at Mia, who could tell that Meagan liked the attention from her dad, and Mia realized how much she missed her own father.

Meagan flipped a page in the book she was scanning. "I think what we have to do with Zac is return him to the scene of the crime. There's something there that might trigger a memory. A smell, a sound, something visual."

Mia nodded, but she knew she didn't want to trick Zac. Though he'd been reluctant to talk about Joel, eventually, he had opened up a bit. Mia thought that Zac trusted her. "It happened at his grandmother's house. He still goes there. All the time."

"I wonder if that's creepy for him," Meagan said, eyes narrowing as she flipped another page. "Where did it happen?" She glanced up. "It was at night? In a bedroom?"

"I think so," Mia replied. She knew only what she'd read in the news clippings from Dana's file cabinet. The first article said that Joel had been sharing a room with his older cousin. Though there was no name given, Mia knew it was Zac. According to the article, the boy had said someone came to take Joel, but then the following day, he couldn't recall anything.

"I wonder if they considered moving, I mean the grandma," Meagan said. "That might be hard for Zac, for Dana, going to where her son had been abducted."

"Maybe they think he'll come back, that he won't know where to find them if Zac's grandma moves."

Meagan shot Mia a look that seemed to say, *what are the chances he's still alive? Why are we even doing this? We're looking for a dead boy.* But then, she stood, stepped over to her desk, sat, flipped her laptop open, and signed on. Her fingers moved over the keyboard, and after a moment, she motioned Mia over.

"Look at this," Meagan said. "Is this the article you read?"

Mia scanned the words on the screen. Though it appeared oddly altered in the larger, digital format and much grainier, she recognized it as the article in Dana's file, the initial report of the abduction. "Yes," she said. "That's it."

Meagan arrowed back, selected another article. The newspaper picture of Dana appeared on the screen, younger, with darker hair, wearing glasses. Her husband stood next to her, attempting to prop her up, but there was something that Mia hadn't been aware of when she'd seen it earlier. There was a disconnect. Two people together, in close physical proximity, yet detached, as if each were adrift in a separate pain. Then a photo of Joel. A photo of Zac's grandma's house.

"He's a cute little boy," Meagan said softly.

A teenager now, Mia thought. If he's still alive.

Dana and Ryan started back to her apartment, barely speaking until they reached the lobby. They stood awkwardly without words.

Finally, she said, "Would you come up?" She motioned toward the elevator. "Maybe if you take a look at some of my old files, you might see something I've missed."

They rode up together in silence, Dana and Ryan both clutching their takeout boxes, stopping once to pick up someone on the second floor who thought they were on their way down.

It had been a while since she'd invited a man up to her apartment. Well, other than Kip, her brothers, but that was different.

As the elevator ascended, she studied Ryan Kelly, who sent her a small, sad smile. There was something appealing about his vulnerability, and at the same time, his physicality, the appealing contrast, his largeness, his strength, yet his sweetness. His willingness to finally open up to her.

Once inside her apartment, Dana opened the fridge to slide in the takeout boxes. She'd barely eaten any of her fettuccini. Ryan had eaten even less of his lasagna. He'd finished his wine, but Dana had left half her glass on the table, with an apology to both the server—for some odd reason—and Ryan.

"You want something to drink?" she asked. She didn't have any alcohol; she'd obliterated the only bottle of wine in her apartment, and the thought of either of them drinking alcohol seemed like the worst way to proceed.

He was standing beside her, then above her as she stooped to slide the two separate boxes onto a lower shelf. He reached in, his arm grazing her awkwardly on the top of her head as she straightened her posture.

"How about milk?" he said. He maneuvered around her and pulled out a milk carton.

He held it at an awkward angle, tilting his head back, pretending to drink out of the carton. Just like one of her brothers, after coming in from baseball practice or a jog, she thought with an inner laugh. But he was merely doing a mimic, a boyish pantomime. He turned and stepped across the kitchen, opened the cupboard, grabbed a glass and poured it half full of milk. She realized that she liked having a man in her kitchen. A milk-drinking man.

This man.

She watched him as he took an enormous drink, then wiped his upper lip like a little kid. They stood staring at one another, and then she said, "I'll go get my laptop. Some files."

She retrieved her laptop from her bedroom, a box of USB drives, a stack of files, some that she'd been storing in the small file cabinet in Mia's room. He was pouring a second glass of milk when she returned. He studied the photos attached with magnets to the fridge.

"My nieces and nephews," she said. There were no pictures of Joel. Not anywhere in her home that visitors would see. She had photos of Joel in her bedroom. But only in a place she never shared with anyone else.

"Cute kids," he said.

"They are. I enjoy them. Especially that little blonde twinkie," she said with a smile, pointing to a picture of Kiki taken about a year ago, her ponytails sticking straight up from her head, wide grin spread over her precious face. "Katherine Pierson-Brown. We call her Kiki. She's my brother's daughter. My brother and his husband."

"Oh," Ryan said, brows rising as he glanced back at Dana. Did he wonder why she hadn't mentioned she had a gay brother, too? "Kiki, cute name. Cute girl."

She set the laptop and stack of files on the breakfast bar, sat and turned on the computer, and popped in a USB stick. He sat, sliding his stool closer to get a good view of the screen.

"When we were doing our series," she said, "the articles on the coverup, we constructed a database, a spreadsheet. When all of the information was gathered and compiled, we could see the patterns, see which priests were being moved about, which priests had gaps in their service. Eventually, we understood these represented periods where they were in counseling and getting psychiatric care, so they could be declared forgiven and rehabilitated."

Ryan nodded, thinking. "You think if we set up some type of

database?"

"Possibly."

"We are aware of only three churches in the Boston area . . . ," he said thoughtfully, and she realized that setting up a database with only three samples would not be helpful. Would they have to wait for a fourth fire, then another? She knew now that abuse had taken place at each of these churches where fires had been set, though she had not been aware of anything at St. Lawrence's until this evening when Ryan told her about his brother. Was this the common factor?

"Did you set up a database, matching abuse victims, to priests, to specific locations?" Ryan asked.

"Many of the interviews we did with victims were considered off the record. A great number of them asked not to be named." She remembered a particular young man who spoke to her once and specifically told her he would not speak to her again. She thought of another who'd refused to meet. She'd spoken to him once on the phone. The following day, he'd taken his own life. "Others, those who decided to sue the Church, were protected by nondisclosure agreements. So, no, there is no specific database for the victims." She had handwritten records in another file, but even back then, entering a name into an electronic system as if this person were merely a statistic seemed to be another form of abuse. "I've got handwritten interview files, but after sixteen years, contact information is likely outdated."

Dana thought of Ryan's brother, Gabe, and the choices he'd made. She knew others had chosen not to come forward, to suffer in silence. Now, were these silent angels about to come forth in a chorus, a host of angels?

They decided, for now, they would concentrate on the empty churches, those sitting unused or on the market. For the next couple of hours, they worked together sifting through files that Dana had examined and organized earlier. She explained the information had not been updated for several years, and Ryan told her he would talk to the Realtor he'd been working with to see if she could get him an updated list of properties currently for sale.

191

Kelly Jones

Again, Dana's thoughts turned to the victims, and she realized if these fires were all related, if the sightings of angel-like figures at each of these places were valid, if they had any connection to the young men in New York, they were most likely dealing with a terrorist group. Though there was no universally accepted definition of a terrorist group, it was generally agreed that violence or the threat of violence for political, religious, or ideological reasons was at the core of such groups. Was it necessary that the group take credit, that their objectives be known? What had the man in New York told Ryan? That the Church must be destroyed to be rebuilt? That it would begin where it began? That it would reach the upper echelons of the Church?

They filled in an electronic calendar, marking the days of the fires. Ryan did this with such ease that Dana knew it was a replica of one he'd already constructed. She had formed a similar chart in her mind, though she had never been told the date of the June fire at St. Lawrence's.

"This is as close as I can get," Ryan said. "Through forensic analysis, we can sometimes pinpoint the beginnings of a fire to a precise time, but this depends on many variables. The fire at St. Lawrence's, since Father Michael didn't make the call until Saturday after the fire was extinguished, could have started late Friday night, early Saturday morning."

"And the fire at St. Al's? Late Thursday, early Friday morning?"

"Yes."

"One in June, another in July, the last in August?" she said. There didn't seem to be a set number of days between fires, though each occurred later in the month than the preceding fire. "One per month? Another in September?"

"It's something we are considering."

They quietly studied the calendar, Dana attempting to see a pattern. "Maybe we need to determine if this is happening anywhere else," she finally said.

He clicked off the database and signed on to a search engine. He typed in *fires churches*.

192

Within a few minutes, they found there had been a fire at an empty church in Pennsylvania, one at a church in upstate New York, but they found nothing more than the brief, no byline articles, similar to those that had first appeared in the *Globe* after the fire at St. Aloysius. One had been nearly a year ago, the other about seven months ago. There were no videos. One of them was a Baptist, not Catholic, church. They also found a mosque in Michigan, a Jewish synagogue in New York State.

If there was any connection to the fires in Boston, there was no evidence of this, nothing to indicate these fires were anything other than unfortunate events. None attributed to arson. The one in Pennsylvania started because of faulty wiring. There was no follow-up report on the one in New York.

"I'm not seeing anything in what's here," Ryan said, "anything that points to these fires having any similarities to those in Boston." He paused. "There are thousands of fires each year, and chances are slim that these are related to what's happening here. I have access to a database," he added thoughtfully, "that might give us more information."

"Is it public record?"

"Most of it is, but it's not online. Someone wanting the information would have to put in a records request."

She realized that would take time, paperwork. "But you have access?"

"I could find some basic information, then if we find similarities, I can make a few calls. I'll have to go down to my office for contact information. And I'd feel more comfortable accessing the data from there."

"It would be helpful to know," Dana said pensively, and then, "The upper echelons?"

Ryan rubbed a finger along his pale brow as if attempting to tame a stray hair, then he pinched his lower lip and ran his hand along his chin.

"Maybe it's time to go speak with the archbishop?" Dana said. "If this is related to what happened years ago in the Church, with the abuse. If this is some type of retaliation, or warning, or prelude to something to come."

"We've spoken with the archbishop," Ryan said matter-of-factly.

She shot him a look of dismay. *Why didn't you take me with you?* she said without words. *You've included me in just about every other aspect of this investigation, other than the fire forensics, which I wouldn't understand anyway.*

"After St. Aloysius, we wanted to know about the insurance. Then, St. Barbara's. Though it had changed hands on paper . . . if arson is suspected, the insurance carrier always comes into the equation."

"Did you ask the archbishop if he thought there was any connection between the fires?"

"He knew of no connection."

"Did you ask him if he had been contacted by anyone claiming credit for the fires?"

"He's had no one communicating prior to or after the fires."

"Did you believe him?" She could hear a roughness in her question.

"You're wondering why I haven't shared this with you sooner? I'm sure you understand why I didn't invite you along to visit the archbishop."

She laughed. "Yes, I can understand why you wouldn't want to take me unless I went in disguise. It's been years since we ran the first article on the abuse and coverup scandal, but the archbishop might recognize me." Ryan nodded in agreement. The old archbishop had eventually been canned because he couldn't hold up under the scrutiny generated from the stories. "Different archbishop, but they probably have a picture of me in the bullseye of a dart target in the office."

"I wouldn't doubt it," he said with a laugh.

"You visited him twice?"

"The first interview was done before you entered the picture, before you stepped into my office."

"But the second interview, after St. Barbara's?"

"I was just beginning to put all this together. Just starting to wonder if it had some connection to Gabe, to the young men demonstrating in New York in front of the church."

"But, you didn't bring this up during your visit?"

"No, of course not."

"You haven't shared this yet with your investigators?"

"I've shared the fact that there have been some unsubstantiated sightings of men dressed in similar fashion, though the witnesses might be questionable—two boys who were looking for ghosts? A druggie at St. Al's?" Dana could hear the defensiveness in his voice. "In our investigations, we deal with quantifiable evidence, not ghosts, angels, apparitions, along with a slew of potentially unreliable witnesses."

"Em would come across as a reliable witness," Dana offered.

"Your investigators are aware of your suspicions about Gabe?"

"We have no evidence," he replied defensively, "nothing to connect Gabe with any of this."

She understood that she was the only one with whom he'd shared his suspicions about his brother. "Is it time to do a story?" she asked.

"We don't have enough facts yet. We've established nothing. Not yet."

"The story would contain only facts. That's how I do it." Now she could hear a hint of defensiveness in her voice. "If we present what we know, someone may come forward with more information. Fact one . . ." She began counting on her fingers. "There have been three recent fires. Fact two, they are all in churches or sections of churches not being used. Fact three, all three fires have some common factors, like where the fires were set, right in front of the main altars. Fact four, a visual. We have the video taken outside of St. Barbara's that night. Print the frame with the—" She stopped for a moment, aware she didn't even know what to call this person. An angel? A terrorist? A boy? A man? "We'll publish it. The person in the gown is a person of interest. Not a suspect, not an accused arsonist, merely a person of interest.

Not Gabe. Someone may come forward with information if they recognize this person."

He didn't respond. He glanced down, then his gaze rose, and his eyes locked on hers. "We're not ready. Not yet. You understand?" He touched her hand.

"Yes, I understand that *you* are not yet ready to go public." She didn't pull back, didn't shake off his touch. She'd just told him how she usually did it. Facts, only. But was she bending to his will, even as she realized someone else, another reporter might, even as they sat, be putting pieces and words together? Was she letting her developing feelings for Ryan influence her work? "Then, we need to do whatever we can to get enough hard facts to put it out there," she said.

"Any ideas?" Slowly he withdrew his hand.

"Maybe we should go higher," she said.

He shot her a puzzled look.

"To the uppermost echelons of the Church," she offered.

"How uppermost are we talking?" he asked.

"I don't mind starting at the top," she said, "working my way down."

He laughed. "You're talking what?" His eyes narrowed.

"All the way to the top."

"The Vatican?"

She nodded.

"You happen to know anyone with Vatican connections?" He laughed again, but it had the ring of fatigue, along with a good dose of doubt. She could see he was growing weary. As was she.

She glanced at the time on the laptop screen. It was 10:35. 4:35 A.M. in Italy.

"As a matter of fact," she said, "yes, I do. Mia's great-uncle, Father Giovanni Borelli."

Mia and Meagan had used up their allotted number of free articles, and the site was prompting them to pay for a subscription.

"Does your dad have an online account?" Mia asked.

"I think so, but . . . I'm sure he does." She hopped up from the chair at her desk. "I'll go downstairs and get his password."

She left the room, returning in less than a minute.

"His office door is closed, so that means he doesn't want to be disturbed. He's probably talking to one of his patients." Meagan rolled her eyes. "He works with a lot of nutcases." She said this matter-of-factly, surprising Mia that she'd use this word to describe her dad's patients. "I'll try later."

But, when she tried about half an hour later, she came back upstairs and explained her dad had gone to bed, so they'd have to wait until morning.

"You hungry?" Meagan asked, and Mia nodded.

The girls tiptoed downstairs and into the kitchen. Meagan sliced them each another piece of chocolate cake. Mia poured two glasses of milk. They sat down at the kitchen table.

"Do you really think we should attempt to do this?" Mia asked.

"My dad always says when there is doubt in taking on a particular task or engaging in a questionable action, ask yourself why are you doing this? What are the consequences of your actions?"

"You are asking why we are doing this? What are the consequences?"

"Yep," Meagan replied.

"I want to help Dana."

"To find her son?" Meagan asked, and Mia heard a hint of skepticism mixed with compassion in her voice.

"You think he's dead?" Mia's voice was low.

"Chances are . . ." Meagan said slowly, hesitantly.

"But he might still be alive."

"You don't want to tell Dana what we are doing?"

"Only if we find him," Mia replied. They finished their cake and milk, rinsed their plates and glasses, loaded them in the dishwasher, then quietly returned to Meagan's room upstairs.

They brushed their teeth, slipped on their PJs, as Meagan called them—though Mia wore an oversized T-shirt and Meagan a ratty pair of sweatpants and cut off T-shirt—and settled into Meagan's queen-sized bed.

Mia lay, unable to sleep, wondering if Meagan was already asleep, when she heard the beep of her cellphone on the nightstand where she'd plugged it in to charge.

She reached over and picked it up.

"Who is it?" Meagan asked.

"It's Zac," Mia told her as she sat up. "It's a text from Zac."

"What's he say?" Meagan was sitting, too. Mia didn't think she'd been asleep either.

"I was fantastic tonight," Mia read from the screen, then told Meagan, "They must have won the game."

"You won!" Mia texted back. Meagan gazed with interest over Mia's shoulder.

"I think he likes you," she said to Mia.

Mia glanced back with a raised brow.

"The game was probably over a couple of hours ago," Meagan said. "Well, he's probably showered now, doesn't want to send his sweety a message when he's all sweaty." Meagan laughed at the alliteration of her words. "I bet you're the first one he sent a message to."

Mia knew it was an out-of-town game, but she didn't know how far away or if his parents had gone. She pictured him sitting on the bus with his rowdy friends, all pumped up about their big win. But, still . . . taking the time to share his good news with her.

"Gotta go," Zac texted. "Coach wants to give me a big kiss for winning the game. Stay tuned for more. Tomorrow they will all be singing my praises. College scouts will be all over this."

"Not too modest. Is he?" Meagan said.

"Proud of you!" Mia texted back, then wondered if this was too personal. It sounded like she thought he was her boyfriend.

"Gma's Sunday," Zac replied. "C U."

Mia didn't remember Dana saying anything about Sunday dinner, but she said she'd pick her up at Meagan's about 3:00. That would give them plenty of time to get to Zac's grandma's for dinner.

"If you go to Grandma's," Meagan whispered as if Zac might

hear their conversation, "we can start doing some on-sight investigation."

Mia didn't even know if they should or could get Zac to bring up memories of what had happened that night. Yet, he had opened up to her a little about his memories of his cousin Joel.

"See you Sunday," she texted back, taking a deep swallow of air as her fingers flew over the keypad, then rested tentatively against her heart.

CHAPTER TWENTY-FIVE

Dana and Ryan moved from the kitchen to the sofa in her living room as they waited, hoping for a response from Borelli. She'd told Ryan in an earlier conversation about Father Giovanni Borelli, Mia's great-uncle, who, along with his sister, Estella, owned a winery in Tuscany. Now, she explained how Father Borelli had since left the priesthood and married.

Ryan's brows shot up at this revelation. "No longer a priest?"

"No, but he was active as a representative of the Vatican at one time, sent to Boston shortly after the scandal broke, though his visit was unannounced, and we didn't meet at that time."

"So, when did you meet?"

"It was later, in Prague. That was almost eight years ago."

"Then, after that, you visited the family in Italy?" Ryan asked, and Dana nodded, aware from his puzzled expression that he was confused about the chronology of their friendship. "Despite this unannounced visit to Boston, you trusted, you trust this man?" he asked cautiously.

"Completely," she said, realizing how important it was that Ryan trust Borelli, too, that this trust was contingent on his trusting Dana. "Yes, I do," she said. "Completely. He's a good man, I value his friendship, and his connections could be extremely helpful." She was about to go into more detail and explain how this friendship had developed and how she knew she could rely on Borelli, when her phone rang. She turned on the speakerphone.

"Mia is okay?" Borelli asked immediately, voice tight.

"Yes, she's doing wonderfully. It's a pleasure having her here with me." Dana wouldn't mention that Mia wasn't here now, that she was spending the weekend with a friend. Dana's email had been vague, and she realized now that he might have taken her late-night, early-morning-in-Italy message as an alarm concerning Mia. She'd written, "I need your help. Please call as soon as possible." She'd said nothing about the fires.

"I take it there is some urgency," Borelli said indignantly, "as there was a tone of distress in your message."

"Mia is fine," she reassured him. "She's making friends, doing well in school. No, it's something else. I hope you might be able to help me."

She told him about the fires at the three churches in Boston, glancing at Ryan as she spoke, waiting for a nod from him before she continued. She explained they'd all been set, almost ritualistically, in front of the main altars. "Young men in flowing garments, long pale hair, appearing almost angelic, or perhaps ghost-like, have been spotted in the vicinity of the fires."

Dana kept eye contact with Ryan as she worked through the critical details, and he seemed fine with what she was sharing. She told Borelli she had reason to believe this might reach beyond Boston, that it might involve a national or even international plot.

"What is it specifically that makes you think that?"

She explained that someone she was working with had spoken to a young man in New York who fit the description of the men sighted at or near the churches at the times of the fires. She told him what the man had said about the destruction of the Church, that it would be done with fire, that it would begin where it all began. That the Church would be rebuilt after being destroyed. Then she said there was a mention of reaching the upper echelons of the Church.

"Implying that those in the upper echelons are involved in this destruction?"

Dana considered this, then said, "Maybe more in the context that the destruction, the fires, would reach the upper echelons." Again, she glanced at Ryan to confirm that this was what he had heard.

He nodded.

"Your archbishop has been contacted?" Borelli asked.

"Local fire officials have spoken with him but learned nothing." Dana knew Ryan had shared none of what she'd just told Borelli with the archbishop.

"I see," said Borelli. He grunted, coughed, and then cleared his throat. "I see," he repeated, and he might as well have said, we both know it is unlikely the archbishop would share sensitive information with law enforcement if it related to the inner workings of the Church, and even less likely he'd share with the press. "The Vatican might be a target?" he asked.

"I'm not sure how to interpret—"

"Others have reported hearing these threats? Seeing these men in other locations?"

"We're not aware, but I'm not sure how seriously people might take someone standing on a soapbox, so to speak, wearing flowing garments, long white hair—"

"Yes," he commented pensively. "The men were seen in New York, yet as far as you know, the fires have all been in Boston?"

"We're still checking on that," Dana replied reflectively as a thought entered her mind. *It will begin where it all began.*

"You're asking if I still have connections," Borelli said, "within the *upper echelons?*"

"Yes."

"You know it's been nearly a decade since I've been active."

She never understood precisely what Borelli did within the Vatican, but she knew he had connections. Even after he'd been retired for several years, he'd enlisted a Vatican pilot, another retiree, to fly them down to southern Italy. At one time, he had served as the Devil's Advocate, looking for reasons to withhold canonization from those being considered for sainthood, those held up as paragons of virtue. Borelli had an understanding of evil, particularly evil masquerading as good. In Prague, when they were trying to determine what had happened to a missing religious icon, she'd become aware that he had connections with a man well versed in the acquisition and disposal of valuable religious artifacts.

"I'm not sure," he added, "if I have any reliable remaining connections."

"But," she said, "you can do some inquiries, see if you can discover anything about such a movement, a movement of young men, who . . ." She didn't even know exactly what she was requesting, but if any of this had reached the Vatican, she hoped Borelli might have access to someone who might know or be in a position to find out.

"Was anyone injured? Killed?"

"Not that we know of. No, not here, not in Boston." Again . . . *where it all began.*

"We?"

"Ryan Kelly, the State Fire Marshal."

"He's chosen to work with you because . . . ?" Borelli released the question with a hint of caution in his words, perhaps a warning. *Be careful whom you trust.*

"He's attempting to determine who started these fires, if there might be more, in his official capacity, but also . . . one of the fires occurred in a small chapel in his home parish." She hesitated, glanced at Ryan. He nodded again. "He thinks his brother might be involved." Dana knew that Ryan had not yet shared this information with his own investigators, but she could see he had no objection to sharing with Borelli.

"He's trying to protect his brother?" Borelli asked, again with caution. Dana knew Borelli had gone out of his way to protect those he loved. *This* he could understand.

She said, "There's more to it than that."

Borelli waited.

Dana glanced at Ryan. "His brother was abused. Years ago. Ryan thinks there might be a connection."

"Retaliation?"

"We're not entirely sure of the motive, but this talk of destruction and rebuilding . . ."

Again, Borelli was thinking, no words coming from the other side. Finally, he said, "I'll see what, if anything, I can discover."

"My love to Gia," Dana said. "She's well?"

"Gia is wonderful," Borelli said.

"You both take care."

When she clicked to end the call, Dana took a deep breath and reached over for Ryan's hand, giving this no conscious thought, just feeling a need for a physical connection.

"Probably a wise decision to enlist this Father Borelli." Ryan tightened his grip on her hand for a moment, and then he released it.

"Yes," she said.

"Though he's no longer a priest."

"No, though, hopefully, he still has connections within the Vatican." Dana went on to explain how she and Borelli had found themselves caught up in political intrigue in the Czech Republic, then in Montalcino, Italy, how they'd worked together to discover who had vandalized a wine cellar and destroyed millions of dollars' worth of wine.

Ryan sat listening, his expression shifting from disbelief, to astonishment, to admiration. "You've certainly used your investigative skills as a journalist in these adventures with Father Borelli. You make my life as a firefighter seem almost mundane." He laughed. "Can I tell you about the time I rescued a cat from a tree?"

Dana laughed too. "I thought that was a cartoon cliché." She was sure as a firefighter, he had stories of his own that were far from *mundane*.

"Nope, real story." He glanced at his watch. "It's almost 1:00 A.M. Maybe my cat story can wait." He stood. "I'll run by my office tomorrow, check out a couple of databases, see if I can find anything that looks like it might be helpful."

"It's already tomorrow." She stood, too. "If you'd like," she offered, "why don't you get some rest here."

"Here?"

"I'll bring you a blanket, a pillow." She didn't want him to think she was offering anything more. "You can crash here." She gestured toward the sofa. "I'll fix some breakfast in the morning, and then maybe I can go with you? To your office tomorrow? Or, we could eat our leftovers for breakfast."

"We could," he said slowly, but she wasn't sure how to read this unenthusiastic response. She wasn't sure if he was mulling over whether he wanted to stay, whether she could go with him to his office, or whether he was willing to eat leftover dinner for breakfast.

When Dana woke the following morning, she was surprised at how late it was, even considering they'd been awake until well into the early morning.

She threw on her bathrobe and opened her bedroom door. The pillow and blanket she'd given Ryan were folded neatly in front of her door. He'd left? She felt a weight of disappointment. She wanted him to take her to his office to review his database. But, more than that, she realized she liked the idea of waking up to Ryan Kelly.

She stepped into the hall, headed toward the kitchen to throw on a pot of coffee, but then she stopped abruptly. She could smell it. Coffee. As she approached the kitchen, she heard something. He was whistling. An unidentifiable tune, but pleasant.

"Sorry I slept so late," she said.

He looked up with a smile. He had placed half a dozen pieces of bacon in her frying pan, and they were starting to sizzle, the inviting aroma mingling with the scent of coffee now. His hair was mussed in a way she found oddly attractive.

"I guess I offered to make you breakfast," she said and then again apologized for sleeping so late. "Or reheat the leftovers." He was barefooted, his blue polo shirt and tan khakis completely wrinkle-free, and she imagined him undressing, carefully folding his clothes, placing them on the chair next to the sofa before slipping under the blanket she'd brought him—

"We can save them for lunch," he said, waving the spatula in his hand. "I like breakfast for breakfast." He shot her another smile. "Sometimes, I eat breakfast for dinner."

"Thank you," she said sincerely. *For not leaving without me,* she wanted to say, but she knew it was more than that. *For not leaving.* "For making me breakfast." *For implying you'll be around for lunch.*

"First up makes breakfast," he said.

"Where'd you find the bacon?" she asked.

"In the freezer."

Oh," she said, barely remembering she had bacon in the freezer. She could see he had grated cheese. A half dozen eggs sat on the counter next to a bowl, a can of mushrooms, some olives, a plastic box with just a few small, wrinkly tomatoes. "An omelet?" she asked.

"I can throw one together with what I found in the pantry, the fridge." He reached into the cupboard and grabbed a cup with such ease it seemed like he belonged in her kitchen. He poured her coffee and motioned her to sit.

So she did and took a long, slow drink of the best cup of coffee she'd had in a very long time as the aroma of the frying bacon surrounded her with comfort.

Mia and Meagan took the bus to the library Saturday morning. When they'd awaken, Meagan had found a note from her dad saying he had an emergency call and would be out for a while. She explained to Mia that she never bothered her father when he was with a patient unless it was an emergency. Getting the password to his online newspaper account did not fall within that category, so the girls decided to go to the library.

They seemed to be the only two in the building who weren't over 60, moms, or kids under five. The children had gone into the children's library, and the older people, who appeared mostly to be homeless men, were scattered about.

They had no trouble getting access to the articles they were looking for and flipped through them on a computer screen, sitting side by side at a library terminal. There were many more articles about Joel's disappearance than what Mia had discovered in the files in her room.

"This happened the night before Easter," Meagan said, scanning one of the articles. "The adults had been out hiding eggs, so there were footprints all over the backyard."

"The footprints matched up with family members," Mia said, summarizing the article as she leaned in toward Meagan to get a better view. In Italy, they celebrated Easter as a religious holiday with chocolate eggs that represented the Resurrection, but there was no Easter Bunny, no adults out hiding eggs that the children believed were hidden by a rabbit.

Meagan glanced at Mia. "According to this article, there were many prints in the damp lawn the following morning, as well as the flower beds, particularly those under the window of the room where the children were sleeping."

"The women had gone out early that morning to hide the eggs." Mia could picture the grownups outside, still early enough that it was dark, hiding Easter eggs. Easter eggs that the children would not find. Easter eggs that were perhaps carefully examined by the police. Had the person who'd taken Joel come into the room before or after the adults crept about the yard, placing an egg under a tree, in a limb, perhaps settling one gently into the earth, peeking out behind a soon-to-bloom tulip or daffodil that had folded its petals in for the damp, dark night? Was the child stealer lurking about even then, moving stealthily up to the children's window, then climbing in after the adults had retreated into the warmth of the house?

"Do you think the police suspected someone in the family?" Meagan asked.

"No one would steal their own child," Mia said.

"Maybe there was an accident," Meagan said, voice low. "And they got rid of the—"

"Don't say that," Mia came back. "Dana and her mom and sister-in-law—the article says it was the women who hid the eggs—they must have obstructed the footprints of the person who took Joel."

"That sounds like sloppy police work to me," Meagan said. One of the articles mentioned a detective, Christopher Prinz. Mia wondered if, after all these years, he was still assigned to the case. "There had to be some footprints somewhere if the grass and garden were damp. If someone besides family members was in the yard. And what about fingerprints?"

Mia shot Meagan a look of concern. She knew Dana would have looked at every possible clue, that she wouldn't let the police get away with sloppy work. Dana herself would cover every inch of that yard, follow the police around. Yet, Mia realized that the yard would have been taped off, that none of the family members would have been allowed inside the cordoned-off crime scene. By the time Dana got to it, most likely, it was covered with additional footprints.

"Does any of this look familiar," Meagan said, shifting to another article. "From when you went there for dinner?" She pointed to a photo of Zac's grandmother's house.

Mia studied the photo carefully. It was taken from a slightly different angle than the one in the first article they'd read. "Enlarge the picture of the house," she said.

"Sure." With a quick maneuver, a click of the mouse, the image expanded on the screen.

Mia could see that something was different about the old photo of the house and how it looked now. In the photo, there was a small room on the back that looked like some type of a screened-off porch. She tried to visualize the exterior as she'd walked out with Zac to see his car, but she didn't recall this room. Had it been removed or perhaps altered? Had some trees grown up covering the windows? She was having trouble conjuring an image because she hadn't looked at the house that closely when she visited.

Mia leaned toward Meagan and read, "The homeowner, Ann Pierson, slept in a bedroom on the first floor on the opposite side of the house. All visiting adults who did not reside in the home, Dana Pierson, Andrew Monaghan, Jeffery Pierson, and Pamela Pierson, were upstairs in bedrooms some distance from the room where the children slept, and none reported hearing anything unusual during the night or early morning."

Mia pictured Dana, a much younger Dana, and Pammie, Zac's mom, tucking the excited children into bed, telling them they must go to sleep so the Easter Bunny could hide the eggs. Then, later, maybe even in the morning, after peaking in on the slumbering boys, tiptoeing out into the yard to hide the eggs. Had Joel already been taken, his mother thinking he was under the pile of blankets on the bed where only one small boy now slept?

"According to this article," Meagan said, finger running down the screen, "the police have determined that there was no forced entry. According to officer Troxell, the window to the boys' room at the back of the house was most likely opened from the inside, or perhaps was never locked." She threw Mia a questioning glance. "Inside job?"

Mia bit down on her lip but said nothing. Again, she pictured the children, Joel, as he looked in the photo in the first newspaper article, though Zac, as a four-year-old, was more difficult to imagine. Two excited little boys, perhaps unable to sleep, waiting for the sweets the Easter Bunny might deliver, imaging the furry, pink-nosed, floppy-eared creature outside their window at that very moment. A rustle in the bushes. A light scratch on the window screen. Perhaps one of the curious boys cranked open the window to peer outside. Could it have been either Zac or Joel who opened the window? A child who allowed a child stealer to creep inside?

"I think one of the kids unlocked the window," Mia said, her voice an unsteady rasp.

CHAPTER TWENTY-SIX

Just as they were finishing a leisurely breakfast, an omelet with wheat toast, bacon, orange juice, and coffee, Ryan got a text message from the Realtor he'd been working with at St. Al's.

"She's emailing a list of Catholic Church buildings currently on the market," he told Dana. "I'll forward it as soon as it comes through."

"Thank you," she said, "and thank you for the delicious breakfast." She took her last gulp of coffee, then rose, lifted the coffee pot, poured the remainder of the coffee into his cup, motioning for him to remain sitting. "I'll clean up," she said as she started clearing the dishes. Ryan did not object. Dana finished her task, retrieved her laptop, opened it, signed on for Ryan, then slid it over in front of him.

"After I've spent the night, made you a delicious breakfast," he said with a grin, "you don't trust me with your password."

His reference to having spent the night made her redden. He was teasing her, she knew. But, he *had* spent the night.

"You are slowly, but surely, gaining my trust," she said with a laugh as she loaded the dishwasher. She recalled how, just last night, she'd presented a case for Ryan trusting her friend Borelli. She squirted some detergent and warm water in the frying pan. Ryan had made far less of a mess than she would have expected. Drew seldom cooked, though he always made a mess when he did.

Sometimes he complained that Dana didn't cook much either. As if it was her duty because she was the wife. She liked a guy who could cook, especially a guy who could do it without completely destroying the kitchen.

As she scrubbed the pan, he sat at the breakfast bar, scanning online news sources, checking emails.

Ryan asked if he could take a shower, if she had an extra toothbrush, that way they could go to his office without dropping by his place.

So, he *was* taking her with him.

She directed him to Mia's bathroom after finding him a new, still-wrapped toothbrush in hers, and also a plastic comb from some promo she'd picked up at a convention. She thought about offering a razor, though when she glanced at the pink and purple plastic-handled disposables in her drawer, she decided not to.

When she handed him the toothbrush and comb, she realized that his pale facial hair was barely visible, though she wondered if she ran her hand along his chin if she might feel the soft stubble. Drew would have half a beard if he missed a day's shaving. Yet, there was nothing soft or un-masculine about Ryan Kelly. He wasn't handsome in the classical movie star sense like Drew, but she was having trouble taking her eyes off of him, studying his face, his slow, careful smile, as he said, "Thank you. For having an extra toothbrush, a comb." Was it merely the newness, the absence of familiarity and history with this man, who had spent the night in her apartment, who'd made her breakfast, that had given rise to these feelings?

She listened to the water in Mia's bathroom as it rattled through the pipes. She waited for the flow to snap off before she hopped into her own shower. She dressed hurriedly, quickly dried her hair, put on the slightest touch of makeup, slipped into her jeans and T-shirt.

He was sitting at the breakfast bar, gazing intently at her computer when she came in.

"I guess you figured out the password?" She sat down. He

smelled clean, fresh, his hair damp.

He shot her a grin. "You didn't sign off. Ready?" he asked, rising.

When they arrived at his office, Dana noticed a few cars parked outside, but they ran into no one in the hallway. Ryan signed on to his computer after pulling up an extra chair for her.

They found two more fires, one in Ohio, one in Vermont, in abandoned churches, though these two had taken place over a year ago, and according to Ryan, there was nothing unusual he could see in the reports. None of these fires had been set before the main altar, and the only one in a Catholic church was attributed to painting rags thrown in the trash, along with cigarette butts, during a remodel.

Dana realized the database was strictly for the states and wondered if there had been others. Was this some international plot? Would Borelli come up with something?

As Ryan made calls, Dana rose and studied the framed photographs on the wall. Ryan, in uniform, stood with Department of Fire Services administrators and other State dignitaries, including the governor in one. He looked very official in his dark, double-breasted suit, rows of gold buttons down the front, a white shirt, black tie, a badge, insignias on his lapels, broad yellow bands on the sleeves. She had never seen him in uniform.

Maps of the different fire districts in the state covered much of the opposite wall. She stood, gazing at the map of the Boston area. Curious, she found the location of St. Lawrence's, then St. Al's, and finally St. Barbara's. In her mind, she traced a line from the location of the first fire, to the second, then the third. The path appeared to form a triangle if she connected fire one, to two, to three, and then back to the first fire at St. Lawrence's. But, if there was a fourth, maybe even a fifth fire, would this shape be altered? She was looking for a pattern in the spreadsheets, the information she and her team had collected years ago. But what if there was a pattern here? And, why was she beginning to believe there might be a pattern, rather than random destruction? She remembered several of the churches on the list she'd been working with, trying to determine where they were located in relation to these three churches. There were so many, it was difficult to do this without referring to the list, a list that would expand, she realized, when Ryan received additional information from the Realtor.

Her cellphone rang. Glancing at the screen, she saw it was Borelli. Ryan appeared to have finished his calls, so she turned on her speakerphone.

"There have been some sightings around Rome," Borelli told her. "The first late last year, one just outside the Vatican walls, this coming from what I consider a reliable source. Young men dressed much as you described. Long pale hair, flowing gowns."

"Did anyone speak to them?" Her heart thumped.

"I'm unable to find anyone who spoke with these young men. But, my friend, my source, described them holding protest signs similar to what you have described. Something about destroying the Church. Rebuilding it."

"What language were the signs written in?"

"English."

"For the tourists?"

"English, most likely the language one might choose to reach the greatest number of people in the city."

Or perhaps they were Americans, Dana considered. "But, no recent sightings? And no fires reported in churches in Rome?"

"The most recent sighting was several months ago. I believe in the spring. I did some checking on my own, walking around the city to various religious monuments and churches, but nothing, no one as described by your Fire Marshal. And, no fires."

"Nothing from within the Vatican?"

"I haven't heard back from my source within the Vatican," he told her. "I'm not sure that I will. My recent marriage hasn't particularly ingratiated me with those positioned in the *upper echelons*." She could almost see him finger quoting the final two words. He paused, then said, "I will continue in my attempt to find something for you. Hopefully, before there is more destruction."

"Yes, hopefully before," Dana said, realizing Borelli, too, thought there was more to come.

"This reference to where it all began?" Borelli asked. "You are aware of the great significance of your reporting in Boston . . . this was instrumental in finally getting the Catholic Church to take a look at the true situation, the evil of what had happened to many children, the Church's failure to acknowledge what had taken place for so many years."

Dana took a deep breath, fully aware that Borelli was acknowledging their work had done some good. Though the Church had been slow to respond, defiant even, the *Globe's* stories about the abuse and coverup forced the Church to consider the evil that had taken place, the harm this had done to so many. And Borelli had also hit on something that Dana, too, had considered. *This is where it began.* Was this why the fires had been set in Boston and nowhere else? Would this destruction spread? Would it reach the upper echelons? The Vatican? St. Peter's? Was this just a prelude?

"Thank you," she said.

"Yes, of course. I'll be in touch then," Borelli said. "I will continue to look into this situation with the angel arsonists."

Angel Arsonists? Is this what they were dealing with? "I would appreciate that," Dana replied.

As they left his office, Ryan told her he'd learned nothing from his calls, that he'd left several messages. They talked about her conversation with Borelli, and Dana suggested that maybe this reference to *where it all began* was not the abuse itself, or the coverup, but the uncovering of the coverup. "This is where it happened. Here in Boston. Our investigation, our writing about it in the *Globe,* was the beginning, finally, of a true effort to uncover the abuse, to begin to seriously address it within the Church."

"So, this might just be the beginning?" Ryan asked. "There will be more at other locations?"

"I don't know. If the fires are beginning here in Boston, then why are these young men protesting, as far as we know, only in New York and Rome?"

"New York? Largest U.S. city? More exposure? Rome? The headquarters of the Catholic Church?"

"But, the fires? Will they reach the upper echelons?" she asked.

Ryan raised his shoulders but didn't reply. There was more to come. They both sensed that. But where? And when?

CHAPTER TWENTY-SEVEN

"Got the Realtor's list," Ryan said, checking his phone as they pulled out of the parking lot at his office. "Looks like a number of churches are still on the market."

"Let's go back to my place," Dana suggested. "We can have lunch, try merging this new list with the one we've been working with."

Back at her apartment, Dana reheated their leftovers for lunch. They spent the afternoon going over the lists, combining them, talking over what Borelli had shared. Ryan received a couple of callbacks on the inquiries he'd made that morning from his office. None of this information led them in any particular direction.

"As far as choosing the churches," he said thoughtfully, "abuse having taken place in each—that seems to be a factor—and none are presently being used, which means there is easy access without having to dodge parishioners, priests, laypeople involved in caring for these buildings. This group has purposely, I believe, not targeted churches that are currently being used for services."

Open the door and see all the people . . .

"No one has been hurt," Ryan added. "These are empty churches."

Dana realized how important it was to Ryan that no one was physically hurt, especially if his brother was involved. Yet, Dana knew that many *had* been hurt. She had seen it up close. Innocent victims, even as protection was extended to the abusers. Then the coverup. Slowly, as these atrocities were revealed, members began to leave the Church, angered and disillusioned. Yet, many devout Catholics still practiced their faith, still attended Mass, and remained faithful. They wanted to see this through, wanted the Church to accept responsibility, to heal, to become whole again.

Ryan glanced at his watch and said, "Let's go get something to eat." He told her about a restaurant recommended by one of his investigators, a place serving great Thai food that was some distance from Dana's apartment.

They took her car as they had when they drove to his office. Ryan told her he'd parked several blocks from her place. She'd commented that he'd probably be stripped, booted, or towed by now, and he just smiled and said he knew a secret parking spot where he could park as long as he needed.

As they hopped in her car, Dana realized they had spent the past twenty-four hours together, mostly working on the story, but they had also gone to dinner, he'd spent the night, they'd had breakfast together at her apartment, gone to his office, and then back to her place for a lunch of leftovers. Now, a second evening together.

The food at the restaurant was wonderful, the atmosphere comfortable with wooden tables and hand-carved chairs with plump, comfortable cushions. Service was quick. Too quick, Dana thought as they lingered over their meal, sipping tea. She wanted more time. To sit and enjoy a conversation that had nothing to do with fires. She sensed they both needed this break.

They talked about Mia, Dana sharing her concerns about letting her spend the weekend with a friend. As Dana spoke of Mia, she realized her mom was probably right about Dana spending too much time alone. Until Mia arrived, she had gotten used to being alone. Open a can of soup for dinner or grab a prepared dinner from the freezer. Mia had changed her life.

Ryan told her how much he missed his daughter, that he often felt as if he hadn't been present enough as she was growing up. Their server checked on them regularly, Dana aware he was eager to free up more space. It was Saturday night, all tables filled, servers scurrying about, taking orders, delivering food, quickly picking up plates.

"I'd like to meet her," Ryan said. "I'd like to meet Mia."

Dana wondered what they would think of one another. "I'd like you to meet her too," she said, wondering if she'd feel differently if Mia were her daughter, then wondering what Mia and Meagan were doing at this very moment—eating pizza and posting photos on their social media sites?

They talked about growing up in Boston, how Ryan had always been a big fan of the Red Sox, how he clearly remembered her dad, even though, after a life-changing injury, he'd gone on to journalism when Dana was still in grade school. She told him about going to games with her dad after that, sometimes with her brothers, sometimes just Dana and her dad.

"You still make it out to Fenway?" he asked.

"Not like when Dad used to take me," she said, feeling the loss again even after so many years.

"We should go," he said.

To Dana, an invitation to Fenway was near sacred. She wanted to reach out and touch him and say, *you can't make that offer unless it's more.* "We should," she said. Was she ready for more? She felt a knot of tension tighten in her stomach, then slowly release when he smiled at her over the table.

"I've enjoyed the last couple of days," he said, reaching for her hand. "Thank you."

"Me too," she replied. Their server checked on them again, asked if they'd like dessert.

"I'm good," Dana said, glancing at Ryan who nodded. The server offered to bring the check.

After he left, Dana said, "I think he's trying to get us to leave."

"I'm feeling comfortable right here," he said, "but, yes, I suppose we should." He glanced toward the door where a line of people waited to be seated.

When the server delivered the bill, they both reached for it.

"I'd like to pay," she said, even as Ryan's hand enclosed hers in an attempt to claim the check. "You paid last night."

"Yes, I did," he replied. "I take it you're not a woman who feels the man should always pick up the bill?"

She laughed nervously, embarrassed by the fact that she'd actually laughed. "No, I believe in equality in a relationship." *What did I just say?* She thought. *Did I just use the word relationship? But, what is this? What are we doing here?* Was the same thought going through his mind?

"Please," she said formally, and he nodded in agreement, slowly releasing her hand.

As they left the restaurant, Dana wondered if she should offer to drop him off at his car, but at the same time, she considered suggesting they go over those files and lists again at her apartment. *We need to consider this or that,* she rehearsed the words in her mind, attempting to think of something to warrant his coming up. Then as they got closer, she blurted out, "Why don't you stay again." She kept her eyes on the road as they took her exit.

"No offense," he said, "but your sofa isn't the most comfortable place I've ever slept."

"You could . . ." She couldn't offer him Mia's bed. Her hands tightened on the steering wheel as she glanced over, eyes on him now. The way he looked at her . . . She felt herself grow warm as the words were coursing through her head. *Bedroom eyes.* "You could stay in my room."

"Then where will you sleep?" he asked with a slow, subtle smile. They pulled into her garage and parked. She turned again and looked at him, neither speaking. Then, he touched her cheek. Her heart was beating much too fast.

"It's a big bed," she said, the words slipping out cautiously as if she was giving this considerable thought. "Big enough for two." She took a deep swallow of air, not believing she'd made this offer. No taking it back now. She wanted him to stay.

His hand, still touching her cheek, moved slowly and cradled her chin, and then he lifted it to the perfect angle, looked into her eyes, and he kissed her. Sweetly, then deeply. Her body quaked. It had been so long. So long since she had felt such intimacy.

Silently they took the elevator up to her apartment. Her entire body shook as she unlocked her door. He took her hand and led her to the bedroom.

"Are you going to talk to Zac tomorrow at his grandma's?" Meagan asked Mia as they lay in bed, neither able to sleep, "about the room where they were sleeping when Joel disappeared?"

"I'm not sure I feel comfortable doing that."

"Maybe it could come up naturally in conversation. You're walking by the back of the house—didn't you say that's where he parked his car? And then you say, 'Oh, is that a bedroom? Is that where you stay when you do an overnighter at your grandma's?' "

"Yes, that sounds like something that would spontaneously pop into my head," Mia said, and then, "Why don't you come with me?"

"Sunday dinner at Grandma's house? You are kidding? That's a family thing."

"I'm not family."

"Sure you are," Meagan said and laughed. "Remember, you're Zac's cousin now." She laughed again, then said, "Let's go downstairs, finish up that pizza." Her father had ordered a large pepperoni and olive that evening, and there was still plenty left. He seemed pleased that the girls had spent the afternoon at the library, though Meagan had told him they'd gone for some art books for their school project. They'd lugged in a pile of books as proof.

"Sure," Mia replied. "I'd go for some pizza."

"What happened?" Ryan whispered, running his hand along the scar on her stomach. They had made love with few words, frantic at first as they undressed one another, then slowly, his hand skimming her body with the lightest touch as they began, his tongue exploring, passion rising, Dana overcome with a hunger she thought had been lost forever.

She was still thin enough that she was not ashamed of her body, and yet, it was a roadmap of her life. The stretch marks from giving birth to her lost child. These would have been evident in the light, but she hadn't flicked it on when they'd entered the room, hands occupied, flying over each other's bodies, undressing one another. They had made love in the dark.

But the scar. Even in the dark, his hands moving over her, it was evident, a ridge, a welt, the scar that she'd had no need to explain to anyone, hidden beneath her clothes. A scar that might attest to her willingness to get involved in danger without much of a second thought. And yet, wasn't this the true danger? The emotional vulnerability. Inviting a man into her bed.

He'd asked before he entered her if they needed protection, and she'd wondered if he thought she could still get pregnant. Of course not, she'd thought, but said, "I haven't been with anyone." She had meant to say *in years*. But it stopped there.

"It's been a while for me, too," he'd said as his hands caressed between her legs, sending a shock through her entire body.

And now, after making love, as he held her, she felt safe, comfortable, yet at the same time completely exposed.

"What happened?" he asked again, a whisper, his fingers tracing along her scar. "I want to know everything about you."

So, she told him about Prague, which, in a quicker version, she'd already shared. She told him about what had happened, how she'd been shot.

His hand continued, carefully, cautiously, stroking her body as they spoke, the rhythm of his touch feeling so natural and right.

"Does it hurt?" he asked.

"It did," she said, "when it happened. Have you ever been injured?"

"Never been shot," he said. "A few sprains. When I was younger, a few scrapes when I was playing sports."

"You're in a dangerous occupation. Ever been burned?"

"I've always been careful," he said, and she wondered if he spoke of more than fire, and she thought how odd it was that this is what had brought them together.

221

Kelly Jones

After a moment, he said, "I like this. I like being here with you. Being close. Together. Talking."

"I like this, too," she whispered.

The following morning when she woke, he was sitting, back to her, on the edge of the bed. She knew it was midmorning, from the angle of light filtering through the window, outlining his body. She could see the well-toned muscles along his shoulders, his arms.

He was studying the picture on the nightstand. Joel.

"Your son," he said.

"Yes," she replied and knew this was one of the reasons she'd never brought anyone to her bed. There had been quick, meaningless affairs. But, never here. Never in this room. "I often wonder what he would look like now. Every couple of years, I get a sketch, an updated, age-enhanced portrait, and I wonder . . ."

"If he's still alive," Ryan said, continuing to study the photo.

"Sometimes," she said. "Yes, sometimes."

He glanced back and reached for her hand. She thought he might say something about his brother, but he didn't.

"I have an obligation this morning," he finally said, turning fully. He had a fine pale fuzz along the upper portion of his well-muscled chest.

"An obligation? You've got a date?" She laughed as she sat up, gathering the blanket around her. They had been uninhibited in their lovemaking, blankets thrown about the bed. But, now, in daylight, she felt modest and shy. Where did they go from here? Was this a mistake?

"A date?" He smiled slowly and said, "It's my week to take Mom to church. Since she moved in with Julie, she could take her, but Mom likes to stick with the old schedule."

"So," Dana said, "you're just up and leaving. No time for breakfast?" She had nothing to feed him anyway—he'd used all the eggs in his omelet. Which made her realize this was their second morning here at her apartment together.

"Would you like to go with me?" he asked.

222

She hesitated, then felt her mouth turn down into a grimace. "To take your mother to church?"

"Too soon?" he asked with a grin, and something about the way he said this, his tone, she knew that this wasn't the end.

"Yes, too soon," she said. She realized they had already gone to church together, an intimate act in itself. Coming before God together. Even though it was all in the line of duty, doing research at St. Lawrence's. But, with his mother? Too much. Too soon.

He reached for her, touched her face, and she thought she must look awful. But, the way he gazed at her, she could see he didn't think that at all. "I like the way you look in the morning," he said. "I like a girl with a natural, honest, unvarnished look."

"Unvarnished?" she said with a laugh. She'd never been called unvarnished before. She wasn't even sure what that meant, but it made her smile, and when he kissed her, she knew it was a compliment.

"I should brush my teeth," he added apologetically.

"You know where your toothbrush is," she said. He had a toothbrush at her house already, and she liked that.

"In Mia's bathroom," he said.

"Maybe you'd best move it in here." She pointed toward the door of her own bathroom.

He sat for another moment, then leaned in and kissed her again. Then he rose and started down the hall, wearing not a stitch. He returned, full-frontal now, holding the toothbrush. "I should probably take a shower before I pick up Mom."

Dana felt herself blush at the thought that his mother might smell the sex on him. Would he tell his mother about her? Surely not the fact that they had slept together, but maybe something like, *I met a girl.* Should she tell her own mother? *I met a guy.*

"Sure you don't want to join me?" he asked slowly, touching her again, running his finger softly over the top of her breasts where she'd pulled the sheet up to cover herself. She felt an electric bolt shoot through her.

"Not for church," she said, "but I probably need a shower, too."

CHAPTER TWENTY-EIGHT

Dana seemed in a particularly happy mood, Mia noticed, when she picked her up at Meagan's. Maybe she had needed a break, some time alone. Mia knew that Dana was used to having time to herself. Maybe this had been good for them both.

Dana came in to meet Meagan and her dad, who said it was a pleasure having Mia for the weekend, that they would love to have her again. Dana said maybe next time Meagan could spend the weekend at their place.

Mia liked that Dana was calling it their place, that she'd offered Meagan an invitation.

On the drive to Zac's grandma's house for dinner, Dana asked her about the weekend and seemed perfectly content with her vague description of the dinner Meagan's dad had made them, their trip to the library to work on a project, then pizza Saturday night.

Dana seemed interested, though not as intent on gathering up every little detail as she had during previous conversations. Something had happened over the weekend that had made Dana seem much happier than usual, much more content and carefree. Much less inclined to pick apart every little particle of Mia's life.

Mia was curious, so she asked, "What did you do over the weekend?"

"Mostly worked on a story about some church fires," Dana replied.

"I heard one of the girls at school talking about a fire in a church that had been closed down," Mia said. "There was another fire?"

"A couple of smaller fires."

"Was anyone hurt?"

"No one hurt."

"Well, that's good."

"Yeah, good," Dana replied, but she was smiling in a weird way that didn't seem to fit into a conversation about fires.

When they arrived at Dana's mom's, they parked out back, and Kiki rushed out to greet them, grabbing Mia's hand, telling her again about her upcoming birthday. Mia glanced over, eyes quickly darting along the back of the house. A room jutted out from the back, but it looked different than it had in the articles she and Meagan had studied at the library. There was a row of trimmed bushes in front of the window. She was sure they were not in the photos they'd seen at the library. The windows were even different, more substantial than those in the room years ago, which seemed more like a screened-in porch. Yet, Mia was sure this was the room where Joel and Zac had been sleeping.

When they stepped inside the house, Mia glanced over at the door leading to the room. It was closed. She wondered if it was locked.

Kiki took her Aunt Dana's hand, and together the three of them went down the hall to the kitchen. After being greeted by Dana's mom, Mia offered to set the table. Soon she heard a car roar up to the parking area in the back of the house. She glanced out the window and saw Zac pull in, hop out of his car, and swagger toward the back door. He wore his baseball cap turned backward.

"Hi," he said, giving his grandma a hug, throwing Mia a friendly smile. "What's for dinner?" He took a sniff.

"Fried chicken," Ann said.

"My favorite," he replied, giving her another squeeze as she grabbed his cap and removed it. Playfully he grabbed it back, held it in front of him, then set it on the kitchen counter next to a stack of mail.

225

"I hear you won the game," Ann said.

"Sure did," Zac came back, even as he threw another grin toward Mia, his dimple deepening.

Mia remembered what Meagan said about Zac being popular, about being surprised that he had suffered such trauma as a small child. Did Mia really want to delve into this? What might it do to Zac, especially if they found something they didn't want to find? What if they discovered Joel was dead?

She had to believe that the police had done a thorough investigation. And didn't Dana's job as a reporter mean that she knew how to investigate? What could Mia and Meagan possibly discover that the professionals hadn't?

"You ought to come to one of my games, Grandma," Zac said.

"I don't know," Ann replied as she lifted several pieces of fried chicken with a fork out of the biggest frying pan Mia had ever seen. She placed them on a platter. "They're always so late, and it's such a drive into town." She handed the plate to Zac. "I don't like to drive at night anymore."

"There's a home game Friday," Pammie chimed in. "We could come pick you up."

"It's quite a drive back here, and don't you usually go for pizza or something after?"

Jeff said, "I could pick you up after work, Mom, then you could spend the night. Zac can bring you home on Saturday."

"What do you say, Grams?" Zac said.

"Well, I might just consider that," Ann replied thoughtfully. "Thank you for inviting me, Zac."

After their dinner of chicken, cheesy potatoes, homemade rolls, green beans, angel food cake, and family chatter, Mia mostly just taking it all in, Zac asked if she wanted to go for a walk.

She glanced at Dana, who said, "Go ahead. I'll help Mom, and Olivia and Quinn can help out too. As I recall, you and Zac did the cleanup last time."

So, they took off, passing through the kitchen. Again, Mia glanced over at the closed door just before they stepped outside.

"You coming to the game Friday?" Zac said.

"I'd like to. I'll check with Aunt Dana."

Zac shot her a look like *did you just call my aunt Aunt Dana?*

Mia laughed. "I told Meagan we are like cousins since I'm living with your aunt."

"Meagan, hmm?"

Mia nodded.

"My mom was asking about her, said she's at St. Gertrude's now. You friends?"

"We've been hanging out. I like her."

"I never really knew her when she was at my school."

"She's had some stuff to deal with."

"Like?"

"I guess we all have stuff."

"Yeah," he said.

They walked out to a vegetable garden, which Mia hadn't noticed before. They sat down on a concrete bench. Mia thought about being back home this time of year. They would be getting ready to harvest the grapes. "I like this time of year," she said.

"Why's that?"

"We harvest the grapes, begin the process of making wine. It's a fun time of year with festivals, celebrations, and excitement. A real sense of achievement."

"You miss your family?"

"It's just my dad and grandma. We send emails every couple of days, but with the time difference, we don't talk that much. My great-uncle lived with us for a while. But, yes, I do miss my family, my friends." She told him a little about her family, the girls at her school back home. "What about you?" she asked Zac. "What's your favorite time of year?"

"I guess I like the fall, too. Football season."

Just like a guy, Mia thought, *tying his life to sports.* "Back home, we're into football, soccer as you Americans call it. But, it's all through private sports clubs, not the schools."

"I'm not much into soccer anymore." Zac got up from the

bench and walked over to where a thick, leafy green vine ran across a patch of dark earth. He knelt down. Half a dozen pumpkins still clung to the vine. Zac turned one over. Someone had carved a name into it. ZAC.

Mia got up from the bench, walked over to Zac, knelt beside him, and gently turned another pumpkin. KIKI. They found two more. OLIVIA. QUINN. Mia thought of Joel, the missing boy, the lost cousin. There should have been one for JOEL, too.

"Grandma makes one for each of us every year. If you carve the name when they are small, it grows as the pumpkin grows. Doesn't do it any harm. We get to take our pumpkins home for Halloween. Then she makes pumpkin pie out of the others for Thanksgiving. Do you like pumpkin pie?"

"I think that's an American thing, too."

"So, I guess you won't be going home for Thanksgiving?"

"Nope, and my family is coming here for Christmas."

"That'll be fun. We always do the big holiday meals here at Grandma's. You think your family will come here for Christmas dinner?"

"We haven't talked about that part of the holiday."

"I hope so." He motioned to Mia, and they started back to the house.

"Where do you stay when you come to your grandma's?" Mia asked as they approached the house.

Zac shot her a puzzled look. "What do you mean?"

"Do you ever do sleepovers?"

He didn't answer right away, but then he said, "Not anymore." He stepped up on the back step. He paused, continued into the house. Then almost as if he were trying to tell her something, almost as if he knew she already knew, he opened the door to the room. A sewing machine stood in one corner, shelves with some fabric on one wall, some cupboards on the other, an ironing board set up near the window.

"There used to be a bed right there," Zac said, pointing. "That's where I used to stay. Joel and I slept in that room, but it isn't a bedroom anymore. And I don't spend nights at my grandma's anymore."

Mia stood gazing into the room, then glanced at Zac, but his expression was unreadable. She couldn't believe he just talked about Joel. *He remembers something.* She was sure he did. This *was* the room where they were sleeping when Joel got abducted. Zac closed the door. Footsteps sounded from above. They heard laughing, then some playful shouts. The others had gone up to the rec room to play games.

"All the bedrooms, other than my grandma's, are upstairs," Zac said. "Sometimes Olivia spends the night, sometimes Quinn. I'm old enough now I stay home alone if Mom and Dad are out of town. Not that they go out of town very often. I haven't spent the night since . . . well, a long time ago."

Mia bit down on her lip. *He remembers something.* She didn't say anything more, but she took a deep breath. *Zac remembers sleeping in the bedroom at the back of the house.* The room now used as a sewing room. There was no longer a bed in the room, but she was sure that Zac had a memory from that night. Maybe it was buried deep inside him. Maybe someone just needed to bring the memory back.

"I hope you know you can talk to me," Mia said quietly as they stepped into the kitchen.

Zac glanced at her but said nothing.

CHAPTER TWENTY-NINE

Ryan called Sunday evening and told Dana he'd enjoyed the weekend, that he'd like to get together again soon.

"We're reviewing a new training program, and I'll be tied up all day tomorrow," he said, "likely most of the week. How about coming to my place tomorrow for dinner?"

His place? There was nothing she wanted more right now than to spend time with him in a way that had nothing to do with the story she was chasing. Nothing to do with fires in churches. She had barely been able to get him off her mind since spending the weekend together.

But, she was thinking of Mia, too.

"Why don't you come here for dinner," she said. "You can meet Mia."

"You're ready to introduce me to *your girl*?"

"I am," Dana replied, even as she wondered—is this a good idea? If Mia were her daughter, would she be thinking about this in a completely different way? *Too soon*, she thought, remembering how she'd reacted when Ryan invited her to go to church with him and his mother. But Mia *wasn't* her daughter. How would Dana introduce him? As the Fire Marshal with whom she was collaborating? Surely not as the man she'd slept with while Mia was away.

"How about 6:30?" she said, even as her mind shifted to another question, mentally spinning through a number of recipes her mother had given her when she got married. She'd done more cooking back then, at the beginning.

"How about 7:00?" he replied. "I'll have trouble getting away any earlier. Busy week, and I have been, well, spending time on . . . I've been thinking about what we talked about Saturday night . . . well, honestly, I've been thinking more about what we *did* Saturday night."

Neither of them said anything for an uncomfortably long time. She heard nothing but breathing, his, and hers. Finally, she said, "Me, too. That was fun." *Fun?* That didn't sound like the right word, but she couldn't put words together that would come close to describing her feelings about the intimate moments they had shared.

"I enjoyed it," Ryan said. "I'd like to spend more time . . . well, more time with you."

"Me, too," she said. And then, awkwardly, after another stretch of quiet, she said, "Have you thought any more about my doing the story?"

"One, two, three," he said, "just the facts?" It didn't appear she had offended him by switching the subject so abruptly, so clumsily. They had both confessed they hadn't been with anyone for a long time, which she took to mean this was something new and important for him, too.

"Yes, just the facts," she replied, "but I would like to include the photo taken at St. Barbara's, a still shot from the newscast." She paused, giving him time to respond, but when he didn't, she said, "I'd like to present what we've got to my editor."

"Why don't you write something up. Let me take a look."

She was about to say, *this isn't how we do it; we don't run a story by the subject of an interview to get his approval. If he talks, we can print.*

She'd been doing this long enough to understand the meaning of *off the record* and knew at times it was an understanding, rather than specifically verbalized. But, approval over the content or wording of an article? This wasn't something she did.

"Will you give me a statement?" she asked. "A quote?"

"A quote?" he answered. "Like?"

"Like, according to State Fire Marshal Ryan Kelly, fire investigators have found similarities in how the three fires were started, though he is unable to share specifics on the ongoing investigations. He believes, based on these similarities, ties could be made to the same perpetrator or perpetrators, and arson is being considered. He asks anyone with information or knowledge of the person in the photograph to contact him. Then, something like, the person in the photo, Kelly emphasized, is not a suspect, but merely a person of interest."

"If I read that," Ryan replied, "I'd automatically think, *oh, yes, definitely a suspect, just don't want to put an accusation out there.*"

"The photo doesn't show the man's face."

"Why don't you put something together. I'll take a look tomorrow."

"Okay," she said reluctantly.

"See you then."

The following day, after Mia left for school, Dana took off for the market to buy groceries. She'd decided to make her mom's recipe for Bar-B-Q ribs. She could do them in the slow cooker so she wouldn't be scurrying about in a frenzy at the last minute. She'd make her mom's scalloped potatoes, too. She could do that ahead, stick them in the oven just before he was scheduled to arrive. She'd pick up a nice loaf of bread, fresh vegetables for a salad. What about dessert? Should she try making a pie? No, that would be pushing her luck. Then, she remembered she had one of her mom's raspberry pies in the freezer. She'd thaw that out.

At home, she assembled the sauce for the ribs, and threw it all into the slow cooker, then took off for her office, spending the morning going over notes with Brenda, sensing Brenda's frustration with Dana's lack of enthusiasm for their eldercare story.

"How do you see this story developing?" Brenda finally asked.

"We need to go deeper," Dana replied. "Find an internal source, someone ready to talk. If we are just talking to those who have suffered the abuse, their families, we're not going to get anywhere."

After they talked about the possibility of finding a past employee of one of these eldercare services, Brenda returned to her desk, and Dana sat, unable to concentrate, thinking of Ryan and the story she really wanted to write. Her thoughts turned to Mia. If Dana introduced Ryan as the Fire Marshal with whom she was working on a story, would Mia find it odd that she had invited him to dinner?

Her story? Their story? With three fires in Catholic churches, someone might take notice, get a jump on the story. But, what *was* the story? She was chasing a story on which she herself did not have a solid grip. She doubted anyone outside of Boston had taken notice since nothing had been made of the similarities in the fires, one that hadn't even been reported, and it didn't appear this was happening anywhere else.

With her eldercare notes still scattered about her desk, she quickly typed up an outline to show Ryan. She emailed it to her personal email, then deleted it from her computer.

"I think we should take Zac into that room," Meagan said. "That's where Joel was abducted. If he's going to bring up a memory, that is the place where it is most likely to happen."

They were on the bus, headed home. Meagan's dad had driven her to school that morning, so they hadn't been able to talk until now. They'd eaten lunch with Marley, and Mia wasn't ready to bring her into their circle of what she was beginning to think of as a circle of intrigue.

Mia felt a tightening in her chest. Meagan had said it could be dangerous trying to pull up repressed memories. Was Meagan considering trying to hypnotize Zac? "If there are memories," Mia said thoughtfully, "wouldn't the police, the professionals, or his therapist—"

"Sometimes, memories might come back or can be altered as one matures. Maybe something Zac saw or heard didn't make any sense to him at the time—he was only four."

"You think he might remember something that he'll understand now that he's older?"

"Such things have happened." Meagan sounded like she knew what she was talking about, but Mia wasn't sure.

"You think he's hiding something?"

"No, not on purpose," Meagan replied. "But, if he feels he can trust us, if he understands we are on his side."

"What do you mean *side?*" Mia asked.

Meagan didn't answer, but Mia could see she was thinking, considering how to reply. Maybe she *didn't* know what she was talking about.

Mia said, "His grandmother still lives there. How are we going to get around that? It's not like we are going to bring her in on this."

"We have to do it at night. It happened at night. The article said her room is at the other end of the house. Maybe she won't know we are there."

Mia swallowed hard. "You want to take Zac and sneak into his grandma's house? But if she hears something, if we sneak in, if it's night, it might scare her."

"True," Meagan said thoughtfully.

"And we still have to get Zac on board. I don't want to trick him into doing this."

"You have to talk to him, then," Meagan said.

"I don't want to hurt him."

"He needs to get this resolved himself. He was there. He's got to have some survivor's guilt." Meagan was talking like a shrink again now, Mia thought. Maybe this was dangerous. They were a couple of kids, amateurs. Yet, Meagan had all those books from her dad . . .

"But, if we find something, discover something, if we find out Joel is dead," Mia said. "Maybe not knowing is better." The bus stopped; a passenger got on. An old man with a cane made his way down the aisle and sat across from the two girls, the only empty seat on the bus. "I imagine his grandma locks the door at night," Mia whispered as if the man might be eavesdropping. "She lives alone."

"We'll have to figure out when she is going to be gone," Meagan said as if carefully constructing a plan. "Don't you think Zac's dad has a key to grandma's house?"

"Yes, maybe. You want Zac to sneak the key?" They were getting ahead of things now, Mia thought with a tightening in her chest. Leaping forward with this crazy plan, if it really was a plan. Mia stared out the window, the knot in her chest tightening, then dropping and exploding with a rumble in her gut. She turned to Meagan. "His grandma said she doesn't go out at night, that she doesn't like to drive at night." It sounded like Mia was trying to talk herself out of this, but then she had a thought. "Zac invited her to the game Friday, and Zac's dad said she could spend the night, go home the next morning."

"So, she won't be home Friday night?" Meagan asked, a mixture of surprise and delight in her voice.

"I think she is considering," Mia said slowly, "though she didn't actually say she'd go."

"That'd be perfect," Meagan replied.

"It would," Mia's said, but her head was spinning as they arrived at Meagan's stop. Zac's grandma lived some distance from Boston, and they would have to figure out how to get there. She patted Meagan affectionately on the knee before Meagan stood and made her way off the bus, turning once, throwing her friend a conspiratorial smile.

When Mia got home from school, the place smelled delicious with an aroma that hit her as soon as she walked in the door. Dana scurried about, humming cheerfully. When she turned, there was a big grin on her face.

"Smells good," Mia said. "What's for dinner?"

"I've invited a friend," Dana said. "Well, a person, a man, with whom I'm collaborating on a story."

"Kip?" Mia asked, wondering if she'd misjudged Dana's and his relationship. But then she remembered Kip had gone out of town for a while.

"No, not Kip. Someone . . . he's the Fire Marshal . . . we're working on the story about the fires."

"Oh, yes," Mia said, curiously. "Do you need some help?"

"No, I've got it all together. Maybe help set the table later. We're eating a little later than usual this evening. Are you hungry? Maybe have a snack?"

Dana was talking fast, tripping over her words, almost stuttering. But, she was smiling. Nervously smiling, Mia observed. Something was definitely going on.

"Sure," Mia said and grabbed an apple out of the fruit bowl and went to her room. She threw her backpack on the bed, hung up her sweater, then glanced over at the file cabinet. She knew more now about what had happened to Joel since she and Meagan had done their research at the library. Should they really continue with this? She pulled a book out of her bag and settled down on her bed to read. She thought about what Meagan said, that the police knew more than what was in the papers. But, she also knew if they had discovered Joel was dead, that would have been reported.

There was still hope.

Later, after Mia helped an increasingly nervous yet excited Dana set the table, the buzzer announced their guest. Within minutes the Fire Marshal arrived. Dana introduced him, and Mia tried not to make it too obvious that she was attempting to determine what was going on between the two of them. He was a nice-looking man, about Dana's age, and he had a friendly smile, a pleasant voice, broad shoulders, and just the right amount of unassuming swagger and confidence. He presented Dana with a small bouquet for the table. She blushed when she said thank you, then reached up into the cupboard, fumbling to find an appropriate vase. It was pretty apparent to Mia that he wasn't just a collaborator on a story she was writing.

It was the best meal Mia had had since she moved in with Dana, who seemed more relaxed as they eased into the dinner. Ryan complimented Dana several times and asked with genuine interest about Mia's life in Italy, her family, her school. He told her he had a daughter in college and asked Mia if she'd decided where she was going to university. She said her father was hoping she'd be back home for at least a year or two, but they both agreed that the best opportunities for further education were probably in the states, at least for graduate studies, though she hadn't decided on a major field of study.

All through dinner, Dana and the Fire Marshal exchanged smiles, laughing nervously. *Yes, something going on here*, Mia mused. She liked the impression he was making, and Mia hoped she was interpreting correctly that Dana and Ryan were doing more than researching a story.

After loading the dishwasher, she excused herself, saying she had homework when she just wanted to gracefully exit so Dana and Ryan could have some time alone, so she could talk to Meagan about their plan.

When she came back into the kitchen about an hour later to get another piece of pie, Dana and the Fire Marshal were sitting side by side, gazing at Dana's laptop as if they truly were working on something. Yet, they were sitting very close, much closer than would have been necessary to each get a clear picture of the computer screen. And, the Fire Marshal's hand was planted firmly on Dana's thigh, though he withdrew it quickly when they finally noticed Mia had come into the room.

CHAPTER THIRTY

Tuesday morning early, Dana went in to see Mac with the story that she and Ryan had agreed on. Ryan had training sessions again that morning and told Dana it would take all day, that he would call later. She was aware he'd set up a special meeting at 6:00 A.M. with the investigators who were working the Catholic Church fires. He'd never shared how much he'd told them about her, if he'd told them anything about what they had discovered, though they had agreed on the quotes that would appear in the story, so she knew they were aware he was releasing information to the press. There would be nothing on their forensic conclusions, though the article would state the Fire Marshal had discovered similarities in the three fires. They had agreed they wouldn't bring Gabe into the conversation, but they had also agreed, if they found evidence that he was involved, Ryan would not withhold this information.

"This is . . ." Mac hesitated after he'd quickly scanned Dana's story. He took a slurp of his coffee. Dana hadn't filled her office cup, eager to present her piece as soon as she arrived. "Three fires?" Mac looked up, catching Dana's gaze.

She told him about her belief that these fires might relate to the past abuse in the Church, that there was credible evidence of abuse in all three churches, and then she paused for a moment to allow Mac to consider that this might tie in with one of the biggest stories the *Globe* had ever published. "We have no evidence of this," she said. "Merely a theory, so we're including none of this now."

"You've no concerns the story is premature?"

"We're *concerned* there might be more fires. If we can prevent another fire, we certainly want to do that."

Mac rubbed a finger thoughtfully over his brow. "*We?* You've brought someone on to help with research?"

"Not yet. The Fire Marshal's been helpful." Dana shifted uncomfortably, feeling an intense heat shoot up from her chest and settle on her cheeks at the mention of Ryan. Mac, rereading the article, didn't seem to notice.

When she added nothing more, he looked up, a troubled crease pinching the bridge of his nose. "This person of interest?"

Dana told him there had been sightings of someone who looked similar to the person in the photo in or near the buildings at the time of the fires. "We are not including this information in the story either. Not yet. Sources are not particularly reliable," she added, "so, we're running nothing at this time. But, here—" she tapped the photo. "We want to put this out, see if anyone comes forward with information that might be helpful."

"This State Fire Marshal? I assume he's a reliable source."

"Yes, of course," Dana answered, but the thought in her head—*I'm sleeping with my source.* Nothing had happened last night after dinner. She'd have loved if he'd stayed, but they both agreed this wasn't something either of them wanted to make public—well, Mia was hardly public, but for now, neither of them wanted to announce that they were . . . what? *Dating?*

Ryan had made it clear he wanted to spend more time with her. "Mia staying with a friend this weekend?" he had teased when Mia went to her room to study. Then he had kissed her, hungrily, as if there was something urgent and forbidden in their being together.

Now, as she sat going over her story with Mac, she could hardly keep Ryan out of her head. She could barely speak of him, even using the title *State Fire Marshal*, without thinking about his touch, their lovemaking. His smile. The way he looked at her.

"The photo's from WBZ?" Mac asked.

Kelly Jones

"I've cleared that. No problem using it."

"Should you be teaming up with one of our crime reporters?" he asked.

"Will you give me some time on my own on this one?"

Mac considered for several moments. "You'll need some help if it goes in the direction you think it might."

"Yes, I know, but for now, let's just put this out—online this evening, print tomorrow. See if we get any response. If we get something helpful, yes, I may need some help then."

Mac took his time to reply, and Dana thought he might not agree to her request, but then he said, "I take it you want off the eldercare story."

"Maybe find someone to help Brenda." Dana wondered if Brenda had said something about her less than enthusiastic attitude.

Mac nodded. "Heard anything from Kip?"

"He's straightening things out. Working on it."

"Good, good," said Mac. "Let me know . . . we can get you some help." He shot her a puzzled look, but she sensed he would wait. They both stood.

"I'm good," she said. "For now."

Dana had attempted, without success, to contact some of the abuse survivors who'd spoken to her years ago, though most of the information she had was outdated. She'd spoken briefly with the sister of one of the victims, who'd told Dana her brother would not speak again to anyone about what had happened to him. The sister refused to give any current contact information.

Yet, Dana wondered if those who had set the fires were victims who had never come forward with their accusations. Like Ryan's brother, Gabe. Something told her these fire starters were not on any of her lists.

She'd been successful in scheduling a meeting that morning with one of the founders of SAVA, Sexual Abuse Victims Advocates, the organization she'd mentioned to Ryan. She wanted to know if they had any knowledge of a group of young men, survivors also,

240

who had opted to take a different route. Several support groups had been formed over the past decade, mostly after the *Globe* series came out. Most were founded on basically one goal—healing for the victims—but this objective veered out in a variety of different directions: accountability, change within the Church, punishment, which always included substantial compensation. The latter had garnered controversial responses, particularly after SAVA had been accused of kickbacks and financial corruption.

J. B. Patterson, the man she was meeting with, was one of the early members of SAVA. Many years ago, when Dana first spoke with him, the young man was infused with such hatred and bitterness, it seemed as if healing would be impossible. She had interviewed him shortly after he had come forward, and it was a painful experience for them both. Kip had been there too, and now she thought with affection about how kind and thoughtful Kip had been.

When Dana arrived at the SAVA office, she realized it had been years since she'd seen J. B. When they met, he was merely a boy. He was now a man. As a victim, he had pulled himself up out of the hole of despair and abuse, and had thrived as an advocate for others.

He invited her into his office and gestured toward a chair where she sat.

"I'm not clear what you're looking for," he told Dana. She'd been vague during her earlier phone call.

"I hope you might be able to help me," she began. "I know there are several groups that have been formed to advocate for abuse victims."

"Yes," he replied, then added, "with varying degrees of success. Those who advocate for healing, who distance themselves from the factions that merely exist for punishment, are generally the most successful." After a beat of silence in which he seemed to be gathering his thoughts, he said, "You're not here to talk about the accusations of corruption within our organization?" He shifted in his chair, back stiffened as if prepared to defend himself.

Dana and her team had done a story on just that subject, though she had not personally interviewed J. B. then. These accusations were still being investigated by law enforcement. In a way, she was surprised he agreed to see her.

"No, that's not why I am here." She gazed around the room. Neat and tidy, nothing on the desk, no stray files stacked on bookcases or cabinets. J. B. wore a perfectly pressed white shirt, blue silk tie, no jacket, though there was one hanging on a hanger on a coat tree in the corner. His hair was neatly trimmed, and she imagined he was a man who never appeared to need a haircut, who scheduled such grooming so regularly and precisely it looked the same from day to day. "Have you been approached by a group," she started in, "or have any knowledge of a group whose purpose is to destroy the Church by—"

"There are factions whose purpose is solely to destroy," he broke in before she could finish. "That is not our goal."

"I understand that," she replied carefully, keeping any form of accusation out of her voice. "This group I speak of, I believe. . ." She hesitated because she had little evidence. "There have been a number of fires recently. In empty Catholic churches."

"St. Barbara's?" he asked. Dana knew this was the only fire that had any noticeable media coverage. The brief *Metro* bleep, reporting the St. Al's fire, would likely have been missed by a casual reader. There was no public report on the fire at St. Lawrence's.

"There were others?" he asked.

"There will be a story in the *Globe* tomorrow. Going online this evening. There have been three fires, three churches."

He didn't ask her to name the churches but asked, "You believe this has something to do with our organization?"

"Not your organization," she replied, "but, possibly, these fires relate to the abuse within the Church."

"Retaliation?"

She considered how much to share. "I believe their goal is to destroy the Church, then rebuild it." She stopped, paused. J. B. seemed to be considering this.

"There are probably more victims wishing to destroy the Church rather than rebuild it. You believe this can be done?"

"This group is rather unusual in that . . ." Dana always stayed clear of giving her own opinion during an interview. It tended to have unintended results, often turning off the interviewee or thwarting the desired openness. She knew when the photo came out in the paper, the picture of the possible angel arsonist might, hopefully, elicit a response from a potential witness. Her email address would be included in the article, and she was trying to get ahead of all that. She guessed she would be sifting through a barrage of responses, some hateful, some hopeful, but very few helpful as she had learned through past experience.

She pulled out her phone, clicked on the video of St. Barbara's and showed J. B. the crowd gathered on the night of the fire.

He studied it carefully and requested she play it again.

"What am I looking for?" he asked.

She didn't want to do what she had casually accused Ryan of doing—leading the witness. "Do you recognize anyone?" she asked.

"Neighbors out in the middle of the night? You think the perpetrator is here?" She didn't answer and he smiled and said, "You see that on TV dramas. The arsonist hanging around."

She nodded. "Maybe in real life too." She wouldn't home in on the suspected angel terrorist in the photo. Not just yet.

She sat, trying to come up with something else, something that might trigger a response, more information, a lead. "Have you had anyone come in seeking help, who, well . . . is there anything unusual about . . ." She considered saying something about the unusual dress and appearance, but she didn't want to plant anything, particularly an image, in his head.

"We are all considered unusual," he said sadly, and she knew this was true. So many of the victims had felt they were different, odd, with something deeply flawed in their very being that had made them targets for this abuse. J. B. rubbed his head, then ran a hand over his temple as if to straighten his mussed hair, which wasn't mussed at all. "May I look at the video again."

Dana replayed the video. Now, she stopped when it came to the frame with the young man with the long hair, dressed in what appeared to be a nightgown.

J. B. studied it carefully, then glanced at Dana and said, "There were two young men that came in to see me, maybe about a year ago."

"Yes," she said hopefully. "Can you tell me something about them?"

"They both said they had been victims. I told them what we might offer in the way of healing, and one said, 'the healing can only begin in the way that Christ began.'"

"Did he explain what that meant?"

"I believe, yes, we spoke of Christ's love for all. How the Father had sacrificed his only son."

"Was there something specific that they requested from you?"

"I'm trying to recall. I think they said it began with the cross. That we must begin as Christ founded his Church on the cross."

"The cross?"

"Yes, but I must admit I didn't fully understand why they had come to me."

"They did not attempt to solicit your help in any kind of. . ." Again, she hesitated. "Destruction?"

"Honestly, I do remember how I found the conversation somewhat difficult to follow. I don't recall any specifics on destroying anything, and certainly nothing about setting fires. I would have reported anything threatening to the police." Again he brushed a hand over his neatly trimmed hair. "I believe I suggested they meet with one of our lawyers, and then the one young man who had done little if any talking . . . yes, it was just one who carried the initial conversation, and the quieter one, the one who had remained silent through the early part of the conversation, became angry."

"Angry?"

J. B. nodded. "He said something like, 'There is another way. The lawyers are just in this for the money.'"

"Another way?"

"I'm trying to recall. I don't believe there was any suggestion of violence. Nothing that would alert me to contact the authorities." J. B. fingered a pen standing upright in a rectangular leather box on his desk. He lifted it, clicked nervously, and returned it to the holder.

"Anything else you could share with me?" She wasn't ready to give up. "The young man in the photo I just showed you?"

He hesitated for another moment of consideration, then said, "The two men, they looked very similar." He stopped.

"Similar to the man in the photo?" she prodded carefully. "Or similar to each other?"

"They looked very similar to each other," he replied. "Almost like twins. But I don't think they were. It was something they had done to look alike."

"How's that?"

"They each had long, pale-colored hair. It wasn't natural, so I know it was something they'd done—dyed their hair so they would look alike. But, not loose, like the person in the photo." Again, he stopped to consider. "Pulled back," he said, "in a ponytail."

"Could either of them have been the person in the video I showed you?"

He glanced again at Dana's phone, but the screen had gone blank. Dana tapped it back on. "This person is turned away from the camera, the face not visible, but perhaps a similarity."

"In their dress, their clothing? The men who came to see you?"

"If they wore garments like this, I would have taken notice." He smiled. "So, no, the way they were dressed was not unusual."

"Did they meet with the lawyer?"

"I could check some of my records, my schedules. I do keep very good records."

Dana had no doubt he kept records, and she felt a nervous twist in her stomach, as if a physical knot had tightened in her gut.

"Let me check with our lawyer to see if I can release any of this information." He was quiet for several moments before rising and then walking her to the door. "It is our policy not to release any information without the consent of our clients," he added solemnly.

On the way out, Dana realized that J. B. had already released some valuable information, but she guessed she would not hear from him again. When she got to her car, she called Ryan, getting only a recording. She left a message, telling him she had something to share, something that might be important. She was sure that someone from the angel arsonists group came to SAVA and spoke with J. B. Were they looking for more members but had stopped because they could see he was not interested in anything that might involve forceful change?

Mia and Meagan talked again about their plans on the way home on the bus. They had reviewed several possibilities during their long phone conversation the previous night. They'd decided to bring Marley in on the plan—mostly because she had a car—but they hadn't explained the details to her yet. They had invited her for a sleepover Friday night, though they were still working on the logistics of this.

"We need to verify that Zac's grandmother is going to the game," Meagan said, "and if she plans on staying in town with Zac's family, and then we need to convince Zac that he's got to go into that room at night. Then we tell our parents we are staying at each other's house Friday night so we can stay out late if we need to."

"I'm not sure Dana will agree to let me stay at your house again. Remember, she told your dad you could stay at our place next time?" Mia swallowed deeply as she considered this proposed deception. "But," she added, considering another possibility, "I think she's got a boyfriend, and maybe she'd like some time alone with him. If we come up with a good reason for me to spend the night at your house, she might not object."

"We could tell Dana we're working on our school project—our Art History, Head Start outreach—and we're using books that are at my house, and there are too many of them to cart over to the apartment. And too heavy. Those art books with the paintings we need to study are huge. Very heavy." Meagan grinned.

"That sounds lame," Mia said, but she smiled, too. "All those paintings are online now."

"Lame, but good enough if she wants some time alone with her guy."

Both girls giggled.

"I've been thinking," Mia said, "The only way to make this work is to tell Zac the truth. You said he has to trust us."

Meagan nodded silently.

"Here's what I'm going to do," Mia said, but at that point, they had arrived at the stop where they parted ways. "I'll call you tonight," she said quickly. "I've got a plan, but I have to call Zac to figure it all out."

Meagan shot her a puzzled look as she headed toward the door of the bus, holding her fingers up in a *Call me* gesture.

Dana got up to heat water and make a cup of tea, then returned to the breakfast bar where she'd spread out a city map after her meeting with J. B. at the SAVA office.

She stared down at the crisscross of streets and highways that made up Boston, again tracing a line from fire A to fire B with her finger like she'd done in her mind along the map on the wall of Ryan's office. Then she lifted her finger and placed it on the location of fire C, St. Barbara's.

She thought of Ryan. She'd called him again and left another message. She knew he was reviewing new training sessions all week, so she told herself not to panic, forced herself to quell the nervous flutters rising inside her. Yet, she knew these feelings were only partially related to the story they were chasing. This rush of adrenaline, or hormones, or whatever it was, felt unfamiliar and odd, in a way that was both pleasant and frightening.

She thought back to her marriage. It had been good in the beginning. After they lost Joel, they had each suffered in their own way. But, it seemed, never together. She'd pushed him away. He'd gone outside the marriage. After the divorce, she'd become involved with men, short-lived affairs without emotion. Was Ryan Kelly a man with whom she could have a true relationship? There were so many things she liked about him. Yet, this mixture of comfort and apprehension was something she couldn't ignore.

She heard the key in the door and looked up to see Mia lugging her overstuffed backpack into the room.

"I won't be home for dinner this evening," Mia announced.

"Oh?" Dana carefully folded the map she'd been studying. She didn't want Mia to ask what she was doing. She didn't want anyone to know until she shared this with Ryan. But, she could tell by the sheepish way Mia set her backpack on the floor, then stood quietly, staring down, that she had no interest in what Dana was doing. Mia had something else on her mind. "So, what's up?" Dana asked.

"Well," Mia started in, glancing up but not meeting Dana's gaze directly, "you remember when I told you Zac had asked for my help with his French?"

Dana didn't remember Mia mentioning this, but she nodded as if to say, *yes, go on.*

"We're getting together tonight. He's got a big test coming up, and I told him I'd help him study. He's got practice after school, so he said he'd just run by, pick me up, then we could grab something to eat and go study."

"Oh, okay," Dana said. She wanted to ask where they were going to study, but she didn't. She'd have to trust Mia here.

"We will probably go to the library. Or maybe a coffee shop. Someplace close by."

Dana thought of suggesting they study here at the apartment.

"We won't be late. We both have to be up early."

"That's nice of you to offer to help Zac. This won't interfere with your own studies?"

"No. I'm fine. I've got some homework, but I should be done by the time Zac picks me up if I start now." She reached down for her backpack, hoisted it to her shoulder, and headed toward her room, Dana wondering what she was up to. *Quit it*, she told herself. What Mia said made perfect sense.

*   *   *

Later, after Zac had dropped by for Mia, thrown Dana a quick hello, and the two left, Ryan Kelly called.

"The story is online," he said bluntly.

"This is what we agreed on," she replied. "I guess I should look again to see if there are any comments." She'd checked shortly after it posted, finding no comments.

"A few," he said. "Nothing very nice."

She turned on her iPad, clicked on the site, and read. He was right—only three comments. One said, *They ought to burn them all down.* Another, *Evil begets evil. Burn in hell.* The third comment said, *The Catholic Church is the devils church.* Oddly, Dana wanted to insert the apostrophe.

"I went to talk to one of the board members of SAVA," she told Ryan.

"SAVA?"

"The organization that advocates for victims."

"Oh, yes, you were telling me about that organization. Did you learn anything?"

"I'm not sure." She told him what J. B. had shared with her.

"So, there are more men involved. It is a group."

"It seems it is, but he didn't share much that might help us locate any of them. He said he'd call if he learned anything, but then he told me it is their policy to allow victims to remain anonymous until they are ready to share."

"Sounds reasonable."

"It does. I haven't heard back from him. I'm guessing I won't."

"Maybe something will come up after the story appears in print tomorrow."

"Maybe," she replied, then, "I have something I want to show you."

"What?"

"It's a visual. I can't explain it well over the phone." She wanted him to come over, but her reasoning was not invented to lure him over—she did have a visual she wanted to share, and it couldn't be done properly over the phone.

"Let me get something to eat, then I'll drop by."

"I've got lots of leftovers," she said. She'd cooked enough ribs to feed an army.

"That was really good. Dinner last night."

"Come by. We'll eat leftovers. I have something to show you."

Zac and Mia grabbed some fast food, ate in the car, then stopped at a coffee shop that was practically empty. Zac had brought his laptop and some assignments that his French teacher said they should review for the test.

When Mia had texted Zac earlier that day, still on the bus, after she and Meagan had parted, the opportunity had practically fallen into her lap. She was trying to come up with some reason to get together that wouldn't involve telling him the real reason she wanted to talk. She had to do this face-to-face. Then he'd mentioned his French test, and now here they were, sitting at the coffee shop side by side.

Mia said, "There's something I want to talk to you about."

"Can you say it in French?" Zac teased.

"I probably could," Mia replied. She glanced around the coffee shop and was glad there was no one there. She'd decided she was just going to be honest, tell him what she and Meagan were up to. If he hated her, that was going to be okay. If he agreed, maybe they could help Dana. Maybe Zac could remember something.

"Is your grandmother going to the game Friday?" Mia asked.

Zac laughed, then said, "I find you Italian girls very confusing. Not that I know any other Italian girls."

Mia took a gulp of coffee. She really didn't want any coffee, she was full of fries and soda and a cheeseburger that seemed to be sitting heavy in her very nervous gut, and now the caffeine was making her jittery, but she thought it would be rude to use the coffee shop to study if they didn't buy something.

"She is," Zac said. "Mom told me Grandma is coming to the game."

"Is she going to spend the night at your place?"

Zac nodded, obviously confused. "Is this going somewhere?"

Then Mia started throwing it all out there, how she'd found the articles in Dana's files, how she and Meagan had talked, how they thought maybe Zac had a memory of what had happened, how Meagan suggested if he went to the room where it had happened, at night, he might remember something.

Zac listened, eyes narrowed, nervously pinching his lip, but it didn't seem he was angry. Then he said, "Meagan?"

Mia nodded. She could barely breathe, the words had come out of her so fast, so furiously.

Finally, Zac said, "I heard she hypnotized Becket." His lips twisted in a weird way, and he blinked several times as if he was thinking this through.

Mia nodded again, and then she started to cry. She didn't know why, but now, after she'd told him their intentions, it sounded stupid and cruel. She didn't want to hurt Zac. She didn't want to do anything that would harm him.

"It helped," Zac said. She could see her crying made him uncomfortable, the way he was biting down on his lip, and she sensed he didn't know what to do or say, so she tried to stop, finally wiping her eyes with the paper napkin. "I don't know what she told Becket," Zac said, "but he's been playing like crazy bad. That means *good*. He's on fire. It's like really weird. Good weird." Finally, he reached out and took her hand. "Please don't cry. I know you just want to help Dana."

"Do you think Joel is still alive?"

"I have to," Zac said.

She stared at him, eyes locked. She thought he was going to cry too, and she didn't want him to. She should never have started this.

"I have to," Zac said again. "I have to believe he's still alive."

"We do," she whispered, an enormous lump lodged in her throat. He was still holding her hand, then massaging it gently.

"I have to believe he's alive," Zac said, "because if I don't, everything that happened is all my fault."

CHAPTER THIRTY-ONE

"If I trace from Fire A, St. Lawrence's . . . ," Dana said, placing a yellow marker on the map, then glancing back at Ryan, who nodded but said nothing. "To Fire B, St. Aloysius," she added as she drew a line connecting the two points. Again, her gaze shot back to Ryan, and she could tell he was still with her, still receptive. *Thank you*, she thought, *for not saying the shortest distance between two points is a straight line.* "Then fire C." She drew another line straight down from St. Barbara's on the map, perfectly intersecting the first line.

"A cross?" Ryan asked skeptically. "You are suggesting the next fire will be at—" He touched the map at the exact point where Dana had ended the second line.

She clicked on her laptop and waited a moment. The updated database, which she'd set up on the screen before Ryan's arrival, listing the empty churches, along with their addresses, popped up. Ryan skimmed the list until he found the address that matched the location where Dana had lifted her marker to indicate where she predicted the next fire would take place.

"St. Judith's?"

"Yes."

"This is one of the churches on the list sent by the Realtor, recently added to your original list?"

"It is."

"Explain," he requested.

She told him what J. B. from SAVA had shared with her, what the two angel-men had told him about the cross. "They said it would begin with the cross. That we must begin as Christ founded his Church on the cross."

"It is a possible theory," he said thoughtfully, rubbing his chin. "Something to consider. A theory. But, a valid theory?" He studied the map, a contemplative crease between his brows. "So, we put a guard, an investigator, at this church every night until—" She heard a roughness in his voice, which she interpreted as doubt, and when he glanced back, she saw the same reservation in his eyes.

"I think I'm on to something," she defended herself.

"I'm playing the devil's advocate here," he said.

"Interesting choice of words," she replied. She thought of Borelli, who had at one time served as the official devil's advocate for the Vatican. "Let me show you something else," she said. She clicked on another file, and the calendar with each of the three fires marked with an X lit up on the screen.

"The dates of the fires," he said thoughtfully.

"Yes," she replied. "All of the fires have occurred at night, toward the end of the week, each confusingly straddling from one day to the next. Two of the fires were reported on a Saturday morning. It's possible a fire could be started on one day, not reported until the next."

"This is true," he agreed.

"Every one of these fires was possibly set on a Friday, and if we go back to the theory of the cross," Dana said, throwing it out slowly. "What significance does Friday have in the liturgical calendar?"

"No meat in the olden days," he offered, "because Friday . . ." He paused to consider. "The day that Christ died." His eyes darted from the screen to Dana.

"In June," she continued, "the first Friday of the month is June second, the date of the fire at St. Lawrence's."

"Assuming the fire was started on Friday, not Saturday."

"If we accept the fires all started on Friday, then July 14, the date of the fire at St. Al's, would be the second week. And the fire at St. Barbara's, Friday, August 18," she added, "is the third week of the month. If we are looking at September, September 22 is the fourth Friday, and if we accept the theory that this is based on the cross, it will be at St. Judith's."

For several moments he did not respond. "It's a neat little package," he finally said. She couldn't read the tone of his voice, couldn't determine if he was considering her theory or if he thought it was ridiculous. *Neat little package?* She guessed he was leaning toward ridiculous.

"There's a definite pattern," she said. "First Friday, second Friday, third Friday—"

"Yes, a pattern," he said slowly.

"As a firefighter, you rely on patterns, fire forensics rely on things like burn patterns and—"

"Well, yes, but that's science."

"And this is religious mumbly jumbly," she replied testily, using the words Ryan himself had used when describing the message imparted by the angel-man he'd spoken to in New York.

"Well, yes," he said, shoulders raised, but he chuckled, obviously aware she'd taken these words from him. "You said you have some leftovers? I'm starving. I think better on a full stomach."

Dana stepped to the fridge, pulled out the leftovers, and arranged them on the small kitchen counter. She felt a little angry, and yet she knew what she had presented would take some consideration. It was reasonable that he would question her theory. What she had just put forward was a bit like something out of *The da Vinci Code*.

Ryan got a couple of plates out of the cupboard. She motioned for him to go ahead. He loaded his plate. Dana spooned up a helping of leftover potatoes on hers.

"Mia's not here for dinner?" he asked.

Dana gestured for Ryan to place his plate in the microwave. "She's studying with a friend." Her words came out with an unexpected tone of concern. She set the microwave timer.

"That's good," he said, throwing her a glance. "Isn't it? She's studying."

"I think so."

"You're not worried about her studies, her grades?" Ryan asked. The microwave beeped, and he took his plate out, then inserted hers. She set the timer again.

"No, it's just that I sense something is going on. She's studying with my nephew Zac."

"That's a problem?" She could see he didn't get it.

"I just wonder if there is something romantic going on."

"That's a problem?" he asked again.

"Zac's a nice boy," she said, "I guess if they got involved . . . but, I just don't know if I'm supposed to handle this like I'm her mother."

"She's how old again?"

"Seventeen."

"Then that's all set by now."

"You mean her moral compass, or whatever we call it?"

He smiled and nodded. When the microwave beeped, she motioned toward the dining room where she'd set out the placemats, silverware, and napkins. They carried their food in and sat.

Ryan lifted his ribs and took a big bite.

"I'm being ridiculous." She laughed nervously. "I mean about Mia and Zac?"

"Probably." He wiped some sauce off his chin with his napkin. "This is really good."

They finished their meal with no further discussion about Mia and Zac or Dana's recently presented theory. As she stared at him across the table, she thought about the night he had spent at her apartment. The second night.

He threw her a seductive grin as she stood, gathering the plates. He touched her wrist, then rose and put his arms around her, nuzzling into her neck. "What time is Mia getting home?" he asked.

"I don't know," she replied, her face growing warm, feeling

completely helpless and defenseless with a plate in each hand, yet at the same time secure and safe in his arms.

"Let's go take a look," he said after a moment, releasing her, taking one of the plates.

"A look?" She asked as they returned to the kitchen and loaded the dishwasher.

"St. Judith's. It's perfect timing. All the fires are set at night."

"Then, you are considering what I've just presented?"

He raised his shoulders, smiled, but offered no verbal confirmation.

"I'll send Mia a text, let her know I'll be out for a bit."

By the time they arrived at St. Judith's, the sky was pitch black. Dana turned off her headlights as they pulled slowly up behind the empty church. It was a large, ancient-looking structure constructed of sturdy red bricks. By the design and size, Dana knew it was one of the earliest churches built in the Boston area. They got out and Dana wished she'd thought to grab a jacket. Summer, though officially not over for a week and a half, was waving farewell. Ryan sensed her shivering and took off his jacket. As he draped it over her shoulders, he leaned into her and kissed her.

After several moments, he drew back and said, "Guess we should take a look."

They started around the building. "Do you know that early Catholic churches were always laid out in the form of a cross?" he said. "The Apse located at the cruciform, the two transepts forming the right and left arms of the church. The nave where the congregation gathers, then the narthex at the lower end."

"How do you know all that?" she asked. *Who is this man?* she asked herself.

"Lots of years in Catholic grade school, then serving as an altar boy. I also took a class in Art History, and one unit was dedicated to early Christian architecture."

"You do not cease to amaze me," she said with great admiration. "Art History?"

"Yep."

A man who eats vegetable lasagna, then digs into a stack of meaty ribs with gusto. A man who obviously works out at the gym. A man who studies Art History and Christian architecture.

"A cross? You do see the symbolism in my suggestion?" she said after a while.

"Christianity is thick with symbolism. It might, indeed, play a part in the destruction of the Church."

"Or possibly the rebuilding?"

Ryan tried the door on the side of the church, rattling the wooden frame as he tested it. Dana thought it might give and admit them, but it did not.

"You think an advance team of angels has been here to scope out the next target?" she asked.

"Possibly." They found a window, the location suggesting it opened into the sacristy, and Ryan had much better luck in prying it open. "I'm going in, and then I'll come around, see if I can open a door for you." She thought of St. Al's, Ryan lifting her up to access the window. This one looked much more difficult, much higher.

"Okay," she said.

He reached into the inside of his jacket, which became an intimate gesture as it was Dana who now wore the jacket. For a moment, his hand rested on her hip, then slid up her torso. He kissed her once more before extracting his cellphone from the inside pocket of the jacket, which rested against her breast. "You've become somewhat of a distraction," he said.

"Just here to help." She gulped, feeling a heat spread through her body.

Reluctantly he turned, clicked on the phone flashlight and shined it into the window. "Go around to the side door and wait for me." Within seconds he had pulled himself up and was gone.

She started around. The streetlight, about half a block away, offered little illumination. A vehicle pulled into the parking lot behind the building, squealed, and pulled out, startling Dana. Were they being followed? No, probably just some kids.

She arrived at the side door. She waited. About ten minutes later, concerned that Ryan hadn't come to let her in, she started back to the window where he'd entered. Her cellphone, in the back pocket of her jeans, vibrated. She pulled it out and clicked on a message from Mia.

I'm home. Going to bed. See you tomorrow.

Then she noticed an email had arrived from Borelli. She opened it.

"*I have acquired access to potentially useful film from a surveillance camera in St. Peter's Square. I have attached,*" he wrote. Dana's heart thumped, even as she guessed it was digital, not actual film, unless the surveillance system at the Vatican had progressed as slowly as the Church itself. She scrolled quickly but found no attachment. Suddenly, she felt a hand on her shoulder. She turned. Ryan stood beside her.

"I was unable to open the door from inside," he said. "Would have required a crowbar. I took a quick look around."

"Did you hear a car pull in behind the building?" she asked.

"Did you see someone, notice anything suspicious?"

"They left quickly."

"Yes, I heard it. Probably some kids. Empty parking lots are great for having a little fun."

"Kids, yeah, that's what I thought. If someone was following us, they would likely attempt to be more discreet."

"Yeah," he said vaguely, then noticed the phone in her hand and gave her a squinty look.

"Borelli," Dana said. "He sent me an email, said there was an attachment, but there wasn't."

"Did he tell you what it was?"

"Video taken in St. Peter's Square. He didn't describe it. I'll call when we get home." She needed access to Wi-Fi for an international call. She glanced at the digital time on her phone. It would be early morning in Italy.

As they walked to her car and then headed back to her house, Ryan explained he'd seen nothing inside St. Judith's to indicate anyone had been there, searching for kindling or planning another fire in front of the altar. "Pretty much the same setup as any Catholic church and, as the other churches where fires have been set, no functioning surveillance."

Where no one was watching, Dana considered. *No one was watching out for those boys, either. No one.*

"But," Ryan said, "you are possibly on to something. The next location, the next church." He was quiet for a moment. "It shouldn't be that difficult to set up surveillance."

Back at the apartment, Dana told Ryan that she should wait to call as it was barely 4:00 A.M. in Rome. As the clock ticked away, both growing weary, she said she could forward Borelli's attachment as soon as it arrived, and Ryan decided to head home.

Two hours later, she called and got a groggy Borelli, who told her indignantly that he had sent the attachments but would try again.

"What's in the video?" she asked.

"Videos. There are several," he explained. "Young men dressed much as you described."

"In St. Peter's Square? Surely, this has alerted the Vatican?"

"I don't know that it has," he said. "With the various religious orders, both Catholic and even non-Christian groups, often in habits or robes, monks, priests, nuns, specific dress for religious orders or sects, frequently visiting the Vatican—if the Vatican panicked every time someone showed up in St. Peter's Square dressed in a robe—"

"Carrying handwritten signs?"

"Yes, flimsy cardboard signs, handwritten as those early sightings, but these were different. Not words as before. But, numbers."

"A code?"

"I believe I've figured this out, though some of the print was partially obscured. I want to see what you think." He released a muffled grunt. "I'll send them again. No, maybe I'll have to get some help. Well, dammit, I can't do it while I'm talking to you on the phone," he added before abruptly breaking the connection.

She waited, finally going to bed and dozing off.

She woke early, before Mia, but still no email from Borelli. For a moment, she feared something had happened to him but then realized if he was getting help, it might take time to find someone he could trust, though it would be midday in Italy now. She waited, spending the next twenty minutes making coffee, sorting through emails, rechecking those she'd received as a result of the online article. She found nothing helpful. She'd hoped the article might even draw out a response from one of those in the terrorist group. Would a terrorist at some time make a demand? Ryan had told her that this wasn't necessarily true. He pointed out several groups, some well-known such as the Boston Marathon bombers, who had no true agenda, no call to action, but wished merely to be noticed.

Mia was up now, eating breakfast. Dana joined her, attempting to act as if everything was normal. When Mia left for school, Dana rechecked her emails, knowing her article had appeared in print that morning. Again, the comments contained nothing helpful. She found one email with a photo attachment—Legolas from the first Hobbit movie. She studied it for some time, struck by how much Ryan's brother Gabe looked like this fictitious character.

At the end of her list of *unread* emails, she found one from a name she recognized: Laura McClellan, the daughter of Mary Cassidy, the woman she'd interviewed when she was still working on the eldercare story.

Dana hesitated, then opened it and scanned the message. Laura wrote that her mother was terribly upset about the fire at St. Barbara's. She insisted she must talk to Dana again. Though Dana was off the eldercare story, the old woman's words had never left her. *You are the woman who lost her child.*

Even as Mary Cassidy's unforgettable words pressed into Dana's head, she wondered if Mary could possibly know something about the fire at St. Barbara's.

You should not have put that priest in prison with a murderer.

Dana knew the priest Mary spoke of was Father Joseph

Jennings, once assigned to St. Barbara's parish, a priest who had abused boys. A priest who had met his demise in prison at the hands of a vicious killer.

Reluctantly, she wrote: Please let me know a convenient time to stop by for a visit with your mom.

She sat, breathing deeply, before hitting SEND.

Just as she was about to give Borelli another call, his email arrived. She opened it, then slowly downloaded the attached videos, staring in disbelief at what she saw.

Immediately, she called Ryan and told him she had to see him right away.

CHAPTER THIRTY-TWO

It was obvious to Dana, as soon as she opened Borelli's attachments, that Gabe was in one of the videos that showed three young men in robes, holding signs of protest, or perhaps warnings of what was to come.

The signs hoisted by the angels did not display words predicting the destruction or rebuilding of the Church as had been seen earlier in New York and Rome, but numbers and letters that were not complete words. In the first video, the angle of the shot did not reveal the full text, but studying the second video and then the third, Dana pieced the messages together. It was not a complicated code, and before Ryan arrived, she had identified the source. A quick flipping through her Bible revealed the threat.

On the first sign: 1 Cor 3:13:

The work of each will be made clear. The day will disclose it. The day will make its appearance with fire, and fire will test the quality of each man's work.

On the second sign: 2 Thess 1:7:

And give relief to you who are troubled, and to us as well. This will happen when the Lord Jesus is revealed from heaven in blazing fire with his powerful angels.

The third sign Dana found the most disturbing. From the Old Testament, Gen 22:2:

Then God said, "Take your son, your only son, Isaac, whom you love, and go to the region of Moriah. Sacrifice him there as a burnt offering on one of the mountains I will tell you about.

Was it possible that the angels were working up to this? A human sacrifice. *Will they listen now?* The angels seemed to be shouting. *Will they hear us now?*

When Ryan arrived and Dana showed him the videos, the first thing he said was, "It's Gabe. He's in Rome." He studied the date stamped on the video—two weeks ago—then added, "I have to find out if he's still there." He rubbed his head, took in a deep breath. "What do these mean?" he said, pointing at the signs, then instantly, before Dana could explain, "They are Bible verses."

"Yes." She showed him where she had marked the verses in her Bible. Silently, he read.

He looked up. "In the Old Testament,' he said, voice low, "God stopped Abraham before he sacrificed his son. But, who is to stop these angels now?"

"We are," Dana whispered.

Mia and Meagan's plan, which so far had come together perfectly, required that Dana didn't become suspicious. Though she had protested at first, after Mia explained why they needed to change their plan and stay at Meagan's, Dana had agreed she could spend another night at her friend's. Hopefully, Mia's dad would not call Dana, and hopefully, Marley, whose mom thought she was staying at Dana's, would not become suspicious.

Friday evening, the three girls attended the uneventful game in which Zac's team scored one single touchdown to claim victory. Marley and Meagan both agreed it was boring, though Meagan leaned over and whispered to Mia, "But the night has just begun."

Zac's grandma was spending the night away from home, Zac had managed to grab a key to her house, and the plan was to meet there after the game.

The three girls pulled up in back of Ann Pierson's house, dimming the lights and proceeding carefully, though there were no nearby neighbors and enough trees around the house, it was unlikely that anyone would see them. They sat in the car, talking little as they waited for Zac. Marley had turned the volume down on the tunes blasted through her iPhone on the car's audio system as they had pulled in, but there was an irritating little thrum coming Mia's way. She asked Meagan, who was in the front seat, to turn it off, which she did. So, they sat, waiting in silence.

"I hope he shows up," said Marley finally.

"I'm sure he will," Mia assured her, even though she wasn't sure he would.

"I'd be more concerned about a no-show if they lost the game," Meagan replied. "If he was feeling shitty about himself, he might change his mind."

The girls had opted out of pizza with Zac's family, Dana, and Zac's grandma because Mia was nervous and didn't know if she could hold it together. But, now, this put them ahead of schedule, and she was having trouble waiting, wondering. What if Zac decided not to come?

Mia opened the car door and hopped out. "Let's take a look," she said as she started up toward the back door. Meagan and Marley followed. An eerie hoot came from a nearby tree, then a flutter of wings, and Mia felt her heart leap.

"Just an owl," Meagan reassured her, even as Mia felt something dart in the dark just inches above her.

"What's that?" she shrieked, then covered her mouth.

"Maybe a bat," Marley offered. "Let's not freak out here. It's not like we're going into a haunted house."

Mia couldn't even think of how to reply. It wasn't a haunted house, but it was a house where a child had been abducted. Yet, she'd been here several times before. In daylight. It seemed different now. She noticed Zac's grandma had left the outside back light on.

Suddenly they were all spotlighted in the headlights of a vehicle as it pulled in, quickly stopping next to Marley's car.

Mia recognized Zac's car. He'd made no effort to pull in quietly and hadn't bothered to dim his lights.

The driver's side door opened, Zac stepped out, cap on his head obstructing his face. Then the passenger door opened, and another tall, broad form emerged. Zac had brought along his friend Becket without even telling anyone he wasn't coming alone.

"Becket," Meagan acknowledged him with a tilt of the head.

"Just here for support," he replied.

Zac held up a set of keys. He walked over to Mia and placed them in her hand as if she were in charge. She felt something inside her chest as hard as a brick. She swallowed, tasting her fear and nerves. "Well, let's do it," she said as if they were about to charge the castle.

When she unlocked and opened the back door, light from the porch fell into the narrow hallway. Zac stepped in first and opened the door to the left, the sewing room, hesitating not a second as if he wanted to get this over with. But then, for several moments, he stood as they lined up behind him. Eventually, he took a step, and they followed him deeper into the room.

Mia wondered if she should turn on the light. "Should we—"

"Leave the light off," Meagan broke in. Her voice sounded authoritative, yet at the same time kind, not bossy. "Let's move over toward the window," she suggested. In the dim light filtering in from the porch light, Mia could see Meagan effortlessly rearranging several items, moving the sole chair, an oversized wingback, toward the window. "Zac," she said softly, "Come sit here by the window."

He complied as Meagan motioned the others to find a place on the floor. Meagan herself kneeled beside Zac. No one spoke until Meagan said, "Let's all get comfortable." The others gathered around, huddled on the floor.

Meagan slowly pulled the sheer curtain away from the window. From her position on the floor, Mia couldn't see anything outside. Several moments passed. Mia tried to sit still, but she could feel her body twitching with nerves.

"You are four years old," Meagan said, voice soft. "You've come to spend the night at Grandma's house. You are excited." She paused, moved in a little closer to Zac, lifted his right hand and held it in both of hers. "You are happy because you know the Easter

Bunny will come as you sleep."

Stillness enveloped them all. Becket sat next to Mia, Marley on the other side. Becket was staring at Zac and Meagan. Marley glanced at Mia, then quickly back, all eyes on Meagan and Zac. The owl in the tree outside let out a low hoot.

"Are you alone?" Meagan asked gently.

"I don't know," Zac spoke for the first time.

"What do you think the Easter Bunny will bring?"

"Mommy said jellybeans and chocolate eggs. I don't like real eggs. They stink."

Becket let out a faint snort that he quickly stifled.

"Where will you find the eggs?" Meagan asked.

Suddenly, Zac stood and Meagan released his hand. He pressed his nose to the window, held still for a long moment, then stood back and pointed. "Out there. Outside."

Meagan rose quietly and stood next to him, leaning in close. Speaking softly, she asked, "Do you see something when you look outside?"

Zac took his hat off and held it in his hand. He rubbed his head, mussing his hair. "Yes."

"What do you see?" Her voice was barely above a whisper.

"I don't know," he answered.

"Can you try to remember?"

For the longest time, no one spoke. "That's okay," Meagan said, "it's okay if you don't remember."

Zac's voice, when he finally spoke again, was low, words catching in his throat. "She said, 'Joel, I want you to come with me. I have something special for you.' "

"The Easter bunny was a girl?" Meagan asked carefully.

"Not a girl, but a grandma."

"Your grandma?"

He ran his hand through his mussed hair again, fingers frantic. He turned back to the chair. He sat down. "I can't talk about it anymore," he said as he slumped, head lowered, both hands cradling his forehead.

"That's okay." Meagan spoke softly.

"I told her . . . 'I'm not Joel.' " Zac's voice was quiet, too. "And she said I have to go back to sleep."

"You went back to sleep?" Meagan asked, voice low, followed by a long stretch of silence.

When it was obvious that Zac was finished, that he would say nothing more, Meagan spoke to him in a whisper that no one else could hear, then took his hand and walked him to the door. Mia sat on the floor, paralyzed, until Meagan glanced back and gestured for the others to follow. Mia left the room last, closing the door, then locking the back door of the house after they had all stepped outside.

Even the night air was still now, as if the birds and bats were in awe of what had just transpired.

What had just happened? Mia wondered. Zac had remembered something from that night. It was not a man, but a woman who had taken Joel. She thought about what Meagan had said about survivor's guilt. The woman had specifically come for Joel. But why? Why did she not take Zac, too? Was that little four-year-old boy, whom Zac had become tonight, feeling the guilt because he had pointed to Joel, then returned to sleep, thinking it all a dream. If he had understood what had happened, might he have alerted the adults before it was too late?

Meagan led Zac back to his car. "You drive," she told Becket as she eased Zac into the passenger side of the car. Zac relinquished his keys without objection.

Once Meagan was back in the car with Marley and Mia, Mia asked, "What now?"

"We're going to get something to eat, go get some coffee. Becket and Zac, too."

"Will Zac remember what just happened?" Marley asked. Her voice was shaky, and when she attempted to start the car, she fumbled a bit, and Mia could tell she too was freaked out by what they had heard.

"He will," Meagan said, "Yes, I believe he will."

267

"He's going to be okay?" Mia asked.

"It's a breakthrough," Meagan said calmly, nothing in her voice to indicate anything but control of the situation. "We learned something tonight that might help."

Mia wasn't sure how this would help. Even if it was true that a woman had abducted Joel, how would they find her? And was Joel still alive, or was it too late? Yet, Mia felt if a woman took Joel, a woman would not harm a child. Women who stole children took tiny newborn babies. Not to harm them, but to love and nurture them. Why would a woman take a three-year-old child?

Why would a grandma come and specifically ask for Joel?

They stopped at a coffee shop, ordered, then sat, no one knowing what to say until Zac spoke. "I'm starting to remember some stuff."

All eyes turned to Meagan. "That's good, Zac. Maybe we can get together later, see if we can come up with a plan."

Zac nodded, but said nothing. Mia had no idea what Meagan meant. Later? A plan? If what Zac said was true, they had something, but what to do with it?

After sitting for some time, awkwardly sipping coffee, eating pastries, the boys each an enormous frosted sugar cookie on top of that, Zac and Becket began verbally replaying every play of the game they had won that evening, as if that was the most significant event of the day. Mia felt something heavy and uncomfortable stir inside her. She excused herself and went to the bathroom, splashing her face with water, wondering if this had been a terrible mistake. Yet, they knew something now. She returned to the table where the others sat quietly.

After they bid their farewells and the girls drove around for a bit, they decided they would go to Meagan's, though her dad thought she was staying at Mia's.

"I'm really tired," Meagan said. "We can sneak in, and Dad won't even know we are there. He's not what you'd call a light sleeper."

"Then what do we tell him in the morning?" Marley asked with an enormous yawn and far less concern than Mia thought their dilemma warranted.

"We'll just tell him we had a change of plans," Meagan replied.

Mia was too tired, too emotionally exhausted to offer any other solution. She knew that Dana would quiz the hell out of them if they showed up at her apartment, but Mia sure didn't want to drive around all night long.

When they got to Meagan's, she was right; they didn't wake her dad. The three girls tiptoed quietly up to Meagan's bedroom.

By Friday afternoon, two days after receiving the videos from Borelli, with information provided through a request to Homeland Security, Ryan knew that Gabe had flown to Rome three weeks earlier. There was no evidence that he had returned to the States. Ryan would be leaving early Monday for Rome, so he and Dana were taking advantage of this time together. He'd asked her to spend the weekend at his place.

"Your request to Homeland Security?" Dana asked late that evening as they lay in his bed. Even without being specific, she knew that Ryan understood exactly what she was asking. They both knew if the arsonist angels were recognized as a terrorist group, it was only a matter of time before the FBI would become aware of what had taken place in Boston.

"Through a friend," Ryan answered vaguely.

With over twenty-five years as a journalist, Dana was aware of jurisdictional squabbles arising between local law enforcement and federal agencies attempting to collaborate, and she also knew Ryan would eventually be pushed aside, particularly if there was any evidence that his brother might be involved in setting the fires. Ryan was not yet ready to let go. And not yet willing to share more with Dana.

How much, if any of this, Dana considered, *should* or *could* be revealed to the public? Would she be looking at this in an entirely different light if she had not become involved with Ryan? Yet, if she hadn't, she would likely be unaware of any of this.

Saturday morning, Dana woke first and lay, studying the room, his room, trying to discover more about this man she was falling in love with. He'd made her dinner Friday night at his place, chicken parmesan, and she smiled at the realization that he was a much better cook than she and seemed to enjoy it.

Ryan's condo was smaller than Dana's apartment and decorated in a way she hadn't expected. His walls were covered with what appeared to be original art, and when she asked, he said most of them he'd picked up at outdoor markets and art fairs. His furnishings were basic—a sofa with a few pillows, a mismatched love seat, a TV tucked away in an antique armoire in the living room. Not that they'd watched any TV, but she'd asked if he had one, just because she was curious. His bookshelf was filled with classics as well as commercial fiction, mysteries and thrillers. Non-fiction on just about any topic one could imagine; geology, current events, history, politics.

His bedroom contained a queen-size bed that took up most of the room. A simple tan bedspread, white sheets with brown and navy stripes, a nightstand with a stack of books, a photo of his daughter. She was pretty and wholesome with auburn hair and a sprinkle of freckles across her nose like her dad.

When he awoke, he reached for her and pulled her closer. "I wish you were going with me to Rome."

"Me, too." She'd considered it, and they'd even discussed it. Mia could probably stay with Jeff and Pammie, but that would mean she'd be staying with Zac . . . or she could stay with Meagan. Mia was at Meagan's now, along with their friend Marley. Mia had come up with some convoluted reason they needed to stay at Meagan's again, and Dana had not objected. But now, she could hardly dump Mia again—she didn't know how long Ryan would be staying in Rome. So, he'd booked a solo flight. Dana had arranged for him to stay with Borelli and Gia.

After showering, Ryan went to fix breakfast while Dana dried her hair, then grabbed her phone and went into the kitchen. She was still getting a few comments on the article that had gone online, emails in response to the print article, but nothing leading to any answers. She lowered herself to the table.

An email had arrived from her editor Mac, asking about a follow-up on the article. Again, he wanted to know if she needed help.

There was another message from Laura McClennan. She said her mother had family visitors on weekends. Too much activity could wear her out. Could Dana come by Monday? Any time after lunch. Maybe about 3:00 was best for her mom. Dana wondered, could Mary Cassidy possibly know something about the fires? Her daughter had told Dana how upset she was about the fire at St. Barbara's.

"What do we do now?" Mia asked Meagan as she plopped a sliced bagel into the toaster. She'd pulled a carton of orange juice out of the fridge, and Mia poured each girl a glass.

"The woman who took Joel came specifically for him. If she was looking for any ol' kid, she would have taken Zac since he was the one who opened the window."

"We don't know that," Mia said defensively, though she wasn't sure why. Zac had been four when this happened, and he needed no defense.

"I thought it was pretty clear that's what happened," Meagan said, glancing at Marley, who was slumped at the kitchen table, dipping a finger into the carton of cream cheese. Meagan handed her a plate with a toasted bagel.

"I'm kind of thinking that, too," Marley said, glancing apologetically at Mia.

"If a woman took him," Mia said, "I don't think she would hurt him or molest him."

"We don't know that for sure," Meagan said pensively. "If we knew the motive . . ."

"How can we figure that out?" Marley said.

"If she specifically came for Joel," Mia said, "maybe it was revenge."

"So, maybe he's not still alive." Marley looked up from her bagel with an expression that seemed to say *I wish I hadn't said that.*

Mia couldn't let herself think this either.

"Revenge . . . against?" Meagan asked.

"Joel's dad?" Mia replied. "He's some kind of lawyer. Maybe a case went bad. But, no," she added, trying to make sense of this, "more likely Dana. She writes articles attacking different businesses or people."

"Or churches," Meagan said. "I Googled her. The big article that made her almost-famous was about priests abusing little kids, mostly boys, then the archbishop was covering up the abuse."

"That's awful," Marley said, eyes wide.

"Don't you think the cops, even Dana, considered all this?" Mia replied.

"None of that was in any of the articles we read," Meagan offered, and Mia remembered they'd talked about the police sometimes withholding information to help solve a case. Mia wondered if they should go to the authorities, but what would they tell them—that Meagan had hypnotized Zac, and he'd remembered that a grandma took Joel? Meagan had said that hypnosis could be dangerous and even bring up false memories by suggestion. But, no one had suggested to Zac that a woman had taken Joel. Zac came up with this on his own. So it had to be true. An old woman had taken Joel.

CHAPTER THIRTY-THREE

After dropping Ryan off at the airport, Dana went to her office to talk to Mac. She knew her editor wanted another story, but she didn't feel they were ready. They had no proof that the men sighted in New York, then Rome, were responsible for the three fires in Boston. She wasn't ready to share Ryan's suspicion that his brother Gabe might be involved, or that it was likely he was now in Rome, or that Ryan had taken off to find him. She knew if there was even a suggestion the fires were related to child abuse by Catholic priests, the archbishop would be breathing down her neck. She had to get her sources, irrefutable evidence, before she did another story. What would she do if it turned out that Gabe was involved?

"I'd like to wait," Dana said after Mac invited her into his office and motioned for her to sit. "We have to make sure our sources, our facts, are right before we put it out there."

"If any of this is true," Mac said thoughtfully, "if it ties in with the abuse in the Church, it could be one hell of a story. But, if you feel we are too early . . . keep digging." He shot her a puzzled look, and she wondered if he could tell she was withholding something. "I'm sensing you're not telling me everything." Nervously, she shifted in her chair, glancing down, hands clasped in her lap.

"If this goes out too early, or if we get it wrong . . ." She looked up at Mac, eyes steady.

"Yes, I agree," he said. "You've got good instincts, Dana. If you feel there is a story, see if you can get something more to verify this tie-in with the abuse. Need some help?"

"Thanks, Mac. I'll let you know."

Again, he shot her a look of concern but did not object.

After leaving his office, Dana sat at her desk, wanting desperately to talk to Ryan, to hear his voice, but she knew he was presently in *airplane mode*. Then she called Kip. Surprisingly, he answered.

"Hey, thought you were off the grid," she said.

"Had to go out for provisions."

She hoped the provisions didn't include alcohol.

"Don't worry," he said, "I'm not drinking. Going cold turkey. It's been almost three weeks now."

Three weeks . . . since Kip had taken off, since she had met Ryan Kelly.

"So, what have you been doing?" she asked.

"Hiking a bit. Reading. There are 78 books on the bookshelf at the cabin. I've read 30 of them."

"You'll come home after you've read them all?"

He laughed, but didn't answer.

"I'm proud of you," she said, sounding like a mother.

"I'm proud of me, too. Hey, I read your article, looked at the photo. What's going on?"

"So, you've got media access in your cabin in the mountains?"

"Nope, but thought it best I catch up with the real world while I'm out here."

For a moment, she wished she were in a remote cabin, too, that all of this was over, that Ryan found Gabe, that their suspicions were all wrong, that she and Ryan, just the two of them, were in a cabin in the mountains.

"That night at St. Barbara's," she said, "did you see anyone who looked like the person in the photo?"

"There were people out from the neighborhood, wearing the clothes they had slept in." He cleared his throat before continuing.

274

"I was drinking that night." He said nothing to defend himself, and Dana did not comment.

She told him about working with Ryan Kelly, what they had discovered at St. Al's, St. Barbara's, and she shared the information about Gabe, information she had not shared with her editor. She told him her theory that the next fire would be at St. Judith's, about the videos Borelli had sent, how Ryan had gone to Rome to see if he could learn more. "Mac wants another story, but we have no proof of any of this."

"We? You and Ryan? You're talking about the Fire Marshal. You're buds now?"

"Yeah," she said, and then, "I think I'm in love." She startled herself by telling Kip this; neither she nor Ryan had used that word.

"Well, that's good," he said, "Really? You're really in love?"

"I am." She smiled.

"You're smiling, aren't you?" he said.

"Yes." She missed Kip.

"I'm happy for you, Dana."

"Me too."

She realized, after they hung up, that she hadn't even told him about Drew and Amy, the baby. As she sat at her desk, staring at her blank computer screen, she realized she hadn't been dwelling on this—the fact that Drew was starting a new life. Maybe she was too. She could picture a future with Ryan. Not a child. No, never a child. But a future.

Dana arrived at Laura McClennan's shortly before 3:00, curious why her mother would want to talk about St. Barbara's. Could Mary Cassidy possibly know something about the fire?

"Thank you for coming," Laura said as she opened the door and invited Dana in. "Mom is not doing particularly well, but she insists on speaking with you."

Laura led Dana down the hall into her mother's bedroom. Mary sat in her wheelchair, an oxygen line now running up to her nose, a portable canister attached to her chair. Her head rested on her chest, eyes closed. A stuffy, unpleasant odor lingered in the air.

"Mom," Laura said gently, approaching her mother. "The lady from the newspaper is here."

Mary's eyes opened, rolled upward, and then she blinked. Slowly she raised her head and reached out for Dana, who stepped closer and accepted her hand. Laura moved a chair in for Dana to sit.

"I don't know," Mary started slowly. "Something strange happened. One day she was gone." She breathed heavily. "Broke her heart, you know." She touched her chest as if she needed to pinpoint the pain. "A mother will do just about anything when she loses a child."

Words wouldn't come to Dana. Mary's grip tightened.

"Who was gone?" Laura asked, leaning in toward her mother. She glanced back, shooting Dana a look that seemed to say, *she's not making much sense.*

"You should not have put that priest in jail with a murderer," Mary said, voice growing in strength.

What *was* Mary trying to tell her? "Why are you telling me this?" Dana finally asked.

"I don't know." Mary's eyes met Dana's and held. "I don't know where he is."

"He?"

"The little boy."

Dana swallowed. "The little boy?" She could barely get the words out. "Little boy?" she repeated, though she didn't know if the words had actually left her mouth.

"I don't know," Mary replied slowly.

An uncomfortable silence filled the stale, heavy air as Dana searched for more words.

"You wanted to talk about St. Barbara's?" Laura asked her mom. "The fire?"

"Terrible things happened there," the old woman said, glancing at her daughter, then looking directly at Dana.

"What terrible things?" Dana's head was spinning, her heart

276

thumping uncontrollably.

Mary's left eye twitched, she took a labored breath, and then something caught in her throat. She coughed, softly at first, then almost violently as she reached up frantically grabbing her oxygen line, pulling it loose.

Quickly, Laura stepped closer and adjusted the oxygen tube. "You okay, Mom?" she asked.

The woman nodded, glanced at Dana as if she wished to share more, but was incapable of continuing. A hopeless expression had spread over her face.

"Mother is very tired," Laura said, "perhaps a little confused." If she had any idea what her mother was trying to tell Dana, there was no indication, her attention now focused on her mother as she placed a protective hand on the old woman's shoulder. She turned to Dana. "Maybe you could talk some other time."

No, no, we must talk now, Dana wanted to shout, but Laura gestured toward the door. Reluctantly, Dana stood and started out of the room, glancing back once, Mary's expression vacant as Laura lovingly rearranged the blanket on her lap. Mary's words, the vagueness, the confusion followed Dana out of the room and then lodged heavily in her mind.

What Mary said made little if any sense. On Dana's first visit, Mary had clearly said, *You are the woman who lost her child.* Now, she spoke of a *she* who was gone. Then of a little boy.

A mother will do just about anything when she loses a child.

You should not have put that priest in jail with a murderer.

Later that evening at home, still rattled by what Mary had said, Dana spread the city map out on the dining room table. She studied it carefully, slowly retracing the cross she had drawn.

She placed her finger on St. Barbara's, then scanned the map, arching in a wide circle. Had Mary Cassidy once been a parishioner at St. Barbara's? Is this why she was concerned about the fire? She now lived with her daughter, and Dana knew that address would be too far away to be within the borders of St. Barbara's parish.

She puzzled over this several minutes, then turned on her laptop and Googled Mary Cassidy. She brought up several persons by that name, finding the one that most closely matched Mary's age. She checked past addresses using a people-finder service for which the *Globe* had a paid subscription. She found a list that connected Mary to a woman named Laura, not Laura McClennan, but the ages seemed to match, so Dana figured this must be the correct Mary Cassidy. A home she had owned over a dozen years ago was inside the borders of St. Barbara's parish. But, what to make of this information? Mary was upset about the fire because this had once been her parish? Yet, again, she had mentioned the priest who had been put in prison with a murderer. Dana knew this was Father Joseph Jennings, the priest who had molested boys at St. Barbara's, who had been convicted and died in prison.

As Dana's eyes again swept over the map, her phone rang. It was Ryan. In a voice weary with travel, he told her he'd arrived safely. He was welcomed by Giovanni Borelli and Gia, though he said they'd spoken little as he was tired and needed some rest, but he wanted to call her right away.

Hearing his voice, she felt a need for his physical presence, and it felt strange and unfamiliar to feel such a longing.

She told him about Mac's agreement to wait on another article and then about her confusing visit with Mary Cassidy.

"That must have been a difficult conversation," he said after she shared what Mary said about the little boy, the priest dying in prison.

"Yes, and puzzling. It seemed she wanted to talk to me about the fire at St. Barbara's. She said terrible things happened there."

"The fire? The abuse?"

"I don't know. She was obviously distraught, and her daughter suggested we talk later."

He was quiet for some time before he said, "I've been thinking about the possibility of a fourth fire. If we accept your theory of when and where, we're running quickly toward the end of the month."

"We are," she said, even as his words twisted in her mind. *We are running out of time. To figure this out before something else, something*

278

dreadful happens.

"Maybe we should tell her," Mia said to Meagan as they sat on the bus on their way to school. "Tell Dana what we've been doing."

"Maybe if we actually find something."

"Yeah," Mia said. She wished Meagan would have said *Joel*, not *something*. That made it sound like they would find only bones, decomposed body parts, a scrap of a kid's pajamas. She thought about how cocky and confident Zac seemed at times, how people could suffer unspeakable grief yet separate their lives into parts. Go on as if everything was normal. Take Dana; she'd lost her child, yet most of the time she was just a normal person. Mia had lost her mother, and it hurt so much, but she'd gone on with her life. So had her dad. People were resilient. Everyone suffered loss, and yet many overcame the grief. Others were haunted forever. She studied her friend, thinking how Meagan had been deserted by her mother. Maybe this was more difficult than a mother who had died.

The two girls sat quietly as they pulled up to the bus stop near St. Gertrude's.

Images of Zac's grandma's house, Sunday dinners, joyful little Kiki, an innocent child, played through Mia's head. The pure untainted joy of a child whose life had not yet been touched by grief. A child who had two fathers, but never a mother. "I just thought of something," Mia said as the two girls hopped off the bus and started toward school. "It's likely that whoever took Joel changed his name."

"This is assuming he's still alive," Meagan said, and Mia could tell she was trying to keep the emotion out of her voice. "You don't give a kid a new name unless you plan on keeping him."

"A kid might accept some lame brain reason for changing his name, but, not his birthday. You can't change the day you were born." Mia told Meagan about Kiki, how the first thing she told Mia when she arrived for dinner at Grandma's was the day of her birthday as she issued an invitation to her party. "A kid never forgets his or her birthday. He might hold on to his birthday. And

279

the kidnapper might think, well, what's the harm of that?"

"So, what do we do with this information?" Meagan asked.

"You know how you see on social media where adopted kids are looking for their birth families?"

"You think we should post this information? Do you know Joel's birthday?"

"It was in the papers I found in the file cabinet," Mia said, thinking. "And Zac mentioned it too." She'd talked to Zac a couple of times since Friday night, and though he'd agreed to get together with Meagan again, he seemed to be making excuses . . . practice all week, an away- game Friday night. "We post something, say he was raised by an old lady. Maybe she told him she was his grandma."

"What if the old lady who took him sold him or gave him away?"

"Well, then he's still alive." Mia gave this more consideration. "And maybe he has some memories of who he was before he was taken."

Meagan didn't respond, and Mia wondered if she regretted what they'd done to Zac, was thinking they should drop the whole thing. "Let's do it then," Meagan said, and her lips lifted slowly and cautiously into a tentative smile. "Let's post something with the information we have. Joel's birthdate."

The next day, Dana called Laura McClennan to ask if she could visit her mother again and was told the doctor had suggested family only. "Your visit seemed to have upset her terribly," Laura said.

Well, it was your mother's request that I visit, Dana was tempted to respond, and your mother has upset me terribly too.

"You said your mother was concerned about the fire at St. Barbara's," Dana replied, "but she said little about this when we talked." She let the words hang openly. Though not in the form of a question, surely Laura understood she was asking one.

"It was our parish," Laura said, "for many years."

"So this upset her, the fire?"

"It did," Laura said. "She seems to be replaying her past right now." Laura might have added, *she's preparing to die,* but she didn't.

After she hung up, Dana wondered if this was all there was to Mary's concerns. Yet, her references to a *she* who was gone, a lost child, a murdered priest. Did Mary Cassidy know more about the fire at St. Barbara's, something Dana and Ryan had not considered?

Ryan called again the following day. He told her that Borelli had been taking him around the city to locations where the angels had been sighted, though they had seen no one and found nothing. "Giovanni is still attempting to find a source within the Vatican to determine if there has been any communication from the Archdiocese of Boston or anyone taking credit for the fires."

"I'm not sure how reliable those old sources are."

"Yeah," he agreed.

"Your investigators' surveillance at St. Judith's has produced nothing?"

"Nothing. Have you heard from SAVA, the victims' support group?"

"No." She told him about her most recent call with Laura McClennan, that the doctor had restricted her mother's visits to family only. "Not making much progress here, either. I'd hoped that first article might produce something, a sighting, maybe even a message from one of those involved in starting the fires. With a statement, a motive, maybe a demand."

"A manifesto?" he asked, and she knew this was a term used to describe the Unabomber's writings. The bomber had requested his beliefs about the evils of technology be published in exchange for an agreement to cease his bombings. The identity of the Unabomber had eventually been revealed through information provided by his brother. With the angels, there was no known manifesto. But there was a brother.

"Or, maybe like Luther," she said, "posting the *Ninety-five Theses*, the beginning of the Reformation."

"I think these arsonists are talking more in terms of destruction and rebuilding in a physical sense."

"Maybe it's simply an act of revenge. If we knew exactly *why* they are doing this—"

"Sometimes there is no why."

They were both quiet, and then he said, "Giovanni suggested we come together for a visit after all this has settled down."

"That'd be fun," Dana replied. She wondered why Borelli would issue such an invitation, what Ryan might have told him about their relationship. That it was more than a professional, working relationship? Obviously, he'd said something.

"I wish you were here. Rome's a great city. And Giovanni and Gia are great hosts."

"I wish I was there, too."

When she returned to her apartment that afternoon, Dana could see from the books on the table that Mia was home. She knocked on her door, and Mia opened it partway and said, "Oh, hi." Her voice carried an edgy lilt. Dana glanced around her into the room.

"Meagan's here," Mia said anxiously. "We're doing homework."

"That's good," Dana said. "Hi, Meagan," she called into the room. "You girls hungry?"

"We grabbed a snack." Meagan now stood behind Mia, gazing over her shoulder. She was substantially taller than Mia. The expression on her face revealed nothing. *Poker face*, the thought came to Dana.

"You want to stay for dinner?" Dana asked.

"We'll be done before that," Mia answered, still planted awkwardly in the doorway. Meagan's expression shifted, uneasy now, as she hovered behind her.

"Okay." *What was going on with those two girls?* Dana wondered as she returned to the kitchen and got herself a drink of water. Mia was acting a little strange, but maybe Mia was thinking the same of her.

Was she missing something? Why was she becoming so suspicious of Mia—with Zac, with Meagan? The girl was doing nothing wrong. Was Dana just suspicious, paranoid about everyone she encountered? She'd barely slept for the past few days. She missed Ryan. She couldn't get Mary Cassidy off her mind.

About forty minutes later, Dana heard Mia's door open, the girls' voices in the hall, words unclear. Had they really been studying? Something was going on, something Mia wished not to share.

Ryan called each day, generally early in the morning. He told Dana if the angel arsonists had been there, they had vanished. There was no sign that Gabe had returned home.

"Maybe he used someone else's passport. They all seem to look alike."

Ryan laughed, but he didn't reply. She was glad he took this as her being frustrated rather than flippant.

"If I don't find anything in the next couple of days, I'm coming home," he announced. "I want to be home by Thursday, the twenty-first, so we can be on-site at St. Judith's." He paused. "And because I miss you."

"I miss you, too."

By the next day, he'd made a reservation to return. Dana would pick him up at the airport.

Early the following morning, the day Ryan was scheduled to leave Rome, the name Christopher Prinz popped up on Dana's phone, identifying an incoming call. Her gut reacted in the way it always did when she saw the name of the detective who'd been working Joel's case for the past thirteen years. Fear, hope, dread, possibility.

She heard from him once or twice a year, a courtesy call—if such a word could be used in this particular case—to let her know nothing had developed. Every couple of years, he'd send an updated drawing. What Joel might look like now. Those were especially heartbreaking. The last time she'd spoken with him was when she phoned to ask if he'd talked to Drew. The one before that, ten months ago.

"Someone is posting on social media," he told her, "looking for a boy whose description, his age, his birthday match Joel's."

"Who? You've been able to track the person?" Her heart leapt with hope, mixed with the knowledge that tracking posts on social

283

media was difficult because these sites refused to release information.

"Yes, I think we have."

"Who?"

"I thought maybe you could tell me."

"What?" she replied, confused. "What do you mean?"

"Someone in your home," he said.

Her mind was flying, shifting, sifting, flinging out every possibility. Both Kip and Ryan had been at her apartment, had access to her internet, her computer.

But, then . . . *Mia. It was Mia. Mia and Meagan.* Could this be possible? Why?

"What did the post say?"

"Here," Detective Prinz said, "I'll read it to you." Dana heard a shuffle of papers over the phone. "We are looking for a boy who was born on March 27, 2001, in Boston, and then later adopted, or possibly raised by his elderly grandmother. His birth name is Joseph Leon, but he was known as a small child as Joel. He was three years old when he went missing. He is now sixteen. If you have any information, please PM."

"Mia." Dana stopped, stood, thinking . . . thinking . . . trying to make sense of what Christopher had just shared. Mia was still in school, in class. Her phone would be turned off.

"Mia Antonelli," Christopher said. "This young woman is living with you?"

"Let me do some checking," she said, words slow and measured. "I'll get back to you."

Reluctantly, she ended the call with Detective Prinz, knowing he had nothing more to share. Dana glanced at her watch, then quickly sent a text to Mia.

Need to talk. I'll pick you up this afternoon. Meagan, too. Let her dad know she'll be coming home with you.

CHAPTER THIRTY-FOUR

For some unknown reason, Dana baked cookies, her favorite, chocolate chip. Then she sat and ate half a dozen as her stomach twisted and turned.

She hopped in her car, drove to Mia's school, then waited until she saw the two girls exit. Wordlessly, they got into the back seat, both toting overstuffed backpacks.

They talked about the weather, which was starting to cool, as they drove home. Mia didn't ask any questions, and neither did Dana. She didn't want to have this discussion while she was driving. The tension inside the car was so thick, if it had been fog, visibility would have been severe enough to ground every single flight at Logan.

When they arrived at the apartment, Mia said, "Smells good."

Dana motioned them into the kitchen.

"You made cookies?" Meagan glanced at Mia as if she knew that Dana never baked cookies.

"Please sit." Dana opened the fridge, withdrew a milk carton and poured a glass for each girl. She placed a dozen cookies on a plate, slid them onto the breakfast bar, and motioned the girls to sit.

"Your message sounded urgent," Mia said formally as she cautiously pulled out a stool and sat. Meagan sat, too, staring down.

"I had a call from a police detective this morning." Dana stood on the opposite side of the bar.

Neither girl said a word, but they exchanged quick concerned glances.

"It seems someone has been posting odd requests on social media. They've been traced to—"

But, before she could finish, Mia was crying. Meagan looked startled. "Maybe I should go," she said.

Dana reached for her hand and pressed it to the bar with much greater force than she'd intended. "No, I think you might have something to add to this conversation."

Then, Mia, through her tears, spoke so quickly with an uncharacteristic accent that Dana couldn't even understand what she was saying.

"Slow down," Dana said. "Then you did send an inquiry, a post on social media? Did you think no one would see it?"

"We were hoping someone would," Meagan said defensively. "That was the point." She went on with a story that Dana had trouble following. *She had hypnotized Zac? He said a woman took Joel?*

This seemed to give Mia new confidence and she jumped in, more coherent now. They thought Joel was still alive. A woman would not harm a child.

By the time Meagan and Mia had worked through the story, Dana was too tense to sit, hands clenching, releasing, unable to look at Mia, not knowing what to say, how to react, her emotions colliding in confusion.

Finally, she stepped over next to Mia and sat. "Have you had any replies?" she asked in a quiet, controlled voice.

"Not one," Mia said, and she was crying again. Dana reached over and took her hand as she felt a single tear flow down her cheek.

Dana's mind was filled with such a blur of thoughts, she was barely aware of where she was headed and, when she arrived at the airport to pick up Ryan, she felt her head would explode as she pulled into the cellphone lot. She wanted desperately to talk to him. And this realization produced another. He was her *person* now—the one she wanted to talk to first.

Ten minutes after receiving his text to let her know he was at the luggage carousel, she pulled into the pickup zone. He'd barely thrown in his bag and hopped into the passenger side, leaned over to kiss her quickly, when words started to flow as Dana explained what Mia and Meagan had done.

"Why would she do such a thing?" she asked as she merged into exiting traffic.

"She's trying to help," Ryan said calmly.

"I know," she said. She wasn't angry but unsettled and anxious, though angry was how she must sound as she described what had happened. His response seemed to steady her now. "Maybe she and Meagan have discovered something we missed completely. If he's still alive, even if he doesn't remember anything about his life from when he was three, maybe they have discovered something." Had this information been locked up in Zac's mind all of this time? Why had none of them—Dana, Christopher Prinz, Zac's parents, Dana's mother, Zac's therapist—attempted to unlock it?

They were protecting him. He had been there when Joel disappeared.

"But, no response to the social media post," she said.

"No one has ever suggested Joel was taken by a woman? An older woman?"

Dana remembered how the police had studied the footprints in the dewy grass that morning. All matched to the three family members, all women, who had been scurrying about the yard that morning hiding Easter eggs. Was there another set of prints, hidden beneath the later prints, or had the abductor, a woman, been wearing the exact same brand and size shoes as who? Her mother? Dana? Pammie? There was so much activity early that morning, the woman having crisscrossed throughout the backyard. Was there another woman? One who had come earlier and already taken Dana's son?

As they settled into the flow of I-90 traffic, Ryan placed his hand on her shoulder and began to gently massage the tightness in her muscles, then up along her neck, the back of her head.

287

"I'm glad you're home," she said.

"Me too."

When they arrived at his condo, he led her to his bedroom, and slowly, softly, they made love, then fell asleep in each other's arms.

She was the first to awaken. She glanced at her watch, realizing she should go home and talk to Mia, let her know she wasn't angry, that she was confused, startled, and caught off guard. Dana wanted to talk to Zac, too, yet she sensed she should do this through the girls, that Zac had come to trust Mia and Meagan.

"I don't want to leave," she told Ryan, "But I need to go, be with Mia and reassure her." As Dana dressed quickly, she realized she'd been so caught up with what Mia and Meagan had done that she'd barely thought about what might happen in the next couple of days. If her theory held up, there would be a fire at St. Judith's the following night, after dark, sometime after midnight. Or the next night, Friday before midnight. And if Gabe Kelly was involved, this could be devastating to Ryan. He was dealing with his own personal trauma, perhaps more imminent than Dana's, yet he had set it aside for her.

"Tomorrow," she said, "after midnight, the fourth Friday of the month."

As they stepped into the hallway, Dana ready to leave, he said, "We're set at St. Judith's." His eyes did not meet hers.

"You're not inviting me to go along, are you?"

"You understand why I can't." He looked at her now.

"Yes," she said. "I understand."

She also understood, as she kissed him goodbye, then started for home, that she could not write this story. If the angels struck again the following night or the next, the story would break. But she was getting too close to Ryan, whose life might be severely affected, to write the story, too close to look at the events objectively. Why had she been unable to admit this earlier? It was because of her feelings for Ryan that she'd been unwilling to let go, but for this very reason she knew she must.

When she arrived at her apartment parking garage, she sat in her car for a moment, then pulled out her phone and called Kip. He didn't answer, so she left a message.

After talking to Mia, reassuring her, Dana prepared a light dinner of canned soup and sandwiches. She spoke with Ryan on the phone but didn't mention her call to Kip. Then she called Christopher Prinz and fell into bed, exhausted. She tossed, restlessly, unable to sleep, as images of her three-year-old son, then an older boy, similar to the sketches Detective Prinz had shared over the years, flashed in her mind.

Then, images of a fire burned in her head. Her body, too, had taken on the heat. A church. A boy. A sacrifice. A terrible vision. A boy, now a man, bursting into flames.

The following morning, Dana sat with a cup of coffee at home, having sent Mia off to school after they'd checked Mia's social media site to which she and Detective Prinz had both been given the password.

There were a number of comments. *Hope you find him. Praying for this boy to be located.* But no replies with any information.

When she spoke to Christopher Prinz the previous evening, they agreed Dana should contact her brother and sister-in-law to talk about what had happened with Mia, Meagan, and Zac. He asked if Dana could arrange a meeting with the girls, Zac and his parents, someplace where Zac would feel comfortable and safe, maybe his own home, Dana's brother's house.

Dana poured herself another cup of coffee, then another. Her phone sounded. Kip!

"You need to head home," Dana said.

"I'm already halfway there."

"You're coming back to work?"

"Headed back before I got your message, but now, sounds like the story on the fires is about to break."

"It's a possibility, but I can't write it."

"Your relationship with Ryan Kelly?"

"That, yes, but there's more going on now." She told him about what Mia and Meagan had done with Zac, about the social media post.

"Could this be something new in the investigation into Joel's disappearance?"

"I'm hopeful," she replied, "but, so far, nothing."

"Probably a good call on the fire story. Yes, I'm ready to get back to work."

"Did you speak with Mac?"

"I did, but before I received your message. We can figure it out when I get there."

"Thanks, Kip."

She clicked off, then stared at her phone for a second and called her sister-in-law.

That evening, Dana, Zac, his parents, Mia, and Meagan met at Jeff and Pammie's with Christopher Prinz and a woman who accompanied him to help with the meeting.

The detective's once dark hair was threaded with gray, his face jowly and middle-aged, and Dana realized she hadn't seen him in years, that their communications had, for the past several years, been through calls and emails. Yet, the sound of his voice, as he introduced the woman who would help facilitate the family meeting, comforted her in its familiarity and, at the same time, reminded her of so many years of failure.

The girls explained what had happened the night they met Zac at his grandmother's house. Zac remained quiet through the explanation, finally saying, "I think I'm starting to remember. I think it was a woman who took Joel away."

Dana, who wanted desperately to believe they had discovered something new, could hear the tentative tone in Zac's voice.

In a separate room, Zac talked with Christopher Prinz and the woman, who the detective had earlier explained to Dana was a specialist in early childhood trauma. Pammie served coffee and cookies while they waited. It all seemed surreal to Dana, and they spoke little as she sat mentally going through every possibility, the few leads, each eventually labeled false, that had come to them over the past thirteen years. Nothing had pointed them in this direction. There was never a suspicion that a woman had taken Joel.

Driving home, Dana considered how this might affect Drew. Detective Prinz had spoken to him, so he was aware of what had been developing, though Christopher had suggested he not be included in the family meeting, not because of any ill will between Dana and Drew, but because it could make it awkward and uncomfortable for Zac, who might not even recognize Drew. During the early years of the investigation, when they were still married, they had worked together, cried together. But it was different now, and it had been for many years.

She called Ryan and told him about the family meeting.

"Where do we go from here?"

"I'm not sure."

"No response, I take it, to the social media post the girls sent out?"

"No, nothing helpful."

"Detective Prinz, he's a good man?"

"He is." A very good man, but as a detective, maybe he was no better than she. For over thirteen years, neither he nor Dana had come up with a credible clue to lead them to Joel.

She wanted to say something to Ryan about what he would be doing that night, but the words, *wish you well, good luck*, didn't seem appropriate. She wanted to be there with him at St. Judith's, not because of the story, but because she cared for him.

"I'll be thinking of you tonight," she finally said.

That night in bed, Dana tossed helplessly, watching the time, slowly moving toward midnight. Nothing from Ryan. An emptiness filled her as she attempted to sleep. Ryan, waiting in a church . . . Dana, always waiting. Each waiting for a lost boy to return home.

Drifting off, she was in the dark, inside a church, crouched behind a pew with Ryan Kelly.

The investigators stationed outside, in the dark. *His* investigators, men without faces, men she had never met. Then, as she turned, dark shadows, silhouettes, in the back of the church.

And then they were gone.

Waiting in the dark.

The sound of her phone woke her from the dream. A text from Ryan.

Nothing. I'll call later.

Dana stared at the word, *Nothing.* Not tonight.

Finally, she fell into a fitful, dreamless sleep.

The following day when she woke, she was well aware that it was Friday. If she was correct, the fire would be tonight, after dark, but before midnight.

She met with Detective Prinz at 10:00.

"What did your child specialist say?" Dana asked.

"She believes Zac believes what he told the girls."

"But, she doesn't believe it is true?"

"No, she didn't say that."

After a long awkward pause, Dana asked, "So, we continue to wait?"

"I'm doing everything I can," Prinz replied, and she knew he was.

Was Dana merely grasping at false hope? Even if a woman had taken her child, they had no evidence of this, no leads to follow. She wanted to believe there would be a response to Mia and Meagan's social media post.

She spoke again with Ryan. Nothing to report.

Again that night, Dana slept restlessly, waking often, checking the time. Midnight, and no call from Ryan. Did this mean nothing had happened at St. Judith's?

The call came early Saturday morning, just after 3:00 A.M. Her stomach lurched, seeing his name on her phone.

"You were right," Ryan said, voice halting. "The fire. St. Judith's. It was Gabe."

CHAPTER THIRTY-FIVE

It felt as if the phone had gone dead. Nothing from Ryan. Then a gasp, a sob.

"The fire?" Dana croaked. "Gabe?" She thought of the bible verses, particularly the last. *Sacrifice him there as a burnt offering.*

"It happened so fast," Ryan said.

"Oh, Ryan, I'm so sorry. He—"

"He's alive, but badly burned."

"He'll be okay?" She took in a deep, deep breath.

"He's at Mass General. It doesn't look good."

"You're at the hospital?"

"Yes."

"Can I come over?"

"Not yet."

"I'll wait until I hear from you, then."

"Yes."

When the phone rang several hours later, it was not Ryan, but Kip.

"I'm home."

"It happened," she said. "Another fire." She told him what she knew.

"God, Dana, I'm so sorry."

"It doesn't look good for Gabe," she said.

"Goddamn."

"Ryan's hopeful. But, yes, it's bad." She didn't know what else to say, so she asked, "You've talked to Mac since you got back?"

"Yes, but I'll leave it up to you to tell him you're off the story."

"Thank you."

The following morning, Dana spoke with Ryan. Gabe had made it through the night.

"What can I do?" Dana asked.

"Pray," Ryan answered. "Please pray."

"Can I come to the hospital?"

"My family is here. Everyone. I'll call you later this afternoon."

Dana thought of how Drew had been excluded from the family meeting. Detective Prinz had said it could be confusing to Zac, who might not even remember his uncle. Would it be painfully confusing for Ryan's family if Dana showed up at the hospital? They didn't know her. Dana's family knew nothing about Ryan either. Kip did, and Mia had met Ryan. Dana sensed she liked him, maybe even had a hint of Dana's feelings for him, though they'd never talked about it. Now, she wanted to be with him.

Later that morning, she met at her office with Kip, and together they went to talk to Mac. He was aware of the recent fire, but nothing had been officially released to the media other than the fact that there had been a fire at St. Judith's.

"I'm taking some time off," Dana said.

"Oh?" said Mac. She could see by his wrinkled brow and squinty eyes that he was confused.

"Some personal things going on." She glanced at Kip, then explained to Mac that there might be a new development on Joel's disappearance.

"I understand," Mac said so sincerely that Dana knew she owed him more. "There's another reason I can't stay on the fire story." She took in a deep breath. "I've developed feelings for one of the investigators."

A stretch of silence expanded through the room. "So," Mac finally said, "I'm assuming Kip knows more about this possible story than I?" He didn't seem angry, more entitled, which at this point he probably was. "Well, then," he said, "If the story is as big as Dana seems to think, I don't believe this is a one-man, or one-woman, show." He picked up his phone, gave it a couple of jabs, lifted it to his ear, then locked eyes with Kip. "Meeting in the conference room. Pronto."

The following day, Ryan asked Dana to join him and his family at the hospital, she fully aware of how odd it was to meet them this way. Yet, they all knew who she was, and somehow it seemed natural for her to be there. Ryan introduced her to his mom, Ella, his older brother Patrick, his sister Julie, the younger sister Birdie, Patrick's wife Steph, Julie's husband Mark. The Kellys, with their pale, freckled complexions, blue eyes, and assorted tones of red hair, would not have been difficult to identify as family.

   Limited visitors were allowed in Gabe's room, and only after scrubbing vigorously and donning protective gear, the risk of infection so great. Dana knew her role was one of offering support, of waiting in the visitors' lounge with family members. Some drifted off to the chapel, and others offered coffee from vending machines. Dana thought of the vigil at St. Barbara's, the parishioners waiting, not giving up, hoping to save the parish. They had been unsuccessful. Now the church was gone, lost in a fire. Would Gabe's fate be the same?

   Ryan's mother said little as she sat between Julie and Birdie, each daughter holding a hand, speaking in soft tones, their mother's eyes downcast, in a trance of grief, or perhaps prayer. When her eyes rose and locked with Dana's, Ella Kelly offered a quiet, knowing nod, and a recognition passed between them. Ella knew. She knew Dana was a mother who had lost her son.

   A short, wiry man with thick, dark curly hair peppered with grey, a stethoscope hanging from his neck, entered the room. He spoke to the family in a measured tone, explaining what might happen next, acknowledging it was a hopeful sign that Gabe had made it through these first difficult days.

Finally, Patrick, the oldest brother, asked, "What are his chances?"

Dana glanced at Ella, who tightened her grip on Julie's hand.

"He's made it through the first couple of days," the doctor repeated, running his fingers absently along the cord of the stethoscope. "This is definitely good news." He paused, thoughtfully. "About fifty-fifty."

The doctor's exit was followed by a long silence. Patrick offered to take his mother home, and reluctantly she agreed. Birdie and Julie said they would hang around and let everyone know if anything developed.

As Dana and Ryan left the room, she studied him carefully. He looked exhausted.

"You want to go get something to eat?" he asked.

"You look tired."

"I am."

"Maybe get some rest." She reached for his hand.

"Good idea, probably. I'll call."

As they walked out, Dana said, "I'm off the story. Kip's back."

"You know the FBI is handling this now. I've held nothing back."

She nodded.

"Gabe will be okay," Ryan said. "I met you because of this terrible tragedy, and we'll get through this together. Thank you for being here." Then slowly, as if he'd given this considerable thought, he said, "I'd like to talk to Kip. The men involved in starting the fires want their story to get out. It's horrific that they felt this was the way to get the attention they need for their stories to have some meaning."

"I'll let him know."

As Dana got in her car and headed toward home, she thought of what the doctor had said—*fifty-fifty*. She would do anything to have those odds of finding her son.

Dana talked to her brothers and their spouses. She told them she was taking some time off work, and then she explained why—she was involved with the man with whom she'd researched the story, the Fire Marshal, Ryan Kelly. She asked for their prayers for his brother Gabe.

She had shared nothing with her mother about Ryan, or what had happened with Mia, Meagan, and Zac. She called.

"I want to talk to you, Mom. Can I come out?"

"Why don't you and Mia come for dinner. I've got a nice little pork roast, and it should be plenty for three."

"Just me, Mom, but not for dinner."

When she arrived, her mother had put on a kettle, arranged oatmeal cookies on a plate, and set out an assortment of teas in a ceramic bowl. They sat at the kitchen table.

"If I'd known you were coming," Ann said, glancing at the plate of cookies, "I'd have made your favorite. I know you don't like raisins."

"This is fine, Mom, really."

The teapot whistled. Ann got up, poured hot water in two cups, placed one before Dana, offered the bowl of tea, and sat again.

As their tea steeped, Dana explained about the fires, she and Ryan working together, what had happened with his brother, that she was taking some time off.

"Because I've developed feelings for Ryan," Dana said, looking at her mom to catch her reaction, which was total surprise.

"Feelings?" she asked. "Romantic feelings?"

"Yes," Dana replied. "And there's something more I should tell you. I know it's a lot, but you need to know." She told her about Mia and Meagan and Zac. When she'd finished, they both sat without speaking. Dana knew she'd dealt her mom a full hand, too many revelations at once, but she seemed to be gathering them up, one by one, turning them over, and then arranging them carefully in her mind.

"There have been no replies to Mia's message?"

"Nothing," Dana said. "We are still waiting." Over the years, she and her mom had silently shared the guilt over Joel's loss. It had never been easy to talk about it. He'd disappeared from her mother's home.

"How sad for you and Ryan. Both to suffer such losses. Gabe is home with his family to take care of him now." Ann's eyes rose to meet Dana's.

"Ryan's hopeful," Dana said. "When he's strong enough, they will begin skin grafts."

"Oh," Ann said, voice quiet. She spooned the teabag out of her cup, wrapped the string around it, then slid it onto her saucer. "You'll introduce Ryan . . . not now, but later after . . ." She couldn't finish her thought, so she shifted and said, "We've never given up hope that we will find Joel."

"No, we haven't," Dana said, even as a recurring thought looped through her mind— even if Joel came back to them, like Gabe, he would not be the same.

Over the next several days, Dana learned what had happened at St Judith's, more from reading the *Globe* stories than from Ryan. Charges had been filed against three young men, two in custody, one in the hospital. The FBI had worked closely with local law enforcement. Ryan Kelly, the State Fire Marshal, was named in the third story as the brother of the suspect Gabriel Kelly, in critical condition from burns suffered in the fire. Ryan was no longer involved in the investigation though he had been instrumental in the early stages, leading them to this group of men, now charged with arson. In her mind, Dana had thought of these victims as boys, but they were all now men. Men whose lives would always be tainted by what had happened to them so many years ago. And now, this.

Through information found by the FBI on a computer used by the angels, it was revealed that they were ready to go public after the final fire, a fire in which an angel would rise from the flames. They planned to ignite the world and reveal their pleas: reform within the Church, more stringent and open reporting requirements for both past and current suspected abusers, and also long-term goals of change, including more thorough vetting requirements for the priesthood, married clergy, and women priests.

This all trickled out, bit by bit, over the following week, then into the next.

There were no further developments in the investigation into Joel's disappearance. It was as if they had leaped forward, perhaps falsely, only to fall back once more.

Dana called Drew. She had nothing to share other than what Christopher Prinz had already told him. *Zac may or may not remember something. A woman may or may not have taken Joel. Mia had posted something on social media, and there were no replies.*

"What do we do?" Drew asked, his voice tense and halting.

"We wait," Dana said.

"Yes," Drew replied, and then, "As we have for the past thirteen years."

Dana knew how difficult this had been for Drew, too. Yet, they had been unable to work through this grief together.

"The wedding's scheduled for this weekend," he said after a long pause in the conversation. "I know Amy would postpone, if . . ." His voice was calm yet strained. Dana knew he was not presenting a case to go ahead with the wedding. He was asking for her advice.

"If we knew something. Oh, Drew, you should probably not. I mean not cancel." Life goes on, she might have said, and for Drew, it seemed as if it had. Not that he had given up. She'd never sensed he had given up. "No, you shouldn't cancel. If anything happens, if we learn anything more—"

"Thanks, Dana," he said. "I'll be available . . . if anything."

"The wedding's here in Boston?"

He hesitated longer than she thought he would. She'd just assumed, since Amy lived in Boston.

"We're flying the families to Hawaii."

She, too, took several moments to respond. "I'll let you know if —"

"Amy says if we need to cancel . . ."

299

"We really have nothing yet, Drew," she replied, knowing how desperately she wanted this to be something. But, it was not. Not yet. "I'll let you know."

CHAPTER THIRTY-SIX

Two days later, as Dana was about to leave for the hospital where she was meeting Ryan, her phone sounded. It was Mia, though Dana knew she was in class and had obviously defied rules and smuggled in her phone.

"We've got a hit," Mia said quickly, voice low. "A response with a private message."

Dana's heart jumped, colliding with a scorching stone rising in her throat. "What did it say?" she croaked.

"I think I might be Joel."

"That's all?" Dana could barely speak, could barely breathe.

"That's all."

Mia explained there was no profile picture on the social media page, nothing but a blank outline of a head, a temporary placeholder. There was little in the *About* information. The boy's name was Joseph Anon. The birthdate listed was the exact date and year as Joel's. There were no posts of any nature on the page. It almost appeared as if it had been set up for one specific purpose— to reply to Mia's.

Dana told Mia she'd pick her up at school. She called Ryan, left a message. She called Detective Prinz. Within an hour, the three of them, Christopher Prinz, Mia, and Dana sat, computer screen in front of them at police headquarters.

Christopher dictated how Mia should answer. "Thank you for

responding. Your parents love you and would like to contact you. I am acting as a go-between. Please, message me again."

Mia's profile on the social media site was a photo in which she appeared young, innocent, with an open heart and mind. A flash of fear shot through Dana. What if this was a stalker? A pervert, intent on luring Mia somewhere unsafe. What could she ask to determine if this was truly Joel? Even as Dana attempted to come up with a better response, Prinz nodded at Mia, and she hit send.

Then they waited. One hour. Two hours. Three hours.

Dana knew how difficult it was to trace the source of a social media post, though Christopher assured her they were doing everything possible. He'd been able to trace Mia to Dana's home because she often posted on various sites, shared with friends back home, mentioned her school, her new American friends, had even shared a picture of Dana she'd taken with her cellphone. But, this boy, this boy who had responded to Mia's post, had no social history, not events, no connections.

Christopher offered coffee, asked both Dana and Mia if they needed something to eat. Dana knew she could not eat, though she sloshed through cup after cup of coffee, her stomach rolling with agitation, her nerves tingling, then jumping from the abundance of caffeine shooting through her. He ordered sandwiches and then, finally, he suggested they go about their day, knowing, Dana was sure, that they would all be monitoring the account.

"No responses, if we get a reply, until we've spoken," he said with an authoritative tone in his voice that was equally irritating and comforting.

Dana and Mia both agreed, and they got back in Dana's car.

"When he responds," Dana said, "you need to ask him to send an email."

"Because that can be traced?"

Dana nodded. "Not always, but much easier."

The following morning, Dana sat at home, reading online articles, trying to keep busy, though she had nothing to work on, no story. She thought about calling Drew, but she knew

Christopher had kept him apprised.

Just after 10:00, she checked Mia's messages.

There was a new one! Just posted. Quickly, heart beating uncontrollably, she read:

"I have lived all of my life with my grandmother. We attend Sunday Mass, but other than that, we seldom leave home. My grandmother has homeschooled me, but she has allowed me to use the small-town library since I was young, and just recently the computers, since I am preparing to take my college entrance exams. She is a kind woman, but many of my questions have gone unanswered. What happened to my parents? Why do I know nothing about my family? Please tell me something about the people who think I might be their son."

Dana called Mia, picked her up, and rushed to police headquarters, where Dana and Christopher Prinz sat, arguing over the next step.

"We should ask for a photo," Dana said. "Let's ask if he can send an email message."

Prinz agreed and Mia sent a new message. "Your father and mother have never stopped looking for you and love you very much. Please send a photo, an email address so we can continue to communicate." Again, they waited for a reply but received nothing. Several times throughout the afternoon, after she and Mia had returned home, Dana checked.

She dropped by the hospital and talked to Ryan, grabbed something to eat at the cafeteria. Ryan said Gabe was still not fully aware of what was going on.

That night, unable to sleep, she sat at her computer, repeatedly checking for messages, and then reading several more stories in various publications about the Arsonist Angels, all originating from the *Globe*, each reporting that one of the men responsible was still fighting for his life.

As she scanned the online news, moving quickly from digital page to page, an obituary photo flashed and disappeared as she robotically clicked to the following page. She arrowed back.

Mary Cassidy had passed away four days ago. Dana scanned the article. She was a widow with one daughter. Then the words *St. Barbara's* popped out on the page. Mary had, as Dana now knew, once been a member of the parish. Chair of the Altar Society, Secretary of the Catholic Women's League, according to the obit. The church had been a big part of her life. Was this why she had been concerned about the fire? Now she was gone, and Dana would never know. Perhaps it did not matter.

Yet, again, Mary's strange words ran through Dana's mind. *You are the woman who lost her child. You should not have put that priest in prison with a murderer. A mother will do just about anything when she loses a child.*

Heat ran up along Dana's neck, onto her cheeks.

She read the obit a second time, looking for something, but what? What if the mother Mary referred to was not Dana, but a different woman? A different mother? A different mother who had lost a child. *You should not have put that priest in prison with a murderer. A woman took Joel.*

Her fingers flew wildly over the keyboard, pulling up a search engine, entering the name Father Joseph Jennings. The first page listed articles about a priest who had molested children, a priest who had died in prison. Articles that Dana had helped to research and write. She signed on to a people search, entered the name Joseph Jennings, limiting the search to the Boston area. There were a number of Joseph Jennings. She attempted to match the correct age, then family connections until she found it—Virginia Jennings, the name of Father Joseph Jennings' mother.

She continued searching, moving from one people finder site to another, locating possible addresses to connect with this name. The last known address, she realized, was on the same street where Mary Cassidy had once lived. The two women had been neighbors.

Then, a dead end. The woman had disappeared. No trace. No forwarding address for Virginia Jennings. No obituary. Nothing.

Dana pressed her hand to her forehead as if attempting to hold everything in. If she let go, her head would explode.

She went back to bed, but her mind was too full for sleep. When she rose again, Mia was in the kitchen, making toast. She'd already started the coffee. Dana poured them each a cup, barely speaking as Mia buttered her toast, spread it with jam, and sat down to eat.

"I'm heading out," Mia said after she'd finished and placed her dishes in the dishwasher. "I'll keep checking messages."

"Me, too," Dana replied. As soon as Mia left, Dana grabbed her phone, her jacket and left, driving much too fast to the neighborhood where Mary Cassidy had once lived, in the neighborhood near St. Barbara's where Virginia Jennings had lived. Another mother who had lost her child. A priest who was murdered in prison. A priest who had once been assigned to St. Barbara's. A man who had once been a child. A child of a woman who had simply disappeared.

She knocked on the door of the house where Virginia Jennings had lived. When a young woman wearing bathrobe and slippers answered, Dana suddenly realized that for others, the day had barely begun.

"I'm trying to locate a long-lost friend," Dana said. "She used to live here."

The woman gave her a puzzled look.

"Virginia Jennings?"

"We've been here for less than a year," the woman replied. "The prior owners were the Murphys."

Dana thanked her and went to the house next door where Mary Cassidy had lived. No answer when she rang the doorbell, so she went to the house on the opposite side of Virginia Jennings'.

An elderly man came to the door, coffee cup in hand. When she told him she was looking for an old friend, Virginia Jennings, he scratched his chin and replied, "We were neighbors for years. My wife and I are the only ones left. All the other neighbors gone, some moved out, others went to nursing homes. Some died." He let out a quiet laugh, then took a slow sip of coffee.

"Do you know what happened to Mrs. Jennings?"

"Ginny? She went by Ginny." He scratched his chin thoughtfully again.

"Do you know where she went?"

"Not sure. She retired years ago. Schoolteacher. She always talked about going to Paris." He shook his head and laughed. "Don't imagine that's where she went. But, come to think of it, she talked about Canada, said she'd like to go up to Canada when she retired."

"How long ago was that?"

"Oh, she retired years ago."

"Is that when she left?"

"No, several years after that, maybe a dozen years ago. Not sure."

"Do you know where in Canada?"

"Sorry," he said slowly. "I don't."

Dana thanked him and started to leave. She turned back. "What did she teach?"

"French. She was a French teacher."

Dana returned home, rushed up to her apartment. From a new file she'd yet to label, she pulled printed copies of the two private messages sent to Mia. They were sent on different days, two separate messages, but just minutes apart, both shortly after 10:00 A.M. She studied the words of the two posts by Joseph Anon, looking for something to lead her to this boy who wrote, *I might be Joel.*

"I have lived all of my life with my grandmother. . . she has allowed me to use the small-town library since I was young, and just recently the computers . . ."

Library? Computers?

Dana clicked on a search engine, pulled up a map, and furiously began to search. For the next three hours, she attempted to find every small town in Canada with a library, realizing the chances of finding Joel in the great expanse of Canada were very narrow.

But then something hit her. The woman taught French. In the province of Quebec, French was the primary language.

She narrowed her search. When she'd come up with a list of 17 possibilities, small cities in Quebec with libraries, she called Prinz.

It took several attempts to explain, the words coming out of her quickly and jumbled. She told him she believed Joel had been taken by Virginia Jennings, mother of Father Joseph Jennings, a priest who had abused children. Dana had written about this abuse and coverup, which had led to his conviction. He had been killed in prison.

"The motive revenge?" Christopher asked.

"Possibly," Dana replied, with the realization that the ultimate revenge would be Virginia killing *her* son. Dana could not go there. A mother would not kill a child.

"I want to make some calls," she said, "but I don't want to use my own phone. Do you have a phone that will not show the number and location of an incoming call?"

Within half an hour, Dana sat at a desk at police headquarters, phone in hand, Christopher Prinz beside her.

After several calls, each answered by a machine, the first real person greeted Dana in French. She took in a deep breath and asked, voice much calmer than she thought possible, "Do you speak English?"

The answer, "Yes, of course."

"My sixteen-year-old son," Dana began, "often comes to the library with his grandmother, and I believe he might be there today. I know his phone will be silenced, and I need to get in touch. We've had a family emergency."

The first few librarians she was able to speak with were kind but unable to help.

Detective Prinz sat listening to the conversations on speakerphone. Dana was surprised he did not object, though after the third call, she sensed by his troubled expression that he was concerned about what she might say if one of the librarians had information on Joel.

She thought of a discussion they'd had years ago after consulting with a specialist in child abduction. Joel might be reluctant to betray the woman he had come to see as his guardian. He'd written in his message that his grandmother was kind. He might want to protect her. Yet, he was curious and wanted to know more about his parents. He knew this woman had lied to him. Dana had to tread very carefully. She glanced at Prinz and sensed he was thinking the same, yet he trusted Dana to be cautious, to continue.

On the twelfth call, trying with difficulty to calm her voice, to remain hopeful, Dana felt a blast of heat course through her body when the librarian said, "Perhaps I know the boy, but I thought, because he always comes with his grandmother, well I didn't know he had a mother."

Dana sensed reluctance on the woman's part, even as her own heart beat rapidly. Detective Prinz stiffened with attention, and Dana thought for a moment he was going to grab the phone from her, but he didn't. Should she tell the librarian the truth? Would she even believe Dana now?

"He is tall and very handsome," Dana said. "He's been coming in, prepping for college entrance exams. They generally come in the morning."

"Oh, yes," she said. "A very nice boy. Very smart. I do hope you are able to contact him, but he and his grandmother left about five minutes ago."

"I'll try again," Dana replied, "he's probably turned his phone on again now. Thank you so much for your help."

Within minutes, Prinz had contacted law enforcement in Sainte-Louisa, a small town in Quebec, describing the situation, relaying the limited information they had, suggesting the librarian might be able to provide additional information, a name and address for the woman and her grandson.

He advised Dana that they should wait until they knew more, though she was sure he realized that she could not wait for any kind of official investigation. Within an hour, Dana had scheduled a charter flight with two seats, after checking and discovering there were no commercial flights available to this small village, but there was a private landing strip.

She called Drew, listening with frustration to his message,

guessing he was now on his way to Hawaii. She left a message of her own. "Call me immediately. It's important."

Then she called Ryan. "I think we've found Joel."

"What can I do?" Ryan asked after she'd offered a detailed explanation.

"Nothing at this point."

"Let me know."

"Yes." Then she asked, "Gabe?"

"The same. Still hanging on."

CHAPTER THIRTY-SEVEN

Dana sat next to Mia in the backseat of the small plane. The weather had turned, dark, ominous clouds threatening, though the pilot had assured them they could beat the storm. She had paid for two seats, one for Drew, but when he finally called, she realized he would have to make arrangements on his own. Then, somehow Mia had talked Dana into taking her along.

Prinz had told Dana that he could arrange a flight for early the following day, but Dana could not wait. She wasn't even sure what she would do when she got there, but she was sure she could find the library. Prinz had warned her that they had no further information, that he had not heard back from the officer he'd contacted in Canada.

She stared out into the dark night, the small aircraft's lights flashing on the wing, the lightweight plane bumping through the murky clouds. She thought of Mary Cassidy. Had Mary known all along that Virginia Jennings—the mother of a priest who had been convicted of child abuse at St. Barbara's, who had been killed in prison—had taken Dana's son? Could this be true? It seemed it was, though there was nothing to officially confirm it. Had Mary merely thought it strange that the woman, as well as Dana's son, had disappeared?

A mother who loses a child will do just about anything.

There was no proof that this boy who had been coming to the

library in a small Canadian town with his grandmother was Joel. They had not heard back from him again. No email address. No photograph. Dana studied Mia, who sat beside her, head pressed to the window, this beautiful girl who had come so unexpectedly into Dana's life. Whom she loved dearly.

When they landed, it was almost midnight. They found a ride into town, arranged by their pilot, and thankfully one of the two hotels in the village had a room.

Dana could not sleep, her body and mind wrapped fragilely, yet ominously, in what she had experienced over the past days, the past weeks. She thought of Ryan, of Gabe. It was as if she were awakening now from a nightmare into a dream. A vision that was not real. None of this was real. None of it made sense. Then, the dream exploded with the sound of her phone. Christopher Prinz.

He told Dana that due to the weather, his flight was delayed. Local law enforcement had contacted the city librarian, who had agreed to go in early to check records for the name and address of the woman and sixteen-year-old boy they suspected was Joel.

"I'm headed to the library as soon as it opens," Dana replied. It was Saturday now, and she knew the library did not open on weekends until noon.

"Can I ask that you wait?" Prinz said.

"You could ask." They both knew she couldn't wait.

She and Mia found a place to have breakfast, where the other diners regarded them with suspicion. Everyone spoke French, though the waitress quickly shifted to English to take their order, even after Mia greeted her with a *Bonjour*.

They finished, both leaving half of their meals of sausage and eggs on their plates, and Dana suggesting they take a walk around town to pass the time—three hours—before the library opened. As they left the restaurant, her phone rang again. Detective Prinz.

"We have an address, just outside of town. An officer from the Sŭreté du Québec is headed out there, to check things out, see what he can discover."

"I'd like to go with him," Dana said.

"Not yet," Prinz said. "I promise, Dana, I'll let you know right away if we discover anything."

Then before she could protest, he hung up.

The next three hours crept slowly, Dana and Mia walking, then waiting outside the library. It had started to snow, a light pure, untainted blanket of white slowly covering the ground. A cleansing smell filled the air. It was beautiful. Peaceful. Pure. When Dana's phone rang, she held her breath.

"It's Joel," Prinz said.

Dana could barely comprehend the words that followed. She feared she might awaken and find herself cruelly pushed out of this dream. Christopher explained the officer had gone to the address the librarian had given him. The woman was in custody. She'd simply asked, "What took you so long?" The boy had been taken to the nearest hospital in Quebec City.

Dana's heart dropped. "Hospital? He's been hurt?"

"No, no, he's okay. But, they want to do a physical, a preliminary evaluation. Do some basic tests."

"Then he's okay?" She was crying now. Mia was staring at Dana, eyes wide.

"It's Joel," Dana whispered into the phone as if she needed to put it into words. She nodded at Mia, who'd said little as they waited. The girl rubbed a tear from her cheek, and Dana put an arm around her as Mia leaned into her shoulder.

"Yes, he's okay," Prinz said.

"He's okay," she said to Mia. "It's Joel. He's okay."

The law enforcement officer, who had come to pick Dana and Mia up at the library, then driven them through the falling snow with deftness, even as Dana's stomach lurched, lead them into the hospital, then stopped in the hallway, stiff and proper in a brown uniform, firearm strapped to his side. He told Dana she would meet first with a woman assigned to the case. Mia could wait in the visitors' lounge.

Dana would remember little about what the woman told her

before she was led into another room.

He sat in a chair and rose to meet her.

He looked less like the age-enhanced drawings, and more like his father than she had imagined. His hair was dark, his eyes very blue. His jaw firm.

"Joel," Dana said. He towered above her. Tall and lanky.

"I think I'm your son." His voice too. His father's, but when he smiled, there was something of her brothers, something of Ben, and Jeff, of Dana's father, of Dana herself.

There was no doubt. This was her son.

She reached out, hands on his shoulders to study him for a moment before pulling him protectively into her arms.

CHAPTER THIRTY-EIGHT

Mia walked on the grounds outside the hospital, through the snow. She had yet to meet Joel. It was the day after his rescue. That's the word Dana had used.

Rescue.

Mia had never seen Dana so happy. Joel's father, Dana explained, was flying in from Hawaii. He'd just gotten married. Dana told her this without anger or resentment. She was smiling too broadly, too filled with joy to allow room for anything else.

Mia had sat on her bed at the hotel the previous night as Dana spoke to Joel's father, describing Joel, how tall and handsome he was.

"Thank you," Mia heard Dana say to Drew. "I think that's best for now. The reunification counselor has been helpful." Then Dana said something about this being the best transition for Joel.

Dana made other calls. Her mother. Zac. Pammie and Jeff. Ben and Sam. Several times, Dana spoke with Ryan. Mia knew he was dealing with the terrible incident with his brother who, along with two other men, had set fire to several churches in Boston.

Mia was glad they had each other. She'd already decided that Ryan and Dana were in love. She could tell by the way Dana spoke to him on the phone, at times leaving the room for privacy, that they were in this together. Dana in her joy, Ryan his grief, yet hope for his brother's recovery.

On the way to the hospital that morning, Dana told Mia that Joel would stay with them when they got back to Boston. Mia felt they would need time alone without her, so, after having lunch at the hospital cafeteria with Dana, while Joel met again with the local police and the detective who'd arrived from Boston, Mia called Meagan and arranged, with her dad's blessing, to stay with them for a while, until Joel got settled. She would present this to Dana later that day.

Now, approaching the hospital's reflection garden, Mia pushed aside a layer of snow and lowered herself to a bench. She imagined in the spring and summer, the garden would be filled with flowers, but now, it was a soft blanket of fluffy white. A single bird, a cardinal, beautiful and red, perched on a dome of snow in the bowl of a birdbath, and then flew into the air.

CHAPTER THIRTY-NINE

Dana knew there was no manual, no guidebook, on how to get to know someone who has always been a part of your life, yet one who has been missing for most of it. The therapist they all met with daily in Boston, individually and separately, helped.

Drew had arranged to fly to Quebec City as soon as he got Dana's message, though his flight was delayed because of the weather. This gave Dana more time with Joel, who stayed at the hospital for another day, meeting with another therapist specializing in recovery and reunification.

During this time, and after their return home, Dana learned from Christopher Prinz, through the Canadian officials, that Virginia Jennings had lived on her teacher's pension and Social Security, that she'd been in Boston for a year after the abduction, then gone to Canada, little Joel curled up asleep in the back seat of her car under a blanket. No one would suspect a grandmother of such a horrendous crime.

Back home, Joel stayed with Dana. Drew agreed this was best for now. She'd settled him in her own bedroom, taking over Mia's. Reluctantly, Dana had agreed to let Mia go to Meagan's. They had not yet decided for how long, but for now this was working.

Often, Dana would enter his room, silently watch as she had when he was an infant. Her eyes carefully following the rise and fall, his breathing. Inhaling, exhaling. Alive. He was alive.

Slowly, Joel was introduced to family members. Dana's mom and Zac had been the first outside of Dana, Mia and Drew, who had flown home together from Canada. Ryan's introduction came about naturally, as did Amy's. Dana's brothers and their spouses, the three younger cousins, came in family groups. The therapist suggested small gatherings to start.

Joel continued to do his studies online, something he had done the past few years with the woman he still referred to as his grandmother. Virginia Jennings had been voluntarily extradited from Canada and was now waiting for a court date, though Christopher Prinz told Dana the woman would likely not live to go to trial. She was 92 and not well.

One evening, during their daily phone conversation, when Mia asked Dana if it was okay if Joel went out with her, Zac, and Meagan, Dana could not come up with words, a sudden panic enveloping her. "Maybe later," she'd finally said, immediately calling her therapist. The paparazzi had been relentless, despite Dana's attempts to protect her son from the media.

She met with the therapist the following day, and though nothing was resolved, and the therapist said little, Dana realized that at one point, she would have to let him go again, that the goal of any parent was to raise a child to be self-sufficient, to forge into the world by himself. It was Dana who suggested that Mia, Zac, and Meagan could hang out with Joel at the apartment.

Less than two months after Joel's rescue, he attended his first Thanksgiving dinner since coming back to them, with Dana's family, Ryan, and Mia, at her mom's.

She was concerned about Joel returning to the place where he'd been taken, and he was aware of his mom's concerns, but as soon as he walked in the first time—a week before the big family gathering—he said, "I'm okay, Mom. This smells like grandma's, and it's a good smell."

Dana watched the family interact with Joel, he throwing his mom a reassuring smile now and then as he visited with his cousins.

After dinner, as the kids helped clear the table, she asked Ryan to walk outside with her. She was so overcome with emotion, she needed just for a moment to step out, to let Joel navigate this on his own.

"The three-bedroom apartment in my building will be available late next month," Dana told Ryan. "It looks like we could be in shortly after Christmas."

"That's great news."

"It will be wonderful to have Mia back again, and the timing is perfect." Mia would be meeting her family in New York for Christmas break, and Joel would spend more time with Drew and Amy during the holidays.

"I know you miss not seeing Mia every day."

"I do. And I'm grateful that Drew and I have been able to agree on what's best for Joel during these past couple of months."

They approached the garden. The foliage and vines were starting to wither. Dana thought about the long winter ahead, then spring, new life. It was as if her own life had started over.

"He's so pure, so innocent," she said. "It's as if this isolation has kept him from the evils of the world."

Ryan put his arm around Dana's shoulder as he listened.

"He asked if he could visit his grandmother," she added quietly. "She's been taken to the hospital." Dana felt a tear slip from her eye. "He still calls her his grandmother."

Ryan didn't respond, just wrapped his arm tighter. He could have said, *this is the woman who raised him*. She did not abuse him physically. But, mentally, she had. She'd taken him away from his family.

"I think he needs to see her again," Dana said. "He's experiencing a rough mixture of emotions. Coming from such a limited, protected environment. Now, thrown into all this . . ." She raised an arm and motioned toward the house. "I wouldn't call it chaos, but lots of people, lots of family. And, then, the newspaper reporters, photographers. I'm doing my best to protect him." She shook her head. "He's still talking about enrolling in school second semester. He and Zac are talking sports." She glanced at Ryan.

"He's got a natural ability. Maybe getting into sports, something physical can help him deal with all this."

"Thanks for taking Zac and Joel over to the school to play ball." Several evenings over the past week, the three had gone to the baseball field at Zac's school, knowing they'd be noticed if they went to a public park. "He does, doesn't he? Have a natural talent." Dana smiled. "I wish he'd been able to . . ." She couldn't finish her thought, not in words. She couldn't look back on all Joel had missed. "I really do hate that woman." She was shaking, her entire body trembling. She pushed her hands into the pockets of her jacket. "Joel asked me if I could ever forgive her."

They'd stopped walking, facing each other now. Ryan reached his own hand into her pocket and took Dana's in his, then rubbed it gently, the friction warming her.

"I don't know that I can," she said. "How can I forgive the woman who took my son?"

Joel walked out of the house, Zac on one side, Mia on the other. Meagan, who had been hanging out at the apartment lately with Joel, Zac, and Mia, was noticeably missing. Mia had told Dana she was spending the day with her mom, and Mia was concerned because Meagan and her mom didn't get along.

"He's doing exceptionally well after all he's been through," Ryan reassured her, tilting his head toward the three teens as they approached. He lifted Dana's hand from her pocket, raised it to his lips and kissed it. "Right now, let's appreciate and be thankful for this."

"That's a good place to start," Dana said.

"Grandma's serving the pumpkin pie," Joel said. "You ready, Mom, Ryan?"

"Yes, ready," Dana replied. She smiled at Ryan, tightened her grip on his hand, then reached out, taking Joel's in her other, and together they all started back toward the house.

Kelly Jones

ONE AND A HALF YEARS LATER

My name is Joe.

This is the name I choose to call myself now. My therapist says this is good. Sometimes I don't know who I am, but if I concentrate on today, look to the future, which my Mom says is very bright, I'm okay.

I don't remember much about the time when I was Joel, but now and then some memories come back. When I first met my Mom, and she held me in her arms, it was the smell I remembered, something warm and comfortable and safe. My Mom still gets these feelings, she doesn't talk about them to me, but I know she's afraid she'll lose me again. I talk with my therapist about that sometimes.

We're on our way to Italy, a graduation gift from Mom and her fiancé Ryan. I'm flying with them now. It's a long flight, and I've got lots of time to think. I really like Ryan, and I can see how good he is for my Mom, a calming presence for her. Ryan has a brother I've never met. He set a bunch of fires to protest the abuse in the Church, which is really weird because my story is sort of wrapped up in all that, too. I heard Mom once, talking to Ryan. She described this evil as a monster masked in piety reaching out its wicked arms, wrapping around the most innocent . . . like ripples from a stone dropped into a pond, spreading farther and farther from the source. But then she laughed and told Ryan that mixing metaphors and similes was at least a venial sin in itself. Some people might think that is strange—laughing at something so serious. But, sometimes, we just have to laugh. I like it when my Mom laughs, and that's something else I remember from when I was little. My Mom's laugh.

Ryan's brother, Gabe, was in the hospital for a really long time, but Mom says he's doing better. When his story came out, it got lots of attention, and support came in from all over the world, enough to pay his medical bills, lawyer fees, and the money he's going to have to pay to fix the churches. I guess everything was settled before it went to court, and Mom says he won't have to go to prison.

My Mom has tried to protect me, keep the paparazzi away, which is kind of odd for her because she used to write for the newspaper, and she admits she was always looking to be the first to get a story. She says in Italy it will probably be a lot easier to be invisible. I was invisible for so many years, it was hard when I became a story plastered all over the news.

I don't remember my Mom and Dad together, so that's really no big deal for me. My Dad is happy with Amy. Sometimes I stay with them. I have a sister. Her name is Nicole, Nicki, and she's just one. I love her so much. I can't picture my Mom and Dad together because they seem happy with who they are with now.

We're going to visit Mia and her family. Mia was there when Mom found me, and I know the story of how she and Meagan and Zac all worked together. When I first came back, hanging out with them really helped. Mia and I keep in touch. I'm excited to see her.

I remember more about the time I was Joseph, when I lived with Grandma Ginny in Canada. It seemed normal, but I know now there was nothing normal about it because what Grandma Ginny did was so wrong. I know she had a son who molested children, though he was a priest. His name was Joseph too, and I think she somehow got things all confused and sometimes thought I was Joseph and she was getting another chance.

I've got two more grandmas now, real grandmas, and uncles, aunts and cousins on both Mom's and Dad's sides. Ryan's family has welcomed me too. Another grandma, more cousins-to-be.

I'm a good person. Oh, I've got my faults. Sometimes I'm not very patient. I want things to happen right now. I've found that sports and being active can help. I finished up my classes at home on the computer after my return, then a year at a private school. I wanted so bad to play sports, but had never done it before. Then, spring semester I tried out for the baseball team and made it. Coach says I'm a natural, and Mom says I got it from my Grandpa Slim Pierson who played professional ball. I never met him.

But, makes me wonder if maybe that thing about nurture vs. nature leans more to the nature side. Most of the time, I feel like I'm part of this family, and Zac has really helped me with that. Sometimes I'm angry that I missed so much.

My Grandma Ginny died. I'm still dealing with that. She saved a bunch of newspaper articles that the authorities found, about her son Joseph dying in prison, stories my Mom wrote, then the stories about the boy who got abducted. I know that was me, that it's all part of my story. Everybody has a story. Mine is just a lot weirder than most.

I was Joel.

Then I was Joseph.

My thoughts jump around a lot.

I'm taking a year off from school. In Great Britain they call it a Gap year. I've got lots of stuff to figure out yet.

My name is Joe, and I'm a survivor.

READERS GUIDE FOR

ANGEL BOY

Discussion Questions

1. Discuss the book title. Who do you believe the angel boy is?

2. At the beginning of the book there is a reference to "unpardoned sins," then later, the idea of forgiveness plays into the story. Is there a difference between pardoning and forgiving? Do you believe there are acts that cannot be forgiven? Are there any in the story?

3. Dana is anxious about having Mia with her for the school year. Why do you believe she is apprehensive? Does her relationship with Mia change over the course of the book? Why or why not?

4. Dana relies on her sister-in-law for advice on teenagers. Do you think she offers good advice? What kind of advice would you offer?

5. When do you think Dana begins to trust Ryan? Do you believe there is a turning point, and do you believe this is a mutual trust? How important is this to the story? How do you think these two are alike? Different? Are similarities or differences more important in a relationship?

6. At times, Dana expresses thoughts on journalistic ethics, but at other times she seems unconcerned. Do you think she makes the correct decisions throughout the story, both professionally and personally? What do you think is the chief factor that influences her to continue working with Ryan?

7. After accusations are made against Kip, Dana considers that, "Women who wanted to get ahead put up with that shit. Younger women just weren't inclined to do so." Do you believe this is true? Do you believe women of Dana's age have accepted behavior that younger women will not? How do you feel about Dana's friendship with Kip? Should she have been aware of his behavior? Should she have done something or said something? How did you feel when he came back to Boston?

8. Fire has many symbolic meanings including birth, rebirth, resurrection, and hope, as well as being the predominant symbol of hell. How does the author use these contradictory concepts of fire both literally and figuratively to tell the story?

9. Mia reflects that, "Everyone suffered loss, and yet many overcame the grief. Others were haunted forever." Do you believe there are losses that cannot be overcome? How does loss define the different characters in the story? How does it affect Dana and Drew's marriage?

10. Should an organization or religion be punished as a whole for the behavior of a few? Why or why not?

11. Were you surprised by the ending of the story? If it were to continue, what do you think Dana would be doing now?

Kelly Jones grew up in Twin Falls, Idaho. She graduated from Gonzaga University in Spokane, Washington, with a degree in English and an art minor. She lives in Boise. Visit her website at kellyjonesbooks.com.

If you liked the book, please post a review on Amazon.com and/or Goodreads.com